Acclaim for Kim Cash Tate

"Tate expertly crafts an intriguing narrative that explores unrequited love, true faith, and the complicated politics of change in the Christian church . . . [An] affecting tale about forgiveness and following God's call."

—*Publishers Weekly* review of *Hope Springs*

"Kim Cash Tate draws us into a world where the dreams, desires, missteps and matters of the heart we discover there mirror our own. She is a master at crafting characters who make you forget you're reading fiction. By the end of *Hope Springs*, you'll feel as if you're cheering on members of your extended family."

—Stacy Hawkins Adams, best-selling author
of *Coming Home* and *The Someday List*

"Tate's amazing ability to connect with the reader on both personal and spiritual levels elevates this novel far above the rest. Those looking for hope and encouragement will find it on the pages of this superb book."

—*Romantic Times* TOP PICK for *Cherished*

"As I read Kim's book *Cherished* the word that came back to me over and over again is grace. Kim has the gift of being able to tell a story so vividly that you forget that the characters she portrays are fictitious and you experience deep empathy for them. You will find yourself in this story. More than that you will discover for the first time or rediscover how deeply you are loved, valued and cherished by God."

—Sheila Walsh, author of *Sweet Sanctuary*

"The author skillfully ties the concept of sexual purity, whether married or single, to the idea of faithfulness on a spiritual level . . . Tate avoids the unrealistic 'happily ever after' ending while still offering a message of faith, hope, and love. Readers will not be disappointed . . ."

—Crosswalk.com review of *Faithful*

"Tate has an amazing ability to put difficult but realistic emotions on paper and show the reader the redeeming love of God in the process."

—*Romantic Times* review of *Faithful*, 4½ stars

"Kim Cash Tate's enjoyable novel is true to both the realities of life and the hope found through faith in Jesus. Romance meets real life with a godly heart. Hooray!"

—Stasi Eldredge, best-selling author
of *Captivating*, regarding *Faithful*

"Three friends. Two husbands. One Romeo. All are shaken to the core as author Kim Cash Tate peels away layers of lies and self-deception to reveal the rotten core of infidelity and its tragic consequences. But this novel is also about hope and healing as her well-drawn characters discover the freedom of being FAITHFUL."

—Neta Jackson, author of the Yada Yada
House of Hope novels, regarding *Faithful*

"*Faithful* by Kim Cash Tate is not only beautifully written, it is a novel that changes you, that makes you question your heart and attitudes. I can't recommend it highly enough!"

—Colleen Coble, best-selling
author of *Lonestar Homecoming*

"Good fiction has to grab me, knock me around, and make me care about what is happening to the characters. But great fiction inspires me. Kim Cash Tate accomplishes it all in *Faithful*."

—Marilyn Meberg, Women of Faith
speaker and author of *Tell Me Everything*

Hope
Springs

Also by
KIM CASH TATE

Faithful

Cherished

Hope Springs

KIM CASH TATE

THOMAS NELSON
Since 1798

NASHVILLE DALLAS MEXICO CITY RIO DE JANEIRO

Published in Nashville, Tennessee by Thomas Nelson. Thomas Nelson is a registered trademark of Thomas Nelson, Inc.

Thomas Nelson, Inc., titles may be purchased in bulk for educational, business, fund-raising, or sales promotional use. For information, please e-mail SpecialMarkets@ThomasNelson.com.

Author is represented by the literary agency of The B&B Media Group, Inc., 109 S. Main, Corsicana, Texas, 75110. www.tbbmedia.com.

Scripture quotations are taken from the NEW AMERICAN STANDARD BIBLE®, Copyright © 1960, 1962, 1963, 1968, 1971, 1972, 1973, 1975, 1977, 1995 by The Lockman Foundation. Used by permission.

Publisher's Note: This novel is a work of fiction. Names, characters, places, and incidents are either products of the author's imagination or used fictitiously. All characters are fictional, and any similarity to people living or dead is purely coincidental.

Library of Congress Cataloging-in-Publication Data

Tate, Kimberly Cash.
  Hope Springs / Kimberly Cash Tate.
    p. cm.
  ISBN 978-1-59554-997-6 (trade paper)
  I. Title.
  PS3620.A885H67 2012
  813'.6--dc23

                    2012007533

Printed in the United States of America

12 13 14 15 16 17 QG 6 5 4 3 2 1

For every soul that's learning to let go

Sanders Family Tree

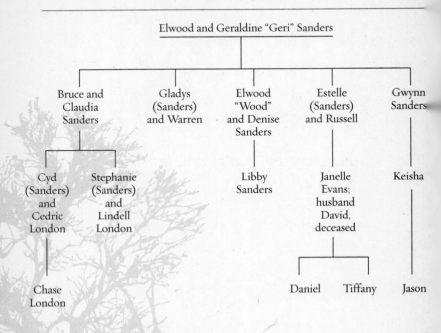

Elwood and Geraldine "Geri" Sanders

- Bruce and Claudia Sanders
  - Cyd (Sanders) and Cedric London
    - Chase London
  - Stephanie (Sanders) and Lindell London
- Gladys (Sanders) and Warren
- Elwood "Wood" and Denise Sanders
  - Libby Sanders
- Estelle (Sanders) and Russell
  - Janelle Evans; husband David, deceased
    - Daniel
    - Tiffany
- Gwynn Sanders
  - Keisha
    - Jason

Dillon Family Tree

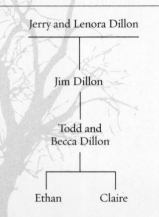

Jerry and Lenora Dillon

Jim Dillon

Todd and Becca Dillon

- Ethan
- Claire

CHAPTER ONE

Wednesday, December 23

S tephanie Sanders London sulked with all the fervor she could muster as she and Lindell rode the escalator up to security in St. Louis's Lambert International Airport. She stared vaguely at the moving stairway, lips pursed, sighing displeasure with rhythmic regularity.

Lindell looked over at her. "Steph, I thought it was settled." He had the nerve to look amused. "We said we were done talking about it."

Her eyes floated to the rafters. "You didn't hear me say a word."

"Oh, cool. Glad I was mistaken."

"I'm just sayin', though, Lindell"—she hit his shoulder—"and stop laughing because I *wasn't* saying a word before but I am now." She adjusted the purse on her shoulder. "I don't see why you're acting like we *have* to go. I'm the one who came up with the idea for this trip, so I should have the right to change my—"

She paused just off the escalator, gaping at the security line that snaked up and down the cordoned rows, spilling into the general walkway, past the Starbucks, ending with an older woman who'd set her bag on the ground and folded her arms.

"That's it. It's a sign. I'm out."

She turned on her heel toward the down escalator, and Lindell pulled her back.

"Where are you going?"

"H-o-m-e."

Lindell looped his hand through her arm and walked her forward as he wheeled their luggage. "It's two days before Christmas," he said. "We knew the lines would be long. That's why we left early."

Stephanie trudged beside him, shaking her head. "What on earth possessed me to suggest traveling for Christmas?"

"To spend time with your family."

"I can spend time with my family *here*, like I do every Christmas."

They joined the back of the line, behind two families who had gotten behind the older woman.

"Exactly. But Pastor Lyles preached that sermon about doing something different this Christmas, taking the focus off of ourselves. And what did you say?" He leaned over, his ear tuned.

"*At the time* I said it might be nice to visit my Grandma Geri, since Daddy said she wasn't feeling too well and I haven't been down there in a long while."

Lindell nodded. "And it was a great idea!"

"Yeah, well, the sermon wore off." She shuffled forward with the others. "I don't want to do anything different for Christmas. There'll be a lot of people staying at her house, and I don't even know them that well—"

"It's family, Steph."

"I stopped going to the reunions and all that after high school because a weekend getaway in Hope Springs, North Carolina, wasn't exactly my idea of a happening time. Nor is *Christmas* in Hope Springs." She sighed. "I mean, Daddy's not even going, and it's his mother."

"Steph, come on . . . your folks were just there in the summer, and they're going back soon. You know they can't miss Chase's first

Christmas." He donned a wry smile. "Guess they want to see Cyd and Cedric too."

Stephanie allowed a chuckle. "You've got that right. Chase is the main attraction." Stephanie's older sister, Cyd, had had a baby in the spring, the first grandchild. "Little spoiled self. And I won't get to see him open the presents I bought him."

"I'm looking forward to getting to know this side of your family. At our wedding I barely got the right names attached to the right faces."

"Shoot, me too. How about this?" She looked hopefully at her husband. "We could rebook the trip for spring, after you get back from Haiti. And I can get Cyd and Cedric to come and bring the baby." She should've thought of that at first. Cyd knew this side of the family much better than she.

Lindell shook his head. "It'll be crazy at work when I get back." Lindell was a doctor and was headed to Haiti for a month on a medical mission trip. He kissed her nose. "We're going. Today. It'll be awesome."

The line inched along, Stephanie retreating into her thoughts. That was another thing, this mission trip. She was happy for Lindell. He'd been excited about it the moment it surfaced and had asked if she'd like to help in an orphanage while he worked with the mobile clinic. But it just wasn't her, so she declined. As the trip got closer, though, and his team had more and more meetings to prepare, she wondered why it wasn't her.

Well. She knew why. She wasn't the servant type. What she really wondered was whether that could ever change. And she surprised herself by sending up a prayer for it to change. And to know whether her life had some kind of purpose . . . besides shopping. Which she loved. But still.

Stephanie sighed, thinking how excited she'd gotten about Pastor Lyles's Christmas message. Seemed to tie in with her prayers.

Visiting Grandma Geri sure sounded like a servanty thing to do. But now the whole thing seemed weird. What would they even talk about? Thank God other family would be—

Stephanie heard her ringtone and dug out her phone.

"Checking up on me?" Stephanie said.

Her dad chuckled. "Now why would I need to do that?"

"Oh, you might've wondered what was going on after that message I left this morning."

"You mean the one asking me to call Lindell and assure him that my family would understand if you changed your travel plans?"

Stephanie sneaked a peek at her husband. She lowered her voice a little. "Wouldn't have hurt to call him, you know."

"I did call him."

"Then why am I at the airport?"

"I told him you were *his* responsibility now, and I'm happy to let him handle you all on his own."

She could hear the grin in her dad's voice and couldn't help but smile herself. "Oh yeah? Then why are you calling?"

"I forgot to tell you there's a big funeral in Hope Springs this afternoon. And I really need you to go."

"Aw, Daddy, now I'm supposed to go to a funeral? You *know* I don't like funerals. They're so . . . creepy."

"They're nobody's favorite thing, Steph, but Jim Dillon was like family. You remember Jim, lived next door to Grandma Geri?"

"The pastor? You grew up with him, didn't you?"

"Yes, but I was older. He was tight with my younger brother, Wood." Bruce sighed. "Total shock. Momma found him slumped over the kitchen table from a heart attack. I looked into making a quick trip, but last-minute flights were either booked or too expensive. So I'm hoping you'll represent."

Stephanie groaned.

Her dad added, "But I do feel bad I forgot to tell you, because I know you didn't pack for a funeral."

"Oh, that's not an issue. I always pack some of everything."

Lindell nodded big, pretending to labor in pulling their luggage forward. Stephanie pinched him.

"All right, Daddy, I'll go." She sighed. Was this another servanty thing? Shoot, after this trip, she'd be servant certified.

"Thanks, sweetheart. And by the way, did you decide to stay at Momma's or a hotel?"

She'd been leaning toward a hotel a few miles away in Rocky Mount, but her dad had encouraged her to stay at her grandmother's.

"Not sure yet," she said. "I've got until six o'clock this evening to cancel the hotel reservation."

"A lot of bonding happens late at night at the house, you know," her father said.

Stephanie quirked a brow. "Is that supposed to be an argument in favor or against?"

"Don't be surprised when you have a great time, Steph," her dad said. "Give everyone our love."

Lindell was looking at the itinerary.

"What time do we arrive?" Stephanie asked, dropping her phone back into her purse.

"Eleven fifty." He tucked the paper away as they moved forward, showing their IDs and boarding passes to the security guard. They headed to the shortest X-ray line.

"So we get the rental car in Raleigh and drive straight to your grandmother's?" Lindell asked. "How far is it?"

"Uh . . . I meant to print out directions." Stephanie reached for a bin for the liquids she'd stored in a baggie. "Something like forty minutes, I think. We'll get a map when we get there."

"Cool. Hope Springs, here we come!"

She pumped her arms in a rah-rah motion. "Awesome!"

Lindell grinned. "See, you're getting the spirit."

She cut her eyes at him as she placed her purse on the security belt.

CHAPTER TWO

J anelle Evans rode a seesaw of emotion the entire road trip
south. Should she be going to Hope Springs for Christmas?
Would it have been better to stay home?

The mile marker winged past: HOPE SPRINGS 10 MILES. This was
her home away from home. She'd spent weeks of summer down here
as a kid, attended almost every Sanders family reunion, celebrated
countless Easters and Christmases. But once she'd had her own kids,
they'd begun building their own Christmas traditions at home.

She and her husband, David, used to pile the family in the car
the day after Thanksgiving to get the tree. They'd make apple cider
and decorate not just the tree but the whole house, inside and out.
And on Christmas morning, David would lead the family in a special
Christmas devotion before the kids tore into their gifts.

But now David was gone and Janelle languished at this time of
year especially, not feeling the joy, not wanting to decorate, prefer-
ring to bury herself under her bedcovers until the season passed. To
the dismay of her family, she'd done that the past two Christmases—
and planned to do it again.

But she'd gotten word that Grandma Geri was under the weather. Then Pastor Jim, a lifelong family friend, died unexpectedly. That gave her mom and her cousin Libby all the extra fodder they needed.

"You should be with your family for Christmas anyway," they said. "Now even more so."

Janelle packed up the kids, left a house with a single symbol of Christmas—an artificial tabletop tree—and started the drive from Maryland to North Carolina, her first such trip since David's death.

She squinted at the highway exit sign approaching. As many times as she'd been here, why did she always get confused at this point? Did she take the first exit into Hope Springs or the second?

"Baby, it's the second. How is it that I always remember, and I haven't been coming down here half as long as you?"

A shiver shot through Janelle, and she was suddenly trembling. This was exactly why she'd stayed away. It was hard enough wading through the painful memories surrounding home, church, and school. Now she'd have to relive the loss here. She sighed, casting a quick glance over her shoulder at the kids. In many ways, this would be harder. These were the people closest to her, and David had come to love visits to Hope Springs as much as she. Everywhere she turned, there'd be a stab of memory, like that stupid highway sign.

She veered off on the second exit and drove a couple miles down a stretch of lonely road. A handful of isolated houses came into view, then that familiar sign: WELCOME TO HOPE SPRINGS—POPULATION 1200. The exit was one thing, the town another. She knew these streets like the back of her hand. Not that there were very many of them.

"So there really is a Mayberry, huh?"

Janelle had laughed at David's remark on his first visit. Now it punctuated the sadness as she made a left onto Main, eyes darting to the clock on the dash—*12:10*. Funeral started at three. She'd made good time.

She drove past the two-pump gas station, long closed, and a smattering of storefronts, plus the Main Street Diner, all with Christmas lights strung. Not a lot of hustle and bustle in the early afternoon—or anytime, really—but a handful of townspeople dotted the sidewalks. Hope Springs always marked a stark contrast to life just outside the nation's capital. Simpler living. Slower pace. Even her driving was unusually sedate.

Janelle turned left again and headed down her grandmother's road, greeted by familiar old homes of varying sizes and states of repair. She bypassed them all and rounded a bend that opened up a different view—a wooded preserve to the left and a stretch of green space on the right. The two houses at the end of the street had been occupied by the same two families for generations, the Sanders and the Dillons. Spending time with one family in Hope Springs meant spending time with the other.

She tapped the brake and gazed at the Dillon home, a two-story white frame house with black shutters and rocking chairs on the front porch. Looked eerily quiet. She still couldn't believe Jim Dillon had died of a heart attack. He was only in his late fifties. Probably thought he'd be pastoring Calvary Church another decade at least.

Janelle continued to Grandma Geri's house, a ranch style that had expanded over the years to accommodate Sanders family gatherings. She pulled onto the dirt and grass that served as a parking lot when family visited, parking next to her parents' car. They'd arrived last night from Florida. When she killed the engine, heads rose behind her and arms stretched with yawning.

"Are we here?" Eight-year-old Daniel rubbed his eyes.

Janelle turned. "Yes, baby, we're here."

They'd driven four and a half hours, and the kids had slept the last two.

Tiffany unhooked the seat belt that crossed her booster seat. "I'm ready to get out, Mommy."

Janelle smiled at her. "Okay, sweetie."

She opened her door and stepped out, leaving the winter jacket she'd worn at the start of the trip. An Indian summer breeze had warmed the Carolina air—and a delicious aroma filled it. She inhaled. Her dad, Russell, and Uncle Wood were probably in the back roasting a pig. Whether the occasion was happy or sad, the prescription was the same—lots and lots of food.

The sliding door opened and Daniel popped out, with Tiffany on his heels. At four she did her best to keep up with her brother's every move. They made a beeline for the house just as Libby was walking out. She spun around.

"Daniel and Tiffany—I know y'all didn't run right past me like you didn't see me."

Daniel stopped with his foot in the door. He and Tiffany turned back around, gave Libby a quick hug, and ran inside.

"That's what you get for being a regular visitor." Janelle hugged her cousin. "They don't think it's anything special to see you."

Since David died, Libby had driven up from Raleigh every few months to spend time with Janelle.

"Uh-huh." Libby looked back at them. "Bet they won't run past my Christmas gifts."

They moved to the door, and Libby paused with her hand on the screen handle. "Before we go in, his name is Al."

"Who?"

"My date."

"Who brings a date to a funeral?"

"Crazy, right? That's what I told him." Libby came closer and whispered, "I told him I was staying through Christmas, and he asked if he could come meet Mom and Dad."

"Oh, he's trying to get in with the family? It can't be serious because you haven't even told me about him."

Libby gave her a look. "Exactly. He can *think* it's serious all he wants. He gives nice gifts."

Janelle shook her head. "You're a heartbreaker, Libby."

The two cousins walked inside, the house relatively quiet still. In the next two hours, the family room to the left would be filled with cousins, aunts and uncles, and family friends, all carrying on pockets of animated conversation. This room was the most recent renovation, added a decade ago and furnished with an eclectic mix of pull-out sofas, recliners, and a corner card table. The bonus this time of year was the beautiful fir tree prominently displayed, with tons of gifts already wrapped and under its branches.

Through the far window, Janelle could see her kids. Must've run through the house and out another door to hang with their grandpa and Libby's dad, Uncle Wood. Al was the only one in the family room, watching something on television.

He got up and smiled as they entered. "I've seen pictures, but now I get to see 'the twins' live and in color."

The same age and inseparable at family gatherings, Janelle and Libby had been dubbed "the twins" as youngsters. But it was especially fitting since their parents really were twins—Janelle's mom and Libby's dad.

Libby put her cheek next to her cousin's, grinning. "Don't we look exactly alike?"

"Uh . . ." Al turned his head sideways for a different angle, trying to mesh Libby's light brown skin and super-short cut with Janelle's maple brown skin and shoulder-length locks. "You're both beautiful, how's that?"

Janelle laughed. "I like you already."

He gave her a friendly embrace. "Nice to meet you."

"Likewise," Janelle said. "So you live in the Raleigh—"

"I know Janelle didn't come in this house and has *yet* to step in this kitchen."

"Uh-oh." Janelle turned toward the sound of the voice. Her aunt Gladys was calling her out.

"Come on in here, girl."

Janelle looked sheepish on purpose as she slow-walked down the hall, seeing them all waiting for her—her mother and Aunt Gladys, and Libby's mom, Aunt Denise. Each had her hands in something, a mixing bowl, a pot or pan. Every burner on the stove was lit, and casserole dishes and desserts lined the counter. But busy as they were, their eyes fixed on her. Janelle knew exactly what they were about to give her—equal parts hug and loving rebuke.

Aunt Gladys, apron tied around her waist, walked away from her pot and held her arms open, scolding in the embrace. "Miss Jan, you know you had no business staying gone for two years. You need your family." Aunt Gladys was the oldest sister in the family, and never one to mince words.

Janelle's mom, Estelle, took a pan of homemade rolls from the oven. "Told her a million times, Gladys—'You don't run *from* your family in trying times, you run *to* them.'" She closed the oven and hugged her daughter.

Janelle gave her mom the eye as she went to hug Aunt Denise. "I wasn't running from family. I've seen you and Dad a lot, and Libby might as well have moved in." She looked over at her cousin, who'd followed her into the kitchen. "Right, Libby?"

"Don't look to me for help." She folded her arms. "I've been telling you the same thing."

Estelle began smoothing frosting over a three-tiered cake. "It's not the same, Jan, and you know it."

"Mom, the world didn't end because I missed two reunions."

"Janelle Evans, I'm gonna put you over my knee and spank you."

Grandma Geri had come in from a side door, toting a laundry basket filled with sheets. The family had gotten her a dryer years ago, but she said certain things didn't feel right unless they hung on her laundry line.

"Momma, all these people around here . . . why are you carrying that basket yourself?" Aunt Gladys went to take it from her. "Please sit down and take it easy."

"Chile, I'm fine. Let me hug my long-lost granddaughter." Grandma Geri set the basket down and started coughing.

She'd always had a commanding presence in Janelle's eyes—tall, relatively fit for her age, always moving and doing. Janelle wasn't sure she'd ever seen her under the weather. She saw her mom and Aunt Gladys look at one another as the cough persisted. Janelle got a glass of water and took it to her. "Grandma, you okay? Let's sit down."

"I'll be"—the cough got deeper—"fine in a minute. Thank you." She took the glass and sipped as Janelle led her to a seat at the kitchen table.

"Momma, if you don't call Doc Reynolds, I will," Aunt Gladys said. "Sounds like you got bronchitis or something."

"I'll be all right." Grandma Geri took a long sip.

"I'm with Gladys," Estelle said. "You've got that nasty cough and shortness of breath. Doesn't make any sense to—"

"Estelle and Gladys, if y'all don't stop worrying me . . ."

Janelle steered a different direction, smiling big at her grandmother. "So you want to spank me now? You already gave me a talking-to over the phone."

"Sounds to me like you didn't get it." The cough was dying down. She cupped Janelle's hand. "I know it ain't easy with David gone, and I been praying for you and the kids . . ." She tightened her grip. "But seem like you trying to make it on your own. Let your family love on you."

Janelle noted the ears around them. The women had gone back to preparing the food, but those pot lids weren't clanging as loudly as before. She sighed. "I know, Grandma. Everything's just been . . . hard, like you said. I don't even know how to explain."

"Sweetheart, what's to explain? You forgot I lost a husband too?"

"But you and Grandpa Elwood had decades together. You saw your children grow up, and some of your grandchildren. You walked with him through his illness." Janelle could feel the emotion rising. "David and I only had seven years. He didn't even . . . didn't even get to see Tiffany's third birthday. He was just *gone*, and I was all alone."

She saw it flash through her mind, all of it still surreal. The call that David had collapsed on the court in a friendly game of basketball. Finding out he had a heart defect. Not even getting to say good-bye.

Grandma Geri tugged softly on her hand. "That's what I'm saying, baby. You're not alone. You've got us *and* you've got Jesus. He's been with you every single second."

Janelle sighed. "I know, Grandma." Dwelling on it only made her sad.

The house phone rang, and she was glad for the distraction. Estelle found the cordless phone on the counter.

"Stephanie? You're on the ground?"

Janelle looked at Libby. "Really? Stephanie's coming?"

Libby looked at her aunt Estelle, presumably hearing it the first time herself.

"Right, head east from the airport," Estelle was saying. "Won't take more than forty minutes." She was smiling. "Can't wait to see you. All right, bye now."

"That's pretty cool," Libby said. "I can't remember the last time Stephanie was here. What made her decide to come?"

"Gladys got everybody thinking I'm at death's door, that's what," Grandma Geri said.

"Momma, I said nothing of the kind." Aunt Gladys was mixing another kind of cake. "But I'm the only one of your children who lives nearby and sees you regularly. So if you want to sue me for telling everybody I'm concerned, then go ahead."

"If it got Stephanie down here, I ain't complaining," Grandma Geri said. "Talk about long-lost granddaughters."

"Are Uncle Bruce and the rest coming?" Janelle asked.

"Bruce and Claudia are spending the holiday with Cyd's family," Aunt Gladys said. She smiled. "They were all here for the family reunion this summer."

Aunt Denise was shaping her famous homemade rolls and placing them on a pan. "You should've seen that little baby boy. Cute as a button." She glanced toward the family room, then looked at her daughter. "At the rate Libby's going, Wood and I will probably have to wait as long as Bruce and Claudia did for a grandchild."

"Or longer." Libby leaned against the counter. "I'm only thirty-four. Lots of life ahead."

"Seeing Cyd with a baby for the first time in her forties . . ." Grandma Geri waved her hand with a little chuckle. "If that didn't tickle me pink, I don't know what would. She's my oldest grandchild, you know."

"We know."

Janelle and Libby laughed at their simultaneous response. Cyd, with all of her professional accomplishments, had always been held up as a model for the younger cousins. Janelle wondered what that must've been like for Stephanie growing up.

Estelle pulled a jumbo pan of baked beans out of the oven.

"So looks like everyone's coming here after the funeral," Janelle said.

"We told Todd we'd take care of everything." Her mother placed the pan on two trivets. "He's got enough on his mind."

Todd was Jim Dillon's son. About the same age as Janelle and Libby, he was part of the cohort of kids that had played in the summers when the Sanders grandchildren visited.

"How's he holding up?" Janelle asked.

"Holding up okay, far as I can see," Estelle said. "You know Todd. He was more concerned about how Momma was doing, now that Jim's not around to see about her."

"Sounds like Todd," Janelle said. "I was hoping to see him before the funeral, but looked like nobody was home."

"He's pulling up right now." Libby was looking out the kitchen window. "He and the kids went over to the church."

"Where's Becca?"

"What did Todd say? Nashton or something?" Grandma Geri said.

"Nash*ville*," Aunt Gladys called over her shoulder.

Janelle chuckled. Her grandmother was known for confusing the endings to place names.

"Anyway," Grandma Geri said, "Becca will be here. She's doing some kind of presentation and had a meeting this morning to get ready for it."

"It's a little more than that, Momma." Estelle smiled over at her. "Todd said she was just added as a speaker with some women's conference—what's the name of it?—something about purpose."

"Worth & Purpose?" Janelle got up to get some water for herself. "I went a few years ago when they came to D.C. Becca's speaking with them? That's awesome."

"What's Worth & Purpose?" Libby asked.

"It's a national Christian women's conference," Janelle said. "One of the biggest. I'm sure there are tons of women who'd love the opportunity to speak on that platform. Becca must be pumped." Janelle sipped some of her water and placed her glass in the sink. "I'm going to talk to Todd before it gets too hectic."

Suddenly she was glad she'd come. The entire road trip she'd been focused on her own loss, and only now gave real consideration to Todd's. Hard to believe both of his parents were gone. His dad was her mom's age . . .

And the surprising news that Stephanie was coming . . . A few years younger than she and Libby, Stephanie had always been something of an enigma, hanging in the shadows of her sister. But that was when she was a teenager. It had been years since Janelle had seen her.

Yes, now that she was here, Hope Springs seemed the only place she should be.

CHAPTER THREE

Becca Dillon took a window seat near the front of the plane, tossed her tote bag into the middle, and reached inside for her iPad.

"You're awesome, Patti. Can't believe how quickly you've done all this for me." She held her phone in the crook of her neck as she powered up the iPad, bottle-blond hair falling in front of her face.

"I'm glad I caught you before the plane took off," Patti said. "I couldn't wait for you to see."

"I hope I have time while everyone's boarding." Becca opened her e-mail and waited for the messages to download. "So you think the pictures turned out well?"

"Fabulous. You're a natural, girl. Even the test shots to get the lighting right turned out well."

"Here it is," Becca said, hunkering down. "Wow, this is a lot. Hope I have time to click through all these attachments."

She glanced up, glad the aisle was still crowded with passengers.

"Ooh, look at the sky on this first one," she said. "You picked the perfect location." She and Patti had spent two hours at the

Missouri Botanical Gardens yesterday. "I look kinda goofy on that one, though."

"Oh, you do not. You were about to ask a question as I snapped. Looks cute and inquisitive to me."

Becca opened the next. "Ah, the one on the boulder where I'm smiling and looking to the side? I *like* that."

"That's my favorite," Patti said. "That wind-in-the-hair shows your personality, looks like you're having fun."

A woman took the aisle seat in her row. Becca lowered her volume. "What about this serious-looking one? I like it, but . . ." She stared at it. "Not sure what it says."

"Says, 'I'm a Bible teacher, a serious one.'" Patti said it in a serious voice.

Becca laughed.

"This is a full flight to Raleigh-Durham," the flight attendant announced. "Please take the first available seat so we can push back and get on our way."

Becca moved her bag from the middle and put it under the seat in front of her. "How will I narrow this down?" She kept clicking through. "You've managed to make me look half decent in more than a few of these." She smiled. "You really *are* good."

In the blink of an eye, it seemed, Becca's life had kicked into another gear. In a matter of weeks she'd be taking the stage with Worth & Purpose, and her redesigned blog was about to go live. Suddenly she needed professional photos for marketing materials and the blog banner, and she didn't want to use the boring studio picture she'd taken more than three years ago.

Becca had known Patti for years. They'd served together on a local not-for-profit board in St. Louis, and she'd heard Patti had a reputation for capturing beautiful, natural shots. These photos were even better than she'd hoped.

"Okay," Becca said, "so if I send you my choices right after

Christmas—not trying to rush you or anything—" She knew Patti would have to enhance the lighting and anything else her photographer's eye deemed necessary.

"Don't be silly. You didn't brave the wind and cold trying to look cute out there for nothing. I know you need these ASAP, so soon as you know which ones you want, I'm on it."

"Really?" Becca was smiling. "You're a gem, Patti. Okay—"

Her phone beeped, and she looked at it. "Hey, Patti, that's my agent. I'll call you . . . Okay." She clicked to take the call. "Nick, hi, I'm about to take off. Hope you've got good news."

"Would a two-book contract fall under 'good news'?" His voice brimmed with excitement. "They loved our proposal."

"Get out of here!" She was whispering, but the enthusiasm was unmistakable. "Two-book contract? Did they *say* they loved it, or are *you* saying they loved it?"

"Talked to the main editor who handles Worth & Purpose's speakers, and those were her words—'I love it.'"

"Get out of here!"

"All electronics need to be powered off at this time . . ."

Becca bowed her head behind the seat. "We've got so much to talk about! I have to tell you about the planning meeting today with Worth & Purpose too."

"Call me when you can, even if it's Christmas. I never take off."

"You're the one who made *me* a workaholic. You're a bad influence." She saw the flight attendant coming toward her. "Okay, gotta go."

Becca powered off her phone and iPad, tucked them into her bag, and sank into her seat—then came forward suddenly again. She'd forgotten to call Todd. *Ugh.*

Things were already a tad strained between them. News of his dad's death had rocked him, and he'd wanted the family to drive to Hope Springs the next day. Any other time Becca would've done all she could to be there for him. She knew how close he'd been to his father. But the timing couldn't have been worse.

Patti had squeezed Becca into her schedule on short notice, and she needed those pictures right away. And the meeting in Nashville was easily the most exciting event of her life—spending the morning with some of the heaviest hitters in women's ministry, talking through her ideas for the conference. The speaking team had already had their planning meeting a month ago, but one of the speakers had to bow out due to pregnancy complications requiring bed rest. They'd contacted Becca three weeks ago and invited her to come on board. Given the upcoming holidays, she had the option of meeting in person or, if time didn't permit, by conference call. She'd jumped at the chance to meet at their offices and had been giddy ever since—until her father-in-law's death . . . and the funeral planned for the same day as her meeting.

Todd had thought it an easy matter. "Can't you contact Worth & Purpose to see if they'll reschedule?" he asked. But Becca chafed. She was the new kid on the block. How would it look if she asked the leadership team to switch gears at the last minute? Plus—and she knew it deep down—she didn't *want* to reschedule. So she asked if the funeral could be set for the afternoon. That way, she could make it after her meeting.

Still, she'd missed the wake the night before. And every day she'd spoken to him, something in his voice let her know that her presence the entire week had been missed. She felt bad that she wasn't with him in Hope Springs. Actually, she felt bad that she'd been enjoying her week. But now she had meant to switch focus, turn all of her attention to Todd, beginning with a call to let him know her flight was on time and she'd definitely be there. How could she have forgotten?

Becca sighed as the plane took off after a long taxi down the runway. She let her eyes close, and her mind couldn't help but drift back to the morning she'd had. She'd been praying and working toward this level of platform for what seemed like the longest time. And it was finally here. As the plane taxied and took off, she thanked God for opening doors that only He could've opened.

"Excuse me for eavesdropping."

Becca opened her eyes again. It was the woman sitting next to her.

"I heard you mention Worth & Purpose. Do you work for them? I went to the conference in Huntsville last year and loved it."

"Oh, I'm actually one of the speakers for the upcoming year." Becca wondered if the excitement of being affiliated with Worth & Purpose would ever get old.

"Wow, really?" The woman looked more closely at Becca. "I'm honored to meet you."

Becca smiled. "I'm honored to meet you too. I'm Becca Dillon, by the way."

"A bunch of us from church are road-tripping again to Huntsville to see you guys in about a month. Will you be there?"

"That's actually the first gathering of the new season. I won't be speaking at that one, but I'll be there."

"Well, I'll be praying for you."

"That means a lot. Thank you." Becca extended her hand. "And tell me your name."

"Name's Judy." The woman shook Becca's hand.

"Thank you so much, Judy. I appreciate your prayers."

Becca sank into her seat again. She'd gotten up early to fly to the meeting and would have loved to catch up on sleep, but there was way too much swirling in her mind. She reached down and pulled a notepad out of her bag. They loved her proposal! She was so excited she wanted to work on the first chapter.

CHAPTER FOUR

Y ou know what, Lindell? You're not allowed to drive anywhere else, ever again."

Stephanie looked out the window of the rental car as Lindell parallel parked, her gaze toward the white-steepled church up the street with all the people heading inside. "I really can't believe this. We should've been in Hope Springs two hours ago."

"I didn't get us *that* lost." Lindell shifted into park and turned off the engine.

Stephanie blank-stared him. "Wow."

Lindell opened his door and Stephanie followed, taking quick strides along the sidewalk that paralleled the long line of cars along the street.

"I didn't even want to come to the funeral." Stephanie stared ahead. "But if I'm gonna come, could I not be wearing jeans? This is so embarrassing."

"Babe, I told you we could've changed at the house. Wouldn't have mattered if we were ten minutes late."

They'd gone by Grandma Geri's house first. Only a teenage

cousin was there, who was babysitting the smaller kids. She'd given them directions to the church.

She held up a hand. "Lindell, I just . . . can't. You have no idea."

It's not a big deal, Stephanie. Let it go and be nice. It's not like Lindell got lost on purpose.

Stephanie huffed. *Lord, You don't let me get away with anything anymore. Can't I enjoy a good attitude for a few minutes?*

And why was God in cahoots with her sister? The voice in her head always sounded exactly like Cyd's.

She peeked at Lindell as they neared the church. "Sorry."

He moved his head closer. "Did you say something?"

She cleared her throat. "I said . . . sorry . . . for getting so upset."

Lindell put an arm around her. "It's all right, babe. I was frustrated too."

There was a line outside the church. They walked up and took their place behind an older couple.

Seconds later she heard, "Stephanie! Is that you?"

Stephanie saw someone farther up in line looking back at her. "Janelle? And Libby!"

Her cousins got out of line—along with a guy she didn't know—and came back and joined them. She gave them both big hugs.

"Look at you, Stephanie," Libby said. "You look good! Love your hair. So thick and pretty."

"Thanks, girl, but I'm about to get the fly short cut like you. That is *fresh*."

She spied Lindell's raised eyebrows over that idea.

"You and Janelle look good too," she said. "Amazing how much you still look the same."

"So do you," Libby said.

Stephanie swatted away the comment. "No need to be kind. I didn't have to wear Spanx last time you saw me."

They laughed and turned to Lindell.

"And this is my husband, Lindell."

Lindell hugged them. "I met your parents at our wedding. It's nice to meet you two finally."

"I was sorry I couldn't come," Libby said. She turned to the guy next to her. "And this is Al. Al, Stephanie and Lindell."

"So what took you so long to get here?" Janelle said as they huddled together in line. "I was afraid you'd gotten lost."

Stephanie brought her gaze over to Lindell.

"Uh," Lindell said. "I thought I could wing it without the map—"

"Even though I specifically *got* a map at the airport . . ."

Quiet, Stephanie.

Hmph.

Lindell was still explaining. "—and somehow got on the wrong ramp and didn't realize we were headed west."

"Ooh." Janelle cringed. "Sorry to hear that."

Stephanie so wanted to add to the story, like how she tried to tell him he was going the wrong way. She chewed her tongue instead.

"Pastor Jim sure was special." Libby cast her eyes about the crowd. "Not too often everybody comes together like this."

"So Calvary is where Jim pastored, right?" Stephanie asked.

"Right," Janelle said. "And his father was the pastor here before him."

"But . . ." Stephanie did a double take of the surroundings. "This isn't the church we went to when I visited, the one our parents grew up in."

Libby pointed down the street. "That would be New Jerusalem, couple blocks down."

"Got it," Stephanie said. "New Jerusalem is the black church; Calvary's the white church."

"And that's exactly how it stays," Janelle said. "Until there's a funeral. Then things turn multiethnic."

They moved up near the entryway, and Stephanie could see that the service had already started. A handful of ushers were moving about, trying to find room for each waiting group. The pews were almost filled.

Libby was turned sideways, able to see who was coming. She suddenly got a look in her eye and turned to Janelle. "Flash from the past."

Janelle looked at her. "Who?"

Libby nodded toward the back of the line. "Kory."

Stephanie had no idea who Kory was, but from the look on Janelle's face, Steph knew she'd find out soon.

Janelle's heart accelerated before she even laid eyes on him. She sucked in a breath, did a slight turn, saw him talking to someone, and turned back. "What's he doing here?"

Libby made a face. "Seriously, Jan?"

"You know what I mean. It's not like he was close to Pastor Jim or anything."

Libby shrugged. "You never know who Pastor Jim impacted. Could've been one conversation."

An usher walked past the two people waiting in front of them and leaned into Stephanie. "Grandma Geri saw you back here and asked me to come get you and your husband. We made room on the first pew."

Libby had a look of mock indignation. "What about us?"

The usher smiled. "Wish we could've made more room near her. But you'll be seated in two minutes."

Libby waved her hand. "I'm just kidding. I know Grandma couldn't wait to see them."

Janelle watched Stephanie and Lindell follow the usher up a side aisle to the front, but her thoughts kept gravitating to who was behind her. She wanted to look again, but didn't. "Is his family with him?"

Libby shifted to scope out the scene better. "He's with his daughter and Kevin and his family."

Kory's older brother, Kevin, had married into the Sanders family—on a great-aunt's side—when Janelle was eighteen. Janelle didn't make the wedding, but that same summer Kory had attended the Sanders family reunion for the first time. She remembered it well, summer before college.

"You know his wife left him, right?"

Janelle was stunned. "Kory's wife? Left him?"

"Left. Him. Girl, I thought I told you." Libby lowered her voice. "As good a man as Kory is, she left him for someone else. It's always the nice guys who finish last." Libby narrowed her eyes as if the woman were standing right there. "I knew she wasn't right when he brought her to the reunion that time. Something about her."

Janelle remembered that summer well too, when she was twenty-six, seeing Kory with his wife for the first time, him seeing her with David . . . "I can't believe it," she said. "How long ago?"

An usher came to get them, and Libby leaned over as they walked. "Earlier this year. Kevin told me at the reunion last summer."

The usher guided them to the left side, second to last row, and they squeezed in as others made room. The Calvary choir, robed in blue, was finishing a slow worship hymn. Todd took to the wooden podium right after.

Libby looked at Janelle. "Todd's bringing the message himself?"

"I was about to ask you that." Janelle shrugged. "I've never heard him speak, but he *is* an assistant pastor at his church."

Todd was staring down at his dad's casket, now closed. He looked somber, but there was a real peace about him.

When he looked up, he took a moment to gather his thoughts. "I remember when I was a boy, I'd come and hang out with Dad at church on Saturdays and sneak up to this very pulpit and play preacher." He smiled. "But I never imagined standing up here for his funeral." Todd paused, then gestured toward the front. "I couldn't be doing this without Pastor Brooks. Most of you know he was my best friend—some might say partner in crime—growing up."

Soft laughter rippled through the congregation.

"Thank you, my friend, for all you've done for me this week, and for the help your congregation has offered. Dad couldn't stop telling me how pleased he was that you're at New Jerusalem now."

Libby sat up in the pew and craned her neck. "I can't see," she complained. "He's not talking about *Travis* Brooks, is he?"

"If you called your grandmother like you should, you'd know the Hope Springs news."

"I know you're not talking."

Janelle stifled a chuckle. "Okay, but I knew that. Pastor Richards retired, and Travis Brooks replaced him. He just moved back a few months ago."

Libby didn't reply, and Janelle let her gaze drift past her cousin to see where Kory might be seated. But Todd had already started into his message, so she turned her focus to the front.

"And the first question people are asking me," Todd was saying, "is 'How are you doing?' A natural question, same question I ask others who've lost a loved one. What's surprising to me, though, is that my answer keeps changing." He looked more engaged now as he looked out among them. "First I was practically numb. I'd only talked to my dad two days before and he was fine. Then he was gone. When I got to Hope Springs and walked into an empty house, the numbness turned to sadness. I realized I hadn't just lost a dad, but a friend, someone I talked to about life, ministry, sports." He took a breath and let it out. "But a new feeling is coming over me, an urgency. I don't know . . ."

He looked as if he were searching for words, discovering for himself whatever was unfolding in his heart.

"There are times in our lives—times like this—when we get an up-close look at death, and it reminds us of our own mortality." Todd stepped out from behind the podium. "The question is, what are we going to do with that close-up view? How will it affect us?" He paused. "Know how it's affecting me right now?"

"Come on, son," an older member of New Jerusalem urged. "Let the Lord use you."

"It's starting to energize me," Todd said. "I *know* the work my dad did at this church and in this town. I *know* he impacted a lot of lives. He used the time God gave him faithfully. I want to take hold of that legacy and do the same. I want to live the rest of my life full-out, all for God, holding nothing back."

"Amen," said someone near them. A few people had taken to their feet, all New Jerusalem members.

Todd's eyes filled with passion. "Anybody else feel like you've been dragging through life, going through the motions? Come on! Why *not* live on fire for Jesus?"

Was that what she'd been doing? Janelle wondered. Dragging through life? David's death had had the opposite effect on her. Instead of turning toward God, she'd shied away. She'd kept going to church, mostly because of the kids, but her faith had taken a beating as she struggled to understand why God would take her husband in the prime of their lives.

She closed her eyes and continued listening to Todd even as prayers bubbled up on the inside. *Lord, I need You. I need You to fill the empty spaces David left.*

Todd shared the gospel at the end of his message, inviting people forward as the New Jerusalem choir sang. After Travis's closing prayer, the pallbearers lifted the casket and led the procession out. Libby's dad was one of them. Uncle Wood and Pastor Jim had spent many a day roaming those woods by their homes as rough-and-tumble boys.

Todd, his kids, and Pastor Jim's two older siblings filed slowly out, with the rest of the church following pew by pew. Weird . . . wasn't Becca supposed to be here by now?

Their row began moving, and Janelle suddenly spotted Kory in the back of the church. She felt awkward, unsure what to say, yet unable to avoid him. Calvary Church had one exit and he was standing right beside it.

Janelle struck up a conversation with family members as the group moved toward the double glass doors. They were all gathered around Stephanie, since so many hadn't seen her in a long time. From the corner of her eye, she saw Kevin head out with his family and Kory's daughter, while Kory remained. She wasn't sure if she was the reason until she got closer and he touched her arm.

"Janelle."

She turned and looked into his eyes. "Kory. Hi."

"I didn't know you'd be here," he said.

His voice was the same; that was her first thought. As if it would change. Her second thought was that he still had that same aura that awakened all of her senses.

"It's been a long time," he added.

"It has."

Same penetrating gaze under thick eyebrows. Same deep brown complexion. She averted her gaze as she moved aside for others to pass, including Libby. Her cousin hugged Kory—and it struck Janelle that she herself hadn't.

Kory gestured to her. "Should we step outside, out of the way?"

She followed him onto the walkway, watching as people got into their cars, powered headlights, and lined up for the short drive to the cemetery.

"I heard about your husband," he said. "I wanted to call you, but . . . I was praying for you."

She looked at him. "I appreciate that, Kory. Thank you." Should she say she'd heard about his wife?

Janelle waited as a few family members stopped to greet Kory and ask how he'd been. When they'd left, she asked, "So how well did you know Pastor Jim?"

"Not well. I've only been to Hope Springs a couple of times, as you know." He cleared his throat. "But both times I had great conversations with him—Todd too. When Kevin said he was coming, I wanted to pay my respects."

She nodded, glancing away again, aware that they were lingering. She saw Al's car drive by and join the lineup. "We'd better be going," she said.

He hesitated. "Kevin said everyone's heading to your grandmother's house afterward?"

Janelle smiled slightly. "Hope so. If not, there's enough food to last a month. You know how they do."

"We'll finish talking there, then?"

About what? She wondered if he had some of the same questions she'd had all those years ago. Or maybe he simply wanted to catch up. Either way, she wasn't sure how she felt about it.

She rubbed her arms through her dress, feeling a chill. Was it the setting sun? "Sure." She began backing away. "I'll be there."

Emotions tumbled inside as she headed to Al's car—and saw a taxi pull up in front of the church. Becca emerged, looking harried. The cabdriver set her luggage on the curb and drove away.

The back door to the limo opened, and Todd got out. Janelle didn't want to stare, but the scene was playing out right in front of her. Her dad stepped out of his car and put Becca's suitcase in his trunk. The exchange between Becca and Todd seemed a little uncomfortable, short though it was. They got in the limo and it drove slowly off.

CHAPTER FIVE

ecca's face was red with embarrassment. How could she have arrived the very moment all the cars were lined up, ready to go to the cemetery? Everything had gone so smoothly with her travel plans—until her plane sat on the runway for more than thirty minutes, waiting for a gate. Now she'd missed the wake *and* the funeral service. And the look in Todd's eyes confirmed what she'd been hearing over the phone—he was hurt.

"And you know what else, Mommy?" Claire said.

Becca leaned in, her arm around her daughter. "What, honey?"

Claire had launched into a monologue the moment Becca got into the limo, which held Becca, Todd, and the kids, as well as Todd's aunt and uncle and their spouses. Claire couldn't fully appreciate her granddad's death, but she couldn't wait to catch Becca up on all the activity and people. In a way Becca was thankful for the distraction.

"I saw Miss Janelle and Tiffany," Claire continued, "and Tiffany is four too, and she lives right next door—"

"She doesn't live next door, sweetheart." Todd sat on her other side. "She's visiting, like we are."

"—and we get to play after . . ." Claire's brows bunched up at her dad. "Where are we going again?"

"To the cemetery. That's where they'll bury your Grandpa Jim. But we know where he really is, right?"

"With Jesus!" Claire stuck her hands straight up in the air.

Two-year-old Ethan's hands shot up too. "De-sus!"

Todd and Becca shared a slight smile, their first since she arrived. When he'd gotten out of the limo he'd said, "Glad you made it," but she wondered if he was really acknowledging that she'd barely made it at all. As a rule he was easygoing, but she couldn't presume on that. Becca caught herself—maybe she already had.

"You've got some precious kids, Todd." His aunt had been playing patty-cake with Ethan. "Wish we could see them more often."

"Me too," Todd said. "Seems like we live the farthest from everybody."

The limo turned into the cemetery and wound through the grounds. Behind them was another limo with more of Todd's extended family, and a long trail of cars. When they pulled up near the burial site and parked, the family filed out and walked toward three short rows of chairs that faced the coffin. Becca sat with Ethan in her lap and Claire beside her, along with Grandpa Jim's siblings. Todd remained standing, talking with people as they made their way over.

Becca watched as Wood and Denise Sanders walked with Grandma Geri across the grass. Todd directed them to the first row of chairs, and Wood paused, gazing at the casket.

"I knew Jim all my life," Wood said. "Loved him like a brother. What you did in that service, making it a charge to live for Jesus—" He gave a slow nod. "You captured Jim's spirit perfectly. That was some message, Todd."

Message? Becca turned slightly, listening.

"Didn't know he had it in him."

A youngish black man had walked up, black-suited, Bible in hand.

Todd gave him a wry smile. "You're the one who encouraged me to do it."

"Good for you, Travis," Wood said. "You know Todd'll stay in the background if he can."

"Yeah," Travis said, "but I told him he should 'say a few words.' Didn't know he would go ahead and preach." Travis had an engaging manner about him. "I hear Calvary members are already whispering about drafting you."

"Drafting me? For what?"

"To replace your dad."

Becca nearly choked on the mint she'd put in her mouth. The thought hadn't occurred to her. Jim Dillon had returned to Hope Springs and taken over as pastor of Calvary Church after *his* father died. Could there be even a remote possibility? She couldn't imagine . . .

"I ain't the least bit surprised," Grandma Geri said. "You've got a shepherd's heart like your daddy. If I had a vote, I'd second it."

"Thanks, Grandma Geri," Todd said, "but whoever made the comment was just being nice. The line of senior pastors ended with Dad. That's not my calling."

Becca let out a sigh of relief.

Travis turned suddenly. "This isn't your wife, is it, Todd? She's way too classy for a guy like you."

"Oh, that's right, you haven't met Becca yet."

Becca felt funny that this was their first opportunity to meet, here at the graveside. She set Ethan down, guiding him to his great-aunt, and stood. "Is this the Travis I've heard so many stories about?"

Todd put an arm around Travis's shoulder. "Yes, this is Travis. The guy who always found trouble to get into and tried to drag me with him. Travis, my wife, Becca."

"So that's the version he's been telling you?" Travis gave her a warm hug. "Pleasure meeting you, Becca." He stepped back, positioned between them. "I'm glad I can set the record straight. We lived on the same street, so on any given day I'd be minding my own business when Todd would knock on the door with some scheme. Now, Todd, I would tell him, you can't do that. Your father's the pastor, it wouldn't look right."

"Y'all were both bad," Grandma Geri said.

They all turned around and laughed.

"Don't take it personally," Wood said. "Momma likes to say Jim and I were bad too."

"That's 'cause you were." Grandma Geri was matter-of-fact. "Thank the Lord you all got some sense when you grew up. Travis, I never would've thought you'd turn out to be a pastor, but you're doing a right fine job at New Jerusalem. And I *did* have a vote for that one."

"So did you vote for me, Grandma Geri?" Travis was grinning.

"You know I did, boy." Grandma Geri started coughing, and it got progressively worse fast.

"Momma, I told you I needed to take you back to the house after the service," Wood said.

"I'll . . . be . . . fine."

Denise reached in her purse. "Momma Geri, I don't know if this throat lozenge would help. I wish I'd brought that bottle of water."

Wood extended his arm to help her up. "I think we should go, Momma."

She waved him away, the cough subsiding. "This'll be over in no time."

Janelle walked up then and gave Todd a long hug. "I was trying to encourage you when we talked earlier," she said, "but you were the one who encouraged me with that message. I'm still thinking about it."

Why is everybody talking about this message?

"You did encourage me, Janelle, more than you know," Todd said.

"Hi, I'm Stephanie, Bruce's daughter." The woman extended her hand to Todd.

"Oh, man, I remember you." Todd hugged her. "It's been a long time. Just saw the rest of your family this summer. And it's a shame we don't all get together in St. Louis."

"Daddy wanted me to tell you how sorry he is about your loss." Stephanie smiled. "My cousins were telling me your grandfather was a preacher, and of course your dad was a preacher, but they didn't tell me *you* were a preacher too." She shook her head. "You got all *in* my mix, talking about living full-out." She gave him an eye. "Thanks a lot."

Todd smiled. "I know Dad's getting a kick out of all this. He liked to tell me I had more preacher in me than I wanted to admit, but who knew it would come out today of all days?" He shrugged. "Trust me, I got in my own mix."

Janelle's cousin Libby hugged Todd next. Then Becca started her round of hugs and hellos.

"The twins, back in town."

Janelle turned, smiling. "Travis!" She embraced him. "Haven't seen you in so long. Weren't you in Dallas or something?"

"Went there for seminary and thought I'd never come back." He smiled. "Never know what God'll do."

"Congratulations, Pastor Brooks." Libby kept her distance of a few feet. "Have to admit I was surprised to hear that one."

They locked eyes for a moment. "It's good to see you, Libby."

Only a few more people were still making their way from the cars. With most everyone gathered, Travis whispered a few words with Todd.

Becca sat back down, and Ethan wriggled away from his great-aunt and toddled over to her. She picked him up, Todd sat beside her, and they listened as Travis spoke final words over Jim's coffin.

It was the first moment since she'd heard of Jim's death that Becca actually focused on her father-in-law, his life and legacy. He'd always been good to her. She wished all the more that there hadn't been a conflict, so she could've spent more time here this week processing the loss and walking through the memories with Todd. She hadn't even been to the house yet, or talked to Todd about what would happen to it. It had been in the family for three generations. Would he sell it? Rent it out?

"O death, where is your victory? Where is your sting?" Travis spoke with fervor. "Thanks be to God, who gives us the victory through our Lord Jesus Christ."

"Amen," sounded all around her, including from Todd.

Would've been nice to hear Todd's message. He didn't speak much at their church in St. Louis. Todd was the low-key assistant pastor, happy to serve as overseer of the church's small groups ministry. His "main" job was as a mechanical engineer at an agricultural company.

Heads bowed as Travis gave the closing prayer. People moved slowly afterward, conversing, many coming to say a few words to Todd.

Travis raised his hands. "The Dillon family would like me to announce that the repast will take place at the home of Geraldine Sanders." He smiled. "Most of you know her as Grandma Geri. If you need directions for how to get there—"

"Boy, you're back in Hope Springs," Grandma Geri said. "Nobody needs directions anywhere."

Travis's eyes twinkled with amusement. "For those who could not hear, Grandma Geri reminded me that nobody needs directions. I don't know why I thought I could give them anyway. Does anybody know street names around here? Hang a left at the Main Street Diner."

"Hey, thanks for the plug." A woman passed by in a black

wraparound skirt, white cotton top, and flats. Her dress was plain, but she had a fresh-faced cuteness about her.

"The diner doesn't need a plug," Travis called after her. "Place speaks for itself, largely because of you, Sara Ann."

"Yeah, yeah." She turned only slightly as she continued walking, a pleasant smile on her face. "Flattery won't get you anywhere, Travis. Now, a big tip? That'll work."

He spread out his hands. "Don't I always?"

Becca was trying to recall if she'd met Sara Ann before, but her attention was drawn to two guys who'd cornered Todd a few feet away on the grass. They were older, and Becca was sure she'd seen them at Calvary Church on prior visits. It was clear they weren't merely offering condolences. Todd was listening too intently.

She guided the kids back to the limo, her curiosity peaking as they waited. Finally Todd opened the door and got in.

The limo wound back through the cemetery toward the exit. Todd seemed lost in thought.

"Well?" Becca's voice was low.

He looked at her. "Well, what?"

"What was that about, the guys you were talking to?"

Todd paused. "They're elders at Calvary. They want to have a conversation about me being pastor there."

Somehow she'd thought it deep down, but it seemed too far out to be so. "You told them no, right? You've always said you're not called to that."

His nod wavered. "I said no, but they asked if I'd be willing to talk about it. We're meeting tomorrow at the church before we leave."

"I'm not understanding," she said. "Why meet with them? We're not moving to Hope Springs."

"I know." He cast a glance out the window. "It's only a conversation."

Becca brushed aside the possibility. "Todd," she said, then hesitated. "I haven't had a chance to apologize for not making the church service."

He watched his aunt give Ethan an animal cracker, then looked at her. "You couldn't help the delay."

"Well, I should've asked to reschedule the meeting as you suggested. I should've . . . I should've been here."

Todd was slow to respond. "Dad always said a person could drive himself crazy wishing for what wasn't, and we should just be thankful for the now." He looked at her. "You're here now." A few seconds passed. "It's an exciting time for you, Bec. I understand that. This is what you've been building toward."

He gazed out the window and Becca let his words settle, thankful for his understanding.

A *ding* sounded in the limousine. She'd forgotten to turn off her phone. She wondered if the text was from her agent or someone from Worth & Purpose. What if she needed to respond right away before they left for the holiday? But no way could she dig her phone out and look at it. This was the time to focus on Todd.

And yet . . . it was killing her. She had to see, and respond if need be. Becca sat tight. They'd be at Grandma Geri's in less than five minutes.

CHAPTER SIX

J anelle checked the makeshift buffet table and saw the baked beans running low. She brought the aluminum pan into the kitchen, scooped several ladles from an even bigger pan into that one, and brought it back as people waited in line in the Sanders dining room. She decided the desserts could use replenishing as well, and headed back to the kitchen to slice more red velvet and lemon cake.

Libby cut her off on the way. "What exactly are you doing?"

Janelle walked around her. "Serving."

"Yeah. For like, the last two hours." Libby followed her into the kitchen. "You haven't even eaten yet."

Janelle grabbed a stack of Styrofoam dessert plates and a knife and began slicing. "Why are you worried about whether I've eaten? I'm not that hungry."

"Really? On the way to the funeral you said you were starving and should've eaten something before we left. Now you've morphed into your mom and Aunt Gladys, making sure everyone else is well fed." She put her hand to Janelle's so she'd stop slicing. "Why are you trying to avoid Kory?"

Their teenage cousin Jackie happened into the kitchen and opened the refrigerator.

"Hey, Jackie," Janelle said, "I need your help a minute. Could you start taking these plates to the buffet table?"

Jackie didn't appear thrilled at the interruption, but she carted off three plates.

Janelle finally looked at Libby again. "Why would I need to avoid Kory? If you hadn't noticed, there are lots of people here, and I thought it'd be nice to help."

"By slicing more cake? Al and I have been keeping Kory company in the family room, and I know he's been waiting for you to come in there. I think you're just—"

"Janelle?" Her mom walked into the kitchen. "Why is Jackie putting more cake on the table? There's plenty. Don't slice up any more, baby, so we can keep it fresh."

Libby made an I-told-you-so face.

"Well, I heard someone say the decaf was running low, so I can get that—"

"Sorry to interrupt."

Kory. Janelle turned to face him. He had changed out of his suit and into a pair of jeans. "No problem. Did you need something?"

"No, I'm good, thanks." He glanced at Estelle and Libby and came a little closer to Janelle. "We're about to leave in a few. Wondered if maybe we could take a walk, talk a little."

"Oh." Janelle remembered the walk they took down the same country road years ago as if it were yesterday. She looked about the kitchen. "I don't know. I was just about to—"

"I got it," Libby said. "Glad to serve." She flashed a smile.

Janelle narrowed her eyes at her, then turned to Kory. "Okay, let me get my jacket."

He opened the screen door for her, and they stepped out into the night. Activity swirled between both houses under well-lit grounds—people eating outdoors in the back, kids running to and fro. Janelle stopped and looked toward the swing set that was about as old as she was. Sara Ann was doing triple duty, giving a light shove to Tiffany, Claire, and Dee, Kory's daughter, all of whom were giggling wildly.

"Mom, Mom, look at us!"

"Wow, Tiffy!" she said. "You all are sailing straight for the moon!"

"Higher, Miss Sara Ann, higher!"

Sara Ann was laughing. "I don't want you to fall out!"

"We're not leaving yet, are we, Dad?" Dee said.

Kory shook his head. "Not yet, sweetheart. You've got a few minutes."

"Aw, Dad, that's all?" Dee yelled, kicking higher.

Kory smiled. "Enjoy it!"

Janelle and Kory started a slow walk up the road in silence, away from the bright lights into the darkened blue sky. She held her arms against the cool temperature as the two of them fell into step.

"I'm glad Dee's having a nice time," she said finally.

"Me too. She was eating beside me, and your daughter asked if she'd like to sit with the girls." Kory looked at her. "Tiffany's a special girl."

"Thank you." Janelle stared at the quiet road ahead of them. "Libby said your wife left, Kory. What happened?"

Kory was staring ahead as well. "We were associates in litigation at a large law firm in Chicago. That's how we met. A bunch of us went up for partner the same year, but the economy had tanked, and we knew they wouldn't promote everybody. But I had worked hard, done well, even brought in some clients. Everyone assumed I'd make it for sure. Shelley had done well, but she hadn't yet developed any business for the firm." He took a breath. "She was promoted. I wasn't."

They took a few steps in silence before Kory continued.

"Then the rumors started about her seeing a senior partner in litigation, who was also married. She denied it . . . until she announced last New Year's Eve that she was leaving to move in with him."

"Wow. Just like that? What about Dee?"

"Shelley said it made more sense for Dee to stay with me. I was the one who basically took care of her." He sighed. "That was the hardest part—convincing Dee her mother loved her even though she left."

Janelle looked at him. "That's so sad, Kory. What did you say when she dropped all this on you?"

"I didn't know what to say at first. I was hurt and angry, couldn't stand the sight of her. I felt like I never really knew her." He kept walking, looking into the night. "I was ready to cut my losses and be done. But in the midst of all that I focused on God again." He glanced at her. "Nothing like heartbreak to lead you back to God. I'd neglected Him all the years I'd been working toward partner. Anyway, it was hard because I knew He was telling me to forgive her and try and reconcile. And that's what I did. Even asked if she'd move with me to North Carolina so we could start over." He retreated into his thoughts a moment. "She said there was nothing we could do. The marriage was over."

Janelle took a moment to think through what he'd said. "So what's the status now?"

"She wasted no time getting an attorney to draft a separation agreement. On New Year's Eve it'll be a year. After that she can file for divorce."

"Will you contest it?"

"No. I've tried to talk to her every step of the way—seemed like God wouldn't leave me alone unless I did." His sigh let her know how hard that was. "Nothing like your wife rejecting you over and over to keep you humble."

"I'm sorry, Kory. I know this was nowhere near what you envisioned for your marriage."

He stopped and turned to her with a curious look. "Are you saying that because you remember?"

Her brow creased, but it took only a minute for his question to register. "That's not why I said it, but I do remember. We were standing in about this same spot. You started that silly discussion of what your marriage would be like."

He had a near-smile. "Oh, it was silly?"

She continued walking. "That's the best word for it. Let's see . . . you and your wife would have breakfast in bed every morning—I guess it would just magically appear."

"We'd train the kids to bring it to us."

"Oh. Okay. All arguments would be decided by a flip of a coin in order to end quickly. And because you're particular about having a clean house, you would assume all cleaning chores in exchange for a limitless basketball and football watching license."

"College and professional."

"Well, of course."

"I said what my *wife* would be like too . . . Too bad I didn't stick to it." He muttered the last part.

"I remember. Beautiful and on fire for Jesus."

"But I was flirting."

Janelle frowned. "Flirting?"

"Don't get me wrong. I meant it . . . much as I could've meant anything at eighteen. But I said it because *you* were beautiful and on fire for Jesus."

She didn't know how to respond, but her stomach did, with a tiny flip.

Kory paused in front of her, hands in his jacket pockets. "I didn't think you remembered that night."

"How could I forget, Kory?"

"I thought you had. Or at least it didn't mean much to you, since you stopped returning my calls."

"*I* stopped returning calls? You were the one who stopped calling. I left messages with your roommate and never heard from you."

"I never got any messages."

Janelle stared at him in disbelief. "I replayed that weekend in my mind so many times. The walks, the conversation. It was like our *souls* connected. Then we went off to college, and when I didn't hear from you after the first month, I almost thought I'd imagined it."

Kory looked into her eyes. "You didn't imagine it. I think we were standing in *this* exact spot when we kissed good-bye. I'd never felt what I felt with you that weekend."

Janelle's breath caught. The wind grazed her face, and their stare lingered long enough for her to remember vividly every second of that kiss. She turned and started back. "It was a lifetime ago. We were kids."

"True." They kept a slow pace. "But even now, it's nice to know it meant something to you too."

"I didn't think I'd ever see you again. Then you showed up years later with Shelley." Janelle tried to hold her tongue, but she had to say this much. "That was interesting. She didn't seem excited to be here."

"No. She didn't want to come. Kevin invited us because Leslie was doing her ballet routine in the family talent show. We'd never seen her perform, and she kept asking if we'd be there. I couldn't say no." He watched a stray cat that had appeared from nowhere and fallen in step with them. "But we only stayed Saturday night because Shelley wanted to get back."

"It was just as well." Janelle didn't mind admitting it now. "It was weird seeing you. I couldn't help it; my heart reacted, and I basically spent the evening avoiding you."

"Like today." Kory glanced sideways at her. "Does that mean your heart reacted when you saw me today?"

If he only knew what was happening inside this very second. When she didn't respond, he pulled her to a stop.

"Janelle?"

She allowed a brief glance. "Maybe. A little." She started walking again. "But it doesn't mean anything. I'm still processing life without David. You're processing life without Shelley. We don't need to go back sixteen years and process that too." She sealed it with the refrain she'd been playing in her head. "Anyway, I'll be gone after Christmas. So it's kind of like that first summer all over again."

"It's nothing like that first summer, Janelle. You said it yourself. We were kids. And technology was primitive compared to now. We can call, text, Skype. We can be friends." The darkness ebbed as they neared the houses. He paused in the shadows. "I don't know about you, but I could use a friend."

She dared to look into his eyes, knowing that on this beautiful late December night with this handsome man—a man her heart knew well—she could easily be drawn in.

"I'll be honest with you," she said. "I'd love for us to be able to build a friendship. But it can't be anything more. Personally, I'm not ready. And God could do a miracle in Shelley's heart and bring you two back together"—she didn't miss the look on his face—"well, He *could*." She looked into his eyes. "But, yeah. I could use a friend too."

He extended his arms, and Janelle moved inside them.

"Merry Christmas, friend," he said.

She closed her eyes, remembering his embrace. "Merry Christmas, friend."

CHAPTER SEVEN

Thursday, December 24

Becca zipped up her suitcase, carried it downstairs, and set it next to the kids' smaller luggage by the front door. She walked past the living room, then backed up. "Claire," she called, "why are all these toys in here? I thought I told you to pack them up."

Claire skipped from the kitchen in a long-sleeved shirt, loose leggings, and bare feet. "I don't have to pack those up, Mommy." She licked her fingers. "We play with them in the car."

Becca mussed her daughter's straight brown hair. "Okay, sweet pea. We'll load everything up when Daddy gets back with the car." She led the way back to the kitchen. "Let's wipe the jelly off your cheek. Good job helping your brother while I finished packing."

"But he won't eat the banana." Claire shrugged as if she'd tired of trying. "All he wants is Frosted Flakes."

"You little stinker." Becca kissed Ethan on the head where he sat at the table. "You'd better eat your fruit. It's good for you."

"No 'nana!" Ethan kicked his legs straight out, happy in defiance, then grabbed another handful of cereal and stuffed it into his mouth.

Becca picked up her laptop from the table and tucked it inside her messenger bag. She'd gotten a little work done on her talk for the conference, based on the direction she'd gotten in the meeting yesterday. But she also wanted to check out the three blog design options that were supposed to be uploaded for her this morning—and she couldn't even *access* them. How had her father-in-law lived like this? Seemed almost primitive to be without Wi-Fi or even a dial-up connection. She felt so detached. Oh, to get out of this little town and feel technologically alive again.

"Mom!" Claire called.

"Oh, Ethan . . ."

He'd reached for his cup and knocked it over, starting a milky stream on course for Jim's Bible, notepad, and reading glasses, still sitting on the kitchen table where he'd left them the morning he died. Todd hadn't had the heart to move them. Becca lifted them quickly out of the way, along with a stack of opened and unopened mail.

"Hand me some paper towels, sweetie . . . thanks." She wiped the mess, picturing Jim here at the table, going through his normal morning routine, unaware it was for the last time.

"Okay, buddy, let's clean you up." Becca wiped Ethan's hands and face, then turned to Claire, who swigged the last of her juice. "Soon as Daddy gets back, we'll be ready to go. Make sure you're not forgetting anything."

Claire hopped up. "I'll go check."

Ethan got down too. "I check."

"Copycat."

"Be patient with him, Claire." Becca started washing the few breakfast dishes they'd used. "He looks up to you. That's part of being a big sister."

Becca glanced at the clock. She'd thought Todd would be back by now. She rinsed her coffee mug and set it in the dish rack, puzzled still that he would even indulge the discussion. She'd told him this morning he shouldn't go. The elders needed to move on, talk to people for whom the position was realistic.

There was no way it made sense for them. Their lives were planted in St. Louis, and her mother was there as well. Her help in taking care of the kids when Becca traveled was invaluable—help they'd need all the more when Worth & Purpose started up. And Todd wasn't even a pulpit preacher. The whole idea of moving to Hope Springs seemed absurd.

A knock sounded at the front door, and Ethan and Claire ran to it. "It's Tiffany!" Claire had her face pasted to the window pane.

"You can open it," Becca said, walking up. "Good morning, Tiffany."

"Hi, Miss Becca. Can Claire come out and play?"

Janelle was with her. "I told her Claire was leaving this morning and probably didn't have time, but she insisted on seeing for herself." She smiled at the girls. "They had a lot of fun together yesterday."

"Fast friends, for sure," Becca said. "I doubt they remember the first time they met; they were only one or two. But they won't forget this time."

"Can I, Mom?" Claire said. "Can I go outside?"

"Let's all go out," Becca said. "It's such a nice morning. No sense waiting for Todd inside."

The girls pounced on a big plastic ball that'd been left in the grass and began throwing it back and forth. Ethan stooped by the porch, fascinated by an inchworm. Becca kept an eye on him as she and Janelle sat in the porch swing.

"You've got perfect driving weather," Janelle said. "What time do you think you'll make it back?"

"It'll be late, close to midnight. And of course we've still got toys to put together, so we could be up all night. But at least we'll be home for Christmas—Ethan, don't put that in your mouth." Becca looked at Janelle. "Boys."

Janelle smiled. "Yep. And this is boy country. I remember the summer when Daniel was three and thought it'd be fun to roll around in the dirt. He picked a dirt pile filled with red ants."

"I remember that. Poor thing was covered with bites. Didn't David take him to the hospital in Rocky Mount?"

Janelle nodded. "I ran for a tube of anti-itch cream, but David wanted to make sure he didn't have some kind of reaction." She laughed a little. "Several hours and several hundred dollars later, they left the hospital with a tube of ointment."

Becca didn't know if it helped or hurt to talk about David. She hoped it was okay. She leaned closer to Janelle. "I'm sorry I haven't been in touch with you. How have you been? What's life been like for you?"

"Don't worry about that, Becca. I haven't been too good about *letting* people stay in touch with me . . . left the Bible study I'd been attending and cut back my involvement at church, missed two family reunions." She sighed. "Been focused on the kids. Trying to adjust to our new normal."

Becca wasn't sure if she should ask, but she plunged ahead. "How's it been financially? I imagine it'd be a pretty rough adjustment, since you left your job when Tiffany was born."

"David was paranoid when it came to money and his family's financial future. Had to save up to buy a car and drive it till it dropped, mortgage had to be affordable on one income . . . Guess it was the accountant in him. He had *two* life insurance policies, through his job and an outside firm. So we're okay for now, but I plan to go back to work when Tiff starts kindergarten next year."

"Don't remind me." Becca looked over at Tiffany and Claire. "Next year'll be a big year for those girls."

Janelle's eyes lit up suddenly. "And a big year for *you*. I haven't had a chance to tell you congrats on the Worth & Purpose speaker spot. That's awesome, Becca."

"So you've heard of them?" Becca didn't take it for granted. There were lots of Christian women's conferences.

"Yeah, I went to a conference with some women from my church, maybe three years ago when they came to D.C. Loved it. Music was great too. I'm so thrilled for you."

"Pray I don't freeze in place on the platform in the middle of my message," Becca said.

"You'll be fine. I'll be praying." She smiled at her. "God's really using you and Todd. So proud of you both."

Becca sat forward. "Okay, you know I missed the service yesterday." She'd told Janelle last night how awful she felt arriving when she did. "What was it about Todd's message that got people talking?"

Janelle thought about it. "Part of it for me was I didn't expect it. I've known Todd since he was little. He had his moments of mischief and all that. But for the most part, he's always been the background guy." She crossed her legs. "But something happened up there. He just came alive. And what he said was exactly what I needed to hear. Made me think about changes I need to make."

Becca pondered that a moment.

"Ha. We talked him up," Janelle said.

Todd's car rolled into the dirt area that'd been fashioned over the years between the houses. Hardly anyone parked in the gravel driveways next to the respective houses. They had this end of the street to themselves, and used every bit of it. Ethan jumped up, ready to run to him.

"Ethan, wait, honey." Becca rose quickly and grabbed his hand until the car stopped moving.

Todd got out, looking cheery. Becca wondered what it meant.

"Hey, buddy," he said. He scooped Ethan up into his arms, regarding Becca. "Are we ready to hit the road?"

"All ready."

"I'm not." Claire was in the grass, arms folded in a huff. "I want to keep playing with Tiffany."

"Honey, don't you want to get home for Christmas?"

"They have Christmas here too, don't they?"

So much for that.

"You'll see Tiffany this summer," Todd said, then glanced at the porch. "Uh, Miss Janelle, you *are* coming down for the reunion, aren't you?"

Janelle came down the porch steps. "You mean now that you've got our girls' hearts set on it? How could I not?"

Todd toted Ethan toward the Sanders home. "Everybody up and at 'em over there, Janelle? I want to say a quick good-bye."

"You know the deal." Janelle followed him to the front, beckoning the girls by hand. "They were just stirring when I left."

Sofa beds with teen bodies sprawled in deep sleep greeted them in the family room when they walked in—as did the smell of bacon. They followed the latter to the kitchen, where Estelle and Gladys were cooking breakfast in their housecoats. Grandma Geri had her coffee at the table, sitting with family who'd camped there for conversation.

Todd stood in the middle of the kitchen and saluted. "Good morning to all—and good-bye. If I don't say it fast, I'll never get out of here."

"I know that's right." Gladys chuckled from her frying pan. "It'll be an hour later, and you'll still be trying to get on the road."

"Boy, get over here and give me a hug," Grandma Geri said. "When you coming again?"

Todd set Ethan down and bent to hug her. "Still got a lot to take care of with Dad's things, so I'll probably be back in a month, if not before."

"I'm gonna really miss your dad," Grandma Geri said. "That was a special man."

The love for his dad showed in Todd's eyes. "Yes, ma'am, he was."

"And you're every bit as special." She took his hand. "You know that, right? God's gifted you."

Todd's face was noncommittal.

"Believe it, Todd."

He gave her a nod. "Yes, ma'am."

Becca hugged Grandma Geri next, then moved person to person as she and Todd said their good-byes. A quick knock on the screen door made them all look. It opened and closed, and a moment later Dr. Reynolds appeared.

"Hey, Dr. Reynolds." Gladys waved. "How is it every family get-together, you happen to stop by right at breakfast time?"

"Yeah, we've caught on to you, Doc." Estelle was peeling potatoes for hash browns.

Gladys turned to Estelle. "We should talk to him about Momma's cough while he's here."

Dr. Reynolds, a distinguished black man in his sixties, had a kind disposition that put people immediately at ease. He knew—and had probably treated—everyone in town, including Claire when she'd gotten severe constipation as a baby during a visit. He was known for stopping by the Sanders home to shoot the breeze during family gatherings, but this visit was out of the ordinary. He had his brief-case, and he had yet to speak. The family looked at him now with tentative expressions.

"Good morning, everyone," he said. "I wish I were just stopping by for bacon and eggs, but I need to speak to Grandma Geri." He stepped closer to her. "Is there someplace we can go for privacy?"

"Momma, what's this about?" Gladys moved closer too.

Estelle had been heating a pan for the potatoes, but she turned it off, set down her paring knife, and went to listen.

Grandma Geri had her hands clasped in front of her. "Right here's fine," she said. "Don't matter to me at this point who hears what you got to say."

Becca looked at Todd, who nodded, gave final hugs, and followed her out.

"What do you think is going on?" Becca whispered outside.

"Grandma Geri must have some health issue. Didn't look good, did it?"

"Whatever it is, looked like they're about to have a serious discussion."

Todd paused. "Actually, Becca, I think we need to have one as well on the drive home."

CHAPTER EIGHT

S tephanie was folding the bedding she and Lindell had used on the pull-out sofa in the living room. Her dad had been right—bonding did take place late at night at her grandmother's house. She, Libby, Janelle, and others had talked and laughed into the wee hours. She'd tried to hang on to sleep as the kids began moving about this morning, but it was futile. Plus the food was smelling too good, and she didn't want to miss out.

Janelle came from the kitchen. "Hey, Dr. Reynolds is here," she said. It was almost a whisper. "Something with Grandma Geri. Doesn't sound good."

Lindell perked up from his spot in a nearby armchair, where he'd moved so Stephanie could make up the bed. He got up, stretching. "Let's see what's going on," he said.

Stephanie went to the kitchen in what she'd slept in—sweatpants and a T-shirt—and stood near the refrigerator with Lindell. Grandma Geri was at the kitchen table with Aunt Gladys, Aunt Estelle, Uncle Wood, and a man who must be Dr. Reynolds. The fairly large kitchen was growing more crowded by the second, with Libby coming now, half-awake, hanging by the door frame. One of the teens had ushered the kids into the family room. Stephanie could hear the sound of cartoons in the distance.

Dr. Reynolds took papers out of a briefcase and set them on the table. Everyone quieted as he cleared his throat and looked at Grandma Geri. "Geraldine, I've known you for more than forty years. Many in this kitchen have been under my care at one time or another. And of course, I had the privilege of taking care of your beloved Elwood up until he passed, rest his soul."

Stephanie was practically holding her breath. What was this buildup about?

He continued. "We have a history that binds us, and I feel part of the Sanders family. So I want you to know I would not come here on Christmas Eve with this news if I didn't think it absolutely necessary."

"I know that, Grayson." Grandma Geri sat a little straighter. "Go on."

Dr. Reynolds took note of the faces surrounding them. "Are you sure you don't want to discuss this privately first, then call everyone in?"

"I'm sure," she said.

"I'll keep it as simple as I can. Dr. Peters called me earlier this morning with the results of the biopsy, and I asked that I be the one to share it with you." His mouth seemed dry. He kept licking his lips. "Geraldine, you have lung cancer."

A flurry of gasps sounded around the room.

"And it's what we call non-small cell lung cancer."

"Have mercy . . ." Aunt Gladys picked up a New Jerusalem fan from the table and swished it before her face.

"Lung cancer?" Stephanie whispered it to Lindell. "I don't remember my grandmother smoking."

"Doesn't have to come from smoking," he whispered back. "But what about your grandfather?"

Stephanie shrugged. She barely remembered him. She was in her early teens when he died.

"I'm confused." Aunt Estelle regarded her mother. "We knew you hadn't been feeling well with the coughing and fatigue, but why didn't we know about the biopsy? Who took you?"

"I took myself." Grandma Geri seemed insulted that she'd presume otherwise. "Contrary to what y'all seem to think, I don't mind going to the doctor. I just didn't want everybody *knowing* I went 'cause you'd worry me to death until I got the results."

Dr. Reynolds added, "From there, I ordered a chest X-ray, which led to the biopsy."

"Momma, you still should've told us," Aunt Gladys said. "But thank God you went when you did."

Uncle Wood leaned forward. "How serious is it, Doc? And how soon will she undergo surgery?"

Dr. Reynolds looked him in the eye. "Very serious. Stage four. The cancer has already begun to spread, and the reality is it's inoperable." He sighed. "Geraldine, you'll receive palliative care, as Elwood did."

Stephanie leaned her head over to Lindell again. "What does that mean?"

Lindell's sigh was sad. "Means they'll try to ease the pain and extend her life as long as they can."

"So chemotherapy, then?" Grandma Geri asked. "Like you did with Elwood?"

Dr. Reynolds nodded. "Yes, chemotherapy. With the hope that it will lessen the symptoms and enable you to live well for as long as possible."

Stephanie looked at her husband. Sometimes she was surprised he actually knew what he was talking about.

"As long as possible?" Worry lined Aunt Estelle's face.

"What's the bottom line, Doc?" Uncle Wood asked. "How long can she expect to live?"

"Wood, there's no way to say with certainty," the doctor said. "Everyone responds to chemo differently."

"Daddy passed pretty quickly from what I remember." Aunt Estelle sounded as if she were talking to herself.

Dr. Reynolds absentmindedly straightened his papers. "Your mother knows better than anybody in this room that God has the final say."

"Yes, He does," Grandma Geri affirmed. "And I got no fear of this thing. I'm fine either way. If I die, y'all know where to find me. With Jesus. And Elwood."

Aunt Gladys gave her a look. "We understand all that, Momma. But we don't want you to give up either. We don't know what God'll do. You could live to be a hundred or more. You have to fight this." She looked at the doctor. "Could Momma go to a treatment facility in Raleigh? She could come stay with us. I'm sure I could call on one of my good friends to help take her to and fro, since my husband and I both work."

"I feel helpless, living way down in Florida," Aunt Estelle said.

"I was thinking the same," Uncle Wood said. "Not much Denise and I can do from Atlanta."

"I think Raleigh's the only viable option," Aunt Gladys said.

Grandma Geri shook her head. "I'm staying in my own home and going to the hospital in Rocky Mount where Elwood went."

"Momma," Uncle Wood said, "the hospital is at least fifteen or twenty minutes from here, and you can't drive yourself to chemo treatments. Who would take you back and forth?"

"I don't know. I can pray about it." Her hands began to tremble. "That's all I want. I don't mind dying, but I want to die in the home I've lived in for over sixty years." Tears slid down her face for the first time since she'd heard the diagnosis.

Aunt Estelle grabbed her hand across the table. "Momma, it'll be okay. We'll figure something out."

"I'll do it." Janelle stood behind her mother, looking pained by all she'd heard.

Stephanie looked at Janelle. *Is she serious?*

"You'll do what?" Aunt Estelle asked her.

"I'll take Grandma to her treatments and help care for her," Janelle said.

Aunt Estelle turned more fully to get a better look at her. "Honey, what sense does that make? What about Daniel's school? Your life is in Maryland."

"What life? It hasn't been the same anyway since David's death." She seemed to think it through on the spot. "It's not like I'm working. Daniel can transfer to Hope Springs Elementary. It'll be like an extended vacation, until Grandma's better."

"Come here, baby." Grandma Geri reached for her.

Janelle walked over and held her hand.

"I can't let you do that, much as you warmed my heart by offering. It's too much."

Janelle bent down next to her. "Grandma, remember you used to tell us, 'Y'all think you're grown,' when we were teens?"

"Mm-hmm." Libby was standing by her dad. "I remember."

"Well, now I *am* grown, and I get to decide what's too much— and I just decided. It's not too much." She smiled. "Besides, what did you tell me yesterday? 'Let your family love on you.' That's what I want to do."

"I also said you needed a spanking 'cause you don't listen." Grandma Geri squeezed Janelle's hand, fresh tears in her eyes.

"That's a mighty special thing you're offering to do, Jan." Uncle Wood looked over at his twin sister. "You raised her right, Stelle."

"Definitely special," Aunt Gladys said. "And you won't be in this alone, Janelle. I can help on weekends."

Libby looked at her from across the table. "What will you do, Jan? Drive home, pack more stuff, and come right back?"

Janelle took a moment to think. "I could leave right after Christmas and be back by the New Year. That'll give me time to square away things at home." She turned to Dr. Reynolds. "Is that okay? Can Grandma wait till then to start treatment?"

"Better be okay." Grandma Geri had recaptured her spunk. "I'm spending my last Christmas holiday with my family in peace."

"Momma, stop talking like that," Aunt Gladys said. "I don't care what the report says. We'll be praying for complete healing."

"Amen" sounded around the kitchen.

Lindell went to talk to Dr. Reynolds, and others stood around listening or talking among themselves. Stephanie was trying to figure out what was going on inside of her. She was saddened by the news and needed to call her dad right away and let him know. But something else was pressing in on her. She eased around family members and slipped out the side door in her slippers, thinking better of it when the chill hit her arms. But she felt the need to keep walking, thinking.

Times like this, she thought of her sister. Cyd always prayed first thing, even when she didn't know what to pray.

Lord, why is my heart beating like this? I feel like I've been running. And You know I don't hardly run.

She continued walking up the road, watching tree limbs sway in the wind, mulling the news. Her grandmother had cancer . . .

Stephanie didn't get overly sad about such things, not when the person was old. Everybody had to die of something, didn't they? Not that she wanted anyone to suffer either. It was just . . . maybe she just found it hard to enter into another person's pain. It required something of her. Required her to care, to feel.

Why was she about to cry?

She waved a hand in front of her face, as if to will it away. She couldn't remember the last time she'd cried.

Okay, Lord . . . what? What is this?

Her mind went to Janelle, how struck she was by Janelle's offer to care for her grandmother. The minute she said it, Stephanie knew she could never do something like that. Would never want to. It took a special kind of person to give that way, a true serv—

She stopped, hands on her hips, weird tears sliding down her face. That could *not* be what this was all about. *Here's the deal, Lord. Yes, I prayed to be a servant, but not that kind. I was talking take-a-meal-to-someone-across-town-when-they're-sick kind of servant, not pick-up-and-move-hundreds-of-miles kind of servant. Anyway, hallelujah, the job's taken. Janelle already filled it.*

She shook her head as if to shake away her ludicrous thoughts.

Lindell's leaving for Haiti next week. You don't have a job either. Nothing's keeping you in St. Louis. You could help Janelle.

"Shut up, Cyd."

Great, she was going crazy. Talking aloud to the Cyd in her head.

"Stephanie, you okay?"

She turned. Lindell was coming toward her. She didn't want him to see her like this. He'd surely ask questions. Had he ever seen her cry?

"I was wondering where you went," he said. He looked more closely at her. "Sweetheart, you're crying?"

He put his arms around her, and she buried her head on his shoulder.

"The news is definitely upsetting," he said. "I'm so glad you felt like we needed to be here for Christmas."

"Yeah, before I changed my mind and wanted to stay in St. Louis. That's the thing, Lindell . . ." She walked a few feet away, processing her thoughts. "I say I want to change and care and all that stuff I'm supposed to say and feel, but deep down I don't want to. You know? Deep down, I'm selfish." She was crying harder, not even understanding why. "I don't want to go out of my way for anybody. I'm not a Janelle."

Lindell came closer. "What are you talking about, Steph?"

She folded her arms, partly because it was cold and partly because she wanted to shield herself against whatever God was trying to do with her. "I think God wants me to spend some time in Hope Springs while you're in Haiti . . ." She wiped a few tears. "Helping Janelle take care of Grandma Geri."

"Wow." Lindell looked aside, presumably processing it himself.

"But I know it wouldn't work," she quickly added. "We can't just leave our home for weeks at a time. Too much to look after—bills, home maintenance. I mean, what if a pipe bursts when it's cold or a bird gets stuck in the chimney—that happened to the Nelsons, you know. Somebody needs to be there."

Lindell brought her into his arms again. "Steph, I have watched God do amazing things in your heart in the two years we've been married." He leaned back to look in her eyes. "You think you're selfish now? Do you remember how you *used* to be?"

The tears had subsided, so she could easily roll her eyes at him.

"I'm trying to encourage you, babe. You've come a long way. We both have. I would never have considered a medical mission trip two years ago." He took her hand and walked with her. "I think it's exciting. You told me you've been praying to have a servant's heart. Sounds like God wants to take you to servant school."

"You didn't answer my concerns, though. What about our house?"

Lindell almost chuckled. "Really, Steph? How much family do we have nearby to check on things for us? And we can pay bills online. The last thing I'm worried about is the house."

"Well, Janelle might not want me here. I might just get in the way."

"True." Lindell stifled a smile. "You'd be remiss if you didn't ask to be sure."

"And I'd miss my family."

He nodded. "Yes, you will. And you'll get to know the family that's here better." He squeezed her hand. "You're not joining the army. It's only a few weeks."

"Hmph. It's kinda like joining the army. Servant school boot camp."

He laughed. "That might be true." He stopped and looked at her. "Not like you have to decide this minute. Let's pray, and whatever you decide, you decide. God can find a way to take you through servant school boot camp in St. Louis just as well as in Hope Springs."

That made her feel better, like her whole life didn't hinge on this one decision. She stared into the distance.

"What?" Lindell said.

"I don't know . . . My thoughts about what I should do keep changing, depending on whether I'm focused on myself or my grandmother." She sighed. "If you ask me, boot camp already started."

CHAPTER NINE

Tuesday, December 29

Todd, help me here." Becca blew out a soft sigh, taking a stab at patience, which was dwindling fast. She swiveled from her computer screen to face him fully. "You're telling me your company is about to lay off a lot of people in your department but you won't be among them."

"Yes. My level is safe for now."

"Yet *this* is your confirmation that we should leave life as we know it and move to Hope Springs? You can't be serious."

They'd been debating this since the road trip home. Todd's meeting with the elders had made an impression and swayed him to at least begin thinking seriously about their proposition. Every day he seemed to be leaning more in favor of the move. But she'd been hanging her hopes on one thing he said he'd need—real confirmation. Given how crazy this notion was, she'd been sure he wouldn't get it.

"I really think so, Bec." He paced in front of her, a distressing sign, since it meant his wheels were turning. "When they told me about the layoffs today, it just clicked." He looked at her, his green eyes twinkling.

"Clicked." She bit her lip, nodding. "What am I missing, Todd? If your job is safe, why would you want to leave?"

He grabbed a chair from the small round table in her office and sat. "When they told me who they were laying off—including a woman who just had a baby and a guy who just bought a house—it struck me that nothing is secure in this world. We hang on to it like it's everything, but it could be gone like that." He snapped a finger. "I felt like God was showing me that instead of trusting in a job, I need to trust where He leads us. You know?"

"Not really." She stared at him. "I'm not seeing why you'd quit a job—that affords us a nice living, by the way—to take a position you've said you're not called to do."

Todd nodded. "That's the other thing God's been showing me."

If I hear that one more time . . .

Todd had prayed and fasted after Christmas, something she'd never seen him do, not apart from some churchwide initiative. Now every time she turned around he had something else God was showing him. And she wasn't excited about any of it.

"I've been running from it, Bec, from my calling," he continued. "Doing what's comfortable. Maybe I feared I wouldn't measure up to my dad and granddad. And frankly, I knew enough to know that shepherding a congregation can be one big headache after another. I didn't want the hassle. But now . . ."

Becca didn't necessarily want to hear the rest. She liked their life just fine before the *But now.*

He sighed. "I don't know . . . I know you're against the move. It's not even that I'm *for* it. I just can't shake it." He leaned forward, elbows on his thighs, and looked her in the eye. "But you're right. I'd be giving up a good salary. I'm out of my mind, aren't I?"

"Yes. You are." She gave him a wry smile, then sighed herself. "I don't get what God is doing. Right when my travel ramps up, we're talking about moving away from Mom? She's invaluable to us. And most of my ministry opportunities are out of town now, but I still get speaking engagements in St. Louis. I would hate to leave the ministry network I've built here." She felt a check inside. "And yet . . . this Calvary opportunity came out of the blue, just like Worth & Purpose. How can I say God is at work with one and not the other?"

Todd stared at her.

"What?"

"I hadn't thought about that. For so long we've been plugging along, taking steps that made sense. Now this 'out of the blue' stuff."

"Kind of like your message at your dad's funeral." He had shared it with her on the way back to St. Louis. "Be nice if 'living full-out' only applied to the things you're excited about." Becca shook her head. "But I'm sorry, I don't think I could ever get excited about living in Hope Springs. I love our life here."

"Sweetheart . . ." He stood and pulled her into a hug. "I love our life here too. I love our church. I love living in a city this size, with everything at our fingertips—shopping, restaurants, museums—"

"—Mom. Cable Internet."

He laughed into her hair. "They've got cable Internet. Dad just didn't have it." He stepped back and looked her in the eye. "Moving back to the place I grew up doesn't excite me either. But hearing from God and trusting Him on a whole new level—that's what excites me." He held her shoulders. "I really do think this is God, Bec. But I'd never accept Calvary's offer without your full support."

She walked to the window. So she could end this with a flat no? Though she wanted to say it, she found it hard. She'd never seen Todd so stirred up about anything related to job or ministry. What if he was right? What if this *was* God?

Or maybe it was some sort of test, God wanting to see if she was willing. But in the end the whole thing would fall through.

She turned back around. "How soon would we have to leave?"

"No telling how long it would take to sell the house in this economy," he said. "Could be six months or more."

A ray of hope poked its nose through. She didn't mind the "when" stretching into the future. More time meant more opportunities to change their minds. But admittedly, the housing issue was one benefit—they'd no longer have a mortgage if they moved into Todd's childhood home. "What would Calvary do without a pastor meanwhile?" she said.

"They were already figuring on an interim preacher while they did a search, so that wouldn't be a problem." He paced a little. "But this isn't a done deal. The elders have to vote, then they recommend me to the congregation for a vote."

Becca gave him a look. "It's a done deal." She swallowed, encouraging herself. *Voicing support only means you're willing. Anything can happen between now and when the house finally sells.* "If you're fully convinced this is God and thus worth the drastic reduction in income and a drastic move to Hope Springs, then I guess . . . fine."

Todd wrapped his arms around her. "I promise you I'll keep praying, and if I get the slightest inkling we're on the wrong track, I have no problem calling it off. And I'm not giving notice at work or church until we see movement with the house." He looked her in the eye. "All the pieces have to fall into place."

Becca nodded and sent up a silent prayer.

Lord, if there's any way we can stay, please . . . close this door.

CHAPTER TEN

Thursday, December 31

Janelle pulled up to her grandmother's house just shy of eleven in the evening on New Year's Eve, car loaded with clothes, books, toys, and everything else she and the kids deemed necessary for a few months' stay. She'd given them a lot of leeway, especially when it grew apparent that they weren't excited about the move. Actually, they'd staged a last-minute revolt. And she'd felt bad that she hadn't truly consulted them. Not that it would've changed her mind necessarily, but she'd learned that when she heard them out up front, the decision, whatever it was, tended to go down better.

Instead, after she'd packed up the car, the kids surprised her with a joint statement—read by Daniel and written in crayon—that they weren't going. Any other time she might've been amused. But they were already running late, and her own emotions about the move were running on high. Thankfully, she'd been able to smooth things over relatively quickly by focusing on how happy they would make Grandma Geri and by allowing them to tote even more stuff to create the feeling of home away from home.

Daniel had run back for his Xbox *and* PlayStation 3, and every corresponding game. Tiffany had carted a huge plastic container with every crayon, marker, and coloring book, and her entire collection of Groovy Girl dolls—which brought tears the first few minutes of the trip. "I won't have *anyone* to play dolls with," she said. Then, clutching one of them, "These are the only friends I'll have."

Janelle pondered the temporary move all the way to Hope Springs. Wasn't easy for her either. For more than two years she'd lived with tangible reminders of David—photos around the house, his books and favorite magazines in the office and family room, jackets and baseball caps in the coat closet, and clothes she hadn't yet brought herself to remove from their bedroom closet. For this trip the only reminder she packed was a single family photo from the nightstand and the journal in which she recorded her thoughts about him.

She had no idea that the emotion of leaving it all behind could be worse than the emotion of living with it. However symbolic, she felt she was making a break—and she didn't know if she was ready.

She cut the engine and glanced back. The kids were wide awake. Tiffany clutched one of her dolls still. Her big brown eyes stared at her mother, and she didn't make a move to get out. Daniel looked down, wearing the same pout he'd worn when she pulled out of their Maryland driveway.

She opened her car door just as her dad and Uncle Wood appeared at Grandma Geri's front door.

"We stayed to help you unload," Dad said, hugging her. "Everyone but your mom and Libby already left for church. Service started at eleven." He opened the back door by Tiffany. "Aww, look at those long faces. You two are usually so excited to be here."

Janelle exchanged a glance with him. She'd called her parents from the car and told them how the kids had protested.

"Nothing to be excited about, Granddaddy." Daniel sounded like an old soul, resigned to his misfortune. "You and Grandma Estelle and everybody else are leaving tomorrow. I have to start a new school. Left all my friends. It'll be the most boring time of my life."

"Yeah." Tiffany liked her role of joint-protestor. "Claire's gone, so I don't have anyone to play with either." She folded her arms. "It's gonna be boring."

"Oh, come on out of the car and give your granddaddy a big hug." Her dad unbuckled Tiffany's seat belt and lifted her out.

Uncle Wood opened the door on Daniel's side. "I can't believe you haven't figured out what a great adventure this'll be."

Daniel got out and looked suspiciously at him. "Mom told you to say that."

"Your mom didn't have to tell me to say that. I already know it's an adventure—I grew up here." Uncle Wood gestured around them. "This is the country, where normal rules don't apply. Do you get to ride your bike to the convenience store to buy candy in Maryland?"

Daniel made a face. "No way. Too far and the streets are too busy."

"Do you get to roam the woods and bring home snakes and play outside after dark?"

His eyes got big. "Never."

Janelle's eyes got big too. She appreciated the pep talk, but Daniel had better not pick up a snake, much less bring it home.

Tiffany tugged the bottom of Uncle Wood's shirt. "What about me? I'm scared of the woods. What kind of adventure can I have?"

Uncle Wood let out a big laugh. "Lots and lots." He picked her up and swung her around, breaking Tiffany's mood. "You ask my twin sister," he said once they'd stopped. "Your Grandma Estelle had lots of girlie adventures growing up."

Tiffany latched onto her sour mood again. "But Grandma had sisters to play with. I don't have anybody."

"Nice try, Uncle Wood," Janelle said.

Uncle Wood gave a hearty laugh. "You look just like your cousin Libby when she was your age and couldn't get her way."

Janelle's dad and uncle grabbed luggage and duffel bags from the trunk, and the group of them moved toward the door.

"How's Grandma?" Janelle asked. "Was she up to going to church?"

Much of the family had stayed in town longer than planned so they could attend Watch Night Service at New Jerusalem. Travis said they'd have special prayer over Grandma Geri and ring in the New Year with praise for what God would do in her life.

"Said she wouldn't miss it," her dad said. "She took a nap so she'd have energy to stay up."

"This week with family has been great for her spirits," added Uncle Wood.

"What about Aunt Gwynn? Anybody hear from her yet?"

Uncle Wood paused before opening the screen door, shaking his head. "Left messages, but nothing so far."

Janelle frowned. "Why not tell her Grandma's sick? I'm sure she'd call then."

"Momma said she doesn't want a sympathy call. She's been praying a long time for real reconciliation."

Libby pulled the door open. "Girl, you barely made it." She stepped back for the crew to walk in. "Hey, Tiffy! Hey, Daniel!"

The kids mumbled hey as they trudged past.

"Uh-uh." Libby tapped them both on the shoulder. "Hugs." She extended her arms.

Daniel and Tiffany brought their heads over for a weak hug, as Libby offered Janelle a sympathetic eye.

Daniel continued on, then stopped and looked around, unsure where to go. "Mom, where am I supposed to put my stuff? Which room'll be mine?"

Estelle was coming down the hall. "We've got it all set up for you," she said, smiling. She hugged them both. "You two are in the middle bedroom. I even put a couple of surprises in there for you."

Daniel looked back at Janelle. "Mom, I'm not sharing a room with Tiffany, am I?"

"Of course you are, sweetheart. There are only three bedrooms."

"But Tiffany can sleep with you, and I can have a room by myself."

"Young man." Estelle was as patient as they came, but she didn't play either. "I didn't have a room to myself until I graduated and went to college, and even then I had to wait two years. Be thankful you've got your own room at home. While you're here you'll be content with what you have." She tipped his chin. "Hear me?"

"Yes, ma'am," came half audibly out of his mouth.

"And anyway, Daniel," Janelle said, "just so you know, Cousin Stephanie and I will be sharing the other room."

Estelle clapped her hands together with a big smile. "She decided to come?"

Janelle nodded. "Talked to her about an hour ago. She's leaving before dawn tomorrow, driving straight through. I'm really excited about it."

"That's awesome," Libby said.

"Warms my heart," Estelle said. "So glad you cousins will get to spend time together." She looked down at Daniel and Tiffany. "Let's put your things down and get you two ready to go." She glanced at Janelle. "We've got to shake a leg."

Janelle's dad carried her luggage into the room her mother and two sisters, Gladys and Gwynn, shared growing up. The room was spacious, with two queen-sized beds, three large dressers, and throw rugs on the hardwood floor.

She threw a suitcase on one of the beds and opened it, taking out the clothes she'd packed on top so she could change quickly. Libby plopped down on the other bed.

Janelle looked at her cousin. "I can see that bracelet sparkling way over here, girl," she said.

"I had no idea Al would get me this for Christmas. Jan, I told him I wasn't looking for a serious relationship."

"Wee-eell . . . you could've refused to take it."

"Girl, please. If he knows I'm not serious and still wants to bless me like this, that's on him."

"I'm surprised he's not with you tonight."

"First I told him I had to work, which I did. We always have an event on New Year's Eve. But I'd worked on all the preplanning and the setup. When I told Dexter about Grandma Geri and the prayer service, he said I should go, that they had it covered." She added, "Have to admit it was a hard call, though. *Everybody* goes to this New Year's Eve bash."

Libby worked for one of the most popular event planners in the Raleigh-Durham area. Dexter Newsome had been featured in national magazines.

"Anyway," she continued, "I left Al a voice mail at the last minute to say the plan had changed. He didn't need to be coming to Hope Springs with me again. It's starting to feel suffocating."

Janelle stepped out of her jeans and lifted her top over her head. "Poor Al. He seemed so nice."

"Poor Al? I doubt I'm the only one he's seeing. At least I hope not."

Janelle pulled on a sweater and zipped her skirt. "So when are you settling down?"

"You sound like Mom and Dad."

"Okaaay . . . is it a weird question?" Janelle sifted through her luggage. Why hadn't she put her makeup bag on top?

"It assumes I'm not 'settled' now. My life feels very settled and comfortable, thank you very much."

"If you say so." She never wanted to judge her cousin's choices, but she didn't know how she could be happy moving from one guy to the next. She found the makeup bag and took it to the mirror. "Are you still seeing that other guy—Tony? I thought he was nice too."

He'd driven with Libby to Maryland to see Janelle on a quick day trip a few months ago.

"From time to time," Libby said. "But he's boring. Never wants to do anything or go anywhere. That trip to Maryland was like living on the edge for him."

Janelle laughed as she powder-puffed her cheeks and nose. "I take offense at that on behalf of all the boring people in the world. We're worthy of love too!"

Libby laughed with her. "You know I love you, but I won't argue. You're boring too."

"Long as you still love me." Janelle quickly applied eye shadow and blush. "On a completely different note, that was an interesting exchange you and Travis had at Pastor Jim's gravesite. I haven't had a chance to ask you about it."

Libby shrugged. "I just said I was surprised to hear he was a pastor. Weren't you, when you first heard?"

"Seemed like there was more to it than that."

"Well, if we're digging . . . I haven't had a chance to ask *you* about that walk you and Kory had."

Now it was Janelle's turn to shrug. "He was just telling me what happened with Shelley. Still can't believe he's going through that."

Libby stared at her. "Mm-hmm. That was it, huh?"

"Basically."

Estelle stepped in. "Girls, we've got to go *now*. It's eleven thirty. Your dad already took the kids to the car."

"Coming." Janelle wedged her feet into her heels, snatched her purse from the bed, and eased out of the room . . . happy to leave that part of the conversation behind.

CHAPTER ELEVEN

New Jerusalem was packed and rocking. The choir clapped and swayed side to side, singing "Great is the Lord, and greatly to be praised," and the bodies in the pews clapped, swayed, and sang with them. Kory Miller stood, watching, wanting to praise. That's why he'd come. He knew this night would be hard, and if he stayed home he'd have to weather a flood of emotion. Not that he wanted Shelley back. He simply grieved the loss of what he'd thought they had, and the loss of a mother at home for Dee.

At Grandma Geri's house after the funeral, Kory had talked at length with Travis. The two men were about the same age and connected easily. Though Travis was a pastor, he was open about having walked a path that didn't glorify God, and how surprised he was that God would even call him to pastor. Kory shared his story as well, and when Travis heard that it was last New Year's Eve that his wife left him, he'd urged him to come to the service tonight.

New Jerusalem was about thirty minutes away from their condo in Rocky Mount, so Kory hadn't even considered Hope Springs in his search for a church. Besides, he favored larger churches and wanted an established kids' ministry for Dee. But after talking to Travis and hearing the message he gave tonight, he was already thinking he'd be back Sunday.

"I'd like everyone to be seated for a moment," Pastor Travis was saying. He walked down the steps from the pulpit area. "We're about to have special prayer for a dear mother in the church, Geraldine Sanders."

Dee patted Kory's arm. "Daddy, only twenty-three minutes and fifteen seconds till the New Year." She had his phone in her hand, using the clock app to count down. This was the first year she'd gotten into the change in calendar year, not realizing its significance in her own life.

Kory acknowledged Dee with a smile and an arm around her shoulder, but he was focused on what was happening up front. Was something wrong with Grandma Geri?

"Grandma Geri, how long have you been a member of New Jerusalem?" Pastor Travis held the microphone in front of her.

Grandma Geri was dressed in white, seated in the front pew. "Elwood and I moved to Hope Springs shortly after we married, when he was working for the railroad. That's when we joined. 'Bout sixty-four years ago."

The congregation reacted with *wows*.

"Sixty-four years." Pastor Travis shook his head, then looked out at everyone. "And a faithful member too. I bet she hardly missed a Sunday in all that time."

Grandma Geri said something, but she didn't have the microphone. Pastor Travis gave it to her. "We couldn't hear you," he said. "Could you repeat that?"

"I said only if I was traveling, because you know I like to stay on the go!"

"Will the members of Grandma Geri's family come forward, please?" Travis watched them rise and move out of the pews. "While they're coming, I want to let you all know that Grandma Geri was recently diagnosed with lung cancer—"

"Oh, Lord, no." Kory spoke to himself, but he heard the same rippling throughout the congregation.

"—but we know our God is a healer—"

"Yes, He is!" rang forth.

"—and we don't intend to go into the New Year relying on a doctor's report. We're relying on the Most High God who has already numbered our days and knows the end from the beginning."

"Amen!"

"I believe all the family is gathered. I'd like to ask the congregation to stand again as we pray."

"Hold on, Pastor," someone said.

The church doors had opened, and Kory turned to see Janelle's parents and her uncle Wood coming in, and Libby—

"Daddy, Daddy, look! It's Tiffany!"

Kory had spotted her at the same time—along with her mother. Janelle must've stayed in town longer than planned. He watched them scurry down the aisle to complete the semicircle that had formed around Grandma Geri.

Those near Grandma Geri laid hands on her, and the others stretched theirs toward her as the pastor prayed. Kory listened to every word, and his heart fell when he heard the cancer was in a late stage. "Heal her, Lord," he whispered in agreement. "You're able."

As the prayer ended and the family took their seats, Pastor Travis headed back to the podium. "Five minutes until midnight," he said.

"No, it's not. It's four minutes and forty-six seconds," Dee whispered.

Kory kept Janelle in view. She and her kids had squeezed into a pew on the opposite side of the aisle.

"As we prepare to step into a new year," Pastor Travis continued, "I want you to remember that one word I gave you. What was it?"

"Press!" the congregation yelled.

Earlier Travis had read the apostle Paul's words: "One thing I do: forgetting what lies behind and reaching forward to what lies ahead, I press on toward the goal for the prize of the upward call of God in Christ Jesus." Then he had led them through an exercise where he'd given several scenarios of what they might have gone through this past year, ending each one with, "But I"—and the congregation filled in the blank—"press!"

"I know some of y'all think I'm too young to know what it means to have to press." He leaned over the podium. "But believe me when I say I've been through some things . . ."

Kory saw his gaze flitter to the section with Janelle and Libby.

"Press, saints. Don't live in the past. Don't let it stop you from living the abundant life Jesus died to give you today. Press on."

The organist struck up a few chords.

"And you know what the organ means," Pastor Travis said. "How many seconds do we have?"

"Twenty!" somebody shouted.

"Stand to your feet and let's count down."

Kory felt the energy around him as voices rose and the organ played.

". . . 18, 17, 16 . . ."

He felt his own energy rising within. He didn't have to focus on what happened a year ago. He could press forward.

". . . 10, 9, 8 . . ."

Thank You, Jesus. Thank You, Jesus, for Your peace.

"Daddy, it's almost here!"

Kory picked her up as the cheers rang out. "Happy New Year, sweetheart!"

Dee threw her arms around his neck. "Happy New Year, Daddy!" She watched people spilling out of the pews to hug those around them. She squirmed to get down. "Can I go say hi to Tiffany?"

Kory glanced in Janelle's direction, but couldn't see her or her children with all the mingling. "Sure, sweetheart."

"Will you go with me?"

He felt awkward. He didn't want Janelle to think he'd shown up hoping to run into her. She'd been hesitant about being friends and certainly hadn't reached out to him yet. He didn't want to push.

"Daddy, come on."

Dee started across the aisle, pulling him along. One thing was sure. He was glad Tiffany had brought his daughter out of her shell. He'd been praying for Dee to find a friend like that in Rocky Mount.

Dee moved through the crowd, finally spotting her quarry. She touched Tiffany's back, and Tiffany squealed when she turned around. "Dee!" They embraced like old friends.

Janelle turned, her eyes warm. "Hey. I didn't know you'd be here."

"Same here. I thought you left a few days ago."

She looked beautiful as always—gorgeous brown skin, beautiful hair—but it was the beauty that radiated from her soul that captivated him from the beginning. Since everyone was hugging around them, he gave her a quick one too. "Happy New Year."

She returned it easily. "Happy New Year, Kory."

They exchanged an amused glance as Tiffany and Dee started in on what they'd gotten for Christmas. Both girls had several pigtails, but Kory could see that Tiffany's hair was much better styled. He had a long way to go in the hair department.

"I was sorry to hear about Grandma Geri," Kory said.

Janelle nodded. "It was a shock to all of us."

"I was just coming to say that, how shocked I am." Sara Ann had walked up beside them.

"Hey, Sara Ann," Janelle said. "I don't know if you remember Kory."

Sara Ann smiled. "I remember pushing your daughter on the swing." She shook his hand and said hello to the girls.

"Do you always come to Watch Night Service?" Janelle asked her.

"I've come the last three years. Because I work at the diner, I miss a lot of Sunday services. But on New Year's Eve the diner's closed, and it hit me one year, hey, that's a service you can make. And what better time to praise God than ringing in the New Year. But Calvary doesn't have service tonight, so . . . here I am." Sara Ann smiled and shrugged, then her brow creased. "And I wouldn't have known about Grandma Geri if I hadn't come. Is she scheduled for surgery?"

"She's not a candidate for surgery—it's too advanced. But she starts chemo on Monday."

"Oh, wow. I'd like to pray with her." Sara Ann glanced toward the front of the church. "She's got a crowd around her right now. I'll drop by tomorrow."

"That sounds great, Sara Ann," Janelle said. "I know she'd appreciate it."

Kory thought about what she'd said as Sara Ann left. "So your grandmother's chemo starts Monday? That must be hard for you . . . I assume you have to head back to Maryland this weekend?"

Tiffany wheeled around with a puzzled look. "But we just got here."

Now Kory looked puzzled.

"I decided to stay with Grandma and help take care of her for a few months," Janelle explained. "We went home and packed up more stuff."

"That's awesome, Janelle. You're really something."

"It's not as selfless as you might think. I thought the change of scenery might be good for me."

It was dawning on him. "So we're practically neighbors."

She allowed a slight smile. "That kinda sorta crossed my mind as well."

"And you know what else that means?"

"What?"

He stepped closer to the girls and held a finger atop each head, pointing downward. He whispered, "These two are practically neighbors."

She whispered back, "I wonder if they know." Janelle moved between them. "Tiffany, Dee, did you know you live near one another now?"

Dee's eyes got wide. "You *live* here now?" She turned to her father. "Daddy, can I spend the night at Tiffany's? I've never had a sleepover before. Please, Daddy?"

"Whoa, sweetheart." He looked into her pleading eyes. "Tiffany won't disappear tomorrow. You'll have plenty of time to play with her."

"But I want to go to her house *tonight*."

Kory gave her the look. "Dee, no whining. It's late and we're heading home."

Janelle moved closer to him and spoke so only the two of them could hear. "She's welcome, you know. She's never done a sleepover?"

"Never."

"You trust her with us?"

"Come on, Janelle." Kory would trust her with his own life. "But she has no clothes or anything."

Janelle gave Dee a once-over. "Looks like she's wearing clothes to me." She smiled. "Let her go with us."

"You're sure?"

"Positive."

He approached Dee with a grave expression. "Miss Janelle just informed me—now don't get upset or anything—that it's okay for you to go home with them tonight."

Dee flung her arms so tight around his waist he was knocked a step back. "Oh, Daddy, thank you, thank you!" She looked back at Janelle. "Thank you, Miss Janelle."

He felt the moment to his core. He'd come tonight to coat the pain, but God had given so much more—that sparkle he saw right now in his daughter's eyes. He'd been praying for a friend for Dee, and never in a million years would he have thought it would be the daughter of Janelle. He couldn't ask for a better influence. And that he might see Janelle more often because of their daughters' friendship . . . He could think of worse things.

CHAPTER TWELVE

Friday, January 1

Stephanie leaned back with a big sigh. "So that's my deal in a nutshell."

She'd arrived in Hope Springs a couple of hours earlier, and though she was curled up on the sofa dead tired, she was having a good time with her cousins.

Janelle and Libby looked at one another, clearly suppressing their amusement.

"Y'all, it's not funny. I'm serious." She propped herself up on an elbow. "I wanted to be real about why I'm here so you wouldn't be thinking it's out of the goodness of my heart. This is straight boot camp for me, and you *will* see me in a funk now and then because it's not my nature to want to help."

Libby laughed outright. "You said that like it's most people's nature to go above and beyond. Your vision is just skewed because you grew up under that sister of yours. And I was cursed to be the 'twin' of this one, who'll drop everything to take care of her grandmother." She crossed her legs. "You didn't hear me volunteer to do a thing."

"I sure wish people would stop acting like I'm doing something huge," Janelle said. "If life were normal and David were still here, I wouldn't have volunteered either. I'm just trying to survive."

"So I can go ahead and tell God I'm cool then," Stephanie said. "I'm no more selfish than the next person. No need for boot camp." She saluted. "Adios, amigas."

"Uh, little cousin, I hate to tell you," Libby said, "but you're here now and might as well do your time—just don't try to recruit me."

"And just 'cause you said that, I'm gonna *pray* God throws you in."

They laughed as cheers went up on the other side of the room. Kory had come to pick up Dee, and some guy—Stephanie forgot his name, but it wasn't Al—had come to see Libby. They'd both ended up in front of the television watching the Rose Bowl game.

"But seriously, Janelle," Stephanie said, "don't assume I'll know how to pitch in. I want you to tell me what I can do to help you. That's why I'm here."

"How long are you staying?" Libby asked.

"Four weeks, which is how long Lindell will be away."

"If it was even four days, it would be awesome," Janelle said. "I really appreciate this, Steph."

"Girl, pray my strength." Stephanie chuckled as she got up. "Anybody want anything?" She looked across the room, but the guys shook their head no. She licked her finger and stroked the air. "One point already for offering my assistance." She got her glass from the coffee table and started down the hall. "Going to get some more Coke and some dip to go with these chips. Thank God this ain't no diet boot camp. I can only combat one vice at a time."

Stephanie opened the refrigerator and got the dip. Then she got ice from the freezer, plunked it into her glass, and opened the fridge again for the Coke. She backed up—"Oh." It was Libby's guy friend. "Excuse me, I didn't know you were behind me."

"No problem." He hardly moved. "How was your drive? You said you came from Kansas City?"

She didn't bother to correct him. She moved around him to pour her drink. "It was . . . long, but good."

He looked at her hand. "Married?"

She looked at him before pouring. "Happily. Why?"

He shrugged. "Just asking."

She carried the Coke back to the fridge.

"You're a good-looking woman, you know that?"

Stephanie pushed the fridge to a close and turned. "Must run in the family, because so is the woman you came here to see."

She picked up her drink and the dip and started back.

Lord, if he says one more thing, I'm going off on him.

The guy returned to the living room minutes later with a bowl of black-eyed peas Aunt Estelle had made before she and Uncle Russell got on the road back to Florida. He sat next to Libby, and they shared it like two lovebirds.

Stephanie hadn't realized how much she and her cousin Libby had in common. She had lived that same life. She glanced over at her cousin. Maybe she was here for more reasons than she knew. She didn't know if Libby would ever listen to her—Stephanie had been *there* too. But one thing was sure . . . the road Libby was on was nowhere near as appealing as it seemed.

CHAPTER THIRTEEN

Saturday, January 2

Becca could hardly keep the tears at bay. She felt betrayed, like the butt of a cruel joke—and the worst part was her own hand had put it into motion.

She cut her eyes over to Todd, who was beside himself with excitement. They were at the dining room table, talking to Connie, the realtor.

"They're preapproved *and* they don't have a house to sell?" Todd said. "This is beyond incredible." He looked at Becca. "Isn't this incredible?"

"A little too incredible." She couldn't feign enthusiasm if she tried. "Why hasn't this family snapped up a house already on the market? There are plenty."

"Ah, you have no idea." Connie put her elbows on the table. "Can I tell you? I got heartburn with these people. House has got to have this and this." She threw up fingers to tick each item off. "Front and backyard's got to have that and that. And they wouldn't bend, not an iota." She gestured to Becca. "And then you called, and it was like a gift from heaven. And this is me talking, who doesn't buy into the heaven thing—no offense, Todd. I know you're a pastor."

Todd smiled. "None taken."

"And, Becca, you won't believe this," Connie continued. "Even though I sold you and Todd this house, I didn't remember its exact layout. But this morning something told me I needed to see it right away. That's why I called, and I'm so glad Todd was here. When I saw it again, I knew this was the house they wanted. I had to get them here as fast as I could."

Becca had called Connie two days ago only to say they were *thinking* about listing their home. She asked if they could get together sometime after the New Year to get an appraisal. If it appeared they could lose money, maybe they'd rethink their decision. She'd been waiting to hear back for a meeting time, but when she returned from her mom's, Connie was sitting in her dining room.

Todd was still smiling. "It's amazing how fast it happened. I didn't have time to call Becca because I was trying to hurry up and get the house in decent shape for them to see it." He looked at Becca. "Thank God the kids were with you at your mom's or I could've never done it. They walk through and *bam*, they say it's the one."

"So beautiful," Connie said. "Just as they knew immediately that all the other houses *weren't* the one, they knew immediately that this was."

Somehow *beautiful* wasn't the word that came to Becca's mind. "I have yet to wrap my mind around this," she said. "Todd let them see the house as a courtesy, but it's not even listed yet. And who do they think they are, demanding we be out of our home in two weeks?"

Becca knew she was on edge, but this was happening so fast.

"Bec, it's not a demand. People state what works best for them, then we counter. Frankly, I don't have a problem with it."

"They're saying two weeks because they've been looking so long—bless their hearts—and they want to get their kids in the neighborhood school and get settled."

"Well, isn't that *their* problem?" Becca's heart rate was accelerating. "Why should I have to rush to move out of my home? Moreover, how do we know this is the best offer we can get? I think we need to list it and find out."

"Bec, really? We have an offer on the table, one that nets us more equity than anticipated, and you think we should wait for something better?" Todd paused for a response, but Becca couldn't think of one. "I know the timing isn't great," he added, "but it has God written all over it—no offense, Connie." He grinned at her.

She grinned back. "None taken."

Becca stared vaguely at the papers in front of her, papers that detailed the hastily written offer on their home. All she could think was she should've waited to call Connie. Then this family would've had no choice but to buy something else, whether it suited them fully or not. She sighed. She'd said she supported the decision. But she'd pinned her hopes on a slow sale of the house.

"You're right," she said finally. "This is a solid offer. But I still don't see how we can be out of here so quickly. Do you know how much work it'll take to figure out what we should take versus what we should give away or throw out? And that's before we actually begin to pack. We don't have professional movers this time around."

"I think we take it one day at a time. We might be surprised by how smoothly it goes."

Becca excused herself as Todd and Connie discussed the things they should counter in the offer—closing date not among them. She walked upstairs, peeking into Ethan's room to make sure he was still napping—he'd fallen asleep in the car. They'd plunked Claire down in the family room to watch a video while they talked, and now, as Becca passed her room, she took in the décor that was barely a year old. In two weeks neither of those rooms would look the same.

She walked into her home office frustrated, feeling her life had left her control. Even if she wanted to move to Hope Springs, now wasn't the time. She needed to focus on preparing her message, working on her book, building her blog. Instead . . .

She turned toward one wall, lined with accordion files and boxes filled with papers and programs, including study notes and drafts of messages she'd given over the years. She'd be organizing all of that instead, determining what to toss, what to recycle, and what to save. This room alone would take hours.

Becca collapsed in her chair, resentment rising. Sure, Todd had been supportive of her Worth & Purpose opportunity, though it meant several weekends away from home. And she appreciated that. But *his* opportunity was turning their lives upside—

Three dings pierced the quiet, and Becca looked at her computer. She'd been away from it all day, which was unusual. She leaned over and awakened the screen, then blinked and moved closer. *Fifty-six new messages? What in the world?*

She skimmed the in-box and saw that most were new Facebook friend requests and Twitter followers, but she'd never had this many in one day. Why the onslaught?

Wait. Had Worth & Purpose announced her as a new speaker? She'd sent them one of her new photos, but she hadn't expected an announcement until after the New Year, if at all. She wasn't a well-known addition to the team. It was more likely that they'd quietly add her picture to the lineup.

She clicked over to the Worth & Purpose window—which was always open—and refreshed the home page. Her gasp was audible. They'd actually posted a "news" item that she'd joined the lineup? It was coupled with the picture she'd sent. She clicked the More button, and it linked to her bio.

With wit and vivacity, Becca Dillon has brought her message of God's grace and love to countless women. Seminary trained, she has been a popular Bible teacher in her local church and at women's retreats, and a featured women's conference speaker. She lives in the St. Louis area with her husband and two children.

She clicked to the page that showed the speaker lineup, and there she was. But she wondered still about the notifications. Did people check the Worth & Purpose site this closely? Or . . . She opened her Twitter screen and saw a flood of mentions. *They tweeted about me?*

Join us in welcoming @BeccaDillon to the @WorthandPurpose speaker lineup. And follow her!

She clicked over to Facebook and saw a similar post about her on their fan page, with numerous "likes" and comments.

She sat back in her chair, her heart *really* accelerating. Somehow it was real now. Really real.

Six more e-mail notifications appeared and Becca sat forward again. Hmm . . . should she create a Facebook fan page now? She had speaker friends who'd done it, but she'd resisted thus far. Now that she might actually garner a decent number of fans, though . . .

She clicked through a couple of Facebook screens to find out how to do it. What would she list herself under? She wasn't a public figure. Wasn't an author either—though she would be. So she chose *writer*, then cut and pasted her bio from the other screen into the information section on the fan page—adding *Worth & Purpose speaker* to the paragraph. Moments later, she'd uploaded one of her new photos and *voila*! She had a fan page . . . with no fans. But hopefully that would change soon.

Another e-mail dinged, and Becca switched to that screen. Katie Flanagan. She and Becca had been on the program together for a few regional conferences, but she didn't know Katie well. She looked at the message.

Hi Becca,

I happened to see the Worth & Purpose announcement on Facebook that you've joined the tour. Congratulations! What an amazing accomplishment. It's always been my hope to join their speaker roster one day, so I'd love to hear how it happened for you. Your life will never be the same, girl!

Katie

"Hey, Bec."

Becca turned as Todd walked in.

"We've finished drafting the counteroffer, and Connie needs your signature," he said. "But I wanted to check with you first. This happened really fast, and the more I think about it, it's fine if you want to wait. It's even fine if you want to call the whole thing off. I want you to feel 100 percent comfortable with where we are."

Becca took a big breath. Seemed like so much had happened just in the last hour. And even the last few minutes.

She stood and looked in her husband's eyes. "I'm realizing more and more how incredibly blessed I am to have this opportunity with Worth & Purpose, and to be able to write a book because of that platform. And neither of these opportunities is dependent upon where we live." She paused, a peace settling within her. "But your opportunity *is* dependent upon where we live, and I want to be supportive. If it means we have to move to Hope Springs, we move to Hope Springs." She smiled. "Thank God there's an airport in reasonable driving distance."

Todd looked surprised. "Wasn't expecting to hear that," he said. "So we're really doing this? Our lives are really about to change?"

Becca's mind went to the flurry of activity on her computer. "I think they already have."

CHAPTER FOURTEEN

Monday, January 4

Janelle had been putting up a brave front, encouraging Grandma Geri, telling her she'd get through this just fine. Using Travis's word—one that spoke to her on many levels—she'd even taken to saying that together they would *press* through any difficulty that arose. But early this morning, on the day of the first chemo treatment, Janelle's resolve had been shaken already.

She'd awakened at four thirty to the sound of Grandma Geri's coughing. She'd heard her coughing in the night almost every night since she'd been there, and always poked her head in the room to make sure she was okay. But this sounded different, moved her out of bed faster. When she knelt at Grandma Geri's bedside, she saw little spots on the sheet and realized her grandmother was coughing up blood. They'd spent the next few minutes in the bathroom, Janelle watching in horror as Grandma Geri vomited blood.

In tears, Janelle had helped her back into bed and then called Dr. Reynolds, who'd said not to hesitate to call, no matter the time. He was calm. This was expected, and he'd already informed Grandma Geri—which explained why Janelle was more panicked than she. He'd said to take her temperature, and if there was no fever, they could simply go to the hospital at the time scheduled for chemo.

Janelle didn't go back to sleep. She powered up her laptop—thankful the family had persuaded her grandmother some time ago to get the Internet—and read beyond the pamphlets Dr. Reynolds had left. Clicking through page after page about this disease and what they could expect, she almost felt sick herself. She felt the urge to close her laptop and pray, an area where she'd slacked off since David's death. It was almost as if she was afraid to pray, afraid to trust, since there were no guarantees. But it suddenly struck her that that's what these next few weeks and months would be about more than anything—praying as never before. And trusting as never before.

Even now, as they walked into the reception area of the hospital's infusion center, she was praying, *Lord, be her strength.*

"Miss Geri!" A middle-aged woman with a megawatt smile approached them in cartoon-figure nurse scrubs. She hugged Grandma Geri. "So good to see you again, though I hate that it's under these circumstances."

Grandma Geri held the woman's hand. "I was hoping you'd still be here. You took good care of my Elwood."

"Had to fight to be the one to take care of you." She looked around conspiratorially. "Got you this." She held up a snack bag filled with craisins, nuts, and pretzels.

Grandma Geri clapped her hands together and laughed softly to herself. "Never heard of craisins till we came here. Elwood and I got addicted to those things." She turned. "Sylvia, this is my granddaughter Janelle."

"Nice to meet you, Sylvia." They shook hands.

"Nice to meet you too. I'm one of the palliative care nurses here." Sylvia's eyes were warm. "It's awesome you're here to support your grandmother. Are you planning to stay with her today for the infusion?"

"Told her not to." Grandma Geri lifted her canvas bag. "Got plenty to keep me occupied." She bowed her head over to Janelle. "I know there's something you could be doing."

"There is. This." Janelle smiled. "Tiffany'll have a good time hanging with Stephanie today."

"Sure is a blessing having Stephanie there," Grandma Geri said. "Feel like I'm really getting to know her."

Sylvia ushered Grandma Geri to a seat in the waiting area, double-checking the chart. "Okay, Miss Geri, you've been to radiology and you've met with Dr. Peters. We just need to wait a few more minutes for the results from your blood work to make sure everything's good. You've been taking your meds, right?"

"How could I forget? My granddaughter pesters me the minute it's time for the next one."

Sylvia fist-bumped Janelle. "I remember, Miss Geri," she said, "when you pestered Mr. Sanders about taking his." She smiled. "It's good for you. It'll hopefully lessen any side effects from the chemotherapy."

"I couldn't get her to eat anything this morning," Janelle said. "Not even a piece of toast."

Grandma Geri wrinkled up her nose. "Felt too nauseous."

"Okay." Sylvia was nodding. "Craisins to the rescue then. Go ahead and try a few, my dear."

Janelle was already counting Sylvia an answer to prayer.

Sylvia put a hand on top of Grandma Geri's. "I know you're familiar with a lot of the procedure, but if you don't mind, I'm going to pretend you know nothing and explain what will happen when we start the infusion."

Grandma Geri nodded.

"This is officially chemo cycle one, day one. The oncologist has ordered five different drips administered through the I.V. I'll tell you about each as we do them. I don't expect you to experience any pain or discomfort while it's being administered, but you let me know immediately if you do."

"Okay."

Sylvia continued. "You'll be laid back and comfy in the recliner.

I've got a blanket in case you get cool. I know you've got your bag of books and magazines there, and there's also a television and DVD player."

"Oh, and I forgot to give you this." Janelle reached into her purse and pulled something out.

Grandma Geri frowned. "What's that?"

"An iPod. I loaded all your favorite gospel songs on here for you to listen to if you want."

"All that music on that little thing?"

"You'll love it, Grandma. Got you a nice soft set of headphones too."

Grandma Geri looked immediately curious. "Can I test it real quick?"

"By all means." Sylvia gave Janelle a thumbs-up.

Janelle put the headphones on her and showed her how to select an album and play it.

Grandma Geri scrolled through. "You got Shirley Caesar on here? Let me see." She pushed a button and a smile spread across her face. "You got to be kidding me. What will they come up with next?" She patted Janelle's knee. "You're an angel, baby."

Grandma Geri had the headphones to her ears still, so Sylvia got up to check on something, giving her a moment. Janelle used the time to check messages. She had a text from Kory. Just one line.

Sheriff served me today.

Kory had been sitting at his office desk for the last half hour, emotions of every sort coursing through his veins—anger, frustration, hurt, resentment. He couldn't believe the sheriff had shown up at his job to serve him with divorce papers. Shelley knew she didn't have to do that. He hadn't stood in her way, hadn't made the process difficult. She could've served him by certified mail and he would've signed for it. Instead she involved an officer of the law and put their domestic issues on blast—in front of colleagues with whom he was still building a reputation. They knew his situation, but this little stunt didn't do him any favors. Made his life look messy, spilling over as it did into the workplace. Seemed her every act was calculated to be vindictive.

Funny she couldn't give half as much thought to her own daughter. She didn't care to truly get to know Dee, made obvious by the Christmas gift she'd sent—a stuffed teddy bear, though for a year and a half Dee had had an aversion to them due to a bad dream. And now that Dee had an opportunity to observe Janelle and Tiffany, she was asking more questions than ever. On the way to preschool this morning she'd said, "Why don't I have a mommy?"

It crushed his heart. "You do have a mommy, sweetheart," he'd said.

"Not a real mommy. Not one that talks to me and does stuff with me."

He'd made excuses for Shelley, as usual. "It's hard because your mommy's far away, but she loves you and will make it up to you."

Then he'd come to work and gotten hit with this.

He was tired of building Shelley up in Dee's eyes. Tired of taking the high road when she was guaranteed to take the low one. And of course . . . *of course* she had to serve him right at the one-year anniversary of the separation. *Was it that bad being married to me, Shelley? You had to rub my nose in it, let me know you want out as fast as you can?*

He grabbed his cell phone from the desk. Without another thought, he dialed her up.

She answered on the first ring. "You must've had a visitor this morning."

Did she sound amused? "What's the deal, Shelley? You hadn't twisted the knife enough, so you had to add a sheriff to the mix?"

"Leave it to you to take it personally. It's part of the process, Kory."

"No, Shelley, it's not part of the process. It's an *option* in the process. But as a litigator, you already know that. You made it personal when you embarrassed me in front of my colleagues."

"What could you be embarrassed about at a country law firm like that? Seriously."

"That's nice, Shelley. This firm and these people are beneath you, are they?"

"They're beneath you too, Kory. Have you forgotten? You were top of your class at Chicago, editor-in-chief of the law review, on the fast track at one of the largest law firms in the world. And you threw it all away."

"Really? That's how you've spun the story in your mind? My version says you sabotaged my career."

He was convinced by now that that's what she'd done. When she and Martin decided they'd leave their spouses and move in together, life would clearly be more convenient if Kory were gone from the firm. Martin had the power to lobby in favor of other associates making partner, and against him.

"You sabotaged your own career," Shelley said, "when you stopped giving 110 percent so you could be home evenings and weekends."

All the frustration he'd felt at that time came bubbling up. "I wanted to be with my daughter and my wife . . . except she was never there."

Shelley didn't respond at first. Then, "You knew my career was important to me."

He nodded, his jaw tight. "I did. Just didn't know how important." Questions he'd had in those first nights after she'd left returned to him. He didn't necessarily want to ask them now, but he was too on edge to stop himself. "Who did you marry, Shelley?

Me or the powerful attorney you hoped I'd become? Did you ever really love me?"

A long pause followed. Finally, "You're a good man, Kory. It would've been hard not to love you. It just . . . wasn't enough."

Kory stared at the court complaint he'd tossed atop his desk. *Shelley Miller v. Kory Miller.* There was nothing left to say. He had to file an answer to the complaint, and he'd do it as soon as possible to move the process forward.

"Kory, so you don't hear this anywhere else," Shelley said. "I'll be scheduling a hearing date at the soonest possible time, thirty days from now. Martin and I are getting married right after."

And he thought the sheriff was the twist.

He lowered the phone from his ear to hang up, but felt compelled to bring it back. "What will you do, Shelley, when you find out that Martin isn't enough?"

Soft laughter drifted through the phone. "I don't think that'll be a problem."

He clicked off, still stewing, when he felt the phone vibrate in his hand. He looked down and answered. "Hey, Janelle."

"Hey. I was thinking . . . why don't you and Dee join us at the house for dinner this evening? Something tells me you could use a friend."

So many thoughts swirled in his head. He said simply, "Thank you," because one more word might've broken him down.

CHAPTER FIFTEEN

Wednesday, January 6

Stephanie was so sleepy her eyes were about to drop from their sockets. She'd jokingly called this boot camp, but the joke was on her—she was being put through her paces. She'd been awakened every morning before dawn by Grandma Geri's coughing, and every morning thus far they'd had an early morning appointment at the hospital. So getting back to sleep was useless. Before she knew it, it was time to wake the kids and get them dressed and fed. After Daniel caught the school bus, she and Tiffany had been playing every conceivable game under the sun—Trouble, Old Maid, dolls, jump rope, even a chalked-up game of hopscotch outdoors.

Now she'd taken a moment to rest her bones on the sofa. She took the liberty of closing her eyes. All she needed was a short nap . . . but she felt a fuzzy sensation under her nose and jumped, eyes wide. It was the stringy hair of a Groovy Girl doll.

Tiffany threw her head back with laughter.

"Tiff, what are you doing?" Stephanie whined. "You're supposed to be taking a nap."

"I grew out of naps."

"That's not what your momma said." Stephanie was almost groggy. "I want you to go lie down for a while."

"I did, but I couldn't fall asleep."

"You only tried for five minutes. Go try again. I want you to lie down until I call you."

Stephanie wanted to give a cheer when Tiffany scurried away, but she was already drifting, one of those deep sleeps you can feel yourself falling into, chest rising and falling, steady breathing moving to a soft—

Pop. Pop. Pop.

Stephanie flew upward, eyes wild. "Tiffany, are you okay? What is that?"

"I'm playing Trouble," she yelled from her room.

Stephanie collapsed back on the sofa. *Lord, You know I don't do kids. This is why.* The only children she'd ever babysat were her friend Dana's. But she'd known Dana her whole life, which meant she'd known Dana's kids her whole life. Those kids knew from the jump how Stephanie rolled—naptime meant naptime.

"Tiffany," she called, "I thought I told you to lie down."

"I *am* lying down. I'm playing in bed."

"Okay, then let me be clearer. I want you to lie down, close your eyes, keep your hands by your side, and count sheep."

Tiffany giggled. "Count sheep?"

Lord . . . ?

"Stephanie?"

"Yes, Tiffany."

"I'm hungry."

Okey-dokey. No nap. Stephanie swung her legs over the side of the sofa and walked into the kids' bedroom. Tiffany was on her bed, drawing circles in the air.

Stephanie sat next to her. "Remember I told you that you needed to eat your sandwich?"

"But I wasn't hungry then."

"Okay. Good thing I left your sandwich on the table. You can go eat it."

"The bread is hard now."

Stephanie took a breath. "Tiffany . . ."

The little girl's eyes lit up. "Can we go to the diner? We haven't been anywhere all week, and Uncle Wood said I'd have adventures. And Claire said they have good milkshakes." She waggled her eyebrows on the last part, as if it were the biggest selling point.

And it was. Stephanie had been good and ready to say no, but the milkshake was enticing. A change of scenery sounded good too. "Only if you eat that sandwich first."

"Okay." Tiffany tore out of bed and ran into the kitchen.

Stephanie stared after her. *No, that little girl didn't just play me.*

Stephanie and Tiffany walked into the Main Street Diner hand in hand for their big adventure.

"Hello there, and welcome!" A woman smiled at them from the hostess podium, grabbing a big plastic menu and a kid's paper one. "Follow me, please."

The diner definitely had a small-town vibe. Servers lingered at tables, talking to patrons as if they knew them. Patrons talked to one another across tables. Décor hadn't been updated in decades, it seemed—red vinyl, really?—but it added to the charm of the place. It was fairly busy for one fifteen. Almost all the tables were full, and many patrons were still ordering breakfast.

The hostess led them to a booth for two. Tiffany slid in and grinned as her legs dangled. Stephanie slid in across from her and accepted the menus with a thank-you.

"What's your favorite milkshake?" Tiffany asked. "Chocolate or vanilla?"

"Strawberry."

She wrinkled up her face. "Strawberry? I never heard of anyone liking strawberry milkshakes. I like vanilla, like Mommy. Daniel likes chocolate." She paused. "Mommy said Daddy used to like chocolate too."

Stephanie's heart took a dive. At four years old, there was probably a lot about her father that Tiffany didn't remember. To have lost a dad at such a young age . . .

Stephanie smiled at her. "I think you should get a vanilla-chocolate mix, and we can call it a Mommy-Daddy milkshake."

"Ewww." Her eyes brightened. "I know! You can get a vanilla-strawberry milkshake and call it a Tiffy-Stephy mix!"

"Um . . . I'm thinking . . . no. But how about a Tiffy-Stephy sandwich—PB&J on one side and turkey on the other."

"Yuck."

"You'll never refuse this . . . a Tiffy-Stephy drink! With chocolate milk and cranberry juice."

"Yuck. Yuck." Tiffany shook her head twice for effect.

"This is my last offer . . . a Tiffy-Stephy hug, with love on one side and sweetness on the other."

Tiffany flung her arms wide as Stephanie rose up and reached across the booth, a slight tear in her eye.

Please don't start this, Lord. I refuse to become mushy.

"Which one of us is the sweetness one?" Tiffany asked.

Stephanie laughed. "Honey, I've never been accused of being sweetness."

"Hey, look at the love. So cool." Sara Ann had walked up. "Can I have one of those, Tiffany?"

Tiffany beamed. "You sure can." She scooted over and hugged Sara Ann.

"Sorry it took so long for me to get to you. This place stays busy lately."

Sara Ann definitely had that natural sweetness. She'd stopped by twice to visit with Grandma Geri, and she just seemed *nice*. Maybe if Stephanie had a Southern accent like Sara Ann's, she'd seem nicer too.

"No problem," Stephanie said. "Our order is easy, one vanilla milkshake and one strawberry."

"Large or small?" Sara Ann asked.

"Small for Miss Tiffany, and . . ." Stephanie glanced down. "My hips are saying ditto."

"Miss." A guy two tables over was flagging Sara Ann, holding up a mug. "Do you plan to refill my coffee today or next week?"

Stephanie's eyebrows rose. She looked at Sara Ann.

"I'm so sorry, sir," she said. "We're short on help. I'm just finishing this order, and I'll grab your coffee."

"Grab it now or I'm out of here."

Stephanie touched her arm. "We're done, Sara Ann. Go ahead and help him." *Though I might have another idea what to do with that coffee.*

"So sorry again, sir," Sara Ann said. "Be right back with the coffeepot." She scurried away.

Tiffany's brow wrinkled. "Miss Sara Ann is so nice. Why was that man mean to her?"

Stephanie looked over at him. "Well . . . I guess he really, really needed some caffeine that very second. And Miss Sara Ann's taking care of so many people that she couldn't get it when he wanted it. She said they need more help."

"Couldn't you help?"

"Well, no, sweetheart. I don't work here."

"That's what I meant. Couldn't you get a job here?" She sounded so matter-of-fact, like it made sense.

"No, actually I can't get a job here," Stephanie said. "My job right now is taking care of you." She smiled, glad for the out.

Tiffany got that wrinkled brow again. "But Mommy said *she'll* be taking care of me a lot of times 'cause Grandma doesn't have to go to the hospital every day. So you *can* do it."

Stephanie leaned over. "Little sweetness one, the other reason I can't work here is because Cousin Stephanie is a little low on patience. I would've—well, I couldn't have handled the situation like Sara Ann."

Sara Ann returned just then and set the milkshakes on the table. "Can I get anything else for you gals?"

Ask what kind of help they need.

No.

Stephanie smiled at Sara Ann. "We're good. These look delicious."

"Can I have a straw?" Tiffany asked.

"Now, how'd I forget that?" Sara Ann fished inside her apron pocket.

Ask.

Ugh.

"Uh, Sara Ann . . . I was just wondering. What kind of help do y'all need here? I'm assuming a full-time commitment, several hours every day?"

She handed out their straws. "Oh no. I mean, that'd be nice, I guess. But we'd take whatever we could get." She looked hopeful. "Why, you know somebody?"

Stephanie peeled the paper from her straw. "Nope. Just wondering."

Sara Ann started toward another table. "All right. Well, point 'em here if they come to mind."

Stephanie bent her head and sucked her shake, marshaling her defenses.

Not doing it, Lord. This wasn't part of the deal. Helping Janelle and Grandma Geri . . . that was the deal. It would actually take away from my ability to help them if I got a job. And I don't even work. I've never wanted to work. That's why I wanted to marry a doctor. She looked up and surveyed the diner. *And if I got some strange unction to work, it wouldn't be here. I mean, seriously . . . maybe the Chanel shop . . .*

"Stephanie, why are you so quiet?"

"Oh." She sighed. "Talking to God. You ever talk to God?"

"Sometimes I tell Him I miss my daddy."

"Aw, sweetheart. I'm glad you talk to God about that."

Tiffany drank some of her shake. "What do you talk to God about?"

"Lately, if I feel like He wants me to do something, I'm usually telling Him why I don't want to do it."

Tiffany gasped. "You tell God you don't want to do something?"

"Yep."

"Does He listen?"

"Good question, Tiff. He does listen actually."

"Do you get your way?"

"So far . . . never."

CHAPTER SIXTEEN

Friday, January 8

B ecca awakened as Todd slowed the car and took the exit
into Hope Springs. It was already dark on a Friday night.
They'd decided midweek to drive down so they could move
some of their things early and assess what needed to be done to the
house. The U-Haul attached to the back made this trip unlike any
other—their first as near-residents.

She had worked much of the trip, polishing her message, then
practicing it for Todd. He'd given great feedback, telling her what
worked, where it lagged, how it resonated overall. Only three weeks
until she'd be on the platform giving it. But she looked forward to
being in the audience for the kickoff conference of the year in two
weeks. Meanwhile, she was enjoying the buildup. She'd been blogging this week about this new phase of her ministry, and she'd been
pleasantly surprised by the feedback. People she'd never heard from
were telling her that they were regular conference attendees and
were already praying for her.

"Soooo ... this is your new normal, folks," Todd said, looking left
and right as he drove slowly down the street. "You got your twenty-
four-hour convenience store by the gas station—always good when

you're hankerin' for junk snacks late at night; your Main Street Diner to my right—but if you're hungry, get there by three; Clotill's consignment shop—will give Nordstrom a run for its money any day of the week."

Becca snorted. "Don't tell Nordstrom they've got fierce competition here. They might put the squeeze on ol' Clotill."

"The great things about this location will be: one, no fast food restaurants—"

"That's not a great thing, Daddy." Claire had awakened about the same time as Becca. "They need a McDonald's."

Todd turned down the road that led to the house. "No fast food restaurants means no fast food calorie temptations for Dad. Two, no Starbucks—"

"My turn," Becca said. "How's that a great thing? I need lattes and frappucinos."

"No designer coffeehouse means no designer coffeehouse daily expenditures."

Becca laughed. "Guess I'll have to learn to make my favorite coffee drinks at home."

They continued down the road and rounded the bend. "What's going on over there?" Becca asked.

Cars covered the grass outside the Sanders home.

Todd pulled into an open spot between the homes. "I don't know. Probably family visiting Grandma Geri."

Becca and Todd had been saddened by the diagnosis and were praying for her. "Have you talked to her since her first chemo?" she asked.

"No, only before. But I talked to Janelle yesterday. Grandma Geri had a couple of rough days and nights, a lot of vomiting."

"We should stop over tonight."

"Absolutely." He looked in the back where Ethan was still sleeping. "We'll take them inside and get settled a bit, then pop over."

They opened the van doors in the back, and Todd scooped up Ethan. Claire climbed down from her seat. "I wanna see Tiffany," she said. Her little feet inched toward the Sanders house.

When Todd and Becca told her they were relocating to Hope Springs, that was her first question. "Will Tiffany be there?" That was all she needed to hop on board.

"Hold on, little lady." Becca took her hand. "We're not heading over just yet."

Ethan was awake now and jumped down to walk up the steps on his own.

Todd unlocked the front door and flipped on the light in the entryway, and Becca stood there, taking it all in with new eyes. This house was very different from their St. Louis home. They were both older houses, but this one was historic-old. Much more character and even a little bigger.

Becca walked farther in, flicking lights as she went, wondering how they would meld the furniture from the two houses. They'd have to give away a lot, and they'd have to totally clear out three of the four bedrooms here. They could keep the guest room furniture in one. Now that she was here, she could see the trip was really needed.

Todd's phone rang, and Becca listened as he answered in the kitchen.

"Hey, Janelle . . . Yep, just got here. We're stopping over a little later . . . Oh, really? Okay, sure. Be right there."

Becca met him as he came out of the kitchen. "What's up?"

"Janelle said they've been taking photos for an album she's putting together for Grandma Geri to flip through while she's doing chemo. They're about to take a pic of my crowd—Janelle, Libby, and Travis—and they want me in it."

"That's a great idea," Becca said, adding, "as long as they keep that camera far from me." Her hair was pulled up lazily for the long drive.

"Come on, kids!" Todd called. "We're headed next door."

"Yaaay!" Claire stretched the word out as she ran down the stairs and to the door, opening it for them all.

They followed Todd to the front entrance. He pushed the door open and—

"Surprise!"

He paused in the doorway as at least two dozen faces smiled at them.

Travis stepped up with a wide grin and pulled him into a handshake-hug. "Come on in, Pastor. This is all for you."

Todd looked tentatively around. "What's all for me?"

"The barbecued ribs in there, for one thing." Travis looked proud.

Janelle raised a finger. "Caveat. Dad and Uncle Wood are gone, so there were stand-ins at the grill. You'll have to test 'em yourself."

Todd glanced skeptically between the two of them. "Travis didn't get near the grill, did he?"

"Oh, so this is what it'll be like having you two around all the time?" Travis said. "And anyway, I wasn't grilling alone. If you don't like the ribs, it might've been my partner's fault. Not saying any names." He fake-coughed, mumbling, "Kory."

Kory looked hurt. "Aw, that's cold, Pastor."

"Todd, Becca, Claire, and Ethan," Janelle said, "welcome to a celebration in honor of you as we rejoice in Todd's acceptance of this call of God to pastor Calvary Church."

Cheers and applause went up. Claire was actually not with her family. She'd already disappeared with Tiffany and Dee.

Janelle continued. "We know the church will undoubtedly have its own official celebration, but your friends wanted to—"

"This is family." Grandma Geri sat in the family room recliner, Stephanie beside her.

Janelle smiled. "Your friends *and* family wanted to throw you a big party soon as we heard."

"But I only told you yesterday we were coming," Todd said.

Janelle gave him a look. "You know it doesn't take long to plan a party and spread the word around here," she said. "What else do we have to do?"

Travis added, "And Janelle had no problem issuing last-minute orders."

"I didn't order you on that grill, I can tell you that."

"This is incredible, you guys," Todd said. "It's been a life-changing couple of weeks for us. It all happened so quickly—"

Becca nodded, eyes wide.

"—but I couldn't have done this if I didn't feel like God was in it. Thank you so much for supporting us. Hey, didn't see you back there, Willard and Skip, and Roy too—my whole elder board is here." He smiled. "Sara Ann, good to see you here. I'm looking forward to chatting with each of you."

He looked at Grandma Geri. "This has been a life-changing time for you too, Grandma Geri, and a tough week. I hope this party isn't too much for you."

"Whose idea you think it was?" She laughed at herself. "I'll say this . . . don't know what this town is coming to, with the two of you as pastors."

"Hadn't thought about it like that," Todd said, "but that *is* rather scary." His eyes twinkled. "And Hope Springs's newest, scariest pastor is itching to visit with *you*, Grandma Geri. But first, can I say one thing?" He waited until some chatter died down. "I'd love to call this a joint celebration, because Becca's got some great things going too." He turned to her. "You want to tell them about it?"

"No, no." She waved him away. "This is your night."

"No fair," Travis said. "Now you've got us wondering. What's the great thing?"

"I'll tell then," Todd said, smiling. "Some of you know Becca's been teaching Bible studies and speaking at conferences for years.

This year she'll be speaking with the Worth & Purpose women's conference in nine cities."

"Whoa," Travis said. "Which means Becca will speak to more people at one conference than Todd and I will speak to in a year—not that I'm jealous or anything." He chuckled. "That's quite an honor, Becca."

"I go to that conference in Greensboro every year." It was the wife of one of the elders from Calvary speaking. "Will you be at that one?"

"Actually, I will," Becca said. "It's in March, I think."

"Road trip!" Stephanie said. "I won't be here, but Janelle can organize it." She smiled over at her. "The whole town needs to go!"

"I'm in!" a few voices shouted.

"I'd be glad to organize it," Janelle said. "Not sure I can go myself, though. I'll have to wait until we get closer to the date to see how things are going."

"You mean to see how *I'm* doing," Grandma Geri said. "You better go on to that conference."

"Having you all there would be awesome," Becca said. "I'd love your prayers too, if you think of it."

"If we think of it?" Sara Ann said. "This is big-time! Don't know if I can go either, since I work weekends, but you better believe I'll be praying."

"Got that right," Grandma Geri said. "Don't let her fool you. That girl's a warrior."

Chatter started up around the room, and Sara Ann came over. "I don't think we've officially met."

Becca shook her hand. "Nice to meet you officially, Sara Ann." She smiled. "So you're from Hope Springs?"

"Born and raised. Graduated high school two years ahead of Todd and Travis."

"Did you leave afterward and come back? That seems to be the trend around here."

"Nope. Went to work full-time at the diner. Been there nineteen years."

Becca was so surprised she might've frowned, but she evened it out quickly. "You've worked at the diner nineteen years? That's . . . all you've wanted to do? I mean, I'm sorry. That didn't come out right."

"No worries," Sara Ann said. "Me and school didn't get along too well. Started at the diner in high school and continued on." She shrugged. "I could never do what you're doin'. You probably went to Bible school and everything."

"I did, but you know . . . not that big a deal." Becca wasn't sure what to say. "I know you've had great experiences at that diner. Ever blog about it?"

Sara Ann looked confused. "Blog?"

"Oh, it's . . . it's sort of posting your thoughts or journaling in your own web space online, and people can comment and dialogue with you."

"I'd need a computer? Nah." She shrugged again. "Been fine without it this long."

"Really? I don't know what I'd do without my computer."

"Hmph." Stephanie had walked up in time to overhear her last comment. "I'm doing my best to find out while I'm here," she said. "Don't know why I'd become such a Facebook addict. I didn't like those folk when I was *in* middle school and high school. Why am I keeping up with them now?"

"Oh, hey, let's make another announcement," Sara Ann said.

Becca and Stephanie looked at one another as Sara Ann waved her hands.

"Can I get everybody's attention for a minute?" Sara Ann put an arm around Stephanie. "I want y'all to meet our newest employee at the Main Street Diner!"

Janelle pumped her fist with a big "Woot! Woot!"

Stephanie looked like she was trying to duck out of sight. When she saw the attention still on her, she said, "Well, I wouldn't say I'm exactly an *employee*. I'm barely even a temp. Just helping out a little here and there while I'm in Hope Springs when I'm not needed here."

"And we'll take all the 'little here and there' we can get," Sara Ann said.

"So if you're able," Janelle further announced, "head on over to the diner for breakfast tomorrow morning. That's Stephanie's big debut."

Stephanie gave Janelle a thin smile. "Thanks so much for that, cousin."

CHAPTER SEVENTEEN

Saturday, January 9

Janelle wasn't sure she could handle this. She'd heard Grandma Geri vomiting in the middle of the night again, which wasn't itself alarming—Grandma had told her not to run to the bathroom every time she "upchucked"—but when it continued over a few minutes, she got up to check. Grandma Geri was slumped over the toilet, sweat beaded on her forehead. Janelle took her temperature, and when it read 103, she remembered the oncologist's words: never ignore a temperature; an infection could be life threatening. She called Dr. Reynolds, and he instructed her to take her grandmother to the hospital right away.

The next few hours were a blur as the hospital fast-tracked Grandma Geri to emergency treatment—X-ray, blood tests, and various drips of antibiotics and other drugs. Turned out she had a chest infection, and her white blood cell count was too low so she had to be admitted.

Somewhere in that blur it hit Janelle that she might be in over her head. While she sat at the hospital, there were four young children sleeping at the house—her own two and Claire and Dee, who had stayed for a sleepover Friday night. Thankfully, Libby had stayed as well, since Stephanie was starting at the diner this morning. But Stephanie would be gone in three weeks anyway, and Libby had her own life in Raleigh. The reality was that Grandma Geri could have an emergency any day of the week, any time of night, for months to come. How could she stand ready to help when she had her own children to look after as well? She couldn't leave them alone in the house.

From the hospital Janelle called Aunt Gladys, who had already planned to spend the day with Grandma Geri, and waited there until she arrived. Now she stared at the countryside as she drove back to Hope Springs, wondering about this other problem she had—what to do today with the kids. Tiffany couldn't be happier, having two playmates to pal around with. But Daniel was another story. His first week of school hadn't gone well. He said nobody liked him, not the teacher or the kids. Janelle had talked to the teacher herself, and the woman seemed great. Daniel just seemed to be having a rough time adjusting, which was showing itself in other ways. He said he wanted his dad, and if anything could break Janelle's heart, that was it . . . because there was nothing she could do about it.

She drove through Hope Springs as the town slowly came alive. Approaching Main Street, she slowed. She hadn't been to the diner in years. As much food as her family cooked up, there was never a need. But a cup of coffee and a few quiet minutes sounded appealing. The kids were likely still asleep. And she'd get to see how Stephanie was faring.

Janelle felt a hint of a smile for the first time this morning. Hearing Stephanie grapple with her "boot camp curveball" had been more than amusing.

Adjacent to the diner was a small parking lot, which was full, so Janelle parked on the street, noting a benefit of small-town living— no meter to feed. A bell tinkled at the opening of the door and the inviting aroma of bacon, eggs, and toast surrounded her. The place was bustling, people seated at booths and tables, servers offering refills of coffee. Should she wait for someone to seat her? She didn't see a sign anywhere. But moments later, Sara Ann appeared from the back.

"Hey! Treat seeing you here." She smiled. "Coming to peek at Stephanie?" She carried a stack of menus that she deposited by the podium near the door.

"Can't say it was the motivation, but a definite side benefit." Janelle glanced around to find her. "She surviving?"

"Totally," Sara Ann said. "She must be back in the kitchen, but I'll take you to her section."

She glanced out the window. A woman in her seventies at least was slowly making her way inside. Sara Ann darted to the door and opened it. "Morning, Mrs. Honeycutt. How are you?"

"Arthritis is giving me a little trouble this morning, but I'm better than I deserve." She kept moving toward the dining room.

"She has a regular table?"

"Same one for years. She and her husband used to come every Saturday morning. He passed away four years ago, and she's kept the tradition."

"Oh, wow." Janelle looked around. "I bet you know a lot of these people's stories."

Sara Ann stared out at the customers. "Like you wouldn't believe." She led Janelle to a small booth. "So if Stephanie wasn't your motivation, what was?"

"Had to rush Grandma Geri to the hospital early this morning." Janelle slid into the booth with a sigh. "Feeling overwhelmed by everything, I guess. Thought I'd get some coffee, take a breather."

"Absolutely. Be right back with a pot. Cream?"

"Thanks."

Sara Ann returned quickly and poured hot coffee into a porcelain mug. She placed a mini pitcher of cream on the table, then reached into her apron and pulled out a small Bible. She handed it to her. "Psalm 121."

Janelle's eyebrows knit lightly as she took it. "Okay."

Sara Ann moved on, tending to other customers. Janelle added cream and sugar to her coffee, stirred, and took a sip. Then she opened the pocket Bible to Psalm 121.

> *I will lift up my eyes to the mountains;*
> *From where shall my help come?*
> *My help comes from the LORD,*
> *Who made heaven and earth.*

She paused right there, staring at the words she'd read. She knew that. She knew her help came from the Lord. She'd said before the first chemo treatment that this would be a time for prayer as never before. But that hadn't been her focus this morning.

She held the mug with both hands, taking a long sip, pondering. Wasn't God the One who'd put it in her heart to help Grandma Geri? If He made heaven and earth, could He not provide what she needed to help her care for the kids as well? He'd already provided Stephanie this month, which was tremendous.

"I hope you don't want anything but coffee, 'cause they got me hopping like a bunny rabbit on steroids this morning."

Janelle looked up, and her stomach buckled.

"And if you laugh, I'm on the first thing smoking back to St. Louis."

"Why . . . would I laugh?" She bit her lip as she gave her cousin the once-over. "I think the Main Street Diner apron is very becoming. Totally love your hair in that bun thing." Janelle reached into her purse. "I've got to get a picture and text it to Cyd."

Stephanie's eyes narrowed. "I wish you would." She turned and hightailed it to her next table as Sara Ann stopped to top off Janelle's mug.

Janelle looked up at her. "What's your deal, Sara Ann?"

Sara Ann set the coffeepot on the table. "What do you mean?"

"You carry a Bible in your apron. You knew exactly what I needed. And watching the way you interact with people around here . . . you're interesting."

Sara Ann laughed. "I hope that's a good thing."

"Oh, I think you're awesome. There just seems to be so much beneath the surface with you." Janelle stared at her, trying to understand what was stirring in her heart. "Do you have a minute?"

"Only a super quick one." Sara Ann slid into the booth across from her.

"Then I'll be super quick." Janelle took another sip of her coffee. "Before David died, I went to this women's Bible study at my church, and I loved it. But everything fell off afterward."

"I can imagine. That was a really hard thing to go through, Janelle."

Janelle nodded, but didn't want to linger there. "Todd's message at the funeral inspired me to look at my life and my relationship with God and make some changes. I want what I used to have, a love of the Bible, and studying, sharing, and praying with other women." She paused to drink her coffee. "I talked to Travis last night and he said New Jerusalem has a Bible study Wednesday nights, but it's for everybody. That's great . . ."

"But . . ."

"I like the dynamic with all women. And I'm thinking it might be nice to take it outside of the church building, draw all kinds of women."

"Wow."

"And I'd love for you to lead it."

"What?" Sara Ann looked genuinely shocked. "No."

"Why not? I think you'd be perfect."

"Perfect? I don't lead stuff. I barely graduated high school. The perfect person is Becca. That's what she does."

Janelle nodded. "She was the first person I thought of and I talked to her last night too. But understandably she said she's got too much going on." She added quickly, "But I honestly think you'd be great. I don't know why, I just do."

Sara Ann moved out of the booth. "Not gonna happen. I read the Bible for me. Who knows if I'm even understanding it right?"

Janelle gave her a look.

"I'm not kidding." She was earnest as she stood by Janelle's side of the booth. "I don't even make it to church on Sunday because of work. Frankly, I'm not getting why you'd ask me."

"Because I've listened to you and I've seen your heart. And you sure knew what psalm I needed." She paused. "I'm not asking you to give a sermon. Just lead us as we study together."

Sara Ann watched the hostess seat a family at one of her tables.

"Gotta go," she said. "But answer's no. Nobody'd show up anyway." She started toward another table.

Janelle looked over her shoulder. "What if one person showed up?"

Sara Ann paused, looked back at her. "Who?"

"Me."

"Oh, Janelle . . ."

"Seriously, if I show up with my Bible, can we have a Bible study, the two of us? It would help just to have that kind of accountability."

"Here? How?"

"What time do you open?"

"Six."

"Do you get a midmorning break?"

"Around ten."

"How about next Saturday at ten then? We'll do it one time, see how it goes."

Sara Ann gave her a look that said her arm was being twisted. "How can I say no if you want an accountability partner?"

"Accountability partner?" Stephanie had been walking past, and she backed up when she heard the words. "Had one all my life. My sister. Now I hear her voice in my head. I don't recommend it." She kept going.

Janelle looked at Sara Ann. "I think I need to work on two of us showing up."

CHAPTER EIGHTEEN

Kory smiled at the sight of the girls trooping over to the Dillon home in a straight line, knees high, arms swinging in time, with Becca at the lead. He got out of his car, and when Dee caught sight of him, she fell out of step.

"Daddy, it's still *morning*. You didn't have to come so early."

Becca waved with a sympathetic smile. "Good morning, Kory."

Kory came closer. "Morning, Becca." He looked into the bright faces. "Good morning, girls. What're you up to?"

"We're gonna help clear out Dad's old room," Claire said, "because it's gonna be mine now."

"And Miss Becca said she'd take us for a Slushee after. Can I stay, Dad?"

Kory noticed that Dee's hair looked a lot better than when he'd left her last night. Janelle must've hooked her up.

Becca aimed a thumb at the Sanders home. "They're whipping up chocolate chip pancakes over there, if that interests you."

"They're really good too," Tiffany said. "My mom makes the best pancakes."

"Is that right?" He rubbed his chin. "I think that means you can stay awhile longer, Dee."

Becca put a hand in the air. "Forward, march!"

The girls marched in time behind Becca, and Kory went the other direction. The side door was open, so he pulled the screen and walked inside. "Hello?"

"Kory, we're in the kitchen," Janelle called.

He continued through the small laundry area and crossed the narrow hall into the kitchen. "Good morning, everybody. Hey, I see the pastor heard about the pancakes as well."

Travis put his fork down and rose to give Kory a hearty handshake. "Right. 'Heard.' Lifelong friend, now neighbor and member of my congregation, and I can't get a personal invitation to a pancake breakfast. Had to hear about it next door."

"It's rough out here, man." Kory joined him at the table.

Janelle looked back from the griddle. "You told me you eat at the diner every Saturday morning."

Travis took his seat again. "That was before my friends moved in down the street. Between you and Todd, I knew somebody'd have breakfast going." He scooped up a forkful of sausage and pancakes. "Don't forget I'm just a lonely ol' bachelor."

"Aw, poor Travis." Libby poured a glass of orange juice.

"Libby." Travis lowered his fork and looked directly at her. "Can we talk before you go back to Raleigh?"

She stared back from where she stood at the counter. "I doubt it. We've got a big event tomorrow, and I'm about to head out."

"Ten minutes, Libby?"

She cut her eyes over at him. "Fine."

Janelle looked back and forth between them, then over at Kory. "Sooo, Kory, can I get you some nice hot pancakes?"

"I thought you'd never ask."

She gestured to two mixing bowls. "I made one batch with chocolate chips and one without. What's your preference, sir?"

Kory smiled. He and Janelle may have met sixteen years ago,

but they still had a lot to learn about one another. "My contribution to my firm's fund-raising cookbook was chocolate chip pancakes and chocolate chip cheesecake . . . recipes honed from years of much love. I'll take the 'with.'"

"Did you just say chocolate chip cheesecake?" Libby took the seat by Kory. "I will personally buy you the ingredients and forget I ever heard of eating right."

"I didn't know you could cook, Kory." Janelle poured batter onto the griddle. "Or are those two items the extent of your repertoire?"

"Do I detect doubt as to my skill level?"

"That's what I heard." Travis was finishing his batch of regular pancakes. "But I'm not saying anything."

Janelle held the spatula aloft. "Skill level? You said that like you can really burn." She cocked her head sideways. "For some reason I just don't see it."

"Okay." A mischievous smile was forming. "I'll take that as a challenge. When I respond, it'll speak for itself."

"Ohhhh." Travis leaned over and fist-bumped Kory. "That's good, that's good."

"You know what, Travis?" Janelle flipped the pancakes. "You might want to stay completely out of cooking conversations."

Travis put his hand to his heart. "See, Janelle, you were a member in good standing till just now." He let his eyes rest on the griddle. "But you can work your way back with another pancake."

Kory laughed and got up to pour a cup of coffee. "Grandma Geri resting?"

"She's at the hospital," Janelle said. "Got a chest infection, and they wanted to keep her overnight. Aunt Gladys is with her. I called a little while ago and she's much better."

"Next chemo treatment is Monday, right?" Travis asked.

"That's right."

"I want to sit with her for a while."

"She'll like that, Travis."

Daniel walked in, his eyes barely open, wearing Spider-Man pj's.

"Good morning, sleepyhead." Janelle lifted a pancake to see if it was done. "Come here and give your mom a hug."

Daniel hesitated, looking around the room.

Janelle put her hand on her hip. "Daniel Evans. I know you're not embarrassed to hug your mom in front of company."

He shuffled over and leaned his head into her chest.

Janelle kissed him on the forehead. "Say good morning to everybody."

Daniel turned. "Good morning, Pastor Brooks and Mr. Miller. Hey, Libby."

"Oh, everybody else gets the formal greeting, and I get 'Hey, Libby'?" She pointed a finger at him. "Ms. Sanders to you, young man."

Janelle scooped the pancakes off the griddle and onto a plate. "Here you go, Mr. Miller."

"Thank you, Ms. Evans." Kory laughed. "But seriously, I understand props for the pastor, but can I just be Kory? I look for my dad when I hear 'Mr. Miller.'"

"I'm trying to shake up the formal thing too," Travis said. "Todd and I talked about it last night. We're still young and not into the formalities. I love that the young people are calling me Pastor Trav."

"I like that," Janelle said. "And you don't have to worry about me being formal. I've known you too long. But you can bring your plate over so I can get back in good standing."

Travis was up in a flash. "Now that's what I'm talking about, Member Evans."

Daniel tugged on her shirt. "Mom, the winter festival is today at our home church. I'm missing everything." His whole body seemed to sag. "What are *we* doing today?"

"I'm not sure yet, Daniel. I want to spend some time next door helping Todd and Becca clean up and get their house ready to move into next week—"

"Aw, Mom, that's boring. There's nothing to do around here."

Kory felt for him. Had to be hard moving to a new place, on top of trying to cope without his dad. He saw it firsthand with Dee.

"Daniel, you might be able to help me with something," Kory said. Daniel looked at him, a tad hopeful.

"There's this new movie out—I don't know if you've heard of it. *Return of the Green Goblin.*"

"Yeah! That's the one I've been talking about."

"The problem is," Kory continued, "I've always been a fan of those movies, but Dee's not, and she's probably too young anyway. And I'm a little embarrassed to walk in by myself, a grown-up without a kid attached. Think you could go with me today?"

Daniel looked at Janelle. "Mom, can I? You *have* to say yes."

Janelle looked amused. "Well. I don't *have* to. But you can go. Yes."

He hugged her waist without hesitation this time. "Thank you, Mom." Then he looked up. "Thank you, Mr. . . . Kory."

"You're welcome, Daniel," Kory said. "I'd like to see what I can do to help out next door first, but we'll go this afternoon, okay? That is, if your mom'll watch Dee for me."

"I'd love to." Janelle turned off the flame under the griddle. "Now go get washed up, son, and then come get some breakfast."

Daniel breezed out with much more pep than he'd entered with.

Travis walked his plate to the sink, rinsed it, and placed it in the dishwasher. Then he said something to Libby. She hesitated, then got up and followed him outside.

Janelle took the seat next to Kory. "I don't know what to say." She looked into his eyes. "Thank you."

He held her gaze. "The feeling is mutual, for all you've done for Dee."

"I'm learning a lot about you as a man, a father . . . a chef." She smiled. "I'm glad we're friends, Mr. Miller."

"Likewise, Ms. Evans." He could get lost in her pretty brown eyes. "Likewise."

Libby shivered slightly and crossed her arms on the back porch swing. She should've brought her jacket, but her mind was crowded with thoughts of what Travis would say. They hadn't had a one-on-one conversation since college, and she'd left the last one never wanting to speak to him again.

Travis bent forward in the swing and shrugged off the jacket to his sweat suit. "Here," he said.

She wanted to decline, but it was pretty breezy. "Thanks." She slipped it on, inhaled his aroma.

The swing moved lazily. They looked out at the backyard that spanned the width of both houses and beyond. In the distance were dormant cornfields.

Travis looked at her. "I wanted to clear the air between us."

"Air is fine, Travis." She surveyed the treetops.

"Libby, clearly you hold animosity against me, and—"

"I don't hold anything against you. I just don't have much to say to you." She pulled his jacket a little closer as the wind kicked up.

He glanced away. "I understand."

"You understand." She looked at him now. "What exactly do you understand, Travis?"

"That I hurt you. I didn't mean to." His eyes were a deep, deep brown. "I was young and immature, and I regret a lot of things . . ."

Their eyes locked for several seconds, then she looked away. "Yeah, I regret a lot of things too."

They sat in silence again. Libby suddenly heard a loud wail in the distance. Had to be Ethan.

"When I think back to that time . . ." Travis spoke slowly, reflectively. "I was leaving Hope Springs for Duke. I had shot up in height that summer, started lifting weights. I was always the kid whose personality made him popular, but now the girls were actually attracted to me." He looked at her and his gaze held. "Even Libby Sanders. I always thought you were pretty when I'd see you in Hope Springs. But I knew you never saw me as special. When we ran into each other sophomore year, it was like you were seeing me for the first time."

True. Libby had gone to a party on her campus, the University of North Carolina, Chapel Hill. When this fine guy started talking to her as if he knew her, she was stunned to realize it was Travis.

"I liked you, Libby. I always liked you." The sun came from behind the clouds. "I'm not proud to admit it, but my head got big with this whole new world that opened up to me. Then I pledged a frat, and I just . . ."

"Didn't want to commit to one girl." She felt her jaw tightening. He looked away.

"Didn't mind sleeping with one, though." The tears revealed themselves, betraying her. "And I'm not saying it was wrong to sleep together—I wasn't into all the purity stuff like Janelle." She swiped a tear from her face. "I just thought you at least *cared* about me." *Ugh. Stop crying.*

He let out a heavy sigh and looked deep into her eyes. "Libby, it *was* wrong to sleep together, and I knew it was wrong. I turned my back on everything I'd been taught and did what I wanted in college." He reached up and lightly brushed her face. "It wasn't until a couple of years after college that I got serious about God again. That's when I left my job and went to seminary in Dallas."

Libby didn't know why she'd tried to imply that sex outside of marriage was okay. She knew the truth. No way you could grow up in the Sanders clan and not know right from wrong. She'd simply chosen not to abide by it.

"And I did care about you," Travis said. "How many times did I try to call you, but you refused to talk to me?"

"Why would I have talked to you at that point? I knock on your apartment door and Debbie answers? I find out you're dating my friend?"

"We weren't dating. She just . . . came over."

"Travis, seriously? You think I want to hear this?"

"I just wanted you to know there was a difference in my mind. You were the one I went places with, held hands with in public."

Libby told herself that it didn't matter now, but her heart latched onto it anyway.

"But I never lied to you, Libby. I told you I wasn't ready to commit to one person. Still," he said, "I apologize anyway for not honoring God and not honoring you."

She stared into her lap. All these years she'd held a grudge, and the only real reason was that he hadn't felt for her what she'd felt for him. She sighed. "I appreciate the apology, Travis, and I understand where it's coming from. Even if it's not really necessary."

The rusty swing was the only sound for the next few minutes as both retreated into their own thoughts.

"So how's life for you now?" he said. "Sounds like event planning is going well."

"It is. I enjoy what I do."

"So, the guy who was with you at the funeral . . . that your boyfriend?"

"Al? No, he's just a friend."

"He looked pretty into you."

Libby didn't say anything.

"You're not seeing anyone seriously?"

She looked at him. "Why?"

"Just asking."

"No. I guess I'm like you were. Not ready to commit to one person."

"Oh, okay." He smirked a little. "Can I ask a question about something else, though?"

"Go on."

He hunkered down with his elbows on his knees. "Seems like Janelle didn't know about us." He looked at her. "As close as you two are, why didn't you tell her?"

Libby took her time to answer, thinking it through for herself. "You and I dated sophomore year and she didn't come down that Christmas or Easter, or I'm sure I would've. But as it was, I avoided it because if I told her, she would've started probing. And she can always read me." Libby paused. "I would've had to admit I was falling for you, and I didn't want to admit that even to myself."

A rabbit appeared from inside a patch of underbrush. Libby and Travis both watched as it scurried out in the open until it found another spot to hide. Travis got up, sending the swing into motion, and walked to the edge of the porch.

Todd suddenly appeared from around the corner. "Hey, there you are," he said. "We're ready to haul some of the mattresses into the U-Haul to take to the homeless shelter. As strong and manly as Kory and I are, we could use a little more muscle."

"You got it, bro." Travis's tone was mellow. "Be right there."

He looked back at Libby. "Just for the record," he said, "I didn't want to admit it either."

CHAPTER NINETEEN

Sunday, January 10

The after-church crowd was thick in the diner. Stephanie had begun to think she'd lost her mind to jump in on the weekend. She'd shadowed Sara Ann for a while first thing yesterday, which helped. Still, she should've wet her feet in a sedate, midmorning, weekday atmosphere, where people read their newspapers, sipped coffee, and let you disappear. *This* atmosphere—long wait, tables filled end-to-end, babies throwing food from high chairs—was *really* testing her nerves.

"Yes, I understand, sir . . ." Stephanie had her pencil to her notepad. "I don't actually know if they'll cook the blueberries inside the pancakes. I know they'll put them on top, though."

"Can you go find out?"

"How about I take the order of everyone at the table, and if they can't put the blueberries on the inside, I'll let you know?"

"I'd actually prefer you find out now." The guy talked deliberately, as if making a management decision. "Because if they can't, I want to order something totally different."

You could actually give me the Plan B order right now, so I don't have to make two trips over here just for you. "Yes, sir."

Stephanie headed to the kitchen. *Be nice. Be polite. Defer to the customer.*

"Ma'am?"

Stephanie paused at one of her tables. *Smile.* She smiled.

"My son's eggs are cold. Could we get another order made fresh?"

"They were cold, really? I'm sorry about that." Seemed like every order she picked up from the kitchen was steaming hot, but she certainly could've missed it.

"Well, they were hot when you brought them, but he wouldn't eat them." The woman smiled. "You know how kids are. He says he'll eat them now if they're made fresh."

Ah, good try. Stephanie leaned over and whispered to her. "If I'm not mistaken, you'll have to pay for a second order. But I can pop this one in the microwave for free."

"Second option works for me," the woman whispered back.

Stephanie took the boy's plate and continued toward the kitchen.

"Excuse me, ma'am, can we get more syrup?" from another table.

"Absolutely, be right there."

She walked extra fast and made it back without another interruption. She put the plate in the microwave and punched the time, then approached Hank, one of the cooks. "Can you put blueberries *inside* pancakes, instead of on top?"

He shrugged. "Sure, we can do that."

"Cool."

She poured syrup into a container, grabbed the plate from the microwave, and headed back, dropping off the syrup, the plate, and returning to the table with Mr. Blueberry.

"Yes, sir," Stephanie said. "We can make it with the blueberries inside."

"Actually, I changed my mind," he said. "I'd like biscuits with gravy and eggs scrambled easy instead of blueberry pancakes."

Stephanie nodded slowly, crossing out the original order and replacing it with the new one.

"But I'm wondering if they'll cook the eggs *with* the gravy instead of pouring it on top of the biscuit afterward."

"Okay, am I being punked?" Stephanie looked around for the camera.

"I'm sorry, I didn't hear what you asked," the man said.

"Uh, nothing," Stephanie said. "I'm assuming you'll want the biscuits and gravy regardless of how it's cooked?"

He thought about it and gave a firm nod. "I'd say so, yes."

"Great. Let me get the rest of your table's order, and I'll put yours in with your preferred method of preparation."

She moved around the table, got their orders, and when she turned, Becca, Todd, and a few others were being seated in her section.

She walked over. "What a really pleasant surprise to see you," she said.

Becca was smiling. "Good to see you too." She was settling Claire in her seat. "You remember Calvary's elders and their wives from Friday night?" She went down the table by name.

"Yes, good to see you again."

Stephanie exchanged pleasantries, but knew she only had a moment. "You all must be looking forward to Todd's first sermon next Sunday," she said.

"Couldn't be more excited," one of the wives said. They all looked to be from Todd's father's generation.

"We're proud of this young man, that's for sure." Willard was beside him and placed a hand on his shoulder. "And praying for him."

Todd held a sleepy Ethan in his lap. "I think I've prayed more the last three weeks than I've prayed my whole life. Not easy following my dad."

Willard looked into his eyes. "I hope you know we're not expecting a reincarnation of Jim. You have your own calling, son, and we believe you're the man for Calvary in this season. We're trusting God to do great things through you."

"Appreciate that, Willard," Todd said.

The blueberry-gravy guy was eyeing Stephanie. She had to get moving. "I'll be right back for your order," she said. "Can I bring coffee, juice?"

She took their drink orders and walked them back to the kitchen, stopping to check on three of her tables. She saw Sara Ann coming out of the swinging doors to the kitchen, moving at a rapid clip with a tray of entrées.

Stephanie submitted her new orders. "And is that my spinach omelet, no cheese?"

Hank had just pan-flipped some kind of omelet in the air. She loved how he did that.

"One and the same," he said. "Sixty seconds."

Stephanie waited, her mind back at Todd's table. Something about that exchange, Todd's comment about following his dad . . . That's exactly how she'd always felt about Cyd. It wasn't easy following her sister—Ph.D., college professor, gifted teacher in classical languages as well as the Bible, encourager, all-around role model. Stephanie never could've been all that, so she didn't bother to try. If anything, she'd done the opposite.

But just now, it clicked—it was never about following Cyd. It was about knowing her own calling and following *that*. But what was it exactly? Where was all this servant training leading? This stint in Hope Springs would pass quickly. What would she do next? Somehow returning to her routine of waking late morning and whiling the day away didn't quite seem like a "calling."

"Yoo-hoo? Stephanie?" Hank's hand was outstretched.

"Oh, sorry. Thanks."

She took the plate and headed back out, certain of one thing. She didn't want her posture to always be resisting. It would be nice to one day have a heart to do whatever God called her to do.

CHAPTER TWENTY

Friday, January 15

Janelle was learning that Grandma Geri's "planned course of treatment" would hardly ever go as planned. She'd been held at the hospital two additional nights, and because of the chest infection, the oncologist delayed the second dose of chemo until Friday. Janelle was getting to know the nurses and other workers in the infusion center. And the treatments, always ominous as a focus, could fade in the throes of a good time—which was exactly what she and Grandma Geri were having.

Janelle laughed. "Grandma, what are you doing? You know an ace doesn't beat a joker."

Grandma Geri kept a stone face, the cards she'd taken up still in her hand. "That's the way we always played it."

"Grandma . . ." Janelle stretched the word, giving her time to recant.

"Well, then let me keep my ace and play another card."

"Grandma, I never thought I'd see the day. You're cheating." Janelle held out her hand. "Those belong to me."

Grandma Geri handed them over, mumbling, "It's the medicine they put in this drip thing."

Janelle shook her head. "I'm keeping a close eye on you from now on."

"Good. You can watch how bad I beat you."

Grandma Geri was in the recliner, hooked to an IV that dispensed the drugs, the machine making a steady rhythmic sound. Janelle had pulled a chair up close to her and set up a tray between them for the card game and snacks.

"Oh!" Janelle said. They'd both played sixes. Janelle held her pile of cards in her hand and waited for her grandmother. "You ready?"

"'Course I'm ready." Grandma Geri lifted the first card.

"I. De. Clare. War!"

Grandma Geri squealed at the last card. "You gonna tell me your jack beats my queen?"

"Ha ha." Janelle glanced pitifully at her pile. "I've only got two cards left. You wouldn't leave your granddaughter broken and card-less, would you?"

"All day."

Janelle cracked up, then looked as the door to the treatment room opened.

"Hey, hey!"

Janelle smiled. "Hey, Pastor Trav."

"Travis." Grandma Geri crooked her finger for him to come closer. "You're just in time to catch this whuppin'."

Travis did a double take as he walked over. "Are y'all playing War? Oh my goodness, it's been years." He folded his arms. "Put it to her, Grandma Geri."

Janelle rolled her eyes at him.

She and Grandma Geri played their next-to-last card.

"Now maybe I forgot this too," Grandma Geri said. "Does an eight beat a five?"

Travis grinned.

"All right, Grandma. Play the last one."

"Bam!" Travis said, capping the loss. "Winner and still champion, Geraldine Sanders!"

Janelle picked up her pencil and made a tally mark. "That's five games to my two. And we're playing until I catch up and pass you."

"Go on and shuffle then." Grandma Geri looked at Travis. "And how you doing today? Out visiting the sick and the shut-in?"

"Only you, Grandma Geri. You know I had to come see my girl." Travis got the only other chair in the room and brought it over. "Question is, how are *you* doing?"

"God gives me grace. And I give Him praise."

Travis smiled. "I remember you used to say that, and I'd be thinking, 'But how are you doing?' Now I understand totally."

Janelle was giving the cards a good shuffle. "Travis, I've been meaning to ask you . . . Todd and Becca get here tomorrow. His first sermon at Calvary is Sunday. Don't you want to hear it? I know I do."

"Yeah, I thought about that too. On the one hand, it's cool that God's got us both pastoring in Hope Springs. But we can't take part in what the other's doing because we're at separate churches and we meet at the same time."

"That's the thing," Janelle said, watching the flutter of the cards as she shuffled. "What if New Jerusalem joined Calvary on Sunday?"

"We can't *not* have service, Janelle. I don't see that going over well. I'm sure people are excited he's back, but you know how it is. Calvary does its thing, we do ours. Always been that way."

"Unless it's a wedding or a funeral." Janelle started dealing the cards.

"Ain't nobody stopping you from going, Jan," Grandma Geri said. "Go on and go."

"I know. I just thought it'd be nice to show full support." She peeped at Travis. "Not that I want to miss my own pastor's sermon."

"At least we record our service, so you could listen later. Calvary hasn't stepped into the twenty-first century with the technology yet." He smiled. "But I bet that's about to change."

Janelle laughed lightly as they played their first cards.

"By the way," Travis said, "I've been getting calls about that Bible study you announced Sunday. People wanting to make sure they heard you right, that it's at the diner and not the church."

Janelle's face lit up. "Really?"

She'd been praying for God to bless this. Sara Ann had tried to back out, just as Janelle had suspected she would, but Janelle asked again if she'd try it once before making a final decision. She didn't tell Sara Ann she'd made an announcement at church. She would've felt too bad for her if no one showed up.

A long beep sounded on the machine, and Sylvia came in to change the fluid.

"How we doing, Miss Geri? Ready for a trip to the ladies' room?"

Grandma laid the card down that she was about to play. "I think I better."

Sylvia helped her up, then pushed the IV pole with her as they made their way to the restroom.

Travis crossed a leg over his knee and looked at Janelle. "How's your cousin?" he said.

"Which one?" Janelle smiled at him.

"All right, make me say it. Libby."

"She's good. Busy."

Travis was quiet a moment. "Is she coming to Hope Springs this weekend?"

"I don't think so. I was surprised she could be here for Todd and Becca's surprise party. The weekends are usually her busiest times."

He glanced away, then looked back at Janelle. "I was thinking about inviting her to church, but I don't want her to feel that I'm pushing or anything."

"She won't come. And she probably *would* feel like you're pushing. But since when would you let that stop you?"

Travis smiled slightly. "Good point. But I don't know . . ."

"Why were you thinking about inviting her?"

Travis was hesitant. "Did she tell you?"

"About the two of you?" At his nod, she said, "Yes."

"She's always been special to me, Janelle. Even in my selfish college mind-set, she was special. My only thought in inviting her was that maybe the Lord would meet her there. I just care. You know?"

Janelle couldn't be more proud to call him her pastor. "Then do what you're led to do."

***

"Up there." Janelle pointed. "Cabinet on the right."

Kory followed her finger and found the home for the plates he'd just dried.

"I don't know why you won't let me help, Kory." Janelle watched from the kitchen table. "It's the least I can do."

"Oh no." He dried another two plates and put them away. "I couldn't have you doubting my ability to clean up after myself too. This is a full-service deal."

Janelle put her chin on her hands. "You don't have to worry about me doubting your skills in the kitchen ever again—cooking or cleaning. You're the man."

He turned and bowed. "Why, thank you. I think we can call this mission accomplished."

She got up. "Not until I get one more sliver of this cheesecake. It really is incredible."

"Better save some for the next time Libby comes. She requested it, you know." He covered the leftover vegetables and put them in the fridge.

"Hmph. You might have to make another one. Even Tiffany and Daniel loved it, and they're not big cheesecake fans. Stephanie's ready to help you take it to market . . . and she means it."

"It was fun cooking for your family." He smiled at her. "Even more fun surprising you."

She carried her dessert plate back to the table. "You certainly did that."

After Grandma Geri's chemo, they'd returned to a house permeated with the aroma of pot roast, potatoes, and green beans. Kory had hipped Stephanie to his surprise, and she'd let him bring his grocery bags and take over the kitchen. Grandma Geri said the roast melted in her mouth, which was saying a lot coming from the family's master chef.

He transferred what was left of the pot roast into a covered dish and put that in the fridge too, then filled the roasting pan with sudsy water. "This needs to soak for a little while," he said.

Janelle savored the last bit of her sliver. "And you need to sit and relax for a while." She thought a minute. Tiffany, Dee, and Daniel were in the family room watching *Toy Story 3* with Stephanie and Aunt Gladys. Grandma Geri had gone to her room to lie down. She put her plate in the sink, saying, "Don't touch it. I'll wash it later," and led him to the living room.

"Ahh." Kory sank into the sofa cushion. "Hadn't realized how long I'd been on my feet."

Janelle sat next to him, mindful to put several inches between them. They'd had little time alone—and even now they weren't *alone*—but she hadn't forgotten how Kory could make her feel.

Kory sat forward suddenly, reaching for something on the coffee table. "This yours?"

Janelle looked closely at the iPod, since she and Grandma Geri both had one. "Yes, that one's mine. Must've left it there after I went walking."

"You can tell a lot about a person by what's on her iPod."

"Oh, really."

"Absolutely."

He manipulated the dial and perused her playlists. "Kirk, Fred, Mandisa, Nicole C. . . ." He nodded, as if he would expect these. "Natalie Grant, MercyMe, Mary Mary, CeCe, of course—who's Alex Williams?"

"Praise and worship leader at my home church. You should check out his album."

"Cool. Hey . . . I see a playlist with my boys. What you know about Da' T.R.U.T.H., Lecrae, Flame, Alien, Ambassador, and all them?"

"Are you serious? You love them too?"

"Saw Alien and Kelli in Charlotte last summer. Unbelievable concert. Okay, what's the Quiet Storm playlist?"

"It's a D.C. thing. The Quiet Storm on Howard University radio, WHUR. Old slow jams."

"The radio station might be a D.C. thing, but these are my cuts." He brought the iPod closer. "Con Funk Shun, Commodores, L.T.D., René & Angela, wow—Atlantic Starr. I haven't heard 'Am I Dreamin'?' in I don't know how long." He put the earbuds in and pushed the play button, his head bopping slowly side to side.

"That's one of my favorites. Let me hear." Janelle took the bud from his left ear and inched closer so she could put it in hers.

Their shoulders swayed slowly together in time. And at the chorus, they simultaneously sang, "Am I dreamin'? Am I just imagining you're here in my life?"

They looked at one another, smiling as she continued with the female lead and he with the male. She swatted his arm when the song ended. "Why didn't you tell me you could sing? You're full of surprises."

"I didn't know you could either." He donned a playful grin. "Let me find another duet for us." He scrolled through the list. "Ohhh.

Anita Baker with Chapter 8? That's, like, top ten old school slow jam."

"Easily." *Just don't play it.*

"I've got to play this."

"Weren't you looking for a duet?"

"Yep, saw a good one. Luther and Cheryl Lynn. But first I have to hear this."

He pressed his thumb on the button. "I Just Wanna Be Your Girl" began to play. In her mind's eye, Janelle was in her dorm room at the University of Maryland, listening to the radio at night. This was a Quiet Storm favorite, and after that weekend with Kory, he was all she thought about when she heard it.

Her eyes closed as she listened, as the words reverberated in her eighteen-year-old heart.

Kory touched her hand. "You okay?"

She opened her eyes and a single tear fell. She swiped it quickly.

"A memory of David?"

She almost felt guilty that it wasn't. "Um, no. But I'm fine."

He took his earbud out and shifted toward her. "I'm supposed to believe that? What're you thinking about?"

She took hers out too and sighed. "The song brought back memories. Freshman year, first semester."

"Freshman year, first semester? Oh, so you got on campus and some guy stole your heart?"

"Before I got on campus." She looked into his eyes. "You were my first kiss, Kory."

He stared at her for long seconds, his eyes soft. "And you wanted to be my girl?"

She looked away.

"Janelle—"

She waved the subject away. "It's silly, just . . . let's move on."

"That's what I wanted too."

Janelle turned toward him again. "So maybe, if it weren't for the missed phone calls and messages . . ." She shook off the speculation. "Wouldn't have worked anyway. We were too young and too far apart."

"Interesting that all these years later, here we are right beside each other."

"Yes, I'd say it's . . . interesting."

A month ago she'd wondered if she could ever move on from David. She still thought about him daily, something he might say to the kids, an inside joke only the two of them would get. She thought her heart would never be drawn to another man. And she still doubted it could—to any man except this one.

He looked deeper into her eyes. "It could still happen, Janelle. It's not too late."

She got up and walked a few feet away. "I can't, Kory. I can't even entertain the thought, not while you're still married."

"Janelle . . ." He came to her. "I'm 'married' to a woman who's engaged to another man. They're tying the knot in less than a month, right after our court hearing. I don't see anything wrong with admitting . . ." He turned her face back with his finger. "With admitting I care about you. I like you. I love getting to know you."

"I love getting to know you too, as a friend. That's what we were sticking to, remember?"

Kory locked eyes with her and smiled.

"What?"

"The irony. That's why I wanted you to be my girl. Because you're different. You're special."

Janelle thought she might melt under his gaze. Though she'd skipped quickly past it, she'd heard his words loud and clear. He'd said it could still happen . . .

As resolved as she was to toe the line with him, it was hard to stop her heart from keeping a calendar, counting the days until he was officially free.

CHAPTER TWENTY-ONE

Saturday, January 16

Janelle arrived at the diner at nine fifty Saturday morning, almost as nervous as Sara Ann. Somehow her focus had gone from personally benefiting from the Bible study to praying that Sara Ann would benefit through recognizing her gift. Except Janelle didn't actually *know* she had a gift. She'd never seen her lead a study. She only had a feeling. And she'd invited others based on that feeling. What if Sara Ann was right, and this wasn't her thing? Janelle would feel terrible if she'd set Sara Ann up for disappointment.

The owner, Lila, was at the podium when she entered.

"Hi, Lila, I'm Janelle. I'm here to meet Sara Ann for a . . . kind of a Bible study."

"I went to school with your mom," Lila said. She came from behind the podium and hugged her. "I'm so glad you talked Sara Ann into this. That girl's been holding Bible studies table to table for years. It's about time it was made official."

"I can't believe that," Janelle said. "Well, I *can*, but . . . that's really neat."

Sara Ann walked over. "My stomach has been in knots all morning because of you. Just thought you should know."

Janelle hugged her. "I've been praying."

"So have I," Lila said. "And I've been telling her all morning to stop fretting and trust God."

"My saving grace is I'm on the clock," Sara Ann said. "I won't take any extra time. I don't even know why you agreed to let me do this."

"As hard as you've worked for me for almost twenty years, this is nothing. I've always asked God to use this diner the way He wants to. This is the best use yet." Lila saw something that needed her attention and zipped away.

Sara Ann sighed. "We might as well head back. I got a table reserved for us toward the back, so we'll be out of the way."

The bell tinkled and three African-American women walked in. Janelle greeted them and turned to Sara Ann. "Sara Ann, this is Beverly, Allison, and Trina. They're all New Jerusalem members."

"Good to meet you." Sara Ann shook their hands. "The hostess should be right over to seat you."

"You know we're here for the Bible study," Beverly said.

Sara Ann looked down and saw the Bibles in their hands, then looked at Janelle. "Oh," she said. "Great. Let's walk this way."

She led them toward the table she'd reserved, which only seated four. Thankfully, there was a free table beside it, which Sara Ann pushed over. "We can go ahead and get settled. I don't know if you're hungry or want coffee or juice or anything, but someone will be over to take orders."

"That's great, I'm starving," Trina said. "I've never eaten here, but it sure smells good."

"Sara Ann?"

They all looked.

Lila had led someone else to the table. "This lady's here for your Bible study," she said.

Janelle was thankful for the turnout, but Sara Ann looked panicked. She extended her hand to the new woman. "Hi, I'm Sara Ann."

The woman shook it. "I'm Jessica. I don't know anyone else here, but I heard the announcement at New Jerusalem and wanted to come."

Janelle stood again and introduced herself and the others to Jessica. Just then Stephanie came over.

She spoke in a low voice to Janelle. "Your girl has been a hot mess this morning, spilling coffee on folk and whatnot. Had *me* praying for her, and you know I'm not an intercessor."

Janelle almost laughed. "I was wondering where you were. Tell me you've got this table."

"I've got this table." She moved toward the middle of their group. "Hello, ladies. My name is Stephanie, and I'll be taking care of you this morning. I'm thinking you might want to get your orders in before you get going." She flipped a pencil from behind her ear. "I'll start on this end."

Janelle watched as Sara Ann took the seat beside her and lowered her head as the women ordered. She knew she was praying.

"Sara Ann, what can I get you?" Stephanie waited, pencil poised.

"Water. Thanks, Steph."

Two more orders and Stephanie was gone. The women trained their eyes on Sara Ann, waiting. She opened her Bible and gazed down at something written on the inside cover. Then she looked up and met their eyes.

"My grandmother gave me this Bible when I was twelve," she said. "And whenever I open it, I see what she wrote and it makes me feel good inside. It says: *To Sara Ann. Love, Jesus.*" Sara Ann waited a moment. "Um . . . when Janelle asked if I would do this, I thought it would be just the two of us. I'm no teacher. I don't have a lesson prepared. No worksheets, nothing. I feel like y'all will leave here thinking you wasted your time. I just want to say I'm sorry."

Janelle put her hand on hers. "Sara Ann, you don't need a lesson. Just share from your heart."

Sara Ann looked down, almost as if she wanted to cry. "Can we pray?"

"Absolutely" sounded around the table. One hand linked with another until a circle had formed.

"Dear God," Sara Ann said, "I don't know enough to give these women what they need. But You do. Would You just meet us here? Would You show us what You want us to know about You? Show us how to love You more. Show us how to make You our all. Amen."

"Well, hallelujah," Beverly said. She was in her forties, a little heavyset, with a disposition both commanding and welcoming, if that were possible. "I can already tell you my time wasn't wasted, Sara Ann. I'm full just from that little prayer. I want that intimacy you obviously have with Jesus." Her eyes misted. "That's why I came. I need Him to meet me."

Sara Ann looked confused. "You were moved by the prayer?"

"Me too." Trina was younger and had a petite frame. "You said, 'Show us how to love You more.' And I don't think I've ever thought about that. How *do* I love Jesus more?" She added quickly, "I don't mean to steer you away from where you wanted to go."

"No, it's fine," Sara Ann said. "Thank you for giving me a direction to steer in." She flipped toward the back of her Bible. "Why don't we turn to John, chapter fourteen."

Together the women read the words that Jesus spoke to His disciples on the night before He went to the cross. Sara Ann spoke briefly, pointing out that four times Jesus told them that if they loved Him, they would keep His commandments.

"It seems to me that the more I'm walking in obedience in every area of life, the more I'm loving Jesus. Here at work I say all the time that if I get a nasty customer, that's a chance to love Jesus, by being kind in return." She looked across the table. "Does that make sense at all, Trina?"

"Perfect sense." Trina was looking at the passage herself. "My supervisor took the credit for something I did. I mean, she straight-up lied. And it's been eating me up. The *last* thing I want to do is forgive her, because she's wrong and she knows she's wrong. But Jesus said to forgive, and if I want to love Him I have to do what He said."

Stephanie brought a tray, set it down on a stand, and began doling out hot plates of food. Janelle felt bad that they all had something, but all Sara Ann ordered was water. A moment later, Stephanie plopped a plate in front of Sara Ann—sausage links, eggs, and a biscuit—and Sara Ann looked up, frowning.

"I knew you didn't order 'cause you were nervous," Stephanie said. "And I *also* knew you'd be hungry when you saw all this food."

"I owe you big," Sara Ann said. She looked to Janelle. "Will you ask a blessing?"

Janelle bowed her head. "Father, we thank You for this food and pray it nourishes our bodies. And we thank You for Sara Ann, who is allowing You to use her today. Bless her, Lord, for being a blessing to us."

As the women took their first bites, Sara Ann leaned in. "Trina, forgiveness has been the hardest area for me. I had to forgive an older neighbor for sexually abusing me over several years. His mother babysat me."

"Lord, have mercy . . . ," Trina said.

Tears welled in Janelle's eyes. "I had no idea you had been through something so awful, Sara Ann."

"And you talk about it calm as you please," Beverly said. "How are you able to do that?"

Sara Ann broke off a piece of biscuit. "I couldn't always. It took a lot of talking to God about it, because I didn't understand why He'd allow it to happen. Not that I'm saying I understand it now." She ate some of her food. "But I guess the point of all of it was, when I was able to forgive him, that's when I felt like my heart opened up to love Jesus even more."

The table was quiet, digesting what Sara Ann had revealed.

"An older cousin abused me from the time I was eight until I was thirteen," Jessica said softly.

The women turned to her and waited.

"I never told anyone until I was twenty-three." Jessica didn't look much older than that now. "I told my mother and she went into such denial about it—his mother and my mother are sisters—that I never brought it up to anyone else again. He's a pastor now. I see him at family gatherings and he acts like nothing happened. Never apologized. Sometimes I wonder if I imagined it all."

Sara Ann got up and went to her, kneeling beside her, hugging her tight. "I know," she said. "I know."

Beverly got up and laid a hand on Jessica, praying silently.

Lila brought a box of tissues over and set it on the table. "I should have thought of this sooner." She pulled a tissue out and gave it to Jessica.

Jessica raised her tearstained face. "I'm sorry." She looked around. "I'll be okay. I don't want to make a scene."

Lila rubbed her back. "Sweetheart, you're fine. Don't let the enemy steal this moment by making you feel embarrassed. Let God do what He wants to do in your heart." She walked away.

"Now why can't I have a supervisor like that?" Trina said, lightening the moment a little.

"I needed to hear this, Sara Ann," Jessica said. "And I needed to be able to talk about it."

"Might help to talk to a counselor," Sara Ann said. "I know somebody good. And let's exchange numbers so the two of us can talk some more." She glanced at her watch. "I don't know if we're doing this again, but if so I know I need to be more organized. At least have a theme or something."

"We had themes *this* time," Beverly said. "Love, obedience . . ."

"And forgiveness," Trina said.

Stephanie breezed over and handed a check to each woman, directing them to pay up front.

"My vote is to do this again," Janelle said. "It was exactly what I needed."

"Have to say this is the first time I've been to a Bible study with bacon," Allison said, "but it was refreshing."

Beverly put a tip on the table, then got up and put her jacket on. "Sara Ann, I think we'll be here next Saturday whether you like it or not."

The rest followed suit, leaving Stephanie a tip and gathering their things.

Sara Ann looked overwhelmed. "I don't know what to say."

"You can say you'll be here," Trina said.

She looked down at her uniform. "I have to be here. I work here."

Beverly hugged Sara Ann, then Trina and Allison. "We'll be praying," Beverly said.

Jessica gave her a long one. "Thank you. I'll be here next time."

Sara Ann squeezed her hand. "I hope so."

Janelle lagged behind, wanting to talk to Sara Ann. Her phone buzzed and she looked at it. "Oh, I've got to go. Kory's on his way to pick up Dee, and they're probably over there running circles around Aunt Gladys."

"Dee stayed the night again?" Sara Ann said. "Those girls are joined at the hip."

"Wait till Claire gets here. Tiffany and Dee were making welcome signs last night, no doubt plotting ways in which the three of them can spend their every waking moment together." Janelle hugged Sara Ann. "Let's talk this week. I was blown away by what you shared, and by the way things went today. I'd love to get your thoughts."

Sara Ann nodded. "God showed me a lot in that little bit of time."

"Me too." Janelle was still trying to take hold of it. "He keeps showing me that it's possible to get beyond painful circumstances and actually live again."

"That's my testimony, Janelle." Sara Ann's expression turned a little playful. "I wonder if this lesson God is teaching you has anything to do with that fella you're racing out of here to meet."

"And on that note . . ." Janelle gave her a quick wave as she dashed out.

CHAPTER TWENTY-TWO

I t had been an awfully long day, and a big yawn told Becca she needed to excuse herself and go to bed—but a little exchange across the kitchen table between Travis and Janelle caught her ear.

"Wait, what's that?" Todd had heard it too.

Janelle and Travis looked at one another. They'd spent the late afternoon and evening helping Becca and Todd move in, along with Kory, who had left a little while ago.

"It's not a big deal," Janelle said. "Certainly nothing you need to concern yourself with the night before your first sermon."

Travis went for another slice of pizza. "Plus you're tired from driving through the night and unloading a moving van. Dude." He gave him the eye as he sat back down. "Trust me. You don't want to hear it."

"Which makes me want to hear it more," Todd said. "I heard you say something about Calvary and New Jerusalem. What's up?"

Janelle took her paper plate to the trash. "I'm baffled that this is even an issue in this day and time, but anyway . . . We had a meeting at New Jerusalem this afternoon, setting up committees for the year." She grabbed a bottled water from the fridge. "Somebody said we need volunteers tomorrow for the hospitality committee, and Sister Taylor asked if I could do it. I said I couldn't 'cause I'll be at Calvary tomorrow."

Todd looked surprised. "You will?"

She stopped and looked at him before she sat down. "Of course. You're my friend, and it's your big day."

"Cool." Todd smiled. "Okay, so . . ."

"So Sister Taylor asked why I was going to Calvary's service and not my own." Janelle looked perplexed, as if she were still in the moment. "Really? You feel the need to call me out and ask why?" She sighed. "I explained that I wanted to support Todd, and she actually said I should show my support by going to the reception Calvary was having afterward, because New Jerusalem members need to support their own pastor."

Becca's eyes got big. "She said it in the meeting?"

"Yes. And got some amens."

"And you know I had to stand up," Travis said. "I told them you and I were best friends growing up, and *I* would be at Calvary's service in the morning too, if I could."

"That's incredible," Todd said.

"But that's not all," Janelle said. "Someone else stood up and said the Calvary reception wasn't an option anyway, because she'd asked and was told it was for Calvary members only."

"What?" Todd looked at Becca, incredulous. "Who would say that? As if it had actually been discussed and determined that it was for Calvary only."

Travis shrugged. "Maybe it was."

"No, I think it was an individual taking it upon himself or herself to make it exclusive. But whatever the case, I'm making it clear that that's not the deal at Calvary." He looked at his watch. "Ten fifteen. I'll have to wait until the morning. I hope it's not too late to rectify it."

Travis pushed his plate aside. "Reminds me of the vacation Bible school fiasco."

"Oh, man . . . I'd never seen my dad that hot."

Becca had never heard this story. "What happened?"

"I don't know about this either," Janelle said.

"We didn't have a youth ministry program growing up," Todd said. "They did a few special things for kids during the school year, and usually nothing in summer. But this one summer"—he turned to Travis—"how old were we, about twelve?"

"Sounds right," Travis said.

"Calvary decided to do a weeklong vacation Bible school program. One of the women had seen it somewhere else and wanted to bring it here. So they made this big deal of it, put a big banner outside the church that they were holding vacation Bible school."

"And New Jerusalem didn't have anything like it," Travis said. "So Todd tells me, and I get hyped about it. We show up together Monday morning."

Becca got a sick feeling in her gut. "And what?"

"The women at the registration table looked at me like I was an alien from outer space."

Janelle cringed. "Tell me no."

Travis gave her a big nod instead. "You would've thought I didn't grow up here, didn't go to school with Calvary kids, didn't go to church right down the street. They said they were sorry, but the vacation Bible school program was for children of Calvary members only." He paused, and it was clear the memory hurt still. "Never mind that right next to me a classmate was registering, and I knew he belonged to a church in another town."

"I went straight to Dad," Todd said. "Right in front of me he called the people in charge into his office. He said if it wasn't open to any kid who wanted to come, he was closing the whole program immediately."

"Did you go, Travis?" Becca asked.

Travis shot her a look.

"I asked him to change his mind," Todd said, "but who could blame him for staying away after that?"

Janelle sighed. "The sad part is all the summers I spent down here as a kid, I never gave much thought to the fact that there was a white church and a black church. Maybe because the church I attended at home was predominantly black. But now that I'm attending a multiethnic church, I see things so differently."

"Now that you mention it," Becca said, "our church in St. Louis has almost a thousand members and only a handful are black."

Travis was pensive. "When New Jerusalem invited me to be senior pastor, I had a lot of reservations. First, I said I wasn't coming back to this small town. I wanted to pastor in a big urban environment. And I was serving at a church in Dallas that was growing in diversity. I liked that. Being back here with the white church and the black church and all the old ways didn't excite me."

"So what made you change your mind?" Janelle asked.

"I prayed about it—prayed for peace about saying no, to be accurate." He chuckled. "But it kept nagging at me, and God kept taking me to Isaiah, to the verse about Him doing a new thing, making rivers in the desert." He sat back, folding his arms. "Let's put it this way. I'm totally walking by faith."

"Wow," Janelle said. "And you didn't know at the time that Todd would be taking over as Calvary's pastor a few months later."

"Huh. That same verse has been coming to me," Todd said. "You know what, Trav? We should start meeting regularly for prayer. It'd be powerful to seek God together about what He wants to do here."

Travis sat forward, a smile coming to his face. "Oh, that gets me excited, bro. Let's do it."

Becca covered another yawn.

"I hear you, Becca," Janelle said. "I'm sleepy myself." She got up and pushed her chair in. "Todd and Travis, y'all can't be hangin' out and talking late on Saturday night like you used to. You got sermons to preach in the morning."

"Isn't that something?" Travis got up and dumped his plate in the trash. "I feel like we're actual adults with responsibilities."

Todd put his arm around Becca as they stood. "Wait till you have a family. That's when it really gets scary."

Becca gave him the eye. "That better be scary in a good way."

Todd flashed his boyish smile. "What other scary is there?"

They walked the others to the door.

"I've been thinking about that a lot lately," Travis said. "Whether I'll have a family one day."

Todd put his hands in his pockets. "You have? Thinking you'd like to?"

"Absolutely. Just need that vital missing component."

"The way those women in your congregation look at you," Janelle said, "I don't think it'll be missing for long."

"Ahh . . ." Becca grinned. "Methinks I'll have a pastor's wife counterpart very soon."

"Ahh . . . ," Travis returned. "Methinks life is never that simple. Both of you just save me a spot at your tables, breakfast, lunch, and dinner."

Becca nodded. "Spot saved and prayers going up for that counterpart."

"Watch out," Todd said. "Things happen when she puts prayer on something."

Travis opened the door. "I've got no problem with Becca praying up a wife for me. Just be specific, is all I ask. She's gotta know how to cook."

"That's it?" Janelle asked.

"Trust me, it whittles the list down real quick." He laughed again. "All right, I'm out."

He and Janelle left and Becca thought about Todd's words as she went up to bed. *Things happen when she puts prayer on something.* She'd asked God for years to do big things with her ministry, and she was watching the answer unfold before her very eyes. She needed to keep praying and believing that this was only the beginning. As bone-weary as she was, she had a great sense of anticipation.

CHAPTER TWENTY-THREE

Sunday, January 17

S tanding in the senior pastor's office watching her husband adjust his tie, Becca suddenly felt the magnitude of the moment. Todd had been given charge over this church and these people. He was responsible for feeding them spiritually, for leading in righteousness, for setting a Christlike standard. It might be a small church, but it was still a big burden.

She took his hand and looked deep into his eyes. "I am so proud of you. You didn't take the position because it benefited you. You didn't take it because it would give you a voice to thousands. You took it just because you knew in your heart that this is where God was calling you. I couldn't be more thrilled for you today." She smiled at him. "And you look way too handsome in that suit."

Todd looked focused. "I wouldn't have done it without your support," he said. "Still hard to believe we actually did this." He nodded to himself. "God's got some purpose. I'm excited to see how it plays out."

"Me too. I think you'll—oh, Ethan, sweetheart, you can't write on that." She spotted him on the floor, pen against the wall. "Where'd you get that?"

It took some tugging to wrest it from his hand, and then he dissolved into crocodile tears.

Becca bent and picked him up. "Ethan, shhh, not now. Service is about to start." She looked to Todd as Ethan did the stiff-bodied, escalating cry move. "Guessing he didn't get the memo about perfect behavior on Dad's first official day."

An elderly woman who volunteered for the church poked her head into the office. "Everything okay? Somebody's awfully upset."

Becca smiled as best she could. "Everything's fine. He's just having a moment."

"Let me see him, Bec." Todd took him as he tried to grab the pen from Becca again, crying still. He looked into Ethan's eyes. "Not acceptable, buddy. You're not getting the pen. Now stop the crying fit." Todd set him in his pastor's chair and got something out of a drawer. "You want the crayon to draw?"

Ethan nodded big, reaching for it.

"You have to stop crying first."

The sobs went to his chest as he sucked in air, finally quieting. Todd gave him the crayon and a piece of paper, then chuckled. "Ethan must've known I needed to focus on something besides my first sermon. Take the edge off a little."

Claire dashed into the office in a pretty dress. She'd been everywhere, checking out the church, helping to fold programs, watching people.

"Mom, guess what? I saw Tiffany come in!" And she was gone again.

Claire had asked this morning why Tiffany and Dee attended a different church, reminding Becca of last night's conversation at the kitchen table.

"Well, honey, that's where their families go and Calvary is where our family goes," Becca had said.

"But why? If we're all friends, why can't we go to the same church?"

"Well, in St. Louis you had friends who didn't go to our church, right?"

"Mom." Claire sighed, as if wondering why she needed to explain. "St. Louis is, like, a thousand people. Of course we went to different churches."

Becca told her Tiffany would be at the service today and let her excitement be the end of it. She couldn't bear Claire making the connection that the difference was the color of their skin.

"We'd better head to the sanctuary," Becca said.

Todd had already had a prayer time with the elders and was standing by his desk, looking over his notes once more.

He kissed her. "Okay, see you in there."

An usher led Becca, Claire, and Ethan to the front pew, left side of the church. It was much more crowded than it had been the Sunday before. Becca looked at the program the usher had given her. A special welcome and prayer for the pastor had been added—and *A word from our pastor's wife, Becca Dillon . . . ?*

Becca consulted Darla, an elder's wife who was seated nearby. She pointed to the program. "No one told me about that. What am I supposed to say?"

"You weren't told?" Darla said. "We thought it'd be nice if people heard from you. Just say you're glad to be here and looking forward to getting to know everybody."

Becca nodded. "Thanks."

Claire tugged at her other side. "Does Dad sit up there?" She pointed to the chair in the raised pulpit area.

"Yes, here he comes."

As the organ started to play, Todd walked in from the back of the pulpit. The choir, also seated up front, stood and began to sing an opening hymn, and the congregation stood and joined in.

The service moved at a fairly rapid clip, almost too rapid. What was she supposed to say? For the first time Becca wondered what kind of role they expected her to play. In some churches, the pastor's wife took on the women's ministry or some other big job. But it wasn't her intent to do anything of the sort. Calvary Church was Todd's ministry. She had her own.

After the offering Darla moved to the podium to introduce her—just as Ethan decided he'd been sitting too long. One of the ushers had planned to watch him when Becca went up. So now, as Ethan slid from the pew, the usher tried to bring him back, which only irritated the little guy. He pulled away and walked a few more paces. Becca rose gingerly and went after him, which made it a game in which he moved faster. She caught him at the side of the pew and scooped him up—bringing an outburst of tears.

Becca caught a look from several people, especially the older women. She hadn't appreciated enough the children's ministry they'd had in their other church. "Oh, Ethan," she said under her breath, "you're in rare form today, aren't you, buddy?"

". . . and so it's with great joy that I ask you to welcome to the Calvary Church family, Becca Dillon."

The congregation applauded, and Becca wondered if she should take Ethan up there and hand him off to Todd as she spoke. But somehow that didn't seem—

"Becca, give him to me."

Becca turned and heaved a sigh of relief.

Janelle's arms were outstretched. "Come on, little man. Daniel's waiting for you."

"Danal?" Ethan calmed immediately as Janelle took him. He was enamored with "big boys" like Daniel.

"Thanks, girl," Becca whispered.

She hurried forward, trying to gather her thoughts.

"Good morning." She smiled big and awaited their reply. "It's such a blessing to be here with you today. I've had the pleasure of meeting many of you already, and I'm looking forward to getting to know each and every one of you."

From up here Becca was struck by how small the congregation

was—maybe a hundred fifty or two hundred people. Hard to believe she'd be speaking to an audience many times that size in three weeks.

She continued, "Calvary Church has a great history that reaches back over a century, and I know Todd considers it a privilege that his family has shared much of that history." She paused when a child cried out, but thankfully it wasn't Ethan. "I'm honored to be part of the Calvary family now myself, and I want you to know that I'm committed to doing all I can to serve alongside my husband. Thank you so much for this wonderful welcome."

Becca took her seat to the sound of applause and Todd was up next.

"I promise you my wife and I didn't plan this." He took his time, looking into the faces, an easy smile on his face. "But she set me up nicely when she referred to the history of this church and my family's part in it. I've been thinking a lot about that. It's because of that history that I almost didn't take this position. I knew I couldn't live up to my dad and granddad. They were huge men of God in my eyes. And I look awfully young to be a 'senior' pastor, don't I?"

Becca glanced at the people nearby. They were warm toward him, smiling.

"But God let me know He wasn't looking for me to recycle old history, but to be part of the new history He would unfold here. I don't know what God has planned for us, but I can tell you I had my first sermon prepared a week ago, and late last night God changed it. He led me to Paul's letter to the Ephesians, where we're told to walk worthy of our calling, with humility, gentleness, patience, and love . . . 'being diligent to preserve the unity of the Spirit in the bond of peace.'"

He took a long pause as he looked out at them. "Today we're going to think about 'walking worthy'—which means walking in unity as one body." He paused again, pensive. "Wouldn't it be interesting if what God wants to do at Calvary in this next season is show us it's not really about Calvary at all? That it's about the body of Christ, of which Calvary is one part? Open your Bibles, please, to Ephesians, chapter four."

Becca peeked again at the expressions of the members around her. Safe to say they wanted to know where Todd was going with this.

CHAPTER TWENTY-FOUR

Janelle raised her camera and caught the momentous embrace, feeling like a proud sister. Travis had just walked into Calvary Church's basement for the reception. When he and Todd saw one another, both official-looking in their suits, they took in the moment—Hope Springs' pastors were together in public for the first time.

"Aw, I love it." Janelle snapped a couple more, taking in the scene with Kory. He'd gone to New Jerusalem's service and come over when it ended. "You can tell they're emotional," she said.

"Travis mentioned in the service that this felt like a big day for him also," Kory said. "Said he was excited about what God was doing on this street."

Several other cameras flashed around the room, including that of Virgil Tenley, the town's newspaper photographer. He stopped by the Sanders family reunion every year to take a group photo of the more than two hundred of them, calling their get-togethers a piece of Hope Springs history.

Andy Walters, a longtime reporter for the paper, accompanied

Virgil. With the crowd gathered around the pastors, he called out, "What's it feel like for childhood friends to return to Hope Springs as pastors?"

The guys smiled at one another. "Unbelievable," Todd said, nodding. "As you probably recall, Andy, we're the ones who made the news for that little fire hydrant prank. Proves God has a sense of humor, I guess."

Janelle chuckled with the rest, leaning over to Kory. "Grandma said they got in big trouble for that. I wish she could be here to see this."

She thought it was sweet that Stephanie wanted to stay home with Grandma Geri. She didn't have to. Aunt Gladys was there. And Stephanie had wanted to hear Todd's first sermon, especially after the way his funeral sermon had spoken to her. But when she saw that Grandma Geri wasn't well enough to go to church, she said she felt like keeping her company.

"I was praying she'd feel better today," Kory said.

"Dr. Peters said we should know this week how she's faring with the chemo."

Andy raised a finger, quieting the crowd. "It's interesting that you're both young, and both lived for several years in urban areas— St. Louis and Dallas. What do you think that will mean for this town? Do you think those experiences will affect the way you pastor here?"

Todd and Travis looked at one another to see who would take a stab at it.

"I think," Travis began, "that God uses who we are and where we've been. He's the One who guided us into those experiences when we left here, and He's the One who brought us back. So I'm looking forward myself to seeing what it'll mean." He put an arm around Todd. "I couldn't be more pumped to have this guy in town with me."

"One more question," Andy said, pausing to jot something down. "Todd, your first sermon at Calvary was about unity in the body. You didn't mention New Jerusalem, but I'm just wondering . . . would you say unity has been lacking between the two churches?"

"No, I wouldn't say that at all, Andy. My dad and Pastor Richards had a great relationship. But there's always room for growth. Unity was on Jesus's mind before He went to the cross when He prayed that His followers would be one. And I think we need to be ever mindful of it as well."

"Amen." Travis stuck out his hand and Todd gripped it—another Kodak moment.

As the crowd returned to the food and punch lines, Janelle walked up to Todd and Travis. "I want to get a picture with you two, like old times."

"When we were packing," Todd said, "I actually found a picture we took the summer before seventh grade. You should've seen what we were wearing."

"Scan it and put it on Facebook, and make sure you tag Janelle," Travis said.

Her eyes widened. "You'd better not!"

Kory took her camera. "I'll take it."

Janelle stood between them and they smiled big, arms around one another's waists.

"Someone's missing from this picture," Travis said.

"Libby."

"I invited her to service."

"I know."

Travis reached for the camera in Kory's hand. "I'll take a shot of you and Janelle. I know she wants one."

Janelle elbowed him in the side, though it was blunted by his suit jacket.

"You would assault your pastor in broad daylight? For telling the truth?"

Kory looked to Janelle. "It's up to you."

"Sure. Let's do it."

It was just a picture, but Janelle's insides twirled a little when Kory put his arm around her shoulder. She looped an arm around his waist just as she'd done with Todd and Travis, but the feeling was different. She was hyper aware of everything about him, even the muscles her arm could feel on his back.

"One . . . two . . . three." Travis clicked, then checked it. "You blinked, Janelle." He turned the camera and showed her. "Let's do another one."

Janelle and Kory moved their heads closer.

"Say cheese," Travis said.

"Cheeeeese."

Travis checked again. "Perfect. Look at that."

Janelle dropped her arm from Kory's waist and took her camera. "Nice."

Kory looked over her shoulder. "Really nice."

"Mom!"

"Dad!"

"Can we go to Claire's?"

The voices hit them at the same time, and Janelle and Kory laughed. "Did you two practice that?" Janelle said.

Becca walked up with a struggling Ethan in her arms. "This little guy needs a nap badly, so I'm taking him home. I told the girls they could come if they wanted. Oh, and Daniel's ready to go too. He said Stephanie can let him in at the house."

"Sounds good," Janelle said.

"Fine with me," Kory said. "Okay if I eat something before I come get her?"

"Take your time," Becca said. "Company for Claire and naptime for Ethan means I can get some things done myself." She marched the troops onward, stopping momentarily to talk to Todd.

"Hungry?" Kory asked.

"Very." Janelle glanced toward the buffet. "The kids had the right idea getting their food at the beginning, though. Look at the line now."

"I was actually wondering if you'd like to go to the diner. I've never been."

Kory drove them the short distance. The place was bustling, but they didn't have to wait, probably because many had gone to the reception at Calvary.

Lila greeted them and walked them to a booth, past Sara Ann, who waved with one hand as she poured hot coffee with the other. She stopped by their table next with mugs filled with fresh brew. "Be right back for your order," she said.

They took off their coats and looked over the menus.

"Are you okay?" Janelle said. "You don't seem totally yourself."

"I don't?" Kory sipped black coffee, put it back down. He sighed. "I guess I'm thinking about the notice I got when I returned home last night. Court hearing is Monday, February 8." He glanced vaguely at the menu. "I'm resigned to it. Just don't know how I'll explain the finality of it to Dee. And I don't know what'll happen when Shelley comes to North Carolina for the hearing . . . if she'll even want to see Dee."

"Of course she will." Janelle tasted her coffee to see if she'd added enough cream and sugar.

"Trust me, there's no guarantee." He took a long sip. "Nothing she does surprises me anymore."

"Hey." Sara Ann looked harried. "How was Todd's sermon?"

"Awesome," Janelle said. "I wish you could've heard him."

"You'll have to tell me about it." She put her pencil to the pad. "But right now it's Sunday-morning busy, so I'd better take your order."

Sara Ann was looking at her, so she went first. "Hotcakes and sausage, please. And orange juice."

"I'll have the same," said Kory, "with two eggs over easy and a side of grits."

Janelle raised her brow. "The hotcakes are pretty big."

"That's what I was hoping."

"Gotta love a healthy appetite." Sara Ann scooped up the menus. "I've got a fresh pot brewing. Be back shortly."

Janelle took a leisurely sip, gazing around the diner, debating whether she wanted to know. "So what was it about Shelley that made you want to marry her?"

Kory looked at her, then away, as if debating whether he wanted to answer. He wrapped his hands around his mug and stared into it. "She and I entered the firm the same year, two out of twelve new associates in litigation—and two of only six black associates out of a hundred in litigation."

"How large is the firm?"

"About five hundred."

Sara Ann topped off their cups. Kory blew off the steam and took a sip.

"You know how it is," he said. "As the only black first-years, she and I gravitated toward one another for advice, information, and whatnot. We'd go to lunch." He shrugged. "The nature of our job meant we worked into the evenings, weekends, so we were together all the time. It was easy to fall into a relationship."

"So the environment made it easy. But what was it about *her*?"

He took a moment. "She was smart, sure of herself. She knew exactly what to say and how to get her way. I was caught up in the hype back then. I'd been heavily recruited by top firms, saw myself making partner, becoming a rainmaker, serving on the firmwide management committee . . . So her style was appealing to me. Also didn't hurt that she was attractive."

Janelle had been tempted to Google her but had decided against it. "So you got married, two up-and-coming power players . . . and what happened?"

"We were fine the first year and a half or so, until I started talking about having a baby. Whenever I brought it up, we'd argue. I assumed Shelley wanted kids like I did, but she didn't. Said they would stifle her career goals. We finally compromised. She said she'd have one, and I said I'd give up my vision of three or four. I thought we were cool. Then Dee was born and—"

Sara Ann appeared and dished out their meals with a flourish. "And two orders of sausage," she said to herself, checking the ticket to be sure she'd gotten everything. Satisfied, she looked up with a smile. "Call me if it's anything less than yummy."

Janelle smiled back. "It certainly looks it."

"Thanks, Sara Ann," Kory said. He prayed over their food and continued. "So, yeah, Dee . . . she changed everything."

"How so?" Janelle poured hot syrup on her hotcakes, then passed it to him.

Kory poured the syrup, then peppered his eggs and grits. "I didn't realize how much I could love a little baby. My world no longer revolved around the firm. I didn't want to work every night and every weekend. I wanted to see the sparkle in Dee's eyes when she looked at her daddy. I wanted to hear the belly laugh when I tickled her."

"And that was a problem?"

"I don't think it was a problem with my supervisors in litigation," he said. "At least at first. When I was working, I was focused and gave my all. Clients complimented my work and gave me new matters to handle. I was doing well." He forked up some pancakes. "But I was no longer concerned with internal politics. I wasn't going to play the game of staying till nine at night just to look committed. I stopped going to cocktail parties and all the other schmooze events with senior partners."

"But Shelley was doing all that?"

He nodded. "And then some. Somewhere in there she started her affair with the head of litigation."

They sank into a silence, eating, thinking. A sadness came over Janelle as she thought of the hopes and dreams people carried into marriage. *Were they ever realized?*

Kory wiped his mouth, stared at Janelle a moment. "So what was it about David that made you want to marry him?"

She smiled at the question. "He was silly. He could find humor and enjoyment in almost anything, and I loved that about him. I could never stay down for long when he was around."

"How did you meet?"

"A girlfriend at church started dating someone, and she kept telling me he had this friend . . ." Janelle gave him a look as she drank some juice. "You know how that is. I said I wasn't interested, wasn't doing a blind date. So she had a cookout and made sure we were both there."

Kory smiled. "And it was love at first sight?"

"More like we hit it off as friends, and the more I got to know him, the more I saw he was the real deal—great to be around, sincere about his faith, hardworking. It was easy to love him."

Kory was almost done with his food. "What's your favorite memory of you, David, and the kids?"

"Hmm, we have a lot of good memories actually." She pushed her plate aside. "Father's Day four years ago has to be near the top of the list. I told David to stay in bed because I'd be making breakfast and bringing it to him. But soon as I went to the kitchen, Tiffany started crying, so I got her from her crib and fed her. Soon as I'm done feeding her, Daniel says he doesn't feel well and wants me to sit with him and read him a story." She laughed. "By the time I'm done with all that, David had breakfast made and on a tray for *me*."

"Aw, that's awesome. Definitely a great guy." He paused, his eyes warm. "I can't imagine having a marriage like that and then losing my spouse. How have you coped? That is, if you don't mind talking about it."

"I don't mind," she said. "It was really hard at first. The first Christmas after David died, I didn't get out of bed until the afternoon. My parents were there, but I didn't want to talk. Phone kept ringing—Libby, Grandma Geri, Aunt Gladys—but I wouldn't talk to them either. I didn't feel like anyone could understand."

"Did you see a counselor?"

"For a while, yes. He said if I couldn't express how I felt to friends and family, I should write it in a journal. That helped some."

"You still journal?"

"Not as much." Time with her journal had really decreased since she'd moved to Hope Springs. She looked at him. "They say divorce can bring almost as much grief as death."

Kory pondered it. "I can see that. Except the memories you're left with are good ones."

"You and Shelley had good memories too."

He let that one hang, staring at the activity in the diner.

"I started praying for her," Janelle said.

Kory looked at her. "Why?"

"She can't be happy living like that, not deep down. She's trying to fill a void that only Jesus can fill."

Kory stared away again.

And Janelle stared at him. Life was strange. She'd had a treasure in David that was taken away. Shelley had a treasure in Kory and let it go. Could Shelley not see the treasure that Kory was?

Seemed awfully plain to Janelle.

CHAPTER TWENTY-FIVE
Wednesday, January 20

Stephanie was having a blast with role reversal.

Daniel had awakened this morning with the flu, which triggered an episode of sadness because he wanted his dad who'd had special ways of caring for him when he was sick. Janelle didn't want to leave him, so Stephanie assured her she'd be fine taking Grandma Geri to the hospital. She'd had an enjoyable time with her on Sunday, which surprised her. For some reason at the start of all of this, Stephanie had regarded time with her grandmother as obligatory, sacrificial even. But the more she got to know her, the more she realized what a pistol Grandma Geri was. When she mentioned it to her dad, Bruce laughed. "You didn't know? You take after your grandmother."

"Over here, Grandma." Stephanie guided her down a different aisle. "The designer sunglasses are this way." Her phone rang and she pulled it out and answered. "Hey, Janelle, what's up?"

"Everything okay? I thought you'd be home by now since it was just a checkup."

"Nope. Doctor said she looks good after her first round. She'll have a CT scan in about ten days. Said we'll know more then."

"Oh, good. So where are you?"

"At the mall."

"The mall? Are you sure Grandma's got enough strength to walk around a mall?"

"The way she's dragging me to and fro? I'm thinking yeah."

Grandma Geri cast an amused glance at Stephanie, but her focus was on the sunglasses in the case.

Stephanie added, "You know she's been losing weight, so I got her some pants and tops. She'll be stylin'."

Janelle laughed. "That's cool, Steph. Can't wait to see."

"I'd like to see that pair on the left." Grandma Geri pointed out a pair to the salesclerk.

"Ooh, those are fly, Grandma."

"What are y'all shopping for now?" Janelle asked.

Stephanie hesitated. "Designer sunglasses."

"Designer sunglasses? For Grandma Geri? Stephanie, that's a nice idea, but she doesn't need that."

"Uh, Stephanie had nothing to do with it. This is all Geraldine Sanders."

Grandma Geri looked back at her, waiting for the clerk to unlock the case. "I told you she'd think I was crazy, didn't I?"

"Is Grandma talking about me?" Janelle said.

"Yep." Stephanie moved closer to watch the try-on.

"Okay," Janelle said. "Why is Grandma Geri looking for a pair of designer sunglasses?"

"I can't exactly tell you."

"What do you mean, you can't exactly—"

"One sec, Janelle . . ." Stephanie lowered her phone a little to hear what the salesclerk was saying.

"You're sure, that pair there? Those are rather expensive."

"Ma'am." Stephanie smiled. She'd learned a lot on the job. "We're well aware of the expense, as I have a pair myself. But if you'd prefer we take our business elsewhere . . ."

The woman had the glasses out of the case and in Grandma Geri's hand in five seconds flat.

Grandma Geri put them on and turned to Stephanie.

"Those are the bomb. Look at you! Here, look in the mirror."

Stephanie put the mirror in front of her, and Grandma Geri profiled this way and that. A big smile came across her face.

"This *is* crazy, isn't it? I mean, I'm eighty-six years old. It's a waste of money."

"It's my money—well, Lindell's—but I'm sure I can say for both of us, go for it." Stephanie reached in her purse, got a credit card, and handed it to the woman.

"Stephanie!"

"Oh." Stephanie brought the phone back to her ear. "Sorry."

"I'm waiting to hear why you can't tell me."

Stephanie sighed. "Grandma, we have to tell her."

Grandma Geri had put the sunglasses back on, checking herself out in the mirror while they were being rung up. She waved a hand at Stephanie. "You go ahead and tell her now."

"All right, this is the deal. Grandma was talking to someone at the hospital who's going through the same treatment for cancer, and the woman told Grandma about her bucket list."

"What's a bucket list?"

"You know that saying about kicking the bucket? A bucket list is a list people make of everything they want to do before they die."

"You are kidding me."

Janelle didn't sound happy, just as Grandma Geri had predicted.

"That is completely morbid and repulsive and utterly—you mean Grandma wanted to make a bucket list and you actually let her?"

"She didn't make a list. She just told me a story about Grandpa Elwood not letting her get the designer sunglasses she wanted decades ago."

"I actually remember that," Janelle said. "Grandpa said he

wouldn't pay a lot of money for sunglasses because all Grandma would do is sit on them and break them. And Grandma had an attitude for days."

"Well, she said if she put together a dream list, that would be on there. And I said let's do it."

Janelle was quiet a moment. "I just hate the idea of Grandma thinking she has to do this thing or that thing before she 'kicks the bucket.' That creeps me out."

"Yeah, we knew you wouldn't like it."

"On the other hand . . . I think it's cute the two of you went shopping and got her some sunglasses." She let go a chuckle. "*That's* what I've got to see."

Libby heard a knock on Grandma Geri's front door and jerked up, realizing she'd fallen asleep on the sofa. She checked her watch. *Nine thirty? Ugh.* She'd driven to Hope Springs late Wednesday afternoon to spend some time with her cousins and Grandma Geri since her weekends were busy. But she'd planned to be out of there by now.

She got up to gather her things and say a quick good-bye—and heard the knock again.

"Hey, Libby, can you get that?" Stephanie called. "I'm in here washing dishes."

Libby opened the door and cocked her head to the side. "Why are you knocking? You know it's open." She left the doorway and kept moving.

Travis stepped inside and closed the door. "You're crankier than normal," he said. "Did I wake you or something?"

She hated that he knew that about her.

"I'm just here to give Janelle something," he said.

Libby walked back toward the bedrooms. "Janelle? Where are you?"

"In here with Daniel."

Libby walked in. Daniel was on his side with a thermometer in his mouth, barely awake. Tiffany was already asleep. "How's he doing?"

"Temperature's almost back to normal. Must've been a twenty-four-hour bug, thank God. But he used that twenty-four to the full. Poor baby couldn't keep any food down today." She kissed his forehead and tucked him in. "Night-night, sweetheart. I love you."

"I didn't know it was so late," Libby half whispered. "I'm about to run. And Travis just showed up."

"Oh, I forgot." Janelle walked with her out of the room. "I asked if he could stop by after Bible study and bring CDs of his Sunday sermon for Grandma and me."

"How is she gonna listen to that?"

"You didn't know she had a boom box in her room?"

"Well, cool. Get your CDs. I'm getting on the road."

Libby packed up her laptop on the dining room table and slipped into her leather jacket. She heard Janelle walk toward the family room.

"Hey, Travis, thanks for bringing those."

"No problem. How's my girl?"

My girl? Libby listened a little more closely as she shouldered her bags.

"She had a good day today," Janelle said. "Got worn out power shopping with Stephanie, so she went to bed after dinner."

"Power shopping, huh?" Travis laughed a little. "I'll pray she rests well tonight. Tell her I stopped by."

"Mom?"

Libby could hear Daniel calling, but Janelle couldn't. She walked into the family room.

"Janelle, Daniel's calling you." She started back toward the door when Travis called her name. She paused, turning slightly.

"Can I talk to you a minute?"

"Not really. Early meeting tomorrow."

He stepped closer. "I thought we ended on a fairly good note when we talked. But you still have an attitude with me, and you didn't reply to my text."

She turned more fully toward him, hands extended in disbelief. "Why would I need to reply? You didn't think I'd actually come to New Jerusalem on Sunday."

"Why wouldn't you?"

"Travis, I hear what you're saying about where you are now, but it's a little hard for me to buy you in the preacher role."

"To *buy* me in the *role*? You think I'm gaming?"

"I've dated so-called preachers before. Who knows?"

She turned, but he took her hand. "Libby, if you want to cast me in a role, let it be that of a friend."

The way he looked at her, the feel of his hand . . . She didn't know what it was, but it made her skin tingle. And for a brief second she allowed herself to remember how much she once cared for him.

She let loose of his hand. "I don't hold anything against you from the past, but I really don't see any role you could play in my life going forward."

He stared into her eyes as if recognizing what was there a moment before. "I understand. Just know that from where I stand, in my heart, that's how I regard you . . . as a friend."

His gaze lingered seconds more, then he turned and left.

CHAPTER TWENTY-SIX

Friday, January 22

Becca could hear applause like thunder as the security detail led the Worth & Purpose speakers and musical artists along a back hallway that led to the arena. The lights had already dimmed, and the worship team had begun singing, which meant one thing—the kickoff to a new season of Worth & Purpose had begun.

The energy and enthusiasm had been palpable from the moment they'd met in the hotel lobby to be transported to the arena. Conference attendees staying at the same hotel had spotted the speakers and artists and rushed to say hello and take pictures. Becca had never seen anything like it. At the conferences at which she'd spoken, there was appreciation shown for the speakers, a picture here and there, but nothing near this level—these were Christian rock stars.

Becca had hung back a little, taking it all in. One woman was making the rounds, asking people to sign her Worth & Purpose shirt. She stopped when she got to Becca.

"Are you somebody?" she said.

Becca was taken aback. "I'm . . . a new speaker with Worth & Purpose, yes."

"Oh, great." She handed Becca the marker. "Then I'd love to have your autograph."

Becca signed it, the first time she'd ever autographed anything, and a few others flocked her way at the implication that she must be one of them. There wasn't time to sign anything more, though, as the head security guy ushered them toward the exit and on board their shuttle. That scene stayed with Becca the entire ride, even as she chatted with speakers and artists she'd admired for years from afar. She was "somebody" now. Soon she'd be recognized and bombarded immediately at these events.

They'd been sequestered so far in the arena, hanging out below in catering, then taking time to pray before the start of the conference. But now, as their heels clicked toward the main area, the energy level was rising again.

The security guy pulled back a curtain and they made their way through one of the entrances. Worship music pulsated through gigantic speakers, but Becca could still hear the elevated cheers and applause when people saw them. Those who would be speaking and singing this weekend made their way to a special seating section. Becca was directed to an area near the Worth & Purpose leadership and staff. She had a front-row seat.

She remained standing with the rest, and as the minutes went by she was amazed by the sight—thousands of women with arms raised. Tears came to her eyes.

Lord, this is such an amazing experience. I can hardly believe that I'm here, that I'm part of this. Thank You for allowing me an opportunity to speak to so many women who long to be in Your presence. Prepare my heart, O God, so that when I take the stage next week in Richmond, You'll be glorified.

When worship ended, a video played on the big screens, one that introduced the speakers in a fun way. Becca had been added too late to be part of it. Wendy Burns was in it, the woman she'd replaced. Becca had heard her speak at one of these conferences before. She'd been with them four years, but there'd been rumors that another national women's conference, For Such a Time, was trying to woo her away with a promise to make her their premier speaker. Becca knew it was useless to speculate, but in this setting speculation was running rampant. What if Wendy Burns had her baby and decided to stay home indefinitely to raise him or her? Or what if Wendy joined For Such a Time? Her departure could open up a spot on the team—a spot Becca could fill next year.

The first speaker, Christa Lane, took the stage after her intro. One of the conference stars who'd been with them almost from the beginning, she was in her late forties, with a beauty that captivated. Becca took in every detail, which was easy to do on the large screen. Christa wore black slacks with a blingy black tank, red leather jacket, and to-die-for black leather high-heeled boots. Her strawberry-blond hair was perfectly coiffed, just above the shoulders. And with every turn and flick of the wrist, her earrings, necklace, and bracelet glistened.

I need more bling, Becca thought. *It shows up great in the lights.* Actually, she needed more clothes. But she wouldn't get her speaker's fee until after next week, and it would be hard to convince Todd she should go shopping meanwhile, given the expense associated with their move. She'd get Janelle and Stephanie to come over and help her piece together something stage-worthy from her closet. But as soon as she got paid, she'd treat herself to something fabulous.

Christa had the audience laughing. She had that way about her, able to make people laugh one minute, cry the next. Becca watched how naturally she moved, how comfortable she seemed. That was one of her prayers, to be natural and comfortable on the platform.

Becca had her phone in her hand. She opened up Twitter and tweeted, *Watching @ChristaLane at @WorthandPurpose kickoff conference. Always moved by her amazing gift*.

Seconds later, Worth & Purpose retweeted Becca, which meant

thousands of their followers saw it. And a minute later, her phone notified her that she'd been mentioned in a tweet. She looked at it.

Love getting to know @BeccaDillon, newest member of @WorthandPurpose speaker team.

It'd been tweeted by one of the other longtime speakers with the team. Having her endorsement, so to speak, melted Becca's heart.

Thank You, Lord, that they're making me feel like part of the team.

Becca retweeted for all of her followers to see, adding, *Love getting to know u too!*

The rest of the evening passed quickly, capped by a concert by Suzy Hill, an award-winning Christian recording artist who brought the house down. Tomorrow would be a full day of messages by other speakers as well as another concert.

The moment Suzy finished, security ushered out the Worth & Purpose team. They followed one another past the rows of women who had floor seats, many of whom smiled and waved at them, through the back hallways, and onto the waiting shuttle.

Becca took a seat near the front. On the way over she'd sat with a woman in the marketing department and got a kick out of learning that she was the one who operated the Twitter account. She looked up now, surprised by who'd joined her—Christa Lane.

"Your message was awesome tonight," Becca said. "I never knew you battled eating disorders."

"This is the first time I'm talking about it publicly," Christa said. "I love that we get to share these intimate pieces of our lives, knowing it'll help others be set free."

"Loved your message, Christa," a member of the worship team said as she boarded.

That sentiment was echoed a few more times at least.

Christa carried on a dialogue with others around them, at one point looking back at Becca. "So how are you feeling about giving your message next week? Nervous?"

"Uh, that's fair." Becca laughed. "Especially after seeing the stage up close tonight, and that jumbo screen."

"You'll do fine," she said. "I'm always nervous too. Feeds the energy."

"No way you were nervous up there."

"Absolutely!"

"Well, there's my prayer request. 'Lord, help me to *use* the nervousness like Christa and not vomit it up in front of everyone.'"

Christa laughed. "I *like* you. So glad you're part of our team. Oh, and I saw your tweet about me. Thank you. I started following you."

"Hey, thanks."

Becca didn't want that to be a big deal to her, but it was. She'd seen Christa's Twitter page. Over twenty thousand people followed her—including almost all Becca's Twitter friends—but Christa only followed back about five hundred. That woman in the hotel lobby came to mind. Becca was somebody now—even to Christa Lane.

CHAPTER TWENTY-SEVEN

Saturday, January 23

I want all the little people to line up right here, shortest to tallest," Stephanie said.

Daniel frowned at her. "I'm not little."

Stephanie stood her five-foot-eight-inch frame next to him and looked down. "Uh-huh, back of the line."

"Miss Stephanie, Ethan's not doing it," Claire said.

Stephanie bent low in front of him. "Ethan, I know you're special in the following-directions department because you're only two and a half, so I'll help you." She took his hand. "Right here, little man." She walked him in front of Claire and stayed beside him.

"Okay, now . . . we'll get our breakfast in an orderly manner, one at a time. Ethan's first."

Stephanie got a paper plate for him and picked him up so he could see the choices. "Ethan, would you like bacon?"

He nodded.

"Very good," she said, putting a piece on the plate. "Eggs?"

He wrinkled up his nose, then shook his head firmly.

"No eggs?"

He shook it again.

"All right. Grits?"

He frowned.

"I don't think he knows what that is," Tiffany said.

Stephanie decided to go ahead and put some on his plate. She scooped some from the pot.

"No want that!"

She put the spoon back and lifted a piece of toast she'd buttered. He shook his head again.

"One little piece of bacon and that's it?"

"Fosty fakes!"

"Come again, little man?"

"He wants Frosted Flakes," Claire said. "That's all he ever wants."

Stephanie looked at him. "I cook up all this good food, and all you want is some processed, partially hydrogenated junk that's been on somebody's shelf for months, if not years, and is probably one molecule away from a plastic bottle?"

He nodded.

"Well, amen, little man. Sounds good to me too."

She took him over to the cabinet, glad to see they had a box, then got him a bowl.

"Claire, go ahead and get your plate, then Tiffany, then Daniel. I think I need to sit next to my friend here."

They all got their food and took a place at the table.

"Can we get some juice?" Daniel said.

"What does your mom want you to drink?"

"Milk."

"Then why you trying to play me? Get the milk."

Moments later Janelle came in with her coat on. "Ooh, lookie here, everyone nice and settled at the table, quietly eating."

"Take a picture because it won't last," Stephanie said. "You *know* it's gonna get live in about three minutes."

Janelle laughed. "Are you sure you don't want to come to the diner Bible study with me? I'm sure Aunt Gladys would watch the kids."

"I told Todd I'd watch Claire and Ethan while he went to his church meeting, so I'm good." She chuckled. "Sent Lindell a text telling him I was watching four kids. He'll wonder what's come over me."

"How's he doing down there anyway?" Janelle asked.

"He said it's hard to explain how devastating and heartbreaking it is, but at the same time exhilarating. Last night they set up their clinic in this tent encampment that had a strep outbreak and served over a hundred patients. Then this boy walks in with a machete wound to his hand." Stephanie bent over to pick up Ethan's sippy cup. "It's really a life-changing experience for him. One more week and he'll be back."

"Which means one more week and you'll be leaving us." Janelle poked out her lip.

"Girl, I know. Time is flying. What y'all gonna do without me?"

"I'm sayin'!"

Janelle kissed Daniel and Tiffany on the cheek. "I'll be back in a little while. Don't forget we're going clothes shopping this afternoon."

"Aw, Mom, do I have to?" Daniel said.

"Yes, you have to."

Janelle looked at her watch. "Can't believe I'm late." She headed for the door. "Call me, Steph, if there's any problem."

"Will do," Stephanie said. "Unless they've got me tied up."

Janelle followed Lila into the diner and saw a cluster of women as they drew to the far section. "That's not all for the Bible study, is it?"

Lila's head nodded up and down. "I guess some of the women told others. It's about double last week."

The women were spread out at three tables pushed close together, with Sara Ann positioned near the center. They'd already ordered and received their food. Janelle tipped to the side with the crew from last week—Beverly, Allison, Trina, and Jessica. She gave them a wave as she sat down.

A woman at the next table over was sharing something with the group.

"So my friends are praying for me to get this job in Charlotte to work in marketing at a top hotel. And I'm telling them that I really believe God is going to open this door because it's exactly what I've been looking for. And sure enough, I get it. We celebrate, they help me move, I get settled. That was seven months ago." The woman, probably in her twenties with long, wavy auburn hair, told the story in a way that held people's attention. "And last week the guy calls me into his office and says he's sorry, but I'm not cutting it." She paused, sighed. "And here I am back in Hope Springs."

"Wow, this just happened," Sara Ann said. "How do you feel about it, Gina?"

Gina let out a breath. "It's not the end of the world. The job wasn't the easiest anyway, far as the people. A lot of 'em were uppity. God's giving me grace and strength, and I know He's got a good plan for me."

"Gina," Sara Ann said, "I'm not asking what promises you can claim. I'm asking how you feel. Because all this came out when I asked if anybody felt disappointed lately. You're disappointed, right?"

Gina hesitated. "I'm disappointed, but I know God'll—"

"Nope." Sara Ann put up a hand, and in her way it was sweet, not off-putting. "Not gonna let you do it, Gina. I want you to sit and stay awhile in it. Are you disappointed?"

Janelle couldn't believe how much more assured Sara Ann seemed this week.

Allison leaned over to the women near her and whispered, "Oh my gosh, this is for me."

Emotion filled Gina's eyes. "Yes. I'm disappointed."

"Why?"

"Because I really wanted that job."

"Why else?"

"Because I really wanted to get out of Hope Springs and now I'm back." She was fighting to stay in control.

"Okay." Sara Ann hadn't moved her gaze. "Why else, Gina?"

"*Because . . .*" She looked aside, holding herself. Then, "I was believing God and praying and had my friends praying—*and He answered.* He could've made it so I knocked 'em dead on that job, but instead they sent me packing. *Why?* Why even answer the prayer if I'm just gonna fail? How do I get the faith to believe Him again?"

"Exactly." Allison's eyes were on the two women.

"I've been wondering the same thing," someone else said.

Sara Ann acknowledged them all with a slow nod, then looked back to Gina. "Have you asked Him how you're supposed to believe Him now?"

"No," Gina said. "I'm supposed to have faith."

"Who gives you the faith?"

Gina stared down for a moment, then looked back at Sara Ann. "God."

"If He already knows you need faith, why not tell Him you're struggling?" Sara Ann scanned the faces. "Why do we think something's wrong with expressing our true feelings and lack of faith to God? We don't have to try to hold it in and be strong around Him. He's strong enough to let us break down and let it all out." She smiled. "And He knows how to build us back up again."

If it were possible, the time after the Bible study was even sweeter. Sara Ann had hopped back to work, but some of the women were slow to leave. The ones remaining had planted themselves at two tables, drinking refills of coffee. Since Janelle hadn't eaten, she'd taken the opportunity to order hotcakes and sausage. Though many were meeting for the first time, the conversation had the tenor and liveliness of old friends.

"Any of you feel like you have to be the strong one all the time?" Bea, a Calvary member in her sixties, raised a hand to her own question. "I feel like I can't be honest about the times I'm feeling low, not even to God." She stared down at a psalm they'd been looking at. "But David had no problem venting to God. I want to learn to sit and stay awhile in my emotions, as Sara Ann put it."

"Me too," Allison said. "And at the same time not give up hope."

"I don't know how to explain it," Gina said, "but I feel like Sara Ann took us on a digging expedition, to get all the stuff out that we didn't want to admit was there. And when she prayed at the end for us to be filled with God's grace and love and strength, ahhh . . . what an exchange." She looked at her friend Mandy beside her. "I am so glad you brought me here today."

Mandy had a sweet smile and bright-green eyes. "I wouldn't have known about it if my great-aunt hadn't told me."

Bea nodded. "Vi told me too." She looked across the table. "You're uncharacteristically quiet over there, Vi."

Janelle looked over at the other table. A petite older woman sat with them but didn't comment.

Sara Ann came by with another fresh round of coffee. "You guys are still over here?" she said.

Vi cleared her throat. "Sara Ann, I've got something to say to you."

Sara Ann set the pot on the table. "Yes, Miss Vi?"

"You know I've known you clear since you came to Hope Springs."

"Yes, ma'am."

"When I first heard about this Bible study you were doing, part of me thought it sounded good, which is why I told people. But part of me was just curious because for the life of me I couldn't see you teaching the Bible." Violet crossed her arms. "Well, you sure showed me."

"I think the proper way to put it," Bea said, "is God showed you."

"You don't have to go agreeing with me, Bea."

Sara Ann bent down and hugged her. "Thank you, Miss Vi. Means a lot that you'd say that."

Beverly looked at the group of them. "It just occurred to me. All of y'all are Calvary members, aren't you?"

Sara Ann laughed. "I guess they still allow me to call myself a member. But yes, I am, and Miss Vi, Bea"—she pointed to each—"Gina, and Mandy."

"So this is interesting," Beverly said. "Almost half of us are Calvary members; the other half are from New Jerusalem. But I think it's awesome that that's not what defines us here."

Janelle sat up and took notice. "That's true. We're just sisters in Christ sharing our struggles and finding encouragement."

"Huh." Sara Ann lingered with them. "I say let's forget the Sunday morning names on Saturday. We should come up with our own name, something to bond us."

Vi stood up. "How about Soul Sisters?"

"All right now, Miss Vi," Beverly said with a big grin. "That sounds like something one of us at *this* table might've suggested."

"If we're sisters in Christ, we're connected at the soul level, aren't we?" Vi looked pleased with herself. "And anyway, I always wanted to be a soul sister."

The two tables roared with laughter.

"Miss Vi, you are a trip!" Beverly said.

"I like it," Bea said. She stood too. "That calls for a Soul Sisters group hug."

"And a picture." Janelle whipped out her camera.

"I'll take that for you," said a gentleman sitting nearby.

The women huddled together.

"Wait! Can I be in it?"

Lila dashed over from the front of the restaurant.

"Only if you're a Soul Sister," Sara Ann said.

Lila put her hand on her hip. "To the very core of my being," she said in an exaggerated Southern drawl.

The women huddled again, hands around one another, smiling big for Janelle's camera and about five cell phone cameras that had quickly appeared.

Janelle was glad they were capturing this. There was something about it . . . something momentous.

CHAPTER TWENTY-EIGHT

Kory woke up Saturday with Janelle on his mind. He hadn't seen her in almost a week—but it felt more like a month. Last night was the first Friday night in a while that Dee hadn't slept over at Tiffany's, so there was no built-in reason for him to see her. But as he did early morning chores around the house, he couldn't help but wonder how he might work her into his day.

He emptied clothes from the dryer to an empty hamper, transferred more into the dryer, and started a new load in the wash. "Dee," he called.

"Yes, Daddy?"

"Time to fold your clothes."

"But I'm watching cartoons."

"Come here, Dee."

He could hear the quick shuffle of her feet coming from the family room and through the kitchen. She appeared in the doorway to the laundry room with a questioning look.

"What did I tell you earlier this morning?"

"Umm . . ." Her mouth curled, and her eyes traveled upward. "You said when my clothes finish drying, I have to fold them."

"When?"

"Right away."

"Why?"

"Well . . . you said last time I waited two days. But I *didn't*, Daddy. I just didn't feel well. Every time I start folding, I feel like I'm gonna faint or something."

Kory managed to keep a straight face. Where did she get this stuff? "Okay, sweetheart, this is what we'll do. You can sit on your bed and fold. That way if you faint, you'll just flop back on the pillow."

"But I don't know *how* to fold, Daddy. I'm too little."

"Dee, I've shown you many times and you do it just fine. And you know I only give you the shirts. Once you get going it only takes a few minutes."

"Daddy?"

"Yes, sweetheart."

"If I do a really, really good job, and don't faint or anything, can we call Miss Janelle and see if I can play with Tiffany today?"

Now she was talking. "Hmm. If the shirts are folded perfectly *and* put away in your drawer. And you're still conscious. Yes, then we can call Miss Janelle."

"Yaaay!" She was jumping around in a circle when Kory's phone rang. "I'll see who it is, Daddy. Maybe it's Miss Janelle!" She ran to the kitchen and grabbed it from the counter. "Oh. It's Mom."

She brought it to him, and he let it ring two more times. "Go ahead and answer it, Dee."

"I don't want to talk to her."

"Yes, you do, sweetheart. I'll stay right here if you want."

Kory knew she had been longing to talk to her mother. But the wait had turned her sour.

Dee lifted the phone and pushed a button to put her on speaker. "Hello."

"Hi, Dee, how are you?"

Kory sighed. Why did Shelley always have the fake sound of a distant aunt when she talked to Dee?

"Good."

"How has your New Year been so far?"

"Good."

"Learning lots of fun stuff in preschool?"

"I guess."

"Tell me what you've been learning."

"Reading, writing, stuff like that."

"Reading and writing? At four? Wow, Dee, that's great."

Yes, Shelley, even the country preschools teach reading and writing.

"I wanted to tell you that I'll be there in two weeks. I'm excited to see you."

Dee's brows knit at Kory. Probably wondering why she didn't know already. "Okay."

"Just okay? Aren't you excited to see me too?"

"Yeah."

"Well, you don't sound very excited." Shelley had a pouty sound in her voice. "What gets you excited these days? Like today. If you could do whatever you wanted, what would it be?"

Dee perked up. "I already asked Dad. Go to Hope Springs and play with Tiffany."

"Hope Springs? That little country . . . Anyway, who's Tiffany?"

"She's my friend."

Kory had no doubt things were about to get interesting.

"I gathered that, Dee. I'm asking how do you know her? Who are her parents?"

"Well, her daddy died. But Miss Janelle is her mom."

"Mm-hmm." The phone went silent. "Where's your dad? I want to talk to him."

Dee's eyes slid up to Kory. "Right here."

"Take the phone off speaker, Kory."

He spoke in a low voice. "Go fold your clothes, Dee." He took the phone from her. "Good morning."

"You just couldn't wait, could you?"

"Pardon me?" He went to the kitchen and opened the refrigerator.

"I know who Janelle is. She was at that family reunion we went to. I *knew* you liked her. And her husband passed? Didn't take you long to get with her, now did it?"

"Let me parse a couple of your suppositions." Kory got a bottled water and took a swig. "Whether I liked Janelle or not back then is immaterial, because I *made* it immaterial by focusing on the one to whom I was married and not allowing my mind to stray." He tipped the bottle up again. "Second, if by 'get with her,' you're referring to physical contact, we haven't so much as kissed. Why? Because Janelle wouldn't go there even if I wanted to. There do exist some people who respect the institution of marriage."

"As if I'm supposed to believe all that. Do your thing, Kory. How cute that she has a daughter who can play with Dee."

Kory could almost thank Shelley for filing the court papers as soon as she had. He was beginning to count down the days. "We're done, then?"

"See you in court."

~

"Remember. Head up—don't look at the ball." Kory moved sideways, guiding him.

"Okay." Daniel was concentrating, trying to look ahead, but lost the rhythm. He hit his forehead in frustration. "Ugh."

"It's okay. You'll get it." Kory jogged to get the basketball and brought it back to him.

"Can you show me again?"

Kory extended his hands and Daniel threw him the ball. He started bouncing with his right hand and moving down the court. "See, I keep my head up. If I'm looking at the ball, how can I focus on the direction I want to go?"

Daniel ran and got in front of him, extending his arms and bending low.

"Ah, you think you can stop me?" Kory dribbled the ball under his leg and switched hands, holding Daniel at bay with the other.

"Aw, cool. Show me how to do that."

Daniel kept up with him, reaching in every few seconds to try to steal the ball. But whatever side he went for, Kory switched. He paused now, bending low, dribbling in place, waiting for Daniel to make his move.

"Come on, Daniel. Try to get it."

"You're gonna fake me out."

Kory eyed Daniel, dribbling to his right. "You're not giving up, are you?"

Daniel threw up his hands. "You're too good. Every time I try to—"

In a quick move, Daniel knocked the ball from him and ran after it when it rolled.

"Oh, you tricked me, huh?"

Kory doubled after him, but Daniel beat him to the ball. Laughing hard, he dribbled haphazardly to the net, stopped, and shot it.

"Did you see that?" Daniel turned, his eyes shining. "That was all net!"

Kory high-fived him. "Beautiful! You know why?"

"That thing you taught me." Daniel demonstrated. "Bringing my arm straight up and letting the ball roll off my fingertips. I did it!"

"You're a fast learner, my man."

His head fell a little. "I still don't have the dribble, though."

Kory put an arm around him. "You'll get it in no time. That's what practice is about. It'll seem like second nature."

"Excuse me."

Kory and Daniel turned and saw the guy who'd been playing the other end of the court.

"Hey, how can I help you?" Kory said.

"Just wanted to say I enjoyed watching the way you work with your son. My fiancée and I are getting married this summer, and I'm looking forward to times like this one day."

Daniel's arm slipped around Kory's waist, and Kory knew Daniel didn't want him to correct the man. He shook his hand. "Congratulations. I wish you all the best with your fiancée and your future family."

When the guy left, Daniel looked up at him. "Thanks, Kory."

Kory gripped him tighter around the shoulder. "Ready for some lunch? I know they're waiting for us."

"Starving."

Kory and Daniel left the gym in Rocky Mount and got in his car, where he'd left his phone. He checked it and smiled. "Told you. Three texts from your mom. 'Where are y'all?'"

Daniel laughed at Kory's spot-on imitation of Janelle's voice.

The day couldn't have worked out better. Shortly after hanging up with Shelley, Janelle had called to say she was coming to Rocky Mount to take the kids clothes shopping. She wondered if Dee would like to go to the mall with them, and even asked if Kory needed her to shop for anything for Dee—an offer he gladly jumped at. He asked if Daniel *really* needed to go or if maybe they could have some time together—and Janelle jumped at that one.

He parked at the fast food restaurant, and he and Daniel walked in.

"There they are," Daniel said.

Dee and Tiffany were waving wildly to get their attention.

Janelle smiled as they came over, looking cute in her white top and jeans. "Did y'all have a good time?" She pulled Daniel into a hug. "You worked up a little sweat."

"Kory had us jogging before we played," Daniel said. "And I kept up with him too."

"Of course you did." She winked at Kory. "You love competition."

Dee stood. "Daddy, look." She threw back her shoulders to show off the design on her shirt: BFF with glittery stars sprinkled all around.

He narrowed his gaze. "What's a BFF?"

"Best friends forever, Daddy! Miss Janelle got it for me. Look at Tiffany! And we got one for Claire too."

"I don't normally buy those fad T-shirts," Janelle said, "but the girls got so excited when they saw them." She shrugged. "I caved."

"Can we order now, Mom?" Tiffany said. "I'm hungry."

Kory glanced at the table. "You waited for us. All right, then, taking down orders." He listened as they listed what they wanted, hoping he could keep track. "I'm thinking I'll need one assistant."

Daniel's hand shot up. "Me!"

He loved that Daniel liked palling around with him. He'd always wanted a son, and since he might never have one, he appreciated any opportunity to pour into a young boy's life.

With two trays piled high with food and drinks—Daniel moving carefully with the lighter one—the guys doled out the goodies.

"Kory, you want to pray?" Janelle asked.

The girls grabbed hands, starting a chain reaction around the table.

Kory bowed his head. "Dear Lord, we thank You for this food and pray it nourishes our bodies. We thank You for this day and for the friendship You've given our families. We pray that it's lasting. In Jesus's name, amen."

"Amen," the kids said, then launched into their food and chatter.

Janelle and Kory stalled, looking into each other's eyes, their fingers intertwined still.

"Amen," Janelle said.

CHAPTER TWENTY-NINE

Tuesday, January 26

Becca felt like a giddy schoolgirl, mixing and matching clothes and shoes from her closet. She brought out a pair of denim jeans and a frilly silk top.

Stephanie angled her head. "Uh, no."

"Yeah, that doesn't do anything for me either." Janelle sat on the floor. "It's cute, but it's not 'stage.'"

"This is exactly why I wanted you two here," Becca said. "You tell the straight-up truth."

She went back in the closet. "Okay, what about this?" She re-emerged with another silk top and blazer over the same pair of jeans.

"Too corporate," Stephanie said. Her legs dangled over the side of the armchair.

"I'm sure that was fine for some of the other conferences you've spoken at," Janelle said. "But you would completely fade in this on the Worth & Purpose stage."

"Oh, I've got an idea." Becca scurried back inside and flipped through the rack, choosing a completely different look—a denim skirt and long white button-up blouse. "This is cute. Right?"

Stephanie stared, then swung her legs to the floor. "Honey pie, let me see what's in that closet."

"I should've thought of that at first," Becca said. "See what you can piece together."

Stephanie took her time, examining each blouse, jacket, skirt, dress, and pair of pants. "Hmm . . . I'm not quite seeing what I'm looking for. Either it's too dressy or not dressy enough."

"What are you looking for exactly?" Becca asked.

"Well, I really never know what I'm looking for. I just know it when I see it. Something fresh." She pondered a moment. "Too bad I'm a couple sizes bigger than you are. I've got a couple pieces we could've tried."

"I didn't think about that," Janelle said. "Becca and I are about the same size. I might have something."

Stephanie looked at her cousin. "Janelle, I don't think I've seen you in anything other than sweat suits, jeans, and a Sunday suit. I can't even picture you wearing anything fresh."

"I'm not saying it's 'fresh,'" Janelle said, "if I even know what you mean. But it's worth going next door and bringing it back. I can also call Libby and tell her to bring some stuff tomorrow. She's got lots of nice things."

Becca and Stephanie chatted as they waited. A few minutes later, Janelle was back with a duffel bag.

"Now, let me qualify," she said. "I knew I'd be here a few months, so I wanted something that would work if Libby invited me to one of her events in Raleigh. But I'm not sure it would work for Becca."

She pulled out a soft black leather jacket, a long silver tank with glittery beading, and dressy denim slacks.

Stephanie stared from the outfit to Janelle. "Cousin . . . that right there is fresh." She turned to Becca. "But it has to be *you*. You have to like it and feel comfortable in it."

"I love it, no question," Becca said. "That fits right in with the types of things the speakers wear. I better try it on, though."

Janelle handed it to her, and Becca went into the closet to change so they could see the full look at once. The first good thing was that it fit. But she couldn't see how it looked on her. She hoped she didn't look dumb.

Becca walked out. "Well?"

"Girrrrl..." Stephanie walked around her, arms folded, nodding. "You look fantastic. But how do you feel? Does it feel like you?"

Becca had that feeling of anticipation again. "I feel like the 'me' I've always thought I could be—confident, stylish, even a little glamorous..." She smiled. "For a Bible teacher, that is."

"A Bible teacher who's on a national stage," Janelle said. "I love the look on you. You look great, Becca."

Becca looked at her watch. "And I'm excited about this prayer meeting. Will you both be able to come?"

"Sister Mitchell is at the house visiting Grandma Geri. She said she'd stay and look after Grandma and the kids while we go over to Calvary."

"Awesome. 'Cause I really want both of you there."

Becca was stunned by the turnout. Several pews were full as she, Janelle, and Stephanie walked in. She had told Todd she wanted to have special prayer before she went to Richmond to speak, thinking he'd simply invite their friends over. Instead he'd made an announcement at church on Sunday. He said they'd be gathering on Tuesday evening to ask a special blessing upon Becca's first weekend with Worth & Purpose.

"Come on up here, sweetheart." Todd was smiling at her, holding a microphone at the top of the aisle.

Janelle and Stephanie urged her down the center aisle. They took a side aisle and eased into one of the pews.

Todd put an arm around Becca and spoke into the mic. "Just before you got here," he said, "I took the liberty of telling these friends how God has blessed you with this platform, both literal and figurative, to tell of His goodness. You've been faithful in teaching His Word, and we believe this is only the beginning of what God will do with the ministry He's given you."

Becca got butterflies in her stomach. She hadn't told Todd that that's what she'd been thinking and praying.

He turned to her. "Bec, you told me you were proud of me my first Sunday here at Calvary as pastor. And I'm telling you in front of everyone here that I'm extremely proud of you, your dedication to the Lord, and your willingness to go where He leads."

Tears formed in Becca's eyes. "Thank you, sweetheart."

"There are a lot of us here, so let's see how we'll handle this." He looked up. "Travis, will you come up, please, so you can lay hands on Becca? My elders, I'd love to have you up here. Sara Ann, you're the one who gave me the idea to announce it."

Becca looked at her and mouthed, *Thank you.*

"And the rest of you, if you could kind of make a circle as best we can around Becca. I know it'll be a big one."

People filed out of the pews and surrounded Becca, and her tears continued to come. *Lord, thank You for this show of love. This means the world to me.*

"Travis, can you start us off?" Todd said. "And we're in no rush. Whoever wants to pray can pray. We'll be here as long as we're here. Amen?"

"Amen!"

Becca lowered her head to soak in every word that was prayed over her. Her faith had never soared quite like this. Just this morning she'd read the words in the gospel of Mark: *"All things for which you pray and ask, believe that you have received them, and they will be granted you."* With so many gathered, praying and asking, she would believe with all her heart that she would receive.

CHAPTER THIRTY

Friday, January 29

Libby almost felt bad bringing Al to Hope Springs. She really didn't want to be bothered with him, but he called just as she was about to leave, asking if she had plans tonight. When he asked to come along, she opened her mouth to say no—but then she thought of Travis. With Al by her side she could avoid the thoughts and feelings that crept in where Travis was concerned. She'd have a buffer.

She was within a few feet of them both now. Al had his arm around her. Travis had the floor.

"First and foremost," Travis was saying, "we're giving thanks to Almighty God. We had special prayer for Grandma Geri on New Year's Eve, and now midway through her chemo treatments, God has given a good report."

"Yes, He has. Didn't I say He would? Glory!" Aunt Gladys waved her hand like she was at church.

"Amen," Janelle said. She was standing behind Grandma Geri, who was seated in one of the family room recliners.

Travis continued. "We don't know what the future holds—for any of us—but today we know that the CT scan shows the tumor has shrunk and the spreading has stemmed. Folks, that's all I need to know to celebrate tonight."

Cheers of agreement went up in the room from friends and family. Many had shown up for the impromptu celebration, including Aunt Gladys and Uncle Warren and two of their grown children.

Travis looked to Todd, who walked over and put a hand on Grandma Geri's shoulder. "All of us are used to Grandma Geri being a pillar of faith and strength," he said, "but a cancer diagnosis is enough to shake anyone." He addressed her directly. "I'm sure you're bearing a lot more on the inside than you're willing to show on the outside. Praise God for news that uplifts and gives you the strength to keep on keepin' on."

"You want to say something, Grandma?" Janelle asked.

Grandma Geri's fingers were clasped in front of her. "If y'all want to know the truth . . . I suppose I always carried more on the inside than out. Not saying that's a good thing." She focused on those fingers. "Family as big as ours, there's always something to carry." She looked into people's faces. "It could be three weeks, three months, or three years . . . I'm going home to Jesus. I don't care so much about the *when*. I just don't want to be carrying as much when I leave."

No one seemed to know what to say.

"Well, you just went and got deep on us, huh, Momma?" Aunt Gladys said. "I don't know what you're planning to unload, but if it's any of my business, please think twice."

"I know that's right," Libby said. "Grandma knows *everybody's* business."

"There's plenty more food," Aunt Gladys announced. "Help yourselves."

People shifted and began to talk and eat again. Libby held her breath as Travis moved in her direction. *Keep going, keep going.*

"Hey, Libby," he said. His eyes always seemed to hold much more than was on the surface.

"Hey, Travis."

He turned to Al and shook his hand. "Good to see you, man." Travis took a step to continue on toward the kitchen.

"Is it?" Al said.

Libby frowned at him. What was he doing?

Travis backed up. "Come again?"

Al seemed to square his shoulders. He was six feet tall, which put him a couple inches shorter than Travis.

"I'm thinking you prefer it when Libby comes to Hope Springs by herself," Al said. "Isn't that why you invited her to church?"

Libby's eyes grew wide. Al was reading her text messages?

Travis looked slightly amused, which was probably more than slightly irritating to Al.

"I invited her with the same motive I invite everybody to church—because I happen to think it's good for the soul." Travis smiled as naturally as if he were talking to Todd. "You're welcome to come as well," he added. "Service is at eleven."

"My Sunday mornings are fine as they are, Pastor Brooks."

Travis spread his hands. "Offer remains open. Like I said, good to see you." He moved on.

Libby spoke under her breath. "What was that about?" She took Al's arm and nudged him toward a corner of the room, out of the traffic.

"I'm not stupid, Libby," Al said. "I can tell something's up between you two. That's why you've been coming to Hope Springs so much lately."

"I come to Hope Springs because my grandmother is sick and my cousins are here. I can't believe you."

"And you're telling me nothing's going on with you and the

preacher? Because you've clearly grown distant." He looked down at her wrist. "I gave you that because I care about you."

Libby sighed. "Al, there is nothing going on between Travis and me, but so what if there were? I've told you time and again that I don't want a committed relationship. And you've apparently been checking my text messages?" She groaned inside as she unhooked the clasp on the bracelet. "I don't think I should keep this." She dropped it into his hand.

"This means we can't keep seeing each other?"

"Not if you expect me to commit to you."

They always say they understand, but in the end . . .

Al hesitated. "What is it, Libby? What keeps you from committing to me?"

She tried not to sigh aloud again. "It's not you. I just . . . I'm not ready to be that serious with anyone right now."

He held the bracelet up. "Wouldn't be right to take it back. I knew the state of affairs when I gave it to you. I guess I just hoped it would help change things."

She was itching to take it back, but then she'd feel obligated to keep seeing him. "I can't, Al."

He turned and walked out the front door without another word.

Libby found Janelle and pulled her into her bedroom, closing the door.

"What's wrong?" Janelle asked.

"Al accused Travis of inviting me to church so he could get back with me."

"To his face?"

"To his face."

"Well . . . why would that be a problem anyway? I thought you and Al weren't serious."

"Exactly! He acted like I'd promised for better or for worse." She held up her arm. "I gave it back."

"I'm glad you did, Libby. That bracelet cost a lot of money, and if he had a different notion about the two of you—"

"Oh! Wait a minute . . ." She held up her phone and pushed a button. After a few seconds she spoke: "Al, I forgot to get my key from you. You weren't planning to go to my apartment when you get back to Raleigh, were you?"

"I do have some of my things there," he said, sighing. "Just call me when you get back, and I'll stop by then."

"Cool. Just making sure." She hung up.

"He has a key to your apartment?"

"Jan, you're not deaf."

"So . . . were you two sleeping together?"

"Janelle . . . seriously? You think the guy would give me a diamond bracelet otherwise?"

"Well, no wonder he thought things were serious, Libby. When you're sleeping with someone, it tends to be serious."

"When *you're* sleeping with someone, it tends to be serious, as in marriage. Al shouldn't have let his feelings get involved."

"How do you keep your feelings from getting involved?"

"I just . . . do. You know I'm not an emotional person. And I'm not letting anyone get close enough to hurt me."

"So that's what you're afraid of?"

"It's not a matter of fear. It's just a fact."

"Sounds like fear to me."

"Oh, you're just gonna *tell* me it's fear."

Janelle shrugged. "You know me. I call it like I see it."

Libby sat on the bed and tucked her legs under her. "Okay, how are you calling it these days with Kory?"

"Love how you changed that subject."

Libby smiled. "Thought you might."

Janelle stretched across the bed beside her. "What do you mean, how am I calling it with Kory? There's nothing to call."

"Really, Jan? You're gonna try that with me?"

"Kory is married, Libby."

Libby looked at her watch. "For another week. Then what?"

Janelle shrugged. "Maybe nothing. Who knows?"

Libby thought about what she was saying. "I'm sorry. I'm being insensitive. It's probably still hard to imagine yourself with anyone but David—which I can totally see. You know how much I loved David."

"I don't think you were insensitive," Janelle said. "David's been gone two years. In my counseling group, they said it's natural to want companionship at this point. Two people in our group have already gotten married again."

"I remember that family reunion when we all met Kory. Seemed like you had fallen in love with the boy by the end of the weekend."

"Oh, it wasn't like that."

Libby raised her eyebrows. "From the moment you met Friday night, the two of you were inseparable until that last night on Monday. You totally clicked . . . So I was wondering, now that you're kind of together again . . ."

Janelle switched to lotus style, sighing. "The truth is I'm afraid to let myself think about the possibility. Whenever I'm around him now, it's just so . . . *nice*. I start to think, *What if?* What if this is really our chance? What if we really fall in love?" She sighed again. "Then I remind myself that life isn't about happy endings. I've seen that firsthand."

"Knock, knock."

Libby and Janelle looked toward the door, then at one another.

"Come in," Janelle said.

Travis opened the door but stayed in the doorway. "Sorry to interrupt. I'm about to go, and Grandma Geri said you put aside my sweet potato pie for safekeeping—thank you very much—and she doesn't know where it is."

Janelle hit Libby's arm. "I didn't tell you—Grandma got a burst of energy today. First time she's felt like baking since the diagnosis. She sent me out for sweet potatoes and a bunch of other ingredients for all the desserts out there."

"I thought Aunt Gladys made those."

"Nope. Grandma. So apparently she knows sweet potato pie is Travis's favorite, and she made him *his own pie*—"

"Why are you acting all surprised?" Travis stepped farther in. "You know that's my girl. We flow like that."

Janelle ignored him. "—and told me to find a hiding place for it so nobody would eat it. Know where I put it?"

"Far left upper cabinet, second shelf."

"Our favorite hiding place for scrumptious desserts." She got up. "I'll go get it."

Travis moved to follow her.

"Travis." Libby got up from the bed.

He turned.

"I want to apologize . . . for what happened out there."

"No need to apologize. Everything's cool."

She wanted to say something more to him, but she didn't know what. And it wouldn't have mattered. He'd already left.

CHAPTER THIRTY-ONE
Saturday, January 30

Stephanie didn't have to work at the diner or take care of the kids, but she was up early anyway, by choice, making the most of the little time she had left. Libby had to get back to Raleigh to prepare for an event. But for now the three cousins had been enjoying morning coffee and conversation at the kitchen table while everyone else slept.

"How'd I miss all that?" Stephanie said. "My man Al went in on Travis, huh?" She chuckled. "Girl, I have to give it to you for giving back that bracelet. I totally kept a diamond pendant a guy gave me, knowing I had no intention of ever committing to him." She looked upward. "Lord, please don't convict me to give it back."

Libby laughed. "Really, Steph? So you've been there? Janelle can't understand why I'd want to date with no desire for commitment."

Stephanie eyed Janelle. "I think there was some kind of mix-up, and *you* were supposed to be Cyd's sister. She used to say the same thing to me." She looked at Libby. "Definitely been there. No desire to commit. No plans to commit. I'll just keep it real—I was engaged to Lindell and still seeing an old boyfriend."

The other women's eyes were wide. "Seriously?" Libby said. "Did he find out?" She sipped her coffee.

"On our wedding night."

"What?" they both said.

"Come on, Steph," Janelle said. "Are you serious?"

Stephanie raised a hand as if giving a Girl Scout oath. "Lindell stepped out of the hotel room to get some snacks, and I e-mailed the other guy, saying I missed him and would call him when I got back from our honeymoon." She couldn't believe it herself now. Sounded like another person. "When Lindell came back in the room, he asked why I had the laptop open. It became a mess from there."

"What did he do?" Janelle said.

Stephanie lifted her mug. "Long story, but our pastor was about to start a series on sex and faithfulness to God. Lindell canceled our honeymoon in the islands, and we were right up in church that next day. I was hot."

Libby shook her head. "The bad thing about it is I can totally see it. That could've totally been me."

"What happened next?" Janelle asked.

"We had to meet in study groups as part of the series—which I didn't like—but God blindsided me. After all those years growing up in church and all those years living like I wanted, it was like He grabbed hold of me and said, 'What are you doing? You don't see this better life I have for you?'" Stephanie paused, reflecting on that time. "Now I'm over two years 'clean'"—she smiled—"committed and faithful to my man."

Janelle smiled big. "I love that. What an awesome God-story."

"Yeah, well, pray for me," Stephanie said, "because it's only by God's grace, and I'm in trouble if it runs out." She shook her head. "That same old boyfriend called me a few months ago and left a message. His voice gave me this little fluttery thing, and I was like, 'Lord, no, I done come too far.'" She pressed a finger in the air. "Delete."

"You need to keep sharing that story, even things like that

temptation you felt, if only for a minute," Janelle said. "It speaks to people when you keep it real."

Stephanie had never thought of sharing her story. Who would she tell? Why would anyone listen to her?

Libby had gotten quiet, focusing on her coffee cup. She looked at Stephanie now. "You said you grew up in church and lived like you wanted. That's me."

She paused so long Stephanie wondered if she would continue.

"I like dating different guys," Libby said finally. "I like the attention. I like the control, especially when they end up being the ones who want commitment and I refuse. I like being untouchable, unreachable."

"What is it you don't want them to touch?" Janelle said.

Libby looked at her. "You already know—that's why you asked. My heart."

Stephanie leaned in. "Have you ever let anyone get that close?"

Libby gazed aside. "Only one person. Travis."

"I had a feeling you two used to see each other, but I didn't know it was that serious."

Libby gave an empty chuckle. "It wasn't, not for him."

The table grew silent.

Stephanie had something on her heart, but she didn't know if she should say it. Didn't know if it would come out right or sound stupid. But it was practically jumping off her tongue.

"Libby, can I say something?"

Libby looked at her.

"Maybe it's not so much about allowing a guy to reach your heart but allowing God to reach it."

Libby gave her a look. "You didn't warn me you were in boot camp preacher school now."

Stephanie got up for more coffee. "Honey, that's about as deep as you're getting from me, because I need to switch the convo up entirely before you hit the road."

"Thank you and amen. Conversation switched." Libby laughed. "So what's up?"

"I don't know why I waited till my last weekend here," Stephanie said, "but I want to sketch out a family tree. I'm not even sure who's all in the family."

"Oh, that's a fun little project," Janelle said. She hopped up, went to a drawer, and pulled out some white paper. "You want to know *all* the Sanders extended family, or are you talking Geraldine and Elwood Sanders family only?"

"Let's start with that, then we can branch out later—ha, didn't plan that."

"Okay, so at the top we've got Geraldine and Elwood Sanders." Janelle drew a big tree with long willowy branches, and at the top of the page, a straight line with *Geraldine (Grandma Geri) and Elwood Sanders*.

Stephanie looked at the paper. "Now let me see if I can do this, and don't laugh that I have to think about it." She paused. "Grandma Geri and Grandpa Elwood's kids were, in order . . . my dad, Bruce; Aunt Gladys; Jan's mom, Estelle; Libby's dad, Uncle Wood . . . That's it, right?"

"And Aunt Gwynn," Libby said.

"Oh, I remember that name. But why don't I hear much about her?"

"Something happened back in the day," Libby said. "All I know is she got pregnant in college and went away to Grandma Geri's sister's house up north. She had the baby—Keisha—and they stayed up there."

Janelle nodded. "We used to go visit them once in a while when I was young, but I don't think Aunt Gwynn has been to Hope Springs since that happened. And she doesn't speak to Grandma Geri. Keisha's never been down here."

"What?" Stephanie was floored. "Whatever went down must've been serious. I wonder if my dad keeps in touch with her. I don't recall us taking any trips—wait a minute. Do they live in Jersey?"

"That's right," Libby said. "We went up there too."

"We *did* visit them," Stephanie said, "but I was so young I didn't know who was who."

Janelle was filling in more names on branches below Geri and Elwood, but Stephanie was so intrigued, she wasn't ready to move on.

"Is there a picture of Aunt Gwynn and Keisha around here?" she said. "I want to see what they look like."

"Long time ago there was a picture of Aunt Gwynn on that living room table with all the other pictures. But it disappeared. I think Grandma took it down because she's hurt that they don't speak."

"There have to be pictures of them, though," Libby said. "Doesn't Grandma keep old pictures somewhere?"

"She sure does," Janelle said. "That would be another good project while I'm here, to put all those old photos in albums for her." She got up. "No better time than now to start. I think they're in this hall closet."

The three of them walked over to see, and Janelle pulled open the sliding door.

"There's another project," Libby said. "That thing's a mess. How could you find anything in there?"

"Good grief," Janelle said. "Grandma Geri must've kept everything from the last century that ever remotely meant anything."

She pushed aside brass and porcelain figurines, candles and candlesticks, vases, magazines . . . "I think I see something." She pulled two big shoe boxes from the back and lifted the lids. "Bingo. This looks like a good place to start."

They carried the boxes back to the kitchen.

"Hey, that's my dad." Stephanie picked up a photo. "Ha . . . wait till I tell him about this. He was *stylin'* in that Afro."

Libby laughed too, looking over her shoulder. "My dad's stylin' right beside him. They thought they were somethin'."

Janelle pulled out a photo. "Here she is. This is Aunt Gwynn." She passed it to Stephanie.

"She's so pretty," Stephanie said. "I wonder how old she is here."

"I'm guessing late teens," Libby said. "Probably around the time she got pregnant."

Janelle continued digging to find Keisha—and pulled out an envelope instead.

"What's that?" Libby said.

"I don't know." Janelle held it up to read the address and stared at it. "It's postmarked last November. And it's from Pastor Jim."

Libby frowned. "Why would Pastor Jim write a letter and *mail* it to Grandma when he lived next door?"

Janelle looked at her. "That's what I'm wondering. It looks really thick."

"Should we open it?" Libby said.

Janelle shook her head. "We can't."

"Well, who's gonna kn—"

"*I'll* know."

The three of them jumped.

"Didn't hear you come in, Grandma." Janelle set the envelope back in the box.

"I see y'all been investigating this morning." Grandma Geri rested herself in a chair.

"We were making a family tree," Stephanie said. "And I wanted to see a picture of Aunt Gwynn and Keisha."

"Grandma, why did Pastor Jim write you a letter?" Libby asked.

Janelle looked at her, probably surprised she'd come right out and ask.

Grandma Geri stared at the envelope. "This was on my mind last night when I said I didn't want to be carrying as much when I leave." She glanced upward. "Didn't mean You had to put things in motion *that* fast." She sighed. "I guess it's time."

CHAPTER THIRTY-TWO

J anelle had planned to attend the Bible study at the diner, but with this impromptu meeting about to get under way, she doubted she'd make it. It was already nine thirty. Aunt Gladys had stayed overnight and joined them in the kitchen. And Grandma Geri had said to call Todd as well. He had brought Claire and Ethan—since Becca was already in Richmond, scheduled to speak in the afternoon—and a couple VeggieTales DVDs to keep all the kids occupied. No one but Grandma Geri knew exactly what was going on, but it was clear it was serious.

Aunt Gladys looked at her mother. "Momma, you want to tell us what this is about?"

"If it's all the same to you," Grandma Geri said, "I want Jan to read the letter. I'll deal with questions after."

Janelle didn't like the sound of that. Reluctantly she took the pages out of the envelope and began to read.

Dear Miss Geri,
    You're probably wondering why I'm writing this letter, since

I see you at least three times a day. But I didn't want to say this in person. Maybe it's that I'm not able to say it in person . . . so much time has passed. I wanted you to read it and ponder it, and let me know your thoughts.

I preached a sermon today at Calvary. It was on Nehemiah 4 in which the people of Jerusalem, while rebuilding the wall, were confronted by the enemy. Nehemiah saw their fear and told the people, "Do not be afraid of them; remember the Lord who is great and awesome, and fight for your brothers, your sons, your daughters, your wives, and your houses."

After I preached the sermon and returned home, the Lord brought my words back to me. He let me know that when I was faced with fear, I didn't fight. I didn't fight for my daughter.

Daughter? Janelle looked immediately at Todd. He looked stunned, and Janelle's own heart began to beat faster.

I hate that I can't even speak of having a daughter, since the fact of her existence has remained a well-guarded secret. As close as you and I are, we never even speak her name—Keisha Rochelle Sanders.

"What?" Aunt Gladys looked at her mother in shock. "Keisha is Jim's daughter? Momma, you knew?"

Todd's head was bowed down. Janelle, Libby, and Stephanie were looking at one another. Grandma Geri simply said, "Go on, Jan."

Janelle cleared her throat to continue.

I've never shared my heart with you about what happened, Miss Geri. I feel a burden right now to make clear to you that I loved Gwynn. I knew her my entire life, but because she was four years younger, which seemed like a wide gulf, I never noticed her in a special way . . . until she came home from college after freshman year. I had just graduated college and was home for the summer preparing for graduate school in the fall. And if you recall, Bruce, Gladys, Wood, and Estelle were all away that summer. Gwynn and I had that summer to ourselves. We took long walks, had long conversations in the porch swing at night, drove more than once to the beach. We fell in love easily. I wanted to marry her even before I learned she was pregnant.

Janelle paused, feeling tears well up in her eyes. She knew the magic he described in that Hope Springs summer, had felt it herself on a small scale. Whatever happened afterward had to have hurt them both.

She continued reading.

My parents and you and Mr. Elwood had begrudgingly endured the romance between us. Oh, you certainly let us know it wasn't proper, that it "wasn't done," but you couldn't stop us from seeing one another. But once she became pregnant, everything changed.

Janelle's eyes bounced to Grandma Geri every few seconds. What was she thinking? How did she feel? Her grandmother sat stoically, giving nothing away.

You all said the baby had to be given up for adoption, discussing it all amongst yourselves while Gwynn and I talked and cried with each other. I was due to leave for graduate school, and my parents were glad for the timing. I needed to go, they said, make a clean break. I could put the summer behind me and move forward with my life. Gwynn would have the baby, put it up for adoption, and then she could return to college and move forward with her life.

The deck was stacked against us. You all may not have realized it, but just as Nehemiah and the people of Jerusalem were confronted with the voice of the enemy, our parents became the voice of the enemy. "A white man and a black woman cannot be together." "It would never work." "You could never marry and raise this baby together. What would people say?"

And I'm ashamed to admit that not only did I not fight for my daughter, I didn't fight for Gwynn. I didn't fight for our love. I accepted the lies, left for graduate school, and moved on with my life. I thought Gwynn would give the baby up for adoption. When I found out she'd kept her, I instantly understood that the fact of my fatherhood would be a secret we would all carry.

But I'm tired of the secret. I want Todd to know his sister. I want to know my daughter, if she's willing. I want her to know she was conceived in love, and that not a day has passed that I haven't thought of her. I want the Sanders and Dillon families to finally be able to embrace the truth that we have been more than neighbors for all these decades. We have been family. But I want us to be in agreement. Let me know.

Signed, James A. Dillon

Janelle slowly returned the pages to a neat fold. Everyone sat in silence.

Finally Aunt Gladys spoke. "Momma, it's only right that we hear from you. What do you have to say about all this?"

Grandma Geri didn't hesitate. "Every word of it is true. Elwood and I, and Jerry and Lenora, didn't know what to do when we saw Jim and Gwynn falling in love. It was obvious, all the time they spent together, the way they looked at each other. We figured it'd fade time they went back to school. But when she wound up pregnant . . ."

Grandma Geri started coughing and tears slid down her face. Janelle got her some water and a tissue.

"I lost my daughter because of it," Grandma Geri said between coughs. "She's never forgiven me. And I don't know my granddaughter." She doubled over, the cough increasing. She took sips of water, and the cough slowly subsided.

"Grandma, what did you tell Pastor Jim?" Janelle asked. "Did you write him back?"

"Said I had to think about it," she said. "Didn't know how it would go over in the family. Didn't know what people would say if he openly acknowledged Keisha as his daughter."

Todd stood. "I'm sorry, I need time to process this."

"Of course you do," Aunt Gladys said. "I think we all do."

Todd went into the living room and got Claire and Ethan, and they left out the front door. The rest of them stared at one another.

Janelle looked at the clock. "The diner Bible study sounds real good to me right now. I'll be a little late but I need it. Anybody want to join me?"

"I'd like to go," Stephanie said. She rose from her chair.

"Libby?"

Libby shook her head. "I'll be doing my processing on the road back to Raleigh."

Grandma Geri was staring down at nothing in particular. Janelle looked at her, wanted to say something to her. But no words came.

CHAPTER THIRTY-THREE

Becca heard the applause as she left the stage, but she still couldn't believe it was over. She'd actually gotten through it, her first Worth & Purpose message, and she hadn't vomited, fallen, or been struck with paralysis onstage. In fact, if she dared believe it, it had seemed to go well.

The audience laughed in places she'd hoped, clapped in places she hadn't expected, and grew very still when she revealed intimate facets of her life. She'd shared this story with friends and with conference audiences of a smaller scale. Now she'd shared it with thousands.

The other speakers were on their feet clapping for her as she returned to her seat. They knew how nervous she'd been. She was the last speaker and had to wait all day to be done with it. They each embraced her, offering encouragement down the line.

"You were fabulous!" Christa Lane said. "You looked so great up there."

One of the musical artists started into a song to close out the conference. Becca let out a breath she'd surely been holding for weeks. Though she'd told the story before, she hadn't known what kind of feedback she'd get in a crowd this size. It wasn't easy telling an arena full of women she'd gotten pregnant at seventeen.

She'd grown up in love with Jesus, been active in church youth group, served as a mentor to younger teens. But when she began dating a boy in youth group, things went further than they'd planned. She'd been afraid to tell her parents she was pregnant, and about the time it became unavoidable, she learned the baby had no heartbeat. She had to undergo induced labor, then deal with the emotional pain of losing a baby and feeling guilty that she was glad her problem had been solved.

In her meeting with the Worth & Purpose team, they'd agreed she shouldn't sugarcoat that last part. There was power in admitting she hadn't been the "perfect Christian girl" even in the way she'd regarded the loss of the baby. That was the point of her message— that there was no such thing as a perfect Christian girl, only a perfect Christ.

As the song neared the end, she took her phone from her purse. Todd had texted first thing this morning that he was praying for her, as had her mom, Janelle, and others. But now it was Twitter lighting up her screen, tweet after tweet that had posted during her message. She scanned a few.

Listening to @BeccaDillon at @WorthandPurpose. Funny, transparent, poignant.

In tears @WorthandPurpose. @BeccaDillon's story is my own. So thankful for a perfect Christ.

"We don't have to hide the shame. God's glory is revealed within it." ~@ BeccaDillon

Becca got tears in her own eyes now. God had truly answered prayer. There were women who'd been touched by the message. She was overwhelmed.

Security came to escort them out. As she walked past the women in the floor seats, many extended their hand to hers. She would meet and greet people on the main concourse level of the arena in a few minutes prior to heading back to the hotel. But first she stopped in the catering area to get her coat and tote bag.

Two members of the Worth & Purpose executive team walked in after her. Becca smiled, thinking they were about to encourage her about her message.

"Becca, we need to talk with you a moment." It was Catherine, the one who'd gotten the vision to start the organization.

"Sure," Becca said.

Catherine led the three of them to a table across the room away from staff who'd gathered there.

Catherine sighed. "This isn't easy for us, and we certainly wanted to wait until after you'd given your message . . ."

Becca had a funny sensation in the pit of her stomach.

". . . but we also didn't think it prudent to wait much longer after that." Catherine sighed again. "Becca, you won't be continuing with Worth & Purpose."

"You mean next year?"

"I mean this year," Catherine said. "Wendy Burns was unexpectedly cleared by her doctor to return. Looks like prayers were answered, and she and the baby are doing fine."

Becca stared at them. "Okay."

"We're very sorry. You did a great job. We were so proud of you. But we did include that contingency in your contract just in case."

Becca didn't know what else to say.

"I know you're scheduled to do a meet and greet right now. Understandably, we don't expect you to do that. You can feel free to head back to the hotel."

"I'd, um . . . I'd like to still do that . . . if that's okay."

"Absolutely."

The women looked at one another, clearly not relishing this task. They all stood.

"We really did love having you, Becca."

She gave a faint smile, the only kind she could, and followed a staff member to the upper level. A line of women was waiting for her. She greeted the first, who began to share a similar story of a teenage pregnancy and the accompanying shame, and the next, who had a different story of shame. On down the line the women bared their hearts. Becca listened. And was thankful for the outlet to cry.

She wished she could stop crying. But back in her hotel room there seemed no end to things that would trigger the tears. She was sure it was self-torture, but she'd check Twitter now and then for tweets from the Worth & Purpose team. They'd gone to dinner, yet no one had asked her to join them like last time. But didn't they know she'd be seeing this? Didn't they care? Did they *have* to post about the grand time they were having with one another? Would it have killed them to make the kind gesture of inviting her? They probably didn't think about it. Just that fast she was nobody again—which made her cry all the more.

Then there were the continuing tweets from women who'd attended the conference, saying she was a great addition to the team. She wanted to scream, *I'm not on the team anymore!*

She heard an e-mail notification and looked up from her slumped position at the desk. Someone had written on her fan page wall how much they enjoyed her message. She clicked to her Facebook window, went to her fan page—now with 317 fans—scrolled down, and clicked *Delete page.*

Are you sure you want to delete this page? it asked.

She leaned forward and not only clicked the answer but yelled it. "YES!"

She slumped back in the chair. She'd have to tell her agent what happened. The book contract would be gone. She'd only gotten it because of this platform, and now it was gone. She was sure the publisher would breathe a sigh of relief that nothing had yet been signed.

Every "blessing" she'd received had been stripped. The tears started again. *This wasn't a blessing, Lord. You let me taste what it could be like, then You yanked it away.* She looked down at the clothes she'd borrowed from Janelle, and suddenly couldn't strip them off fast enough. She got up, took off the jacket, tank, and denim pants, and put on a pair of sweats and a T-shirt. She walked into the bathroom and washed off all the stage makeup. Then she went and found the Worth & Purpose program in her tote—the one she'd tucked away as a keep-sake—and slung it into the trash.

Her phone notified her she had a text. She walked to the desk where she'd left it and looked. It was from Janelle: *I just know you knocked it out of the park. Can't wait to hear!*

Becca didn't know what to text back. She didn't know what she'd say when she got home tomorrow. She didn't know what she'd do from here.

CHAPTER THIRTY-FOUR

Sunday, January 31

Stephanie was glad she could visit New Jerusalem once more on her last Sunday in Hope Springs. She'd worked at the diner on Thursday and told Lila she was willing to work Sunday, but another server had been hired in the interim.

Stephanie loved Living Word, her home church in St. Louis. Dr. Lyles, the pastor she'd grown up with, was a gifted preacher whose Bible studies were used around the world. She was blessed to sit under excellent teaching week after week. But here in this little country church it was clear—Pastor Travis was gifted as well.

She leaned over to Janelle. "Is he always on fire like this?"

Her cousin nodded. "Every time I've heard him. When he starts teaching, he's in another zone."

Kory sat on the other side of Janelle, with Daniel beside him. Tiffany and Dee were beside Stephanie.

"Without Christ, you couldn't string a coherent thought together," Travis was saying. "You couldn't walk and chew gum at the same time. Matter of fact, without Him, you would start to tilt as you walk"—people chuckled as he demonstrated—"because the earth would move off its axis and throw everybody and everything into chaos. Why? Because 'in Him all things hold together.'"

Travis walked down from the pulpit area and looked among them. "You can try to live without Him if you want to—and believe me, I tried. I found out how empty that path was and how messed up my life had become. And in all my trying, I hurt people." He paused with a sigh. "And when you hurt people because *you* tried to live without Christ, it's the worst feeling in the world. And you can't always go back and fix it."

Stephanie and Janelle looked at one another.

Travis concluded his sermon a few minutes later, and as the worship team began playing softly, Stephanie leaned over to Janelle again. "Between Travis and Todd, Hope Springs has got a pair of gifted preachers."

"You just never know who God will raise up."

They watched as people came forward for prayer and were directed to the side for further counseling. In a few minutes Travis said the benediction.

Stephanie high-fived Tiffany and Dee. "You girls did really well. I didn't hear as much giggling as I expected." She was well aware it helped that they had candy to suck on.

Kory drove them all back to the house, and Stephanie checked the cars out front.

"Looks like Todd's back from church but Becca's not here yet," she said. "I can't wait to hear how it went."

"She didn't answer my text," Janelle said, "but I know she was busy. I checked her blog this morning, thinking she'd post after the conference like she did last week, but nothing new was up there."

When they stepped inside, Stephanie stopped to inhale. "Mmmmm."

"Tell me about it," Kory said.

They entered the kitchen where Aunt Gladys was holding court by herself, working pots and pans, checking the oven.

"Aunt Gladys, you didn't have to do all this. You've got it smelling like Thanksgiving in here."

"I can't have my niece leaving without a special meal. That's not how I roll."

Stephanie laughed, hugging her. "Thank you."

Kory got some chips and dip and planted himself at the table with the Sunday paper.

"How's Grandma Geri doing?" Janelle asked.

"Stayed in bed mostly," Aunt Gladys said. "No coughing episodes or anything. I've been checking on her."

"Still withdrawn?" Janelle asked.

Aunt Gladys spooned out a bit of collards to taste. "Hard to tell if it's the illness or the secret being out or both. But she's not herself."

News had traveled fast on the Sanders family grapevine. By the time Stephanie and Janelle returned from the Bible study, Aunt Gladys had called all of her siblings, save Aunt Gwynn, and told them what happened. Stephanie's dad then called to get her perspective, and Janelle's mom called her. And Stephanie was sure they'd talked to Grandma Geri and probably Todd too.

Calls had also gone out to Aunt Gwynn from all her siblings, but no one had spoken with her personally. With all the voice mails, she knew the secret was out and likely didn't want to talk.

The side door opened and Claire dashed past the kitchen, then dashed back, poking her head in. "Have you seen Tiffany and Dee?" she asked.

"Good afternoon, Claire." Janelle was smiling.

"Good afternoon, Miss Janelle."

"I think Tiffany and Dee are out back. And, Claire?"

"Yes?"

"Let us know when your mom gets back."

Claire shrugged. "She's already here."

Stephanie looked out the window. "She sure did ease in without us seeing." She glanced at Janelle. "Should we give her some time?"

"Much as I've been praying? I'm going to get the report."

The two of them got their jackets and walked over, entering the screen door. "Hello?"

"We're in the kitchen," Todd said.

But when they got in the kitchen, only Todd and Ethan were there. Ethan was eating a sandwich.

"We're looking for Becca," Janelle said. "Excited to hear how things went."

Todd cast a glance in the direction of the staircase and sighed. "She's up in our room, but she's not doing well. They let her go right after her message."

"What do you mean, 'let her go'?" Stephanie asked.

"They brought her on board to replace a speaker who was having complications with her pregnancy. But the doctor cleared her to return. Becca had to step aside."

"Oh no," Janelle said. "I mean, it's great for that speaker and her baby, but Becca was really looking forward to spending the season with them."

"And beyond," Todd said. "She was praying to continue with them next year. She had her sights set on an upward trajectory for her ministry, and now she sees it as plummeting."

"But she shouldn't see it that way at all," Janelle said.

"I've been telling her that," Todd said. "When she told me last night what happened, first thing I said was, 'God still used you in a big way on that platform, and now He's got another plan. He wasn't surprised by this.'"

"She wasn't hearing it?" Stephanie asked.

Todd shook his head. "Not at all."

"Can we go up and talk to her?" Janelle said.

"Please do."

Stephanie and Janelle ascended the steps slowly. What could they say in the face of such disappointment? The door was open and Becca was stretched across the bed.

Janelle rapped lightly on the door. "Becca?"

She rolled to her side. "Come on in."

They pulled off their jackets, laid them on a chair, and sat beside her on the bed.

"Todd told us what happened," Stephanie said. "I think it stinks that they couldn't give you a good twenty-four hours to enjoy your moment. I mean, who does that?"

"Well." Becca stared downward. "Finding out today, tomorrow, or in two weeks would've been worse. I'm glad they told me when they did."

"How did the actual message go, Bec?" Janelle asked.

"Great, I think. I got good feedback from the other speakers and from people in the audience. I think a lot of women connected with the message. I was on a high until I got the news."

"Which gives it a double stink," Stephanie said. "Just my opinion."

"Becca, that's awesome news," Janelle said. "Praise God that you got up on that stage and knocked it out of the park, just like I thought you would. God is faithful."

Becca's eyes shifted. "I'm having a hard time with that."

Janelle paused. "With what?"

"All the prayers that were prayed, all the verses I clung to . . . 'All things for which you pray and ask, believe that you have received them, and they will be granted you.'" Becca had raised herself up and spoken with authority; then she sank back down. "I memorized that, I *believed* that. So I asked God to prosper my time with Worth & Purpose, and to bless my ministry so I could continue with them, not only *this* season, but next year and into the future." She raised her hands in disbelief. "And I got axed my first day on the job!"

Janelle looked sad for Becca. "You really shouldn't see it like that. You did well. It just happened that you got the opportunity because you were replacing someone and the woman came back. But don't let that take away from God's faithfulness in working through you yesterday. How many people heard you speak?"

She shrugged. "I don't know. Maybe five thousand."

Janelle looked at her. "That's five thousand women you potentially impacted who could go on to impact someone else because of what they heard."

"Shoot, now that you put it that way," Stephanie said, "I agree . . . yesterday was incredible all by itself."

"Incredibly humiliating," Becca said. "I've been *blogging* about this, how excited I was about this opportunity, how I was believing God to do great things. I just want to shut the blog down and hide in a hole."

Janelle sat up. "Becca Dillon, you have no reason to hide or to be humiliated. You—" She stopped abruptly.

Becca looked up. "What?"

"At the diner a couple of weeks ago, Sara Ann was encouraging us to sit down in our disappointments and pour our hearts out to God." She looked at Becca. "I see so clearly how God used you yesterday, and I automatically wanted you to see it and be strong. But you know . . . it's okay to be disappointed."

"I'm disappointed, but it's more than that." Becca sat up. "I'm having a hard time believing God for anything related to ministry again. I'm not even sure I *want* to do ministry again."

⌒

Stephanie was full from the meal and the love everyone had shown. They'd even gone around the table and let her know what it meant to have her there this past month. Grandma Geri had made it to the table and started off the words of encouragement. Becca had come, in spite of her heartache, and Todd as well, though he didn't quite seem himself. And no wonder, given the bombshell he'd heard yesterday. And Libby had come from Raleigh—with a guy named Omar—both of them sitting across the table from Travis. Strange vibe *that* was.

Now, at dusk, Stephanie was taking a walk alone, thinking through her life and what her time in Hope Springs had meant. She missed Lindell terribly and looked forward to seeing the rest of her family, but she didn't want to lose the connections she'd made here. And there was so much unresolved . . .

Her phone rang and she reached into her jacket pocket and frowned slightly.

"Hey, babe, something wrong?" She'd just talked to Lindell two hours ago. They hadn't been able to talk every day while he was in Haiti, and certainly not twice a day.

"I felt like I needed to call you back," he said. "You sounded kind of sad."

"Oh, I didn't mean to." She really hadn't. She'd shared some of what had been going on in Hope Springs, but thought she'd done a good job of sounding upbeat and ready to get home. "Babe, I'm the last person you should be worried about while you're down there. I'm fine."

"I know, but . . . I prayed about it, and I don't see why you need to leave Hope Springs tomorrow."

"Why do you say that?"

"You set your departure date to match mine, but seems like Hope Springs is your own little mission trip."

He paused to answer someone's question, and she could hear voices and outdoor noise in the background.

He continued, "I've never seen you this into anything. Just the way you update me about your grandmother and the time you spend with her . . . this is impacting your life. And it's a season you will likely never have again. Not trying to be morbid, Steph, but I'm a doctor.

Grandma Geri's prognosis isn't good. You're spending valuable time there, and there's no reason for you to rush back."

"Are you saying you don't miss me?"

"I miss you so much I call you way more than I should," he said. "But it's not about me. I'm seeing that more than ever down here. Sometimes we have to live sacrificially, think of others. That's what you're doing. And I feel like I need to support you in that."

The wind whipped across Stephanie's face as her mind walked through all he was saying. "So what do you think? Another week or so? I don't want to be gone from home *too* long."

"I think God will let us know. Babe, I've got to go. I love you."

"Love you too. Call me the minute you reach the States."

"Will do."

Stephanie held the phone. *Really, God? You would have me spend more time here in Hope Springs?* She hadn't considered the possibility until Lindell suggested it. And it let her know how far she'd come in one month. She wasn't fighting it.

CHAPTER THIRTY-FIVE

Wednesday, February 3

Chemo on Wednesday provided the first opportunity for Janelle to really talk to Grandma Geri about Aunt Gwynn and Pastor Jim, though she hadn't planned to bring it up. She had the playing cards, DVDs, and magazines ready as usual. But instead Grandma Geri wanted to unload more of what she'd been carrying.

"She sees my sister as her grandmother, you know." Grandma Geri had focused the conversation on Keisha.

Janelle was still making sure she had all the pieces. "That's Aunt Floretta, right? Your sister in Jersey? So when Aunt Gwynn left Hope Springs, she went to stay with her?"

"That's right. Gwynn couldn't go back to school, and she couldn't stay here. Would've been too much talk. The plan was that Floretta would take care of her while she was pregnant, and then Gwynn would come back."

"But she never did."

"No. She decided to keep the baby." Grandma Geri paused. "Elwood and I told her she couldn't bring the baby to Hope Springs. What if people saw a resemblance or somehow or other put it together that it was Jim's? We thought we were persuading her to go ahead and give the baby up. Instead we convinced her to stay away once she kept it."

Janelle was careful. "Grandma, why did you and Grandpa worry so much what people thought? Seems like that's what drove this whole thing."

Her grandmother took a minute to respond. "That's just how it was. You didn't do certain things. You didn't get pregnant, and you certainly didn't get entangled with another race. Gwynn managed to do both."

"So Aunt Floretta helped raise Keisha, didn't she?"

"Gwynn and Keisha lived with Floretta for years. Floretta was like a second mother to that little girl. To this day Keisha calls her Grandma." Grandma Geri looked away.

"And you kept in touch with Aunt Floretta?"

"That was my only connection with my daughter and grand-daughter," Grandma Geri said. "Floretta would try to get Gwynn on the phone, but she'd refuse."

Janelle was silent a minute, mulling her family history. "I knew Aunt Gwynn got pregnant in college and had to leave, and you and Grandpa wanted her to give the baby up for adoption. And I knew she went to stay with Aunt Floretta." She tried to put herself in her aunt's shoes. "I always thought she stayed away from Hope Springs because she was bitter toward you and Grandpa—which I guess is true. But I'm sure a lot of it was not wanting to be near the Dillons either. I couldn't imagine seeing his parents time and again, knowing they couldn't or wouldn't acknowledge Keisha as their grandbaby. And I especially couldn't imagine seeing Jim with his family. I can see why she stayed away." She realized what she'd just said. "Sorry, Grandma."

Grandma Geri seemed to be mulling their history as well. "I've sent letters apologizing over the years because I hate how it all happened," she said. "But for the life of me, I don't know if we would handle it any differently if we could go back. I know what life would've been like for them, for all of us."

"For a while," Janelle said, "till people got over it. And so what if they didn't? Aunt Gwynn, Jim, and the baby could've moved elsewhere."

"Jan, it always sounds plain in hindsight."

Janelle lapsed into her own thoughts for a while. Then, "Mom and Dad used to drive up to Jersey sometimes when we were young. So I got to know Keisha a little even though we never really kept in touch." She looked at her grandmother. "Have you met her even once?"

"Never. Only seen pictures."

Janelle didn't know what to say.

❧

Janelle heard a light knock on the side door Wednesday evening as she and Stephanie cleaned the kitchen. "Hello?" a voice said.

"Come on in, Todd."

Travis was with him. The guys were dressed in slacks and button-downs, their Wednesday evening Bible study attire.

Stephanie looked over her shoulder from her place at the sink. "I guess we should feel guilty that we weren't at Bible study tonight—at either church."

Travis pulled out a chair and sat down. "From what I'm hearing, that Saturday morning diner study is what's happening. I'm thinking about crashing."

"I've heard the same," Todd said.

"So what's up, guys?" Janelle said. "This is looking rather official."

Todd glanced at Travis. "I'm on a mission. Travis is here for moral support, I guess." He gave a wry smile. "I was hoping you could help me."

Janelle sat down at the table.

"I know your family's trying to get in touch with your aunt Gwynn, but my focus is on Keisha. I wondered if you could call and introduce us."

"I don't know, Todd. It's been years since I talked to her. I'm not even sure I have the right number."

"If you don't, could you get it?"

"I guess . . . but there's no guarantee she'll get on the phone. Do you know what you'll say?"

Todd sighed. "No idea. I don't even want to plan it out. I'm praying for God to make the rough places smooth."

Janelle nodded. "I like that. I'll start praying that myself." She got up and found her phone. "Want me to try right now?"

"That's what I was hoping."

Stephanie put the last pan she'd been washing in the rack to dry and came to the table.

Janelle took a breath and tapped in the number. In light of everything that had happened, she didn't know what to say to her own cousin. How much did Keisha know?

"Whoever's number this is," she told them, "it's ringing." Seconds later a woman answered. "Hello . . . is this Keisha?"

"Yes, this is Keisha. Hi, Janelle."

"How'd you know who it was?"

"You're in my contacts," she said. "You must have had the same number for a long time."

"Likewise." Janelle smiled into the silence. "How have you been?"

"You don't have to make small talk, Janelle. I know why you're calling."

"You do?"

"Mom said everyone's trying to get in touch with her, that you all know who my father is now."

"So you already knew?" Janelle hadn't been sure.

Todd was focused on Janelle's every word.

"Yes, I knew."

She sounded so calm. Janelle was the one who had to get her bearings. "Well, I'm actually here with, um . . . your brother, I guess I could say. Jim's son, Todd. He wants me to introduce you two, if that's okay."

Keisha didn't respond.

Janelle looked at Todd. "Keisha?"

"I'm not sure, but if he's sitting right there . . . you can put me on speaker."

Janelle wasn't so sure this was a good idea either. "Okay, just a sec." She put the phone on the table, making a face at Todd to warn him it might not go well, and pushed the speaker button. "Keisha, as I said, Todd is here with me. Just to tell you a little about him, he's my age, thirty-four, married, with two kids who are four and two. They moved to Hope Springs from St. Louis about a month ago. He took over as pastor of Calvary Church." She paused to see if Keisha would say anything, but she didn't. "And, Todd, this is Keisha."

Janelle didn't know what else to say. She was pretty sure Keisha was married, but she didn't know about kids.

Todd leaned forward. "Hi, Keisha, I'm so glad to meet you by phone."

"Did you already know about me?" Keisha asked.

"No. I learned for the first time on Saturday."

"I knew about you," Keisha said.

Todd cleared his throat. "I'd love to know more about you. Are you married? Any kids?"

"I got married four years ago. We have a boy, Jason, who's three."

"That's awesome," Todd said. "And you live in New Jersey?"

"That's right, in Neptune."

"So if you don't mind my asking," he said, "how long have you known who your dad was?"

"My mother told me the whole story when I was twelve."

They all looked surprised.

"Really?" Todd said. "Wow. Did you . . . did you ever want to come to Hope Springs to meet this side of your family?"

Keisha hesitated a little. "Well . . . from what I understood, it was never really an option." She paused. "Do you mind if I speak plainly?"

"Please do," Todd said.

"I'm sure you have warm and fuzzy feelings about your family, Todd. And I understand your dad just passed, so I'm mindful of showing respect. But the truth is that your grandparents didn't want me because I'm black, and your dad went along with the status quo for most of my life. I honestly have a real problem with your grandfather calling himself a pastor—your father too—and yet living with the obvious prejudice they had toward black people."

Janelle looked at the rest of them with wide eyes.

It took Todd a few seconds to recover. "You don't mince words, that's for sure. In all fairness, Keisha, I hear what you're saying about Granddad, but I don't see how you could say that about my dad. In his letter to Grandma Geri, he spoke of his love for your mother."

"He was willing to live his life without telling a soul about me. If I were white, would that have been the case?"

"I think back then any pregnancy out of wedlock was taboo, especially in a small town. It often meant the girl going away—"

"Or it meant getting married, if you were the right color."

Janelle had never heard such pointed discussion, but then, she'd never spoken with someone who'd had to reconcile such family history. "Keisha, I'm kind of surprised you answered the phone given the way you feel about everything."

"My mother is the one who would rather avoid than engage, so she doesn't answer calls. I don't have a problem engaging the issue. I'm glad it's finally out."

Todd gave them a tentative glance before he continued. "Keisha, what would you think about meeting in person? My family and I could plan a trip up there or . . ."

"Or my family could come to Hope Springs?" Keisha chuckled for the first time, but she didn't sound amused.

Janelle weighed her next words carefully. "Actually, Keisha," she said, "it might be a good time to consider coming to Hope Springs. I don't know if you've heard that Grandma Geri has advanced-stage lung cancer. I know that she's . . . Well, she's never met you either."

Keisha was slow to respond. "I'll have to give it some thought, to know if I can open myself up to meeting Todd or my mom's mom. It would have to be from the heart, from a real desire to establish a relationship, and I don't know if I'm there yet. I'll pray about it."

The four of them in Grandma Geri's kitchen looked somber.

Todd stared at the phone, nodding. "Thank you, Keisha. Do you mind if I get your phone number from Janelle?"

"I don't mind."

"Take care, Keisha," Janelle said, and ended the call.

"Well, that was interesting." Stephanie blew out a breath and sat back.

Todd looked troubled. "I've always seen my dad and granddad as great men of God. She nicely and calmly called them prejudiced. That's taking it a bit far, don't you think? Janelle, Stephanie . . . your grandparents took the same position."

"They all accepted the status quo regarding skin color," Janelle said. "What I heard Keisha saying is that she expected more from them as pastors."

"No matter how nice and calm Keisha sounded, we'd be crazy if we didn't understand how hurt she has to have been over all this,"

Travis said. "Neither set of grandparents wanted her around, and that came to include her father as well, who never acknowledged her until late in his life. Jim had a good heart. But when you look at it from her perspective . . ." He shrugged. "Can't say I blame her."

Todd retreated into his thoughts.

"I was just thinking," Stephanie said, "how powerful the status quo can be. People just don't want to break from the norm."

"That's interesting, Steph," Janelle said, "because that's been on my mind even before this revelation, and now even more so." She looked at Todd and Travis. "I was planning to talk to the two of you this week about that very thing."

CHAPTER THIRTY-SIX

Saturday, February 6

A week after her dismissal from Worth & Purpose, Becca was still struggling to get her bearings. She had no problem sitting down in her disappointment, as Janelle had advised—her problem was getting back up. Maybe if she could've found that hole to hide in, she could've recouped by now. As it was, life kept finding her—throwing reminders of what could've been.

Her agent had called first thing Monday morning. As if she needed confirmation, he let her know she wouldn't be getting a book deal after all, ever. She'd footnoted that last word in her mind, because it was true. Only the big-platform people got nonfiction book contracts. Those playing small ball could stick to their blogs. And she wasn't even sticking to that.

She had yet to update it. People had been posting comments on her last entry, asking how things went, letting her know they'd been praying. She couldn't address it yet. She wanted to get to a better place first, a place of peace, where she could say God must have a better plan and purpose and mean it. Or where she could quote, "All things work together for good . . ."—one of her favorite promises—and believe the promise applied to her and this situation. She felt silly for even redesigning the blog. If she hadn't paid a fee for it, she'd delete it just as she had her Facebook fan page.

Becca groaned aloud, hearing her own funk as she swept the kitchen floor. She wanted to break out of it but she couldn't. She wished Worth & Purpose had never entered her orbit. That's what bothered her most. She wished God could just tell her why He opened the door only to slam it shut. *What was the point, Lord? What were You trying to teach me? That I should never dream? That I could never have ministry success?*

"Hey, Bec, I've got an idea to run by you."

Todd had gone over to the church for an early morning meeting. The kids were sleeping late.

She held the broom. "What's up?"

"At the meeting this morning we were talking about ministries already operating at Calvary and ones we'd like to implement." He grabbed a banana from the fruit basket on the counter. "Calvary has never had a formal women's ministry. There was a unanimous feeling in the group that you'd be the perfect person to head that up."

Becca shook her head. "Sorry, Todd, but that doesn't sound appealing in the least. The women's ministry at our old church had Bible studies on Tuesday morning and Wednesday evening, retreats, fun Friday night workshop sessions. If I *were* interested, that's the kind of ministry I'd want to head up." She looked at him. "What do they even do here?"

"I think that's the point, Bec. We'd need someone to fashion a women's ministry. But you're right, it won't be like our old church. We just don't have the numbers."

"Well, even if they had the numbers, I doubt I'd be interested. I don't want to give a single thought to 'ministry.'"

Todd looked out the back window as Becca continued sweeping.

"Have you heard anything from Keisha?" she asked. She'd been trying not to let her issues take precedence over what Todd was going through.

He glanced back at her. "No. But we only talked to her Wednesday. I'd be shocked to hear from her again this year, quite frankly."

"I know we keep saying it, but I still can't believe your dad was in love with Gwynn—and they conceived a love child. That just blows my mind."

"Yours?" He faced the window again. "It's almost tragic in a way, to love so deeply but have that love denied because of the thinking of the time."

She whisked under the table. "I'm really hoping you and Keisha can develop some kind of relationship."

"I'm praying about that," he said.

Becca couldn't say the same. She didn't have the faith to pray and believe for much of anything right now.

Her phone dinged on the counter, letting her know she had a text.

"I know it's Janelle," she said. "She's been trying to get me to go to the Bible study at the diner this morning."

"I think it'd be great if you went," Todd said. "At the least you'd get out of the house, get your mind off things."

And get away from that computer. She kept finding things to look up despite herself. A little while ago she'd gone to the Worth & Purpose website and seen that the site had been scrubbed of her existence.

She sighed. "I may as well." She was curious what a "diner Bible study" was like anyway, especially one led by Sara Ann.

❧

Becca walked into the diner with Janelle and Stephanie, a little late. The hostess led them to an area where several women were gathered.

Becca noticed the cross-section right away—black, white, older, younger. And they all looked actively engaged in the discussion.

The three of them completed a third table, clustered together in a corner of the diner. The woman next to Becca smiled at them. "We're talking about the promises of God," she said, "focusing on promises we don't hear very often."

Sara Ann was at the middle table and had the women laughing about something. "I don't see why y'all don't think this is fun," she said. She was grinning. "All right, any more promises we don't hear people claiming very often? I haven't heard anyone say, 'Whom the Lord loves, He chastens.'" She laughed at the grumbles. "What? It's a promise, ain't it?"

"I've got one."

A hand went up at the table next to Becca. "'In this world you will have trouble. But take heart! I have overcome the world.'" The woman looked up from her Bible. "Call me weird if you want, but I like that trouble is guaranteed—seriously! It comforts me because things *do* go wrong."

"That's for sure," another woman said, as heads nodded.

"So I tell myself, 'Beverly, this shouldn't shock you. What did Jesus say? You're gonna have trouble in this world.' And I remind myself that He's overcome the world."

"I love that," Sara Ann said. She looked around for others.

Another hand went up. "I've got one, only because God hit me over the head with it this week. 'Before honor comes humility.'" The woman was older and looked familiar, probably from Calvary. "I tend to want the honor, but not the humility," she said. "But humility brings us closest to Christ. At least that's the message God wants me to get. I'm still working on it."

Becca was still staring at the woman after she'd finished. It was as if she'd been talking only to her. The words had hit Becca over the head too, like a two-by-four.

Sara Ann had already moved on to someone else, so Becca got up and tiptoed over to the woman, crouching down beside her. "Excuse me, what verse is that?"

"Proverbs 15:33."

"Thank you."

Becca went back, leafed through her Bible, and read it again.

"Before honor comes humility."

She didn't know why it was hitting her, but it was. Humility. Such an obvious, everyday word, but suddenly she wasn't sure what it meant. Not in the way she needed to. What was it supposed to mean *for her*?

Becca felt such a stirring inside that she knew one thing for sure—she had to find out.

CHAPTER THIRTY-SEVEN

L ibby, you're using all the red!" Tiffany came around the table, picked up the bottle of red paint, and moved it closer to her. Libby put her fists to her hips. "Tiffy, are you being stingy? After I bought all this paint in Raleigh and brought it with me? I know you didn't think it was just for the kids." She went and got the bottle and poured more red into her paint tray.

Janelle watched with amusement. "Tiffany, you should know better than to mess with Libby when she's working on a master-piece. She thinks she's got skills."

"She *does* have skills." Becca peeked at Libby's work while she helped control Ethan's wildly flinging paintbrush. "Those red apples on the tree are popping."

"Why, thank you." Libby bowed. "Is it too late to pursue the path of starving artist?"

Stephanie broke her focus on her own creation and looked up. "Long as you're willing to starve."

"Good point." Libby twirled her brush in the air as if considering. "I'll be at work on time Monday."

"Mommy, I need help." Claire held her brush above the white paper. "I don't know how to paint a Chihuahua."

"Has to be a Chihuahua?" Becca chewed her lip. "Can't be any old dog?"

"Of course not, Mom." Janelle winked at her. "We watched *Beverly Hills Chihuahua* last night, remember?"

"Oh, what was I thinking? Of course it has to be a Chihuahua." Becca looked at Claire's paper. "But, sweetheart, I wouldn't know how to draw one."

"I can do it." Daniel was standing over his paper, putting light strokes of blue on the sky.

Claire gave him a skeptical eye. "Can you really?"

Tiffany gave a matter-of-fact nod. "Sure he can."

He took the same brush and with a few strokes painted a Chihuahua on the newspaper covering the table.

Claire's face lit up. "That's my Chihuahua!"

A rap on the door sounded as Daniel walked around to paint the dog on Claire's paper.

"It's Dee!"

Tiffany and Claire threw their brushes on the newspaper and dashed to the side door with their paint smocks on.

Janelle followed and opened up, looking first at the little girl with the big smile. "Hey, Miss Dee."

"Hi, Miss Janelle," Dee said, but Janelle barely heard it because Tiffany and Claire had her by the hands, pulling her inside, exclaiming, "Come on, we're already painting."

Janelle looked up then, and instantaneously she was in Kory's arms.

He held her with a sweetness. "I haven't seen you since Sunday." She felt his breath on her ear. "That's six whole days . . . feels like forever."

"For me too. Even though we've talked on the phone, it's not the same."

She allowed herself to savor the feel of her head on his shoulder, his arms around her waist, the scent of his sweater. But only for a moment. She stepped back and led him inside.

He smiled as he entered the kitchen. "You all have quite the art lab going on. Thanks for inviting Dee to join the fun."

Someone had already put Dee in a smock and tied it in back. Libby was outfitting her with a brush, paper, and a plastic tray to squeeze her paints into.

"Libby's idea," Janelle said. "I was wondering what the kids could do on a lazy Saturday, and she said she'd bring paint."

Janelle and Kory stood a little away from the table. He lowered his voice. "I can think of something for the two of us to do. Why don't we go for a ride?"

Janelle replied with a semi-frown. "A ride where?"

Kory shrugged. "Wherever."

"I can't. Aunt Gladys is with Grandma in the family room, but we've got a house full of kids here. Wouldn't be right for me to just leave."

"Go!"

Janelle smirked at the women. "I thought this was a private conversation."

As she turned back to Kory, her heart skipped a little. Time alone with him would indeed be very special. And he was right, the "where" didn't matter.

"Hey," she announced, "Kory and I are going for a little ride. We won't be long."

"Take your time," Libby said, face to her painting. "We got it covered."

Janelle grabbed her jacket and followed him out. He walked to the passenger side, opened the door, and she brushed past him as she got in. She could count on one hand the number of times she'd ridden in the car with him. Still felt like a new experience, one that gave her a feeling of anticipation.

"Where to?" he asked over the start of the engine.

"I have no idea," she said.

"How about Stony Park?"

"Isn't that in Wilson? Never been, but I've heard some of my younger cousins talk about it." She narrowed her eyes at him playfully. "Is that where you took your high school sweethearts?"

Kory drove off, wagging his eyebrows at her. "I shall neither confirm nor deny."

A short ride down the highway later, Kory took the Wilson exit. Signs appeared almost immediately, directing them to the park. They drove about two miles, then turned into the park, and the sunlight dimmed slightly as they rode beneath a canopy of trees. They weren't lush, as they were in summer, but the overhead effect was beautiful nonetheless.

Kory took a road that branched left. Janelle hadn't seen a single soul yet, maybe because it was winter. Everything was peaceful. Even the two of them had lapsed into a comfortable silence.

He parked the car in an almost empty lot, and they got out and started walking. Janelle shivered a little with the forties temperature and zipped her jacket to the top. Kory took her hand, rubbing the back with his thumb. They nestled closer together as they stepped onto a walking trail. In that moment, there wasn't a single place she'd rather be.

His hand wrapped tighter around hers. "I think this is the closest we've ever come to a date."

She watched their feet walking slowly in sync. "But it's definitely not a date."

"Okay. What should we call it?"

"Two friends taking a Saturday afternoon stroll."

". . . holding hands, hearts beating wildly . . ."

Janelle laughed. "Hearts beating wildly? You might be a bit of a romantic, Mr. Miller."

"Maybe a little," he said.

The tree-lined path narrowed, moving them closer. Janelle looked up at him. "How are you feeling? About Monday?"

"It's been on my mind a lot this week. If I'm feeling anything, it's relief. I'm ready to put this part of my life behind me."

"Not even a little sadness?"

He thought about it. "For Dee, yes. She didn't ask to be caught up in all this. But not for me. Not anymore."

"Is Shelley coming to the hearing?"

"She said she is. I don't know when she's flying in. She told Dee she wanted to see her, but I haven't heard anything from her since."

"What does Dee think?"

"Hasn't even mentioned it, which is weird because she doesn't forget things like that. Maybe she's guarding against disappointment in case she doesn't see her, or I don't know . . . I'm seeing distance between the two of them as far as Dee is concerned. Maybe she just doesn't care."

"Oh, I hope it's not the latter." Janelle's heart went out to the little girl. "She needs her mother. I really hope they get time together."

Kory sighed. "If Shelley doesn't start making a real effort soon . . . She hardly knows Dee at all."

They continued in silence, which made every other sight and sound come alive. "Are you hearing all these songs out here? It's like we happened into a bird convention."

"Look up there." Kory pointed to a tree branch directly ahead of them.

"Ooh, pretty cardinal. So striking against the bare branch."

The bird looked as if it were staring at them, so they stopped and stared back. Janelle took a tiny step forward and imitated a birdcall. It flew away.

Kory looked at her as they walked on. "What was that?"

"I was trying to speak its language."

"You probably spoke the blue jay war cry or something. He thought you were the enemy."

Janelle laughed. "Well, we certainly don't want to start a war— wait, I just thought of something," she said. "There are no snakes out here, are there?"

"Probably only nonpoisonous ones."

"*Probably* . . ." Janelle stopped dead in her tracks and surveyed every inch of space around them. "If I see a snake of any sort, I'll have a heart attack on the spot."

"They're not thinking about you." He tugged her along. "You gotta get a little tougher, city girl. You're in the country now."

Their path forked, and Kory took them right. They came to a picturesque spot with a beautiful lake view. Two mountain bike riders came whizzing by, and they moved quickly aside. Janelle turned and kept looking, thinking it'd be nice if she and Kory did that one day. She hadn't been bike riding in years.

"Speaking of the country," he said, "any idea how long you'll be down here?"

She'd wondered herself lately. "It's hard to say. Grandma Geri's doing fairly well, considering, and her chemo will be done soon. But I'm not sure what it means. If the chemo did what they hoped, it might mean she has a year instead of a few months to live." Her eyes were focused on the water. "I don't know if I'll go back home after this school semester or what. I'll have to see how she's doing."

"Do you want to go back?"

Goose bumps came with the question. "We still have our house in Maryland and other commitments we've put on hold."

"Janelle." He moved in front of her, still holding her hand. "Would you consider relocating permanently to North Carolina?"

"What reason would I have?"

"Me. Us."

Janelle sighed and let his hand drop for the first time since they'd started walking. "I can't go there, Kory. I can't think of the future, can't think in terms of an *us*." She walked ahead.

He pulled her to a stop again. "Can you in two days?"

She looked at him, but barely. "I don't know . . . Thinking about the future is scary regardless."

"It's scary for me too." Kory's eyes bored into hers. "But somehow, it's a little less scary when I picture you in it."

"Kory, still . . . asking if I'd relocate is awfully premature. Technically, we've never even had a date."

"Okay." Kory took her hand back. "Will you go on an official date with me? How about Monday night?" His boyish grin penetrated her soul. "We don't have to go anywhere or do anything. Just being with you is enough."

This was the moment Janelle had longed for sixteen years ago, hearing him say he wanted to be with her, to build an "us." If anything, this moment meant more, knowing that after so much time had passed, they had found their way back to one another.

She looked deep into his eyes. "It's a date, Mr. Miller."

He lifted her off the ground in an embrace. "I don't think I've ever been this happy about a *date*."

She continued gazing into his eyes as he lowered her slowly to the ground, his arms locked tight around her. Their faces touched, and she knew if she closed her eyes she'd be lost in his embrace. Lost in the feeling of a kiss she'd known only once . . . and had never forgotten.

So she kept her eyes open and took a small step back, grabbing his hand instead. She would save the kiss. For their first date.

CHAPTER THIRTY-EIGHT

Sunday, February 7

J anelle, it's not a big deal if I stay at the house."

"And it's not a big deal if you wear those jeans to church."

Libby plopped on the sofa and clicked the remote to catch the Sunday news programs. Janelle walked to the television and turned it off.

"Janelle, please. Get in the car. Go to church. Leave me in peace."

"But you're not listening to me," Janelle said. She sat next to her. "You said you would go if you had brought the right clothes, and I'm telling you it doesn't matter. I think it's awesome you want to go. Don't let something like that stop you."

"*Want to go* is an exaggeration. I said I was *willing* to go, and only because Grandma is finally up to going and said she wanted all her granddaughters to go too. I thought it would be nice to give her that, but then I realized I didn't have any clothes."

"People wear jeans all the time to my church in Maryland."

Libby looked at her. "Huh. Funny you're wearing a skirt today. Oh"—she sat forward and flung open her hands—"because you're not in Maryland! You know no one wears jeans at New Jerusalem."

"Want me to change and put on jeans?"

"Don't be silly."

"Mommy," Tiffany called. "Aunt Gladys said her and Grandma Geri are about to leave for church."

"Come here, Tiffy," Libby said. "Let me see what your momma put on you."

Tiffany came skipping in.

"Don't you look cute . . . in your nice church dress and patent leather shoes." Libby gave Janelle the eye.

"I'm ready," Stephanie called. "What's the verdict, Libby?"

"Not going," Libby yelled back.

"Even if I'm wearing jeans?"

"Let's see."

Stephanie strolled into the family room, modeling her denim down the carpeted runway, then striking a pose. "You know I get excited when it comes to breaking protocol. Come on, girl."

They heard the side door open and tiny feet running through the house, then they heard squeals.

"Tiffany, what's going on?" Janelle called.

Tiffany and Claire appeared in the family room.

"Claire's going to church with us!" Tiffany said.

They all looked at Claire. "Your mom and dad said it's okay?" Janelle asked.

"I asked and Dad said why not?"

The girls held hands, yelling, "Yaaay!" all the way out the door.

Libby raised her brow at the two of them and got up. "Oh, I'm *so* going to church today."

Libby wished she had a video camera to record facial expressions as their carload strolled up the walkway and into the church building.

It was bordering on comical. The second glances and stares almost made them seem like celebrities. She wondered which was drawing more attention, Steph's and her denim against the backdrop of suits and dresses, or Tiffany and Claire holding hands and swinging them as if they had not a care in the world.

"Hey, there's Dee!" Tiffany saw her friend coming through the glass door.

Janelle gave her a look. "Shh . . . inside voice, Tiff."

Kory and Dee walked in, and the girls did their best at low-volume squeals. Kory walked straight to Janelle and hugged her. Libby loved that he didn't play coy. Janelle was obviously special to him, and he made a point of showing it.

As they waited for an usher to seat them, Libby saw that Travis had gone out front to talk to people coming into church. The women in particular seemed quite enamored with him. There was no doubt he looked especially handsome in a suit.

Someone opened the door wide, and Libby caught Travis's eye from just inside. She turned away slightly. She hadn't expected to see him before the service. And afterward she'd be able to slip out. She moved up with her group, waiting for the usher to return.

"Good Sunday morning."

Great.

"Good morning, Travis." Janelle and Stephanie said it simultaneously.

Kory shook his hand. "Hey, good morning, Pastor Trav."

"Daniel, my man." Travis gave the little boy a super firm hand-shake that made him laugh, hugged Tiffany, then stopped. "And Claire? Does your dad know where you are?"

Claire giggled. "Yes."

Libby looked at him. "Good morning."

"Good morning, yourself." He smiled at her. "You know you didn't have to dress up."

"You're funny."

He held her gaze. "Good to see you here."

An usher led their group up the center aisle. Libby saw her grandmother and Aunt Gladys in front. They filed into a pew almost two-thirds of the way back and chatted until the band started playing. Five people came out to lead praise and worship, which was new. Libby remembered only a choir before.

The congregation stood, and Travis moved up the side aisle to the front row. Libby wished Janelle was sitting near her—Stephanie, the girls, and Daniel were in between—because she wanted to ask about these little changes. Seemed like Pastor Richards used to have a processional down the middle aisle to start the service and he sat on the platform.

Since she didn't know the words to the first song, and there was no big screen, Libby's eyes drifted around the sanctuary. The makeup of the people had changed too. When she used to come on visits to Hope Springs, she'd said that everyone was her grandmother's age—an exaggeration, but only a slight one. She never would've thought New Jerusalem could draw an influx of people her age and younger. She wondered what they'd do if they outgrew this place. It was already crowded, and people were still arriving.

A family with young kids came in, and behind them, a woman. Everything about her was striking—clothes, hair, poise. Libby saw an usher approach her, but she only whispered something and remained where she was. Libby guessed she was trying to find her family—until she realized who the woman was and which family she was trying to find.

"Excuse me." Libby moved quickly past Stephanie and the kids to get to Janelle. She spoke into her ear. "You will not guess who just walked in."

Janelle shifted her head slightly to see, then shifted back. Her eyes said it all. She whispered to Kory, whose head snapped back. He looked forward again, his mind clearly figuring what to do. He whispered something to Janelle, left the pew, and walked to the back. A minute later he and Shelley had left the building.

Kory's heart was beating fast, and he couldn't fathom why. He knew Shelley was coming to Carolina for the court hearing tomorrow, and he knew she wanted to see Dee. But showing up unannounced like this made him think she was up to something. The last thing he wanted was for Shelley's antics to interfere with him and Janelle.

He walked outside, well away from the front entrance, before confronting her. "What are you doing here, Shelley?"

Her hair blew in the breeze. "I thought you'd be pleased that I came to church."

"How did you know what church I attended?"

"You haven't changed the password on your bank account. I saw the canceled checks."

How could he have overlooked that? He hated the thought of her in his business. He knew what he'd be doing when he got home.

"Instead of snooping, you could've just *asked*. Would've been nice to know when and where you were planning to pick up Dee."

She tucked her hair behind her ear. "I do want to see Dee, but my main motivation was seeing you."

"Me." She was definitely up to something. "Why?"

"I need to talk to you."

"We're talking right now."

She held her arms through her coat. "Kory, can we go somewhere? It's cold out here."

"Shelley, I'm not in the mood for games. Tell me right here what you need to talk to me about."

She hesitated. "I want to talk to you about postponing the court hearing."

He stared at her, trying to keep his head about him. "We can talk in my car."

He'd parked on a different street around the corner. Leading the way, he went to the driver's side, opened it, and unlocked the other door so she could get in. He started the engine, turned on the heat, and looked straight ahead.

"You won't even look at me, Kory?"

"Why do you want to postpone the hearing?"

Shelley sighed. "Martin and I are no longer together."

He looked at her. "What does that have to do with the hearing?"

"Kory, I feel like you're being so cold toward me."

He stared at her, awaiting an answer.

She looked down at the handbag in her lap. "He decided to go back to his wife. And he chose to wait until a week before the hearing when I had completely planned our trip to the justice of the peace and a celebration afterward, and after everyone in litigation had been made aware." She blew out a breath. "I was humiliated. Stayed out of the office all week, and I don't know if I'm going back."

"I'm sorry, Shelley," he said. "I must be slow. I got nowhere in that story any illumination as to what it has to do with our divorce hearing."

Shelley looked out the passenger window, then back down at her bag. "It was like everything you've ever said came back to haunt me. You told me the things I was chasing after would leave me empty, and it was true. You told me I'd find out that Jesus is who I really need." She looked up at him. "And now I know how true that is too."

"All of a sudden you've seen the light." He nodded. "Okay. That's wonderful."

"Kory, I have. I . . . I see how wrong I was. What I did to you . . . to our family . . . I've never apologized, but I'm sorry."

Am I in the Twilight Zone?

"Shelley, God has already brought me to the place where I can forgive you. I accept your apology." He paused. "And really I wish you well on your newfound spiritual journey. That's an awesome thing."

"Well." She took more than a few seconds to continue. "I had hoped we could share the journey . . . That's why I wanted to postpone the hearing, so we could talk about maybe reconciling."

His incredulity was so great he almost laughed. "You . . . want to talk about reconciling? You can't be serious."

"I knew you would respond that way, especially after what I did to you and the way I've behaved since. But, Kory, I know you understand that people can change. I've *changed*. I'm not the person I was before." She touched his arm when he looked away. "I know you loved me at one time. I know you believe in reconciliation, because you tried to reconcile after I left. I'm asking you now to give us another chance."

Kory looked her squarely in the face. "You're right. I did try to reconcile. I was willing to forgive you for the affair and try to rebuild our marriage for the sake of our family. You laughed in my face, more than once, and I finally had to move on." He adjusted the heat down. "So, no, Shelley, I'm not interested in giving it a chance. My plans are to proceed with the divorce hearing tomorrow."

"Will you think about it overnight?"

"There's nothing to think about."

She was silent. Then, "Can I spend time with Dee today?"

"Of course you can. As much time as you'd like."

"That was Janelle you were sitting with in there, wasn't it?"

"It was."

Shelley looked away.

"Sermon's probably almost over," Kory said, "but I'd like to go back in. You're welcome to do the same. We can talk afterward about plans for Dee."

She nodded.

Kory turned off the engine, got out of the car, and shut his door. He waited for Shelley to get out, clicked the remote lock, and walked back inside.

CHAPTER THIRTY-NINE

J anelle felt her heart breaking into a million tiny pieces.

She'd heard what happened with Shelley, and she'd heard Kory's response. But she could also hear what God was saying deep inside. And it was killing her.

"Janelle, I don't understand why you're upset." Kory gently pushed the hair from her face and wiped her tears. "It's nothing for you to worry about."

As much as she'd tried to hold them back, her emotions had reached the point of no return. A steady stream of tears fell as they sat on Grandma Geri's back porch swing. How could she convey what was in her heart when she barely understood it . . . and certainly didn't like it?

She tried again to collect herself. "You know I've been praying for her. I've been praying for God to get hold of her heart, help her see that what she did was wrong, and set her on a new path in Christ. And that's just what you're saying has happened."

Kory gestured with his hands. "No, I'm saying that's what *she's* saying has happened. Shelley is a con artist. I learned that the hard way. She knows what to say and how to say it. I believe she was truthful about one thing—she was humiliated. And now to save face she wants to show the world, 'I didn't want Martin anyway. I wanted my family back all along.'" He added, "She also doesn't like that her relationship with Martin fell apart, yet she sees me building one with someone else."

"I know she's been all the things you've said. But who's to say she hasn't changed? Redemption is possible for us all."

"You're right, and I'm not saying there's no way she could've changed. But I *am* mindful of her history, so it's hard for me to believe it simply because she says it." He focused on Janelle. "But even if I believe she's changed, I don't see why you're upset."

"Because I feel like you need to go back to her."

"What?"

"Kory, she's saying she's changed and wants her family back. God is a God of grace and mercy and second chances—"

"Yes. And He can be that to her, without me."

"But what if He wants her to experience that *through* you." Saying it made her heart hurt more.

"Janelle, if God wanted me to reconcile with Shelley, don't you think He would tell *me*? Don't you think He would give me the desire?"

"Did you pray about it?"

"I can't count the number of times I prayed about it."

"I don't mean all the months prior. After you talked to her today?"

"No. I have a peace about moving on."

"That's just it, Kory. That's what's upsetting me. Because I *don't* have a peace about moving on. I don't want to be what stands in the way of God healing your marriage." Emotion welled afresh. "I feel like I have to let you go . . . before we've had a chance to really be together."

Kory closed his eyes, hands clasped atop his head. "I can't believe we're having this conversation. This can't be happening, not when we're so close . . ." He got up and walked to the edge of the porch. "Why did she have to show up today? Why is she still messing up my life?"

Silence engulfed them as he looked out at the horizon. Janelle couldn't believe this was happening either. She'd felt like a schoolgirl dreaming about their first date tomorrow night. She'd even written a journal entry this morning, thanking God for the special man David was and acknowledging that no one could take his place—but thanking Him also for allowing her heart to expand far enough to give someone else a place. She knew David would want her to enjoy the companionship of another man. It seemed so perfect that that man would be Kory, the one she had dreamed about so long ago.

Kory came to her and took her hand, lifting her out of the swing. He put his arms around her and held her. "I never told you this," he said, his voice a soft caress, "but after spending that first weekend with you, after that long walk on the last night and that kiss, I knew I had fallen in love with you." His lips brushed her face as he spoke. "It may have been silly and immature. It may have been just for that moment in time. But I loved you. And deep within me lodged the thought that one day we would be together."

Fresh tears streamed down Janelle's face.

"We grew up, we lost touch, we got married," he said, "and I let the thought go. But it returned when I saw you again at the funeral. And I wouldn't have thought it possible, but those same feelings from that night returned as if it were yesterday." He lifted her face with his finger. "Janelle, I love you."

"That's why it hurts, Kory. Because I love you too."

He brought her close, and she could feel his tears on her cheek. They stayed that way forever it seemed, afraid of what would happen when they let go.

"What if I pray, and I still don't feel God is telling me to reconcile? What if I go forward with the divorce tomorrow? What then?"

"I don't know. I just know I have to give you the space to do whatever God wants you to do. If you go through with the divorce . . . if the reconciliation doesn't happen . . . I can't think beyond right now."

"We might still have our first date tomorrow night."

"Don't, Kory." She couldn't set her heart on it. She looked into his eyes. "Promise you'll pray. Ask God His will. And whatever happens, we'll trust Him."

He sighed. "I'm having such a hard time with this, but I can do that. I promise I'll pray today, tonight, tomorrow morning. And we'll trust."

They lingered minutes more in the embrace. Finally Kory sighed again. "I guess I need to go."

Janelle couldn't speak. Certainly couldn't bring herself to say the word *good-bye*. She simply memorized the feel of his arms around her.

He slowly pulled away, kissed her cheek, and was gone.

⤾

"Have you flippin' lost your mind?" Libby had jumped up from the sofa and started pacing as if ready to right a wrong. "Tell me you've been inhaling meds at the hospital. Because that's the only explanation for sending that man back to his wife."

Janelle had come into the family room and collapsed on the sofa, her head resting on the arm. She spoke from the crook of her own arm. "I didn't send him back to his wife. You could say I sent Him to the Lord to ask what to do about his wife." She wanted to cry again. "I told him to ask God His will."

Libby came and stood directly in front of her. "You. Are. Crazy." She plunked down with a sigh on the sofa beside her. "I don't even know what else to say."

"Ummm . . . yeah, I'm having a hard time connecting the dots on this one," Stephanie said. "He wants to be with you. You want to be with him. You're looking kinda crazy to me too."

"Everything in me wants to call him back," Janelle admitted. "Maybe I *have* lost my mind." She sat straight up. "I'm calling him."

"No, Janelle." Becca had put Claire and Ethan down for a Sunday nap—along with Todd—and come to watch a movie with them. "You haven't lost your mind. You said you felt God wanted you to step back and give their marriage a chance. It had nothing to do with you and everything to do with Him. You wanted His will. How can that be cra—"

She stopped speaking, and Janelle looked up at her.

Becca rose from the recliner. "That's it." She stared into the distance. "Just like that."

"What?" Janelle said.

A fresh energy started Becca pacing in front of them. "I haven't been able to let go of that verse we heard yesterday at the diner—'Before honor comes humility.' Came home, looked up verses about humility . . . but it was like, whatever I was supposed to get was out here somewhere." She circled her hands in the air, then looked at Janelle. "And then I heard myself saying it to you."

"Okay, Janelle might understand what you're saying, but I'm not following." Stephanie shifted on the sofa. "You gotta break it down for a sista."

"Uh, I'm not following either actually," Janelle said.

"Okay." Becca was pacing again. "You know how the woman yesterday said we're most like Christ when we're humble? He *emptied* Himself, it says in Philippians, and God wants us to empty ourselves and be filled with Him . . . that's humility."

She sat back down on the edge of the recliner. "When I told Janelle that what she did had nothing to do with her and everything to do with God, that's when it hit me. For her it wasn't about self.

And it seems so unusual that someone would do that because, well, we all tend to be about self . . . I know I am." She sighed.

"I was focused on what being part of Worth & Purpose would do for me and my ministry. It was tempting to get caught up in the feeling that I was 'somebody' now, just because of the numbers . . . as if God didn't value all ministry the same." She shook her head. "What Sara Ann is doing in a diner in Hope Springs, North Carolina, is powerful ministry. What you all are doing for your grandmother is powerful ministry. Janelle, what you just showed us in that selfless act with Kory is powerful ministry . . . I'm ashamed that I thought of one as 'bigger' and more important than another."

"The best part, Becca," Janelle said, "is now you see God's purpose in it all. It wasn't that He wasn't answering your prayer. He had a better blessing to draw you closer to Him."

"So basically . . ." Stephanie was pondering. "You're saying Worth & Purpose was your boot camp experience like Hope Springs was mine."

"And Kory was mine." Janelle sighed.

Libby groaned. "I still think it's crazy. If I had a man *half* as good as Kory . . ."

"You'd do what?" Janelle asked. "Commit?"

"I didn't say that."

"What would you do?"

"Maybe I'd *think* about committing."

"What about Travis?" Stephanie said. "If you ask me, he still cares about you."

Libby was quiet. "He's a pastor. He has to."

Stephanie looked at her. "You know what I mean."

Libby stared downward for a long while. "Even if he did care, he couldn't act on it. I'm not . . . I'm not someone he could commit to. I don't live that type of life."

Janelle hadn't seen this vulnerable side of Libby in a long time. "Libby, what are you saying?"

Libby shrugged. "I've been intimate with other men, and I can't even talk like it's in the past. He needs a godly woman, and that's not . . . me." She shrugged again. "Which is fine. Can you picture me with a pastor? Small-town pastor at that? Please."

Janelle knew better and was struck by one thing—she and her cousin were on two different paths, living totally different lives, yet found themselves in the same place . . . each unable to have the one man her heart desired.

CHAPTER FORTY

Thursday, February 11

J anelle and Kory didn't get their first date Monday night. She knew what time the court hearing had been scheduled for—ten thirty a.m.—and she'd watched the hospital clock attentively. Kory was there, she just knew it. He would call or text her afterward to let her know he'd prayed and had a peace still about going forward. He and Shelley were officially over.

Eleven o'clock came, then eleven thirty, then three o'clock as they drove out of the hospital parking lot. By nightfall, she'd swung to the exact opposite—he and Shelley were back together. And as she awoke Thursday, that's where she remained.

Janelle lingered in bed. She had an hour before she needed to awaken Daniel for school. Grandma Geri had finished her third round of chemo and had an appointment with her oncologist late morning. Janelle hadn't heard her stirring yet. She had an urge to write in her journal.

From under the covers, she turned on her bedside lamp, hoping she wouldn't wake Stephanie in the other bed. She reached for the journal on the nightstand, opened it, and took the pen from inside. She turned to the last page on which she'd written, skipped a line, and wrote the date—February 11—and waited for words to spill from her heart.

Dear God,

It seems so strange to write to You about another man. For the last two years these pages have filled with the ups and downs of life without David . . . mostly the downs, as You know. But this morning, Lord, I really need to talk to someone about Kory. And You're the only One who can understand because You understand me better than anyone.

You know how deeply I feel, how much I like to reflect. You know how I love to dream even as I project the practical, commonsense side of myself. When Libby and Steph and Becca asked how I was doing this week, I told the truth. By Your grace I felt strengthened to move on again. But that wasn't the whole truth. How could I tell them that from that short period of life with Kory, I had something to mourn?

Janelle wiped her tears with the sleeve of her pajama top. She didn't care how much she cried. She wanted to cry. If she let all her tears out now, maybe they'd be done.

But, Lord, You know . . . I dreamed of our lives becoming one. I dreamed of our families becoming one. I saw in Kory a father for Daniel, and in Daniel a son for Kory. I dreamed of being a second mother to Dee, and oh how I dreamed of Dee and Tiffany as sisters. I could see that, Lord, the two of them growing up together, in the same classes, sharing clothes and shoes, talking into the night. I saw Kory as the strong man Tiffany will need in her life, a man who will love her unconditionally so that she'll have no need to seek pseudo love from an immature boy.

And, Lord, I dreamed of Kory as my husband. I knew he

still belonged to someone else, and You know how hard I tried not to think it. I would've never told him that. But in those unguarded moments of my soul, I dreamed of knowing his every mood, what he's like on lazy days around the house, how much he whines when he's sick. I dreamed of being his wife, of loving him with abandon and revealing myself without reservation.

And now, Lord, once again I must mourn—this time the loss of a dream. The loss of what almost was. It would seem almost silly if my heart weren't aching so.

She picked a tissue from the box and dabbed her face and another to blow her nose.

But, Lord, as much as it hurts, I pray Your best for Kory and Shelley. I pray that You heal their marriage. Renew their hopes and dreams and establish them. Be the bridge that leads them back to a strong connection of the heart. And sweet little Dee . . . thank You for returning her mother to her. I pray that you bond them as mother and daughter.

Her chest heaved from the quiet sobs that remained.

And finally, Lord, help me to cling to You, not David or Kory or even my grief. I want to cling to You and trust You. Help me to believe that You are working all things together for good in my life despite how it looks or feels.

Yours
Janelle

She stared at the page, then tucked the pen back into the journal and closed it. All the emotion had left her tired. She could sleep another two hours at least, but she forced herself up and out of bed. In the kitchen she started a pot of coffee. As she made her way to the bathroom, she heard a loud thump—and the sound of someone crying out.

Her heart was thumping itself as she rushed to the bedroom and stooped beside her grandmother.

"I don't know what's wrong," Grandma Geri said. "I tried to get out of bed and I just fell. I can't move."

Janelle jumped up. "I'm getting my phone to call 911. Be right back."

She ran and got her phone as Stephanie came out of the room.

"What's going on?" she said.

"Grandma can't move. I'm dialing 911."

Janelle ran back to her grandmother's side, Stephanie at her heels, telling the operator the emergency and her grandmother's overall condition.

"The ambulance will be here shortly, Grandma."

"I'll go call Dr. Reynolds and Aunt Gladys," Stephanie said.

Janelle sat beside her grandmother on the floor, holding her, feeling helpless, trying to be strong. She hoped nothing was broken. Grandma Geri continued to moan. "Dear Lord," Janelle prayed aloud, "please help my grandmother. Whatever's going on, please get her the help she needs quickly and heal her."

Daniel and Tiffany appeared at the bedroom door, looking frightened.

"What's wrong with Grandma?" Daniel said.

"I don't know yet, sweetheart. Say a prayer."

Janelle could hear the ambulance, and then Stephanie opening the door.

Todd entered with Stephanie and the paramedics, who brought a stretcher into the bedroom. Janelle moved out of their way and stood near the door.

"What happened?" Todd asked.

"She said she fell getting out of bed. She can't move." She paused, watching the paramedics tend to her. "I'm scared, Todd."

Todd closed his eyes, and Janelle knew he was praying.

"Why don't you let me take the kids to my house," he said. "That way you and Stephanie can both go to the hospital. I can get Daniel to school."

He ushered the kids to their room to get what they needed. Janelle and Stephanie watched the paramedics lift Grandma Geri carefully onto the stretcher and move her out. They got into Janelle's car and followed the ambulance, answering a call seconds later from Travis, who'd seen them pass his house. They talked to Libby on the way as well.

At the hospital, Grandma Geri was taken directly to an examination room, leaving the granddaughters to wait. Their time filled with phone calls and texts from family wanting updates, which they didn't have. Janelle had gotten up twice already to ask for one, and at the hour and a half mark was about to ask again when Aunt Gladys arrived.

Worry etched her face. "What have they told you?"

"Nothing," Janelle said. "I was just about to ask—"

"Janelle?"

"Hi, Dr. Peters," Janelle said. "This is my Aunt Gladys. I think you've met Stephanie."

They exchanged greetings and Dr. Peters got down to business. "We've ordered additional tests, but based on my preliminary examination, we're dealing with metastatic bones disease."

"What exactly does that mean, Doctor?" Aunt Gladys said.

"It means the cancer has spread to her bones, which weakens the skeletal system. In this case it has spread to her spine." Dr. Peters spoke in a low tone, as others were in the waiting area.

"Wait a minute," Aunt Gladys said, perplexed. "A little over a week ago the CT scan showed the tumor had shrunk. We thought she was doing better."

"To the naked eye the tumor appeared to have shrunk." Dr. Peters looked a little perturbed. "Quite frankly, the radiologist who told you that misread the scan. It's not my practice to give patients CT scan results based on observation only. I like to have the full report with actual measurements that can be compared to the original scan. That's why I was planning to meet with Mrs. Sanders today." He sighed. "The full report shows the tumor has actually grown."

The women looked at one another.

"That is simply not acceptable, to get a family's hopes up like that . . ." Aunt Gladys paused, releasing a sigh of frustration. "You said it has spread to her spine. And she couldn't move this morning. Please tell me she's not paralyzed."

"I'm afraid that is her current condition, yes. It was not totally unexpected. Bone metastases are fairly common in advanced-stage lung cancer."

"Now that I think about it," Janelle said, "Grandma complained a couple of times lately about a sharp pain, but she couldn't pinpoint it, and then it would disappear."

"That's usually one of the first signs," Dr. Peters said. "You'll be able to visit with her shortly, but we'll obviously be keeping her here as we move forward with additional tests."

Janelle, Stephanie, and Aunt Gladys went to the cafeteria to grab a bite and make calls. By evening Libby, Todd, and Sara Ann had come. Becca stayed home with the kids.

Most of them had been in Grandma Geri's room for quick visits. Janelle and Libby were in there again now. The nurse had told them to keep it brief. Visiting hours were almost over, and their grandmother needed rest.

Grandma Geri was hooked to monitors, her bed inclined slightly, legs stretched beneath a blanket like normal. Except she couldn't feel them.

Propped against the pillow, her head was turned toward her granddaughters. "Now you two know I don't have much time."

Libby held her hand. "Grandma, why are you saying that to everyone who comes in here? You're being pessimistic."

"I'm being *realistic*." She starting coughing and holding her chest, and took the water Janelle handed her. After a sip, she continued. "I want to get on with that bucket list I started."

Janelle looked at her. "You want to go shopping again?"

"No, nothing like that," she said. "I'm talking about the daughter I haven't seen in decades, and the granddaughter I've never seen. I don't want to look down from heaven and see them at my funeral—if they'd even come. I want to see them while I'm alive."

Janelle glanced at Libby and back to her grandmother. "We left messages for Aunt Gwynn today, and I exchanged texts with Keisha." She was happy that Keisha responded. Nothing lengthy—just *Thank you for the update*—but a response nonetheless.

"I need you two to pray about this thing," Grandma Geri said. "Gwynn hasn't called anybody back in who-knows-how-long. Getting her here would take a miracle."

"I've been praying already—"

"Well, step it up, Jan," she said. "I don't have long."

Libby sighed. "Grandma, please."

The door opened behind them and Travis appeared.

He stayed by the door. "Is this an okay time? I wanted to see my girl before visiting hours ended."

Grandma Geri's face brightened. "Come on in here, boy."

There were no more chairs, so Janelle got up. "Go ahead and sit. I've been in and out of here all day."

Libby gave Janelle the eye as Travis took the seat next to her. Janelle eased out of the room.

~⌐~

How quickly the dynamic had changed. One minute a peaceful family gathering with her grandmother and cousin. The next, a gathering in which she felt jumpy inside and found it hard to focus—all because of a one-person switch.

Libby held her hands in her lap, debating whether to get up herself and leave as the two of them talked.

Travis leaned forward on his elbows, always comfortable in conversation with Grandma Geri. He wasn't focusing on her current state. He had her laughing as he told the latest happenings at the church.

"I'm serious, Grandma Geri. Sister Mason volunteered to make sweet potato pies for pastor's appreciation. Now you know I'm all about some sweet potato pie—"

"Shirley can't cook no sweet potato pies. They never turn out right."

"I'm sayin'!" Travis had the biggest grin on his face. "So I said, 'Sister Mason, nobody can make hot water cornbread like you. Could you please do me a favor and make that instead?'"

"What she say?"

"She said Brother Mason never liked her cornbread, so she didn't think anyone else liked it either. Said she'll make a batch for the church and one for me to take home—and you know I love when I can take some food home, since I can't cook."

"Will you *please* find you a wife? Don't make no sense that you're still single, all these nice young ladies running around here."

Libby was sure of it; she should've left.

"I might not get married," Travis said. "I might be like the apostle Paul and live a life of singleness, eating fast food." His brow wrinkled. "I wonder if he ate fast food."

"Oh, you'll get married," Grandma Geri said, "if I have to find you a bride myself. Got a bunch of grands and great-grands, you know. One sitting right here."

Libby's stomach went from jumping to double Dutching. "I think that's enough, Grandma."

Grandma Geri looked at her. "I done told you I don't have much time. So I'm gonna say whatever I need to say."

She started coughing again, and Libby gladly got up to pour

water for her. She handed it to her grandmother. "Should I call the nurse?" she asked.

"I'm fine," her grandmother coughed out. "Stop trying . . . to . . . change the subject."

Libby watched her closely anyway, ready to call the nurse if it persisted much longer. She refused to look at Travis.

Grandma Geri started right in when her coughing subsided. "Now, Libby, those guys you've brought to the house are nice enough young men."

Libby guessed she should be thankful her grandmother's mental faculties were still sharp.

"But ain't none of 'em in the kingdom, are they?"

Why, oh why is she questioning me in front of Travis? She cleared her throat. "Grandma, is this really necessary right now?"

Travis was looking downward. At least he was kind enough to give the appearance of having sympathy for her.

"Life is not complicated, baby. The wrong choices—no matter how right they seem at the time—can follow you the rest of your life. You see that with me and Gwynn. Obeying God is always the right choice. Always." She cut an eye over to Travis. "Now that young man *is* in the kingdom, just so you know."

Libby found that last part amusing, though she wouldn't show it.

A nurse pushed the door open and entered. "I'm going to have to ask you two to let Mrs. Sanders rest," she said.

Libby wanted to tell her she was ten minutes late.

"I was just getting a second wind," Grandma Geri said.

"Grandma, you were in rare form this evening." Libby kissed her cheek. "Rest well. I'll see you tomorrow. Love you."

Travis hugged her. "The church is praying. God's got you. Grace and peace, Grandma Geri."

They walked out into the hall and started toward the waiting area. After a few feet of silence, Travis looked over at her. "Sorry you had to go through that."

Libby shrugged, following the tiled squares down the hall. "Just Grandma being Grandma."

"For the record, marrying you wouldn't work anyway."

Her stomach jumped, thinking of the reasons she herself had said he couldn't marry her. "Why not?"

"You can't cook either."

She laughed. "I beg your pardon. I've learned a lot over the years."

"You learn how to cook?"

"Depends on how you define 'cook.'"

Travis laughed heartily. After a few moments, he said, "How are you doing? This was a tough day for your family."

"Very tough." She looked at him. "Paralyzed? It's horrible the way cancer ravages the body. I'm thankful she's in good spirits despite everything. But it's starting to hit us that Grandma may not be with us long. I can't imagine what our family will be like without her."

"Or Hope Springs, for that matter," Travis said. "What would it be like for the Sanders family to be gone from that house at the end of the street? I can't imagine."

"I honestly hadn't thought about that," Libby said. "What will happen to that house? We have to keep it. Where else would we have our family reunions?" She shuddered. "I don't want to think about any of it. One day at a time."

Almost to the waiting room, she stopped and looked at Travis. "I want to thank you for always being there to lift Grandma's spirits. You're a special man." She paused. "A true man of God."

"I love your grandmother. Always have, even when I was giving her fits as a boy running in her garden. We had some fun down at that house."

"Ooh, remember we used to play hide-and-seek at night? Don't laugh, but I thought it was scary. I wanted somebody to find me so I wouldn't be alone in the dark."

"You don't remember that time I found you behind the water tower, do you?"

Travis had turned that penetrating eye thing on. Libby took a steadying breath.

"I remember. One of y'all mischievous boys had changed up the rules. If you were the one seeking, you could pick one person you found and kiss them." Libby laughed at the memory. "And Janelle said she'd only play if the kiss could be on the hand."

"And when it was my turn to look, I found you and picked you as the one I wanted to kiss."

Libby laughed again. "And I said, 'I ain't kissing you.' So I held out my hand, and you kissed it."

"What you don't know," Travis said, "is that I refused to wash my face that night, because my lips had touched Libby Sanders's hand."

"Stop lying."

"I'm serious."

They stared at one another, the history between them coursing through their veins.

"We'd better get back to the waiting room."

He didn't say anything. Wouldn't break their gaze.

And Libby felt a pull like none she'd ever felt before.

"You're right," he said. "We'd better get back."

CHAPTER FORTY-ONE
Saturday, February 13

The hospital had become the campout spot. Janelle and Stephanie had been there since morning with the kids, and Becca was just now arriving with hers. Janelle got up to greet her.

"How's Grandma Geri doing?" Becca asked.

"About the same. Aunt Gladys is in there with her now."

"Mom," Daniel said, "can we *please* go hang out with Kory? Doesn't he live near here? There's nothing to do in the waiting room."

"Yeah, we could go see Dee," Tiffany said. "Mommy, will you call them? I want Dee to sleep over with me and Claire tonight."

"You guys, I told you we're not doing that anymore. You just have to accept it." Janelle gave Becca an exasperated look.

Becca set Ethan down, keeping an eye on him. She nodded toward Todd and Travis on a sofa in the waiting room. "Looks like they're in deep conversation over there. About the meeting tonight?"

"Yeah, we were all talking about it. I guess there's never been one like this with both Calvary and New Jerusalem members. It's pretty historic."

"Todd's not so sure it'll go well."

"Travis either. And if it doesn't, I'll bear the brunt of the blame, I'm sure."

"Don't say that—Ethan, come here, sweetie."

Stephanie went after him. "I'll watch him," she said. She gathered all the kids around her.

Becca continued. "There were a lot of factors that went into this meeting. The whole revelation about Jim and Gwynn played a big part, and the Bible study at the diner. You were just the one who had the lightbulb moment that put it all together."

"Speaking of lightbulb moments," Janelle said, "I'm still thinking of the one you had about humility. How are you feeling about everything now?"

Becca's pause was thoughtful. "Honestly, it's still hard, still disappointing, still a little embarrassing. Still hard not to focus on *me*." She gave a wry smile. "I need a lot of work in the 'emptying of self' department. Have to keep telling myself it's *His* ministry, not mine. God should be able to do what He wants with it, right? He might know a little about how it'll fit with everything else He's got going on earth." She laughed lightly at herself.

"Are you praying about what's next?"

"I'm praying about what's *now*." She pointed at Claire and Ethan. "I don't even want to think about 'next.' And I definitely don't want to chase after anything, even if it's only in prayer. I want to learn how to chase after God."

"Amen, Becca. I need to learn that too."

Todd and Travis came over to the women.

"We need some feedback on how we're thinking about approaching this tonight," Todd said.

"In other words," Travis added, "we want to know whether we'll get thrown out of town."

Janelle and Stephanie arrived late at New Jerusalem, twenty minutes after the meeting had started. They had waited together with Aunt Gladys to talk to the doctor about Grandma Geri, and it had taken longer than expected. They hightailed it over to the church as soon as they got back to Hope Springs.

The church was absolutely packed, with some standing in the back and to the sides of the pews. Travis and Todd had designated New Jerusalem as the location because it provided more seating than Calvary, but she didn't think they expected it to be *this* full. The scene struck her the same as at Pastor Jim's funeral. Something beautiful about seeing both congregations together.

Janelle looked around, half wondering if Kory might be there. After all, he'd joined New Jerusalem and had been very much interested in the preliminary discussion about this. But she doubted he would bring Shelley here. They'd probably find a church together in Rocky Mount.

"The bottom line is this," Todd was saying. "As people of God, we have to be willing to examine ourselves. Romans 12:2 tells us not to be conformed to this world but to be transformed by the renewing of our minds. Only then can we do God's good and perfect will." He looked out at the sea of black faces and white faces. "In this world—in this country—we are separated by skin color, and we understand the ugly history that fueled it. But we are citizens of a different kingdom. We belong to Christ. And in Christ's kingdom we don't regard one another according to the flesh. We are one."

Janelle didn't think she'd ever seen the church this quiet. Not a single *amen* answered Todd's words.

"And so," Todd said, "we wanted to set a biblical foundation at the outset, with the hope that the balance of the meeting will proceed within that framework. Pastor Travis will share what we are proposing."

Travis came to the podium without notes. Taking his time,

he regarded every section of the sanctuary, moving his gaze along slowly. Interesting the effect it had. Some seemed to squirm a little, uncomfortable with the pause.

"I grew up in Hope Springs, as many of you did," he began, "and I had no concept of the term 'the body of Christ.' I had no concept of what it meant to be one in Christ. I had a better understanding of race and division than reconciliation and unity, and my understanding of race and division came mostly from the churches. I wonder if God is pleased with that." He inserted another pregnant pause. "Here in Hope Springs recently we've seen a change. And sad to say, it didn't start in the churches. It started in the Main Street Diner with Janelle Evans and Sara Ann Matthews, and it has flourished with members of both Calvary and New Jerusalem."

Janelle glanced across the aisle where she'd spotted Beverly and Allison earlier.

Soul Sisters, Beverly mouthed and smiled.

"Pastor Todd and I have been greatly encouraged and motivated by the example of these women. They've shown us not only what's *possible* here in Hope Springs but what's *preferable*. And I commend them." Travis nodded to Sara Ann, who sat near the front. "With that backdrop we are proposing the following—that members of Calvary and New Jerusalem come together for a joint service the first Sunday of each month. We believe this will foster oneness in the community and in our hearts. We believe it will promote fellowship and love within the body, and as the world sees our love, God will be glorified. Details such as location will be worked out. For tonight we want to open up discussion on the proposal."

Todd rejoined Travis at the podium.

"We're asking you to stand when it's your turn and state your comment or question as loudly as you can," Travis said.

Todd pointed near the back. "Pervis Mitchell."

Pervis, a Calvary member probably in his sixties, stood. "I want to know who would preach on that Sunday."

His voice barely projected. Janelle only heard him because she stood near him.

Someone repeated it to Travis and Todd, and Todd repeated it for the crowd. "We thought a simple way to do it was to alternate," Todd said.

A middle-aged woman in the middle stood before she was acknowledged.

"Go ahead, Delores," Todd said.

"My question is about the music. Which choir would sing? And whose band would play? New Jerusalem's music hurts my ears."

"Well, funny you say that." A New Jerusalem woman stood. "I was about to ask the same questions, because I find Calvary's music on the boring side."

Chatter started up within the pews. Todd and Travis looked at one another.

"Listen," Travis said into the mic. "We knew people would have these questions, and we appreciate them. But concerns about music shouldn't override the biblical goal of unity. Amen?" He paused but got no response. "Pastor Todd and I would love to see the formation of a combined choir for the joint service. It would actually be a great thing to gain a better appreciation of each other's cultural styles and tastes."

Two elders—one from Calvary and the other from New Jerusalem—stood together. The Calvary elder spoke first. "I was just sitting here talking with Larry, and we feel the same way. You were each brought to pastor your individual church, not to go radical and attempt to merge the two churches. We understand that you two are personal friends, but this is beyond the pale. And it should've been brought to the elder boards first."

Todd spoke. "Willard, let me make clear that we are not proposing a merging of the churches. Calvary will remain Calvary; New Jerusalem will remain New Jerusalem. Travis and I remain pastors of our individual churches. We are simply talking about coming together as members of one body to celebrate Christ on the first Sunday of each month."

Todd seemed to be finished but then added, "When you brought me on, you told me you were trusting God to do great things through me. I'm sure New Jerusalem felt the same regarding Travis. We believe this is one of those great things. We worship within two blocks of one another, and most of us hardly know each other between the churches. Do you not see a benefit to this from God's perspective?"

Neither elder responded but they sat back down.

Randy, a New Jerusalem member, stood. "No offense, Pastor Travis," he said, "but I probably wouldn't come on the Sundays Pastor Todd is preaching. Just being real. I joined New Jerusalem because I like to hear *you* preach."

Chatter erupted again as members of both congregations echoed the likelihood that they too wouldn't come if the other pastor were preaching.

Sara Ann stood amid the chatter.

Todd raised his hands. "We want to hear everyone, but one at a time, please. Sara Ann, go on."

"I wasn't going to say anything, since I can't make Sunday service anyway because of the diner." She spoke loudly and clearly. "But this is actually breaking my heart." She looked into the faces of those assembled. "You all wouldn't come if the other pastor is preaching? I thought the word was from the Lord, and Todd and Travis were simply the vessels. You're worried about music? Is the music for you or for the Lord?" She turned to the elders. "You're concerned about your individual churches? Whose church is it? Yours or the Lord's?

"I didn't want to do the diner Bible study. I didn't think I *could* do it. But I found out it wasn't about me. None of this is about us." She glanced up at Todd and Travis. "I don't know what will happen with this joint service idea. I pray it goes forward, because I've seen the blessing of unity and fellowship with my Soul Sisters. And I pray both churches get to experience it."

She sat down, but others popped up. Gina, Bea, Violet, Trina . . . one by one, the Soul Sisters stood. Janelle, Stephanie, Beverly, and Allison moved forward up the center aisle, and they all made their way to the front. Becca, who'd been sitting up front, joined them, and they summoned Sara Ann forward as well. The women hugged one another as a group, and then Beverly turned to the pastors.

"I don't care if nobody else shows up for the joint service, I think I can speak for the Soul Sisters in saying *we'll* be there."

"Yeah!" The group pumped their fists.

Janelle had tears in her eyes, thankful for the way God had moved Sara Ann.

People in the pews began to stand now, one here, one there, showing their support for the joint service. A little less than half had come to their feet in the end.

Janelle could tell Todd and Travis were greatly moved. Neither had words. So Trina began singing a song the Calvary choir was known for.

Voices joined in and before long the sound of beautiful worship filled the sanctuary.

"How great is our God, sing with me, how great is our God . . ."

CHAPTER FORTY-TWO

Saturday, February 27

No, it's definitely lopsided." Janelle's head went lopsided as she looked at it. "It's too high on the right."

Stephanie held her hands out wide like a picture frame. "I don't know. Looks even to me."

Todd and Travis, perched high on a pair of ladders, looked at them impatiently from either end of a banner strung across the family room.

"Hanging out on ladders is not my favorite thing," Todd said. "Are we good or are we not?"

"Mom, can you come here a minute?" Janelle called.

"What is it, sweetheart?" Estelle called back. "I'm making the roux for the macaroni and cheese."

"Oh no, go on and tend to that," Travis told her. "That's much more important."

Janelle made a face at him. "Jackie, are you in there?" she called.

Their teenage cousin, Aunt Gladys's granddaughter, had arrived in town that afternoon. She bebopped into the family room, texting on her phone, and looked up. "Ooh, that thing is lopsided." She turned to Janelle. "Did you call me?"

"That was all I needed, my dear." She looked at Stephanie. "Get your eyes checked."

Todd and Travis adjusted the banner, came down, and the four of them stared at it.

Happy 87th Birthday, Grandma Geri! it said.

Janelle sighed, trying to push away the sadness. "Okay. I can do this."

"We *have* to do this," Stephanie said. "We have to stay upbeat."

They'd been giving one another pep talks all day. It had been hard watching Grandma Geri since she'd gotten home from the hospital. She'd stayed there eleven days, undergoing various tests and close monitoring. Though still in fairly good spirits, it seemed ever since the paralysis she'd been going downhill physically. She stayed in bed mostly, wasn't eating much, didn't even want a birthday party. She said a big family celebration would only remind her that *all* her family wasn't present.

But that was the point of the party—to gather all the family. After Grandma Geri charged Janelle and Libby to pray that she could see Aunt Gwynn and Keisha, Libby had been planning. She'd never been responsible for a Sanders family gathering before—the older generation planned; her generation showed up.

But she went to work and put Janelle and Stephanie to work, calling every single person in the Sanders family directory plus family beyond the immediate clan. They wanted the family reunion vibe of summer—festive, overflowing with food and fun.

Except how could it really be fun? They knew why they were gathering. Barring a miracle, this would be Grandma Geri's last birthday. And how could it be fun when she was deteriorating before their very eyes?

And there was the matter of Aunt Gwynn and Keisha. If they didn't come, the entire purpose for the event would have failed. And if they *did* come and it didn't go well . . .

Still, for the sake of Grandma Geri and the occasion, Janelle and Stephanie had vowed to exude joy. And Stephanie had additional incentive. Lindell and the rest of her family were coming.

Janelle picked up her notepad and placed a check by *banner.* "All right, what's next? We don't have much time before cars start arriving."

Stephanie looked at the list. "We're rolling. Food preparation duly delegated to the elders, cleaning detail duly delegated to the youngsters. Balloons on the way."

"We picked up the cake," Janelle added. "What about the video?"

"Check," Travis said. "Got it from Terry."

"Cool, thanks." Janelle couldn't wait to surprise Grandma Geri with it. The media guy at New Jerusalem had put together a celebration of her life, with pictures they'd given him and interviews he'd done of family members and church members.

"Where is Libby?" Stephanie asked. "Isn't she supposed to be handling this day-of-event stuff?"

"Good question," Janelle said. "She should've been here at least an hour ago."

Todd rested in a recliner. "What's the latest on Keisha and her mom?"

"First she said she couldn't come, then she was thinking about driving down with her husband and son, but her husband had a conflict." Janelle raised a brow, not wanting to admit she was skeptical. "Uncle Bruce offered Keisha and Aunt Gwynn his airline rewards tickets, and there's a flight that leaves in an hour. I don't know if they'll be on it."

"We haven't told Grandma any of this," Janelle added. "If it doesn't work out, she'll never know it was a possibility."

The door burst open, and Daniel, Tiffany, Claire, and a gaggle of other kids came tearing through the family room on their way to who-knew-where.

"Hey!" Janelle and Todd called at once.

"Come back here," he added.

Those kids had been on the go ever since Aunt Gladys's grand-kids—six of them under ten—showed up. Janelle's dad and Uncle Wood were at their usual post outdoors, grilling and keeping an eye on the kids, supposedly. The late February weather was unseasonably warm, and Janelle figured the children had a touch of spring fever.

The stampede was much slower in reverse.

"Yes, Daddy?" Claire asked, looking innocent.

"You know you don't run through the house."

"All of you know that," Janelle said. "And, Daniel, you were lead-ing the pack, and I know you know better. If you want to run, stay outdoors. If you come inside, you'll sit down and do something pro-ductive—or maybe take a nap."

They were out the door in a flash.

Stephanie laughed. "Girl, you said *nap*, and that was all she wrote."

"It's a shame," Janelle said. "I hear myself issuing the same threats they gave us when we were running around here. *Nap* was the biggest threat of all."

"Shoot, Grandma Geri would make *me* take a nap." Travis laughed. "I was like, 'I can just go home,' and she'd say, 'Boy, lie down and close your eyes.'"

"So many memories," Todd said. "I know we want to keep it upbeat, but wow . . . whenever the Lord sees fit to take Grandma Geri home, that'll be the end of an era on this street. What if y'all sell this house and another family moves in? How weird would *that* be?"

"No one wants to talk about it," Janelle said. "But the reality is, a lot of decisions will need to be made, sooner rather than later."

They heard a rap on the door.

"That's the balloon delivery," Stephanie said. She went to open the door—and squealed.

Janelle looked and squealed herself. She hadn't seen Uncle Bruce, Aunt Claudia, or Cyd in years.

"Y'all are here!" Stephanie embraced Lindell tight for several seconds, then kissed him. "I missed you."

Janelle smiled at the teary sound in Stephanie's voice.

Lindell kissed her again. "Missed you too, babe."

Stephanie hugged her mom and dad next, then—"Oh, look at Chase!" Stephanie lifted him from Cyd. "Hi, sweetie! You're so big now. And your birthday's coming soon." She kissed his cheek. "You didn't forget Aunt Stephy, did you?"

Chase wrapped his arms around her and laid his head on her neck.

"Aw, you're gonna make me cry," Stephanie said. "Oh, I guess I should greet your parents, huh?"

"Yeah, we were wondering." Cyd had a big smile as she hugged her sister.

Janelle opened her arms wide to hug Cyd herself. "So happy for you," Janelle said. "Last time I saw you, you were single. Now you're married with a baby." She turned to her husband. "Hi, I'm Cyd's cousin Janelle."

Cyd's husband hugged her. "Hey, Janelle. I'm Cedric. Great to meet you."

"So wait . . ." Janelle glanced between the two of them. "You and Lindell are brothers, right?"

Cedric smiled. "I claim him sometimes."

"How long are you all staying?" Janelle asked.

"Unfortunately, this one's a quick visit," Uncle Bruce said. "We fly back tomorrow evening."

"But Stephanie and I are driving back together," Lindell said.

Janelle looked at her cousin. "So you're leaving us for real this time?"

"For real." Stephanie hugged Lindell's waist. "I miss my hubby."

Todd and Travis had come over to greet everyone.

Uncle Bruce hugged Todd. "Still can't believe your dad is gone. Knew him all his life. And, son, I'm really proud of you for what you're doing at Calvary." He grabbed Travis's hand and brought him to a hug. "You too, Travis. Stephanie's been updating me. Both of you have grown up to be fine men of God."

"Thanks, Bruce." Travis had a gleam in his eye. "But you said that like you're surprised."

Uncle Bruce laughed. "Uh, a little." He glanced around. "Momma's in her room?"

Stephanie nodded.

As he and the others started down the hall, the door opened again. Libby walked in, followed by Omar, the guy she'd brought a few Sundays ago to dinner. Janelle had to give it to her—he was good-looking.

"Hey," Libby said, "sorry I'm late. Y'all remember Omar, right?"

"How's everybody?" he said, shaking each hand. "Nice to see you all again."

"You as well," Travis said.

Travis looked as if he were about to approach Libby to greet her, but she turned to Omar.

"Let's find my mom and dad," she said. "I want you to meet them."

～⌒～

Grandma Geri was all dolled up in her wheelchair, surrounded by a family room full of loved ones. Aunt Gladys had gotten her a new outfit, and she and Estelle had helped their mother dress and do her makeup. They'd also gotten a stylist to come shape up her short 'fro—her new style when her hair began falling out. After resting earlier she'd been out socializing for more than two hours, opening gifts, ordering people to eat—even if she didn't eat herself—and getting a kick out of her video, telling them to rewind it twice. Much as she'd said she didn't want a party, she was wearing it well.

Janelle left the main party site and went to the living room to see if she'd left her camera there. She picked it up, and when she turned, she was facing Kevin, Kory's older brother.

"Hey," she said, ready to move around him. She'd already made casual—and quick—conversation with him and his family.

"Janelle, can I talk to you a minute?" he said.

Her heart slipped into an erratic beat. Didn't help that he and Kory favored one another. "Okay."

"Kory told me what you did, and I wanted to tell you how much I admired that."

"Okay." She didn't know what else to say.

"I hope you know how much he cared about you."

Past tense. Nice. Thanks for clarifying that, Kevin. She had nothing to say to that either.

"Well. That's all I wanted to say," Kevin said. He turned to leave.

Don't do it, Janelle. Do not *ask him*—"Kevin?"

He turned around.

"So . . . they're together?"

"Shelley's with him and Dee at the house, yes."

"Okay."

Instead of going back to the party, she went to her room, closed the door, and sat cross-legged on the bed. There was no other explanation for Kory not calling the last three weeks, but hearing it—*knowing* it . . .

In the morning she'd sort through her feelings in her journal. With God's help she'd get to a place where she could pray for him and Shelley again—wasn't this news an answer to her prayers? But right now, it hurt. And she only wanted to cry.

Janelle still had the camera in hand. She turned it on and pushed the button to view the pictures. She scrolled through ones just taken today, then back, back she went until she got to Todd's reception at Calvary and the pictures she'd taken with Kory. The only ones they'd ever taken.

She stared at the two of them, his arm around her, her head tucked close to his chest. She remembered his words, his tone, his touch, his feel. She moved her finger to the button and clicked the picture into the trash. Then the next. And she had her cry.

Minutes later, she heard a quick knock at the door, and then it opened. Libby stuck her head in. "Janelle, there's a taxi—what's wrong?"

Janelle swiped her face. "Nothing." She jumped up. "A taxi's here?"

"It's coming down the road, and it's got to have Keisha in it at least. People are headed outside."

Janelle followed. They took the side door near the kitchen, and indeed, most of the family stood in the dark to greet the yellow taxi. Looked like the driver had his high beams on, which wasn't unusual around there if you didn't know your way, but it prevented them from seeing who or even how many were in the car.

Several seconds passed, then a back door opened and a woman stepped out.

"Is that Keisha?" Libby said. "I can't hardly tell with that stupid bright light in my eyes."

"I don't know if that's Keisha, but whoever it is isn't alone, because she's helping somebody else out, an older woman. That must be Aunt Floretta."

"I didn't know she was coming," Libby said.

"Me either."

Janelle expected the door to close, but a third woman got out. Everything in her seemed to pause—she knew it must be Aunt Gwynn.

Libby knew too, because they were both struck silent.

The driver gave them their luggage, and the taxi with the bright lights pulled away. The three women stood in place, looking at the house, the family that had gathered outside, and each other.

Uncle Bruce, Aunt Gladys, Estelle, and Uncle Wood were the first to go to them. Seeing their parents move, Janelle and Libby were seconds behind. Faces were lost in hugs, questions lost in tears. Janelle hugged Aunt Floretta and then Aunt Gwynn, who was then corralled by her siblings to a separate powwow. She then hugged Keisha, who even in the dark looked pretty much the same—smooth café au lait skin, wavy hair layered short, maybe a little leftover baby weight.

"I'm so glad you came." Janelle wished she could stay a week so they could talk all day and night.

"I honestly wasn't sure until the last minute. I didn't want to come without my mother, and the only way my mother would come was if Grandma came. I ended up charging a ticket for her."

Janelle and Libby glanced at one another. It was strange hearing Keisha refer to Aunt Floretta as "Grandma."

"Your very first time in Hope Springs," Libby said. "This is truly a moment."

Keisha looked around. "I'm looking forward to tomorrow when I can see the town better." She looked to where her mother appeared to still be in deep conversation with her siblings. "It's weird. My mother has her memories to contend with here; I have none."

Cyd and Stephanie came over and hugged Keisha as well. As they all shared small talk, Janelle said, "Forgive me for staring. You and your brother have the same eyes." She spun around. "Where is Todd?"

He was in the distance, giving the family space. Janelle waved him over.

"Todd, this is Keisha. Keisha, Todd."

They took one another in, and the resemblance really was obvious.

"Can I . . . hug you?" Todd said.

Keisha seemed overwhelmed, perhaps more than she thought she'd be. She didn't answer. She just reached for him and they embraced.

Janelle wanted to cry again, happy tears this time.

"You said you wouldn't come unless you were open to building a relationship," Todd said. "I'm hoping this means . . ."

Keisha nodded with a slight smile. "I'm open."

Aunt Floretta had moved inside with other family members, to where Grandma Geri had remained in her wheelchair. More family came to greet Keisha, many for the first time. Keisha was a little guarded, not at all chatty, trying to feel her way in a new environment with a lot of new family.

"Should we go inside?" Janelle asked her.

Keisha looked back at her mom. No telling how long the five siblings would be in conference. "Might as well," Keisha said.

But when Keisha began to move toward the house, Aunt Gwynn called to her. "We'll go in together," Aunt Gwynn said.

The rest of them walked on into the house. Family was still gathered around Grandma Geri, but much more somber, no one knowing what to expect. Grandma Geri looked more nervous than Janelle had ever seen her, fidgeting with a napkin, leaving it in shreds in her lap. Janelle grabbed one of her hands and held it. She prayed what she'd been praying for weeks.

Lord, please bring peace where there's been strife. Bring healing where there's been hurt. Bring forgiveness where there's been bitterness. May Your love flow in our hearts.

Janelle tried to read her mom when she walked in, but she seemed lost in her own thoughts. Same with each one who entered after her. None of the usual banter. Almost a heaviness.

Aunt Gwynn walked in next with Keisha. In the light Grandma Geri's youngest looked a lot like her older sisters, but with a leaner frame. She wore a sweater with matching cardigan and slacks, small pearl earrings in her ears. Her hair, layered short like her daughter's, looked recently styled. Life appeared to be treating her well, at least on the surface.

With all the remodeling the house had to look vastly different. This family room didn't exist when she left home. Aunt Gwynn didn't look at anyone in particular, just at the room, the ceiling; then she disappeared down the hall, Keisha by her side, as they took in the rest of the house. Hardly anyone spoke. They waited until the two did what they needed to do and made their way back.

Janelle could hear them coming, and Aunt Floretta met them down the hall. They paused there in conversation, then continued on, only to the edge of the family room. There they stood.

Family members looked at one another. What now? The principle players were in the room, but they couldn't be made to talk. Meanwhile, the party had come to a screeching halt.

Suddenly Keisha moved out from her mom and "grandmom." She walked over to the wheelchair and knelt in front of it. "I'm Keisha," she said, extending her hand.

Grandma Geri's eyes bubbled with tears. She stared at Keisha as if noting every aspect of her, then she ignored her hand, pulled her close, and hugged her. Keisha leaned in, returning the embrace.

Janelle had never heard her grandmother weep like that, not even when Grandpa Elwood died. Her upper frame shook as she held tight to her granddaughter. "I'm sorry," she said. "I'm so sorry. I hate that I never knew you. Please, please forgive me."

Libby looked at Janelle as if trying to hold back tears, but it was useless. There was hardly a dry eye in the family room.

Janelle was surprised to see that Keisha was crying too. She pulled back a little, looking Grandma Geri in the eye. "I spent a lot of my life being bitter about what happened, and I'll bet you've spent a lot of your life regretting it. I don't want to talk about that anymore." Keisha wiped tears from her face. "I want to talk about you. I want to get to know . . . my Grandma Geri."

"And I want to get to know my Keisha."

Grandma Geri embraced her again, then Keisha sat on a chair next to the wheelchair, holding her grandmother's hand—mostly because Grandma Geri wouldn't let her go.

An awkward silence seeped in again. Did they resume mingling and chatting? Wait to see if Aunt Gwynn would come forward?

She did finally, slowly. She sat on the sofa a few feet from the wheelchair, though it wasn't clear if she was making herself comfortable or opening up dialogue.

"This is very difficult, being here," she said finally, seemingly to everyone. "I've been gone almost forty years, and though from time to time I've seen my sisters and brothers and their kids, and a few others of you who've come to Jersey, most of you are practically strangers." She looked out among them. "It cost me a lot, staying away. But neither could I come for many reasons. So I buried the past. Ran from it mostly. Who knows what the right thing was to do? Maybe I should've shown up at a family reunion one year with my daughter and faced my mother, Jim, and all my demons." She shrugged. "Who knows?"

Aunt Gwynn took her time, almost emotionless. "So now I'm supposed to make my appearance in Hope Springs after all these decades, rush to my ailing mother's side, and say all is forgiven so she can feel . . . oh, I don't know . . . freer as her life nears an end. Is that what we're doing here?"

Grandma Geri had a tissue Aunt Gladys had slipped her. She clutched it in her lap, looking at the floor.

"See, it's real nice," Aunt Gwynn said, "that my daughter can say she doesn't want to talk about the past, because she didn't live that past. I did." Emotion was entering into her voice. "I was the one who was told not to bring my baby back here if I chose to keep her. I was the one made to feel like I'd done something horribly wrong because I'd fallen in love with a white man. Do you know I've never fallen in love with anyone else my entire life?"

She took a breath, looked at no one in particular.

"So maybe you're wondering why I came." She was back to her collected self. "I came for my daughter, because she asked me. She wants to get to know her grandmother, and I will not discourage her. That's her choice. As for me, I still cannot think about my mother—my churchgoing, Bible-reading, always-telling-me-right-from-wrong mother—without seeing her face as she sent me from home and handed me an ultimatum about *my* baby. God help me, but I'm not ready to forgive her."

She stood. "Wood, you said you'd take me to my hotel?" She headed for the door.

"Gwynn, don't leave like this." Aunt Gladys stood as well. "What happened was terrible, but you've got to put it behind you for your own good. You've got to make peace."

"Gladys, I told you outside. This is where I am and I'm not going to pretend." She looked at her brother. "Wood, will you take me or not?"

The pain was evident in Uncle Wood's eyes. "'Course I'll take you, Gwynn."

He picked up her luggage near the door and they walked out.

Keisha spoke with Grandma Geri in low tones. Janelle's mom, Aunt Gladys, and Aunt Denise went to the kitchen, where they would begin cleaning and dissecting everything about the night. The rest seemed to grope for what to do next.

Libby needed air. She walked out of the house a few seconds after her dad and watched him and Aunt Gwynn pull away. The entire episode had shaken her. She wished they hadn't had the party, not when it only gave Aunt Gwynn a forum to voice decades of bitterness. Grandma Geri would never forget the things she said, and in front of everybody. As sick as she was, to have to endure that kind of pain . . .

But Libby knew it was more than that. She took a few steps in the gravel, looking into the night sky, the silver moon. She'd seen in her aunt Gwynn a glimpse of herself—the running, the rebellion. Would Libby find herself in that same spot twenty years from now, alone, hardened . . . sad? That's what struck her the most, that Aunt Gwynn was sad, whether she realized it or not. She'd locked herself in a prison and didn't know how to get out. And hadn't Libby? Hadn't she locked up her heart, not knowing how to—

She turned when she heard footsteps coming toward her.

"Travis, I can't. Not now." She turned back around, her heart beating through her chest.

"Just wanted to see if you were okay." He stopped in front of her, his presence causing her to shiver. "You looked upset in there."

Her feelings were a contradiction. She wanted him to go. She wanted him to hold her. "Hard not to be upset." She couldn't look at him. "But I'll be all right."

"Okay."

He started back to the house.

"Travis . . ."

He paused. "Yes?"

She closed her eyes, not wanting to reveal her thoughts. But she wanted to know. "Am I a project to you?"

He walked back to her. "What do you mean?"

"Do you feel like you hurt me in the past, so you have an obligation to act like you care, invite me to church, and all that?"

"It's no obligation. I do care about you, Libby."

"As a pastor?"

"As a friend."

Quiet engulfed them for a few moments.

"So I see you and Omar are hanging in there."

"Yeah. Things are going well."

"Seems like a nice guy."

"He is."

They both stared into the night sky.

"Libby, I . . ." He turned to her, and his brown eyes spoke in earnest, looking deep into hers, grappling. He sighed. "I'd better go."

She watched him walk back into the house, sure of what he'd said. He could see her as a friend but nothing more. He knew the life she'd been leading, the kind of life that disqualified her from his.

CHAPTER FORTY-THREE

Monday, May 3

They'd been told "any day now" a week ago, and family and friends had been squeezing in moments with Grandma Geri.

A hospice nurse had been coming regularly to the house for the past month—Dr. Reynolds too—but Janelle didn't need either to tell her that her grandmother was fading. Every day Grandma Geri appeared a little more shrunken, like the air in her earthly body was being let out. Today her breathing was more labored than ever, as if her spirit were giving a gracious warning that it was heading home.

They all seemed to sense it. Aunt Gladys, Estelle, and Uncle Wood were in the room. Libby had come from Raleigh last night after an event and was lingering this morning. Todd and Becca had made their usual morning visit but hadn't yet left. Same with Travis. He'd stopped by for a "quick hello" on the way to run an errand, and more than an hour later he hadn't left the room.

The older generation was telling funny stories from their growing-up years, and Grandma Geri listened, smiling, saying little. Though it was a beautiful warm, sunny day, she had two blankets atop her regular comforter, pulled to her neck. Her arms lay outside the blankets. Janelle held one hand, Libby the other.

Grandma Geri opened her mouth to say something, and everyone quieted. She spoke so softly it was hard to hear.

"Church," she said. "Yes-ter-day."

"Oh, the combined service." Todd nodded his head. "It was beautiful, Grandma Geri. We'd been planning it for two months, but it was better than we hoped and prayed for."

"Starting it on the first Sunday in May was perfect," Janelle said. "The weather was gorgeous. Seemed like it spurred people to come out."

There were people who stayed home too, and had been vocal about opposing it. But no point dampening Grandma Geri's spirits with that.

"Location was perfect," Todd said.

"I wondered what it would be like, having it in the high school," Aunt Gladys said, "but it was really nice."

"Yeah," Todd said. "But it was kind of funny seeing all those spring hats against the backdrop of the basketball nets."

Grandma Geri's eyes smiled.

"And you should've heard Travis's sermon, Grandma," Janelle said.

"I'm telling you," Estelle said. "Resurrection Day might've been last month, but you got people fired up talking about what it means for our lives today, knowing Jesus is risen."

Libby cast a downward glance. She hadn't been to church in Hope Springs since the one service when Stephanie was there.

Travis acknowledged their words with a thin smile. He'd been quiet, standing against the dresser.

They heard the side screen door open and bang close. Sara Ann came to the doorway, Ethan on her hip. She'd stopped by to see Grandma Geri and ended up hanging around to help with the kids.

"Sorry to interrupt," she said. "Is it okay to take Ethan to the little park up the street? Claire and Tiffany want to go."

"Sure," Todd said, "but you've got to keep a close eye on that one."

"No problema," she said, whipping out her secret weapon in a bottle. "He stays close to me as long as I'm blowing bubbles. Be back soon."

Becca smiled as she left. "Soul Sisters was awesome this weekend too. That Sara Ann is something."

Grandma Geri started coughing, a weak, raspy, quiet cough, but it commanded everyone's attention.

The screen door opened and banged shut again, and Janelle expected to see Sara Ann back with another question. But she gasped at the sight that appeared before them. "Keisha!"

"I didn't know you were coming," Libby said.

Keisha walked farther into the room. "It was a surprise. My aunts and uncles chipped in and blessed me with a plane ticket so I could be here."

Janelle looked over at them. They knew how much this would mean to Grandma Geri.

"And we just talked to you yesterday, so that was pretty sneaky," Todd said.

Keisha hugged her brother. "I know. I wanted to tell you."

Janelle moved so Keisha could sit next to Grandma Geri.

Grandma Geri looked long at her, licking her lips, and tears began to roll down her cheeks.

Keisha held her hand tight, looking into her grandmother's eyes, her own tears streaming. She hadn't seen Grandma Geri since the party in February. She had to be shocked by how different she looked.

Grandma Geri opened her mouth, and they all leaned in to listen. "Thank . . . You . . . Jesus."

She kept her eyes on Keisha as the raspy cough returned, lifting her head from the pillow. Then her head fell back softly again and she quieted. Her eyes closed.

Janelle knew immediately and began crying. No one said a word. Uncle Wood left the room. Aunt Gladys and Estelle stroked their mother's hair and kissed her cheek. Becca wept silently. Todd's head was bowed.

Travis moved from the dresser finally and stood over her, staring. Janelle had never seen him cry, but he didn't hide it. His tears fell and fell. Libby got up tentatively and touched his shoulder, and they held one another.

Janelle touched Keisha's shoulder. "She had a peace about going once she saw you one last time."

Keisha couldn't respond.

Janelle wondered what was going through her cousin's head. She wondered if she might be thinking that between the last visit and this one, she had her own Hope Springs memories now . . . and unlike her mother's, they were good ones.

CHAPTER FORTY-FOUR

Saturday, May 8

J anelle sat graveside, staring at the white roses laid atop the coffin. Family members had each been given one when they arrived at the cemetery, and they'd placed them there at the close of the graveside service.

There were dozens and dozens. Janelle hadn't seen this much family at the reunions. They'd come from Grandpa Elwood and Grandma Geri's sides, three to four generations deep. Grandma Geri herself had one brother and two sisters living, all of whom were there, including Floretta. She'd come down by car with Keisha and her husband and son. The only conspicuously absent member of the family was Aunt Gwynn.

Almost everyone had moved on to Grandma Geri's house. Janelle couldn't bring herself to leave.

She continued looking at the roses—Todd's idea. He and Travis had sat down with Grandma Geri more than a month ago, at her request, to go over her wishes for her funeral. Though Travis was her pastor and the service would take place at New Jerusalem, she'd wanted Todd to take part as well. Travis gave the eulogy; Todd followed with a sharing of the gospel. She knew Grandma Geri was looking down from heaven, proud of her boys.

Janelle hadn't been especially sad at the church or here at the cemetery. She'd gotten out her sadness earlier in the week—or so she thought. Today had felt like a celebration, a rejoicing that Grandma Geri's suffering had ended and she was with the Savior.

But the sadness returned as everyone headed to her grandmother's. The house would overflow with people, but most of them would be gone by tonight, all of them in a couple of days. And soon she'd be gone too. It hadn't hit her until now, but when the school year ended for Daniel in three weeks, there'd be no reason for them to stay. They would pack up and head home to Maryland. Her extended time in Hope Springs was just about over.

It would be yet another loss. No more extended visits with Libby or daily chats with Todd and Becca. No more Travis stopping by for pancakes. No more New Jerusalem or Soul Sisters. She would greatly miss those Saturday morning gatherings.

She'd go home . . . to what? Home reminded her that there was no more David. Maybe she should sell that house and move. That would help, but she felt the loss in her soul. Would it ever subside?

Well. It *had* subsided; not totally, but for a brief time she'd made room for someone else. But that was no more too. Everything was "no more."

The sadness overtook her as she stared at the casket, and she began to weep.

Why, God? Why am I always experiencing loss?

She felt a hand on her shoulder and looked up.

Libby sat next to her. "Jan, I've been waiting for you in the car. Let's go. Don't sit here by yourself. You'll only feel worse."

"You don't have to wait for me," she said. "I can walk back."

"No, you can't. Just the drive to the front of the cemetery is ridiculous."

Janelle shook her head. "Well, I can't leave yet. I need some time."

"Okay, I'll wait." Libby walked back across the grass.

Janelle settled back into her thoughts. *Lord, I don't know what to do. Part of me wants to stay down here, but what sense does that make? Stay down here and do what? And would I stay in Hope Springs or Raleigh, near Libby? I don't know . . . Maryland is still my home. I love my church family there. I do have friends there.*

But no matter what I do, I'm sure that'll get taken from me too. Right, Lord? That's just my fate. Don't enjoy anyone or anything, because I'll look up and it'll be gone. And You know what? I'm tired of asking why. It is what it is. And I have to deal with it. I have to just deal with a life of perpetual sadness.

She pulled a tissue from her purse, blowing her nose as her eyes reddened with tears. She felt a hand on her shoulder again.

"Libby, will you *please—*" She looked up, and everything in her world stopped.

He lifted her by the hand to her feet and brought her into his arms.

Her heart pounded inside her chest. Why was he here? Why was he holding her?

She backed up. "Kory, what are you doing? That's not . . . we can't . . ." The sobs that had gathered in her chest wouldn't let her finish.

He wiped the tears from her left cheek, then the right, and ran his finger slowly along her brow. "I'm sorry about the loss of your grandmother. You've been through so much."

She turned away from him slightly, looking toward the casket. She only nodded.

"I went by the house, and Todd said you stayed behind at the cemetery. I decided to come here instead of waiting there."

"You didn't have to come at all." Janelle focused on the casket still. "In fact, it would've been better if you hadn't."

"I almost didn't," he said. "That's why I didn't make the service. I was trying to decide."

"And you decided what? You'd come to Hope Springs, do the obligatory condolence thing, and leave—Kory, I can't. You made the wrong choice."

She turned to go and saw in the distance there was only one car. "What happened to Libby?"

"I saw her when I drove up and said I'd give you a ride back."

She groaned. "Would've been nice if Libby had asked if that was all right."

"I told her I wanted to talk to you."

She tossed her eyes. "Kory, what is there to say?"

"Shelley and I aren't together, Janelle."

She looked at him dead-on. "Since when?"

"She left two months ago."

Janelle stared at him, processing. "So you two were working on your marriage, and she left again? How did you feel?"

"I wasn't hurt like before, if that's what you're asking." He sighed. "After you and I talked, I prayed like we agreed. I prayed hard. And I was really thrown when I felt like God did want me to cancel the hearing and try to reconcile my marriage. You have no idea how much I struggled with that."

They sat back down and Janelle listened, staring at the ground.

"I kept hearing Him say I didn't have to trust *her*, but to trust *Him*. So I let her move in with us, in the guest bedroom. I told her we were taking it slow as far as the marriage was concerned, but I wanted to support her in her spiritual growth. So we found a church nearby and started going."

"How were things with her and Dee?" Janelle asked.

"Iffy. Dee had a wall up. She was afraid to trust her too, thinking Shelley would leave again."

Janelle waited for him to continue.

"It was weird," he said. "I felt the same way I felt after she left the first time, that I didn't really know her. When we were together before, she was at the firm day and night. Now I was around her more, and we hardly had anything to talk about. And it was clear she was restless." He leaned forward, elbows on his thighs. "But I was trusting God, so I hung in. The important thing, I kept telling myself, was that she was going to church, hearing truth. But on the third and fourth Sundays, she said she didn't feel well and stayed home. By the fifth, she was gone."

"Did she say why she was leaving?"

"She said Martin wanted her back, and after living with me again she was convinced we were never meant to be." Kory sounded matter-of-fact.

Janelle looked at him. "Why didn't you—?" She looked away. She didn't know if she wanted to know.

He sat up and looked at her. "Why didn't I call you then? If you only knew . . . I was ready to call you the moment she left. But I felt this check. Like, *not yet.* I felt like God wanted me to wait until the divorce was final. But it was delayed because the court tried to say this was a new separation, and we'd have to wait another year." He gave her a look. "You know I was ready to argue that one myself in court."

"What happened?"

"My lawyer submitted a brief on the point. The good thing was her lawyer submitted a brief arguing the same point. The court agreed and scheduled the hearing. It was final on Tuesday." His eyes were warm. "But I knew you were grieving, and it didn't seem like the right time to tell you. Kept going back and forth about whether today was the right time, but I just couldn't wait any longer." He touched her face. "I had to see you."

Janelle stared into his eyes. "I honestly don't know what to say."

"Was it true what you said before?"

"What did I say?"

"That you love me."

Her insides twirled. She couldn't believe she'd said it then, but she'd thought she might never see him again. "It's true."

He pulled her up again and put his arms around her. "Tell me again."

She wrapped her arms around him. "I love you, Kory."

"I love you too, Janelle."

He looked deep into her eyes, and she couldn't believe they had this moment, after all this time, all these years. He kissed her, then kissed her again, and her skin tingled as they allowed it to linger.

"Say yes," he said, their lips still touching.

Her heart leaped. "To what?"

"To our first"—he kissed her—"official"—kissed her again—"date."

She laughed. "Absolutely yes."

They kissed again, and Janelle let out a little giggle.

"What?"

"I feel like Grandma Geri is watching us."

He peeked over at the coffin. "She is, just not from there."

He took her hand and walked closer to the coffin. They stood there silently for a few moments, then Kory let go of her hand suddenly and moved to get something. She watched him pick up a rose that someone must've dropped. He placed it atop the coffin, then took her hand and walked her across the grass to his car.

"Where's Dee?" she asked.

"One guess."

"At the house with Tiffany."

"You're brilliant." He smiled. "The hardest thing about waiting was having to endure a constant barrage of questions from Dee about why she couldn't go stay at Tiffany's."

"So you were hearing it too? I wish I could've seen the BFF reunion."

"It was quite a sight." He looked at her. "But you know what got me? Daniel running to me when he saw me and throwing his arms around my waist."

Janelle got a lump in her throat.

"And so," he said, "I hereby submit the Dee-Tiffany reunion and the Daniel bear hug as my evidence."

"Evidence?"

"In support of your need to relocate to North Carolina—although I stipulate that a move to Maryland could be considered for Dee and me."

Janelle smiled. "There are more reasons for us to come here than for you two to go there." Were they really talking about this?

"Ah, so I don't have to use as much oratorical persuasion as I thought?"

He unlocked the passenger door and opened it for her.

She paused. "Well . . . there's still a lot to consider. It's a big decision, and I can't just base it on *you*. I've learned how quickly things can—"

He slowly kissed her on the lips. "I thought it would help to employ a different brand of persuasion."

She wondered if he knew how well that was working for him.

CHAPTER FORTY-FIVE

Sunday, May 9

Stephanie and Lindell boarded the plane for St. Louis behind her mom, dad, Cyd, Cedric, and Chase. Stephanie paused halfway down the aisle while they put their luggage in the overhead bin and got situated. She reached over and pinched Chase's cheeks as he stood bouncing on Cyd's legs, that big smile on his face, then she continued on.

"Babe, where are you going?" Lindell said. "There're two seats right here behind them."

They were on Southwest Airlines and could sit where they wanted.

Stephanie kept going, putting a few rows between the two of them and the rest of the family. She stopped near the back. "I wanted to be able to talk in private," she said.

She stood aside as Lindell threw their carry-ons overhead, then let him have the window seat.

He buckled his belt. "I could tell you were preoccupied. I know it was hard saying good-bye to Grandma Geri."

Stephanie pushed her handbag under the seat in front of her. "Bittersweet," she said, looking for the second part of her seat belt.

She found it under her seat and clicked them together. "Grandma always said don't be sad, because she'd be with Jesus and Grandpa Elwood." She smiled faintly, thinking about it. "But I regret taking so long to get to know her. I can't believe I only spent real time with her in the last few months of her life."

"Don't focus on what you didn't have, babe. The time you *did* have was sweet." He held her hand across the armrest. "Cyd even said she envied how well you got to know Grandma Geri because of the concentrated time you had with her."

"Yeah." Stephanie sighed. "It was definitely a special time. I'm still trying to understand it, though. Was that *all* it was about, getting to know Grandma Geri? Helping to serve her?" She added quickly, "And if so, fine. It was more than worth it. But I feel like there's more. Like I'm supposed to *do* something, but I'm not sure what." She looked at her husband. "That's what I wanted to talk to you about."

A teenager took the seat next to Stephanie, with her family across the aisle.

"I know what you mean," Lindell said. "I still have an unsettled feeling after Haiti. It's almost like, how can life still be the same?"

Stephanie nodded, wide-eyed. "Exactly. I'm doing the same thing I was doing before Hope Springs—basically nothing. Looking at church ministries, but can't figure out where to plug in." Her brows knit. "Lately I've been thinking about a job. What do you think?"

"How about the pancake house near church?"

She let go of his hand so she could swat his arm. "I'm serious! But hey, now that I've got experience . . ."

"Well." He thought about it as the attendant gave instructions in the event of an emergency. "You majored in criminology. Maybe you're supposed to be serving criminals in some way."

She rolled her eyes. "Yeah, right. I had no idea what I wanted to do in college. I only majored in that so I could take classes with a guy I was dating." She shot him a look. "Don't judge me."

He shook his head at her. "I knew exactly what I wanted to do, and I'm doing it," he said. "For the first time, though, I'm questioning. But I don't think God could be telling me to leave my profession. Could He? What else would I do?"

Stephanie's eyes got wide again. "Nooo, He couldn't be saying that. That was my calling, to marry a doctor." She leaned over with a big smile and kissed him, then took his hand again. "The funny thing is, after Hope Springs, I'm open to just about anything. I just want to know what it is."

"This can't be a coincidence," he said. "Both of us having these feelings."

The engine roared as they taxied down the runway and took for the skies. They both sank into their thoughts for several minutes, then Stephanie turned toward him.

"Several rows away, and I *still* hear her."

Lindell chuckled. Stephanie had told him how God spoke to her in Cyd's voice. "What did she say?"

"That we need to pray, because one thing is sure—after these experiences we've had, we'll never be the same." She looked into his eyes. "Our lives are about to change."

READING GROUP GUIDE

1. Stephanie heard a sermon that inspired her to do something selfless for Christmas. But the sermon "wore off," and she wanted to change her mind. When you receive inspiration from above to step outside your comfort zone, do you follow through? Is it hard?

2. Todd's dad's death motivated him to stop dragging through life and live full-out for Jesus. Do you ever feel that you are dragging through life? Would you say you're living full-out for Jesus?

3. Sensing God might be at work, Becca agreed to support Todd's call to pastor Calvary Church and move to Hope Springs. But she secretly prayed that God would close the door. Do you ever "agree" to something openly, while praying in secret that it doesn't happen?

4. Stephanie wanted to get to a point where she had a heart to do whatever He called her to do, without resisting. On which end of the spectrum do you more often find yourself, resisting or having a heart to do God's will?

5. When her grandmother had to be rushed to the hospital, Janelle felt overwhelmed by all she'd taken on. Though she knew the Lord was her help, the crisis took her focus off of Him. Do you remember that the Lord is your help when a crisis hits?

6. Sara Ann didn't feel qualified to lead the diner Bible study, though she had a deep relationship with God and studied the Bible regularly. If you feel God is calling you to do something, do you focus on your own qualifications? Or do you trust God to equip you?

7. At the diner Bible study, Gina found it hard to "sit down in her disappointment." When you're disappointed with God, do you admit it to Him and yourself?

8. Because of past hurts, Libby had built a protective shield around her heart and didn't want to commit to anyone, not even God. Have you ever been there?

9. In Becca's mind, Worth & Purpose was "big" ministry, the platform she'd been working toward as she moved through all the "lower tiers" of ministry. Do you tend to think of some forms of ministry as more or less significant than others?

10. Janelle let Kory go, telling him she didn't want to be what stood in the way of God healing his marriage. Would you have made that choice?

11. Have you ever felt like God was taking you through a spiritual boot camp? Describe.

12. Do you seek humility—being emptied of self and allowing God to fill you totally?

13. Though several decades had passed, Aunt Gwynn couldn't bring herself to forgive her mother for the pain she had caused. Have you ever held on to unforgiveness? How did you get past it? If you're holding on to unforgiveness right now, are you willing to seek help in breaking free?

14. Stephanie got to a point where she was open to doing God's will, whatever it might be. Can you say the same?

ACKNOWLEDGMENTS

With this novel more than any other, I was amazed at what God was working in my own life that correlated with what was unfolding in the story. I don't outline prior to writing, so when I say I was amazed, I'm talking literal *Are you serious, God?* moments as my fingers flew across the keys. I'm thankful for the very real and personal ways in which God speaks and guides me as I write. I'm thankful, too, for the people He graciously placed in my path:

My editors, Amanda Bostic and L.B. Norton—thank you for seeing what I can't see and for helping to shape these characters, places, and situations I craft in my head. I love this team!

My publisher, Allen Arnold—thank you for your encouragement and wisdom, and for always making yourself available. You are a consummate leader, and I'm privileged to know you.

Becky Monds, Katie Bond, Eric Mullet, Ruthie Dean, Kristen Vasgaard, Ashley Schneider, and Jodi Hughes—thank you for the creative energy and hard work you put into Thomas Nelson Fiction. I'm amazed at what you do and thankful to be a part.

Tina Jacobson—you are much more than a literary agent. Thank you for your counsel and your desire to see me be all that God has called me to be.

Edna J. Cash—thank you for being everything from a personal intercessor to a personal editor, not to mention mom and sister in Christ. I will never know this side of heaven the extent to which I'm blessed because of you.

Earl and Joyce Cash—thank you for your constant love and for going above and beyond in your support of my novels. Who knew I'd have personal publicists in The Villages? I love it!

My blog family—you have encouraged me, prayed for me, sharpened me, and walked alongside me. I can't thank you enough for being there—not just for me, but for one another.

Bill, Quentin, and Cameron—I thank God for the privilege of growing with you, of enduring life's twists and turns with you, and of experiencing God's faithfulness with you. You are God's precious gifts to me.

To you, the reader—I'm so thankful that you would give of your time to read *Hope Springs*. Please know that I prayed for you before you picked up the book. And as you close it, I pray that God will speak to you powerfully as to the plans He has for your life. I also want to extend to you an invitation to join our active blog community at KimCashTate.com

"Tate has an amazing ability to put difficult but realistic emotions on paper and show the reader the redeeming love of God in the process."— *Romantic Times*

AN EXCERPT FROM
faithful

CYDNEY SANDERS JUMPED at the ringing of the phone, startled out of slumber. She rolled over, peeked at the bedside clock, and groaned. She had twenty whole minutes before the alarm would sound, and she wanted every minute of that twenty. Only her sister would be calling at five forty in the morning. Every morning she called, earlier and earlier, with a new something that couldn't wait regarding that wedding of hers. Not that Stephanie was partial to mornings. She was apt to call several times during the day and into the evening as well. Everything wedding related was urgent.

Cyd nestled back under the covers, rolling her eyes at the fifth ring. Tonight she would remember to turn that thing off. She was tired of Stephanie worrying her from dawn to dusk.

Her heart skipped suddenly and she bolted upright. *The wedding is tomorrow.* The day seemed to take forever to get here, and yet it had come all too quickly. She sighed, dread descending at once with a light throbbing of her head. She might have felt stressed no matter what date her sister had chosen for the wedding. That she chose Cyd's fortieth birthday made it infinitely worse.

She sank back down at the thought of it. *Forty*. She didn't mind the age itself. She'd always thought it would be kind of cool, in fact. At forty, she'd be right in the middle of things, a lot of life behind her, a lot of living yet to do. She'd be at a stride, confident in her path, her purpose. She would have climbed atop decades of prayer and study, ready to walk in some wisdom. Celebrate a little understanding. Stand firmly in faith. Count it all joy.

And she'd look good. She was sure of that. She'd work out during her pregnancies, and while the babies nursed and sucked down her tummy, she would add weights to the cardio routine to shape and tone. As she aged, her metabolism could turn on her if it wanted to; she had something for that too. She would switch up her workout every few weeks, from jogging to mountain bike riding to Tae Bo, all to keep her body guessing, never letting it plateau. Her husband would thank her.

He would also throw her a party. She wasn't much of a party person, but she always knew she'd want a big one on the day she turned forty. It wouldn't have to be a surprise. She'd heard enough stories of husbands unable to keep a party secret anyway. They'd plan it together, and she would kick in the new season in high spirits, surrounded by the people she loved.

Now that she was one day away, she still had no problem with forty. It was the other stuff that had shown up with it—forty, never been married, childless. Now, despite her distinguished career as a classics professor at Washington University in St. Louis, she was questioning her path and her purpose and dreading her new season—and the fact that she was forced to ring it in as maid of honor in her younger sister's wedding . . . her *much younger* sister.

She was still irritated that Stephanie kept the date even after their mother reminded her that October 18 was Cyd's birthday.

"Why does that matter?" Stephanie had said.

The only thing that mattered to Stephanie was Stephanie, and if she wanted something, she was going to make it happen. Like now. She cared not a whit that she was ringing Cyd's phone off the hook before dawn, waking Cyd and the new puppy, who was yelping frantically in her crate in the kitchen.

Cyd gave up, reached over, and snatched up the phone. Before it came fully to her ear, she heard her sister's voice.

"Cyd, I forgot to tell you last night—*stop*," Stephanie giggled. "You see I'm on the phone."

Cyd switched off her alarm. "Good morning to you too, Steph." She swung her legs out from under the warm bedding and shivered as they hit the air. The days were warm and muggy still, but the nights were increasingly cooler.

From a hook inside the closet, she grabbed her plum terry robe, which at Cyd's five-nine hit her above the knee, and slipped it over her cotton pajama shorts and tank. Her ponytail caught under the robe and she lifted it out, let it flop back down. It was a good ways down her back, thick with ringlets from air drying, a naturally deep reddish brown. Her face had the same richness, a beautiful honey brown, smooth and flawless.

Stephanie was giggling still as she and her fiancé, Lindell, whispered in the background.

I can't believe she woke me up for this. Cyd pushed her feet into her slippers and padded downstairs with a yawn to let out the puppy. "Do you do this when you're talking to Momma?"

Stephanie fumbled with the phone. "Do what?"

"Make it obvious that you and Lindell spent the night together?"

"Cyd, we are grown and will be married to*morrow*. Who gives a flip if we spent the night together?"

"Stephanie . . ." Cyd closed her eyes at the bottom of the stairs as all manner of responses swirled in her mind. Sometimes she wondered if she and Stephanie had really grown up in the same family with the same two parents who loved God and made His ways abundantly clear. Much of it had sailed right over Stephanie's head. Cyd had attempted to nail it down for her over the years, particularly in the area of relationships, but Stephanie never warmed to any notion of chastity, or even monogamy. In fact, when she'd called to announce her engagement six months ago, Cyd thought the husband-to-be was Warren, the man Stephanie had been bringing lately when she stopped by.

But Cyd had vowed moons ago to stop lecturing her sister and pray instead. She took a deep breath and expelled it loudly enough for Stephanie to know she was moving on, but only with effort.

"So, you forgot to tell me something?" She headed to the kitchen, where Reese was barking with attitude, indignant that Cyd was taking too long to get there.

"Girl, listen to this," Stephanie said. "LaShaun called Momma yesterday, upset 'cause we didn't include a guest on her invitation, talking about she wants to bring Jo-Jo. That's why I *didn't* put 'and guest' on her invitation. I'm not paying for that loser to come up in there, eat our food, drink, and act a fool. And why is she calling now anyway? Hello? The deadline for RSVPs was last month. Can you believe her?"

"Stephanie, was there a need to call so early to tell me this?" Cyd clicked on the kitchen light.

"Don't you think it's a trip?"

"Okay, yeah."

"I know! And you know Momma. She said, 'That's your cousin. Just keep the peace and let her bring him.' I'm tempted to call LaShaun right now and tell her both of them can jump in a lake."

Cyd headed to the crate under the desk portion of the kitchen counter. Tired though she was, Reese's drama tickled her inside. She was whimpering and pawing at the gated opening, and when Cyd unlocked it, the energetic twelve-week-old shot out. A mix of cocker spaniel and who knew what else, with dark chocolate wavy hair and tan patches on the neck, underbelly, and paws, she'd reminded Cyd of a peanut butter cup the moment she nabbed her heart at the shelter.

Reese jumped on Cyd, then rolled over for a tummy rub. Three seconds later she dashed toward the back door. At her age she could barely make it through the night without an accident. If Cyd delayed now, she'd be cleaning up a mess. She attached the leash and led her out.

"Well, what do you think?" Stephanie asked.

"About telling LaShaun to jump in the lake?" Cyd turned on the lights in the backyard and stepped outside with Reese, tightening her robe.

Stephanie sucked her teeth. "I mean about the whole thing."

"Well, Momma and Daddy are paying," Cyd said, since it seemed her sister had forgotten, "so if Momma doesn't mind Jo-Jo coming, why worry about it? You'll be so busy you probably won't see much of them anyway. No point getting your cousin *and* Aunt Gladys mad over something like this."

"Whatever," Stephanie said. "I should've known you'd say the same thing as Momma. I still might call LaShaun, just to let her know she should've called me directly, not tried to go through Momma."

"All right, go ahead and ponder that. I've got to get ready for class and—"

"I wasn't finished," Stephanie whined. "Did you talk to Dana?"

"I talked to her last night. Why?"

"So she told you about the shoes?"

"Mm-hmm." Cyd moved to different spots in the yard, tugging on the leash to get Reese to stop digging and do her business. A light popped on in the house next door and she saw Ted, a professor in the chemistry department, moving around in his kitchen. Many of her colleagues from Wash U lived in her Clayton neighborhood— six on her block alone.

"I wasn't trying to be difficult," Stephanie said, "but something told me to stop by her house yesterday to see for myself what kind of shoes she bought. You said they were cute, but those things were dreadful."

"Stephanie, they're flower-girl shoes. All flower-girl shoes are cute. Mackenzie tried them on with the dress when I was over there last week, and she looked adorable."

"The *dress* is adorable—because I picked it out—but those tired Mary Janes with the plain strap across the top have got to go. Is that what they wear at white weddings or something?"

"I don't know. Google it—'official flower-girl shoe at white weddings.'"

"Ha, ha, very funny. I'm just sayin' . . ."

Cyd led Reese back into the house, half listening as Stephanie droned on about some snazzier shoes with rhinestones Dana could've gotten and why she shouldn't have trusted Dana to make the choice in the first place.

She'd get over it. Stephanie did a lot of complaining about a lot of people, but there was no doubt—she loved Dana. Dana had been like family ever since she and Cyd met on the volleyball team in junior high, when Stephanie was just a baby. Stephanie had always looked up to her like a second big sister, and when Dana got married and had Mackenzie and Mark, Stephanie actually volunteered to babysit regularly. Those kids adored "Aunt Stephanie," and when it came time to plan her wedding, Stephanie didn't hesitate to include them . . . even though a couple of great-aunts questioned her appointing white kids as flower girl and ring bearer.

". . . so, long story short, I asked Dana to take 'em back and find some shoes with some pizzazz.'"

"She told me she's not hunting for shoes today. She doesn't have time." Cyd stopped in the office, awakened her computer screen with a shake of the mouse, and started skimming an e-mail from a student.

"She told me that too," Stephanie said. "So I'm hoping you can do it."

"Do what?"

"Find some cute shoes."

"I have to work." And even if she didn't, she wouldn't get roped into this one. She'd gone above and beyond for Stephanie already. This week alone, she'd taken care of several items Stephanie was supposed to handle. If her sister wanted to sweat the flower girl's shoes the day before the wedding, she'd have to do it alone.

"But your class is at eight o'clock. You've got the whole day after that."

Cyd donned a tight-lipped smile to beat back her annoyance. "Stephanie, you know that teaching is only part of what I do. I have a paper due for a conference coming up, and I'm already behind."

She unhooked Reese's leash and watched her run around in circles, delighted with her freedom. But when Cyd headed for the stairs, Reese fell quickly in step. No way would she be left behind.

"How can you even focus on work today?" Stephanie sounded perplexed. "Aren't you just too excited about the big event? Girl, you know this is your wedding too."

Cyd paused on a stair. "How is this my wedding too?"

"Since it looks like you won't be getting married yourself"— Stephanie had a shrug in her voice—"you've at least gotten a chance to plan one through me. You know, living vicariously. Hasn't it been fun?"

Cyd held the phone aloft and stared at it. Did Stephanie really think these last few months had been *fun*? She had involved Cyd in every decision from her dress to her colors to the style, thickness, and font of the invitations to the type of headpiece Mackenzie should wear—all of which *could* have been fun if Stephanie had really wanted her sister's opinions.

What Stephanie wanted was for Cyd to accompany her about town to every wedding-related appointment, listen with interest as she debated with herself about gowns, floral arrangements, and what to include on the wedding registry, and affirm her ultimate picks. She also wanted Cyd to handle whatever she deemed drudgery. And Cyd didn't mind; as the maid of honor, she thought it her duty to address invitations, order favors, and the like. What bugged her was Stephanie's ingratitude, which wasn't new but had taken on a high-gloss sheen. It was Stephanie's world, and everyone else revolved around it, especially Cyd, since in Stephanie's opinion she didn't have a life anyway.

Now she was telling Cyd—matter-of-factly—that it looked like her sister wouldn't ever be getting married. Cyd wished she could dismiss it as she did Stephanie's other flippant remarks. But how could she, when her own inner voice was shouting the same?

Tears crowded Cyd's eyes, and she was startled, and grateful, when the phone beeped to announce another call. She didn't bother to look at the caller's identity.

"Steph, that's my other line. I've gotta go."

"Who would be calling you this early? Besides me, that is." Stephanie chuckled at herself. "Probably Momma. Tell her I'll call her in a few minutes. By the way, what did you decide to wear to the rehearsal tonight?"

"Steph, really, I've got to go. Talk to you later."

Cyd clicked Off, threw the phone on the bed, and headed to the bathroom. She couldn't bear more wedding talk at the moment, and if it was her mother, that's all she would hear.

She peeled off her clothes, turned on the shower, and stepped under the warm spray of water. Now that she was smack up against it—the wedding, the birthday—everything seemed to rush at her. She wouldn't mind being forty, unmarried, and childless if she'd expected it. But from a young age she'd prayed repeatedly for a husband—and not just a "Christian" but someone on fire for the Lord. And she'd believed deep in her heart that God would answer.

Cyd looked upward, past the dingy housing of the lightbulb, as tears mingled with water, questions with accusation.

I trusted in Your promises, Lord. You said if I delighted myself in You, You would give me the desires of my heart.

The tears flowed harder. *You said if I abide in You and Your words abide in me, I could ask whatever I wish and it would be done. Haven't I delighted myself in You? Haven't I abided in You?*

The story continues in *Faithful*

ABOUT THE AUTHOR

KIM CASH TATE is the author of *Cherished, Faithful, Heavenly Places*, and the memoir *More Christian than African-American*. A former practicing attorney, she is also the founder of Colored in Christ Ministries. She and her husband have two children.